# *The Citadel*

Dianis, A World In Turmoil Chronicles
Book Three

Frank Dravis

# Copyright

The Citadel
Dianis, a World In Turmoil chronicles
Book Three

ISBN-13: 978-0-9996886-3-2
PB

Six Factors Publishing LLC
N1358 State Highway 35
Stoddard WI 54658

www.dianisworld.com

Isuelt Map: Jerry Mooney

# Table of Contents

# Cast of Characters

## Protagonists

- **IDB (Interspecies Development Branch), Avarian Federation**
  - Achelous Forushen, former chief inspector of Civilization Monitoring
  - Anna Lexa, armorer, IDB Central Station
  - Baryy Maxmun, deceased sociologist
  - Clienen Hor, director of IDB Margel Damansk
  - Ivan Darinarishcan, chief of Ready Reaction
  - Illian Meridia, Agent Ready Reaction
  - Jeremy, IDB Dianis artificial intelligence (AI)
  - Lieutenant Hearter, commander, enforcement cutter *IDBS Shields*
  - Outish, planetary astrobiologist
  - Sergeant Mears, senior NCO, enforcement cutter *IDBS Shields*

- **Avarian Federation (The Human Galactic Federation)**
  - Admiral Feall, Battlegroup Commander
  - Captain Trich, captain of *AFS Tempest Dare*
  - Major Vuulanin, Marine adjutant, *AFS Tempest Dare*

- **Mother Dianis (Religion of Life Believers, Provincial Dianis)**
  - Alex, Defender
  - Christina Tara, Al Suri Ascalon Defender

- **Doromen (A Race of Humans, Provincial Dianis)**
  - Cordelei Greenleaf, sixthsense diviner
  - Lettern Stouttree, IDB Agent, Civilization Monitoring

- Margern, Wedgewood town chairwoman, sister to Woodwern
- Mbecca, sixthsense healer
- Ogden, master weaponsmith, warden of the Second Ward
- Rachael Stouttree, sixthsense kinetic, sister to Lettern
- Sedge the Warlord, mercenary, Wedgewood garrison commander
- Woodwern, Mearsbirch clan chairman

- **Alor of Tivor (Duchy of Tivor, Provincial Dianis)**
  - Captain Enderma, Tivor Marines
  - Eliot, Marinda Merchants huntsmaster
  - Lieutenant Rayamars, Tivor Archers
  - Marisa Pontifract, Princess House Marinda, Marinda Merchants owner
  - Ropert, Aorolmin of Tivor, the duke of Tivor

- **The Silver Cup Couriers Guild**
  - Prince Fire Eye, prince of the wryvern nation

# The Matrincy (Avarian Federation)

- Councilor Margret, Special Investigations
- The Matriarch, Matrincy Grand Councilor, senator Avarian Federation

# Antagonists

- **Nordarken Mining (Avarian Federation)**
  - Rocl Binair, senior vice president of Resource Production
  - Quorat, deceased exploration contractor

- **Contract Miners (Galactic Independents)**
  - Bleep Nuts, mining contractor

- Haz, mining boss
- Junko, mining boss
- Krch, Tweeunar geologist

- **Empire of Nak Drakas (Provincial Dianis)**
  - Commandant Fritach, Washentrufel (Drakan secret service) commandant
  - Decurion Uloch, Drakan Hoplite commander
  - Emperor Elixir Tyr Violorich, Drakan Empire supreme leader
  - General Lord Orn Blannach, Drakan military supreme commander
  - Khajeet, Warkenvaal aide to Major Startoren
  - Larech, Washentrufel agent
  - Major Startoren, Washentrufel station commander

- **Diunesis Antiquaria (Religion of Paleowrights, Provincial Dianis)**
  - Captain Irons, Scarlet Saviors captain
  - Predicant Greglor, Viscount Helprig assistant
  - Viscount Helprig, Paleowright bishop

# Map of Continent of Isuelt

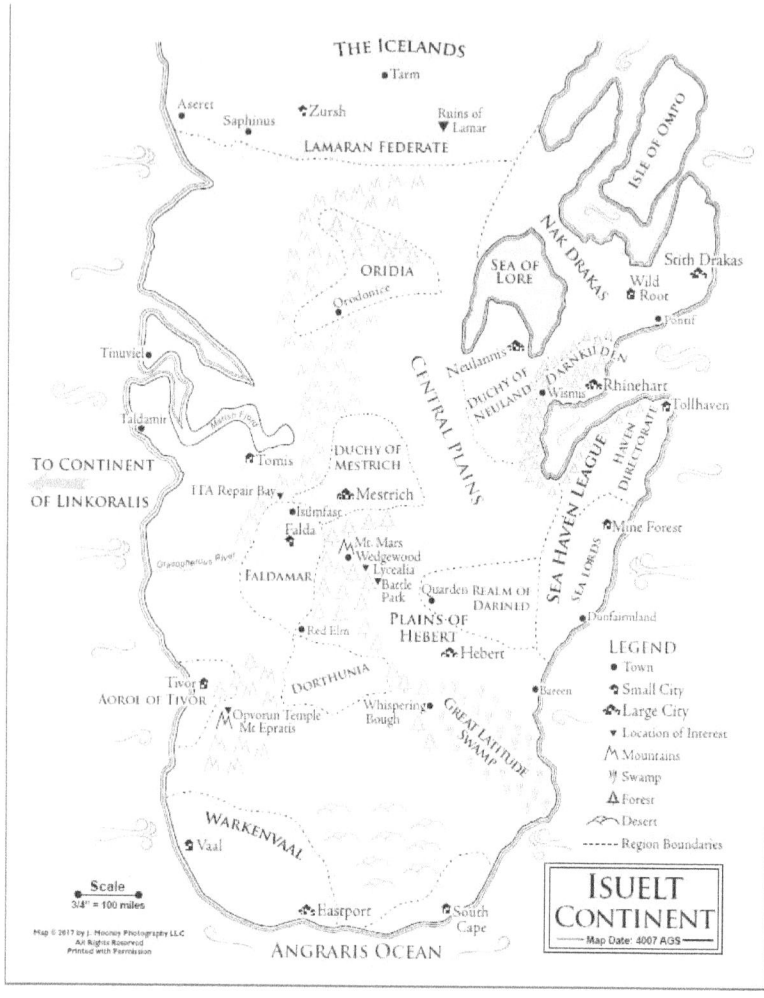

THE ICELANDS
• Tarm

Aseret
•
Saphinus
•

⛊ Zursh

Ruins of
▼ Lamar

LAMARAN FEDERATE

ISLE OF OMRO

NAK DRAKAS

SEA OF
LORE

ORIDIA
•
Oredonice

Stith Drakas

Wild
⚑ Root

• Ssnif

Timuviel •

Neulanms ⚑

DUCHY OF
NEULAND

DARKALDEN

• Wisms

⚑ Rhinehart
⚑ Tollhaven

Taldamir •

Maron Fork

CENTRAL PLAINS

HAVEN
DIRECTORATE

TO CONTINENT
OF LINKORALIS

⚑ Tomis

DUCHY OF
MESTRICH

⚑ Mestrich

SEA HAVEN LEAGUE

SEA LORDS

⚑ Mine Forest

HA Repair Bay ▼

• Isdmfasr
Falda
⚑

Glycophenitus River

FALDAMAR

Mt. Mars
• Wedgewood
▼ Lyceaita
▼ Battle
Park

Quarden REALM OF
• DARINED

• Dunfarmland

• Red Elm

PLAINS OF
HEBERT

⚑ Hebert

LEGEND

Tivor ⚑
AOROL OF TIVOR

DORTHUNIA

Whispering •
Bough

GREAT LATITUDE SWAMP

• Bareen

• Town
⚑ Small City
⚑ Large City
▼ Location of Interest
M Mountains
⩊ Swamp
△ Forest
⌁ Desert
------ Region Boundaries

M Opvorun Temple
M Mt Epratis

WARKENVAAL

⚑ Vaal

Scale
3/4" = 100 miles

Map © 2017 by J. Mooney Photography LLC
All Rights Reserved
Printed with Permission

⚑ Hastport

South
⚑ Cape

ISUELT
CONTINENT
Map Date: 4007 AGS

ANGRARIS OCEAN

# *Map of the Margel*

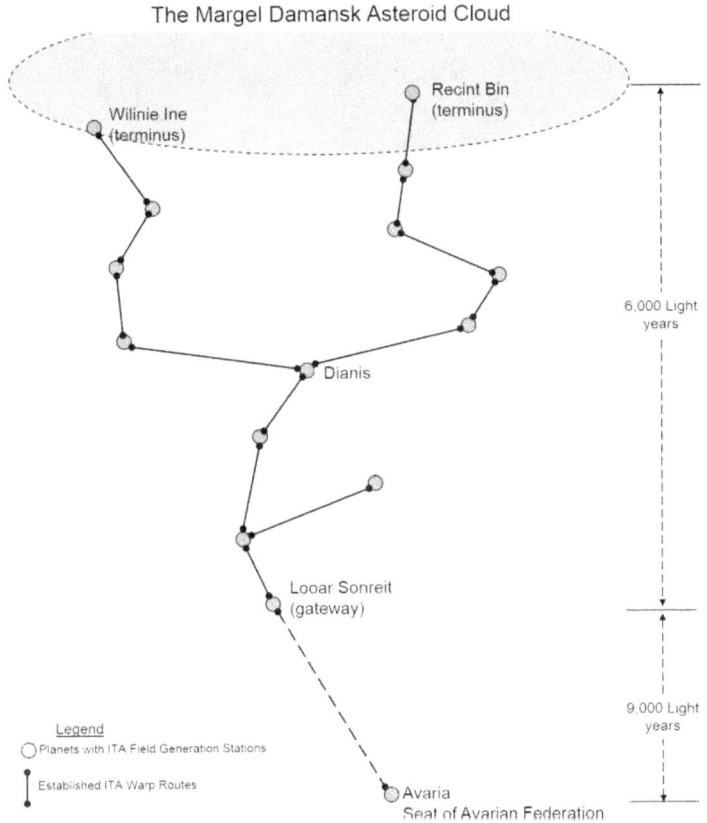

The Margel Damansk Asteroid Cloud

Recint Bin
(terminus)

Wilinie Ine
(terminus)

Dianis

6,000 Light
years

Looar Sonreit
(gateway)

Legend
⬭ Planets with ITA Field Generation Stations

▮ Established ITA Warp Routes

9,000 Light
years

Avaria
Seat of Avarian Federation

Margel Damansk Arm of ITA Transportation Network

Norma Spiral Arm, Milky Way Galaxy

# Map of the Citadel

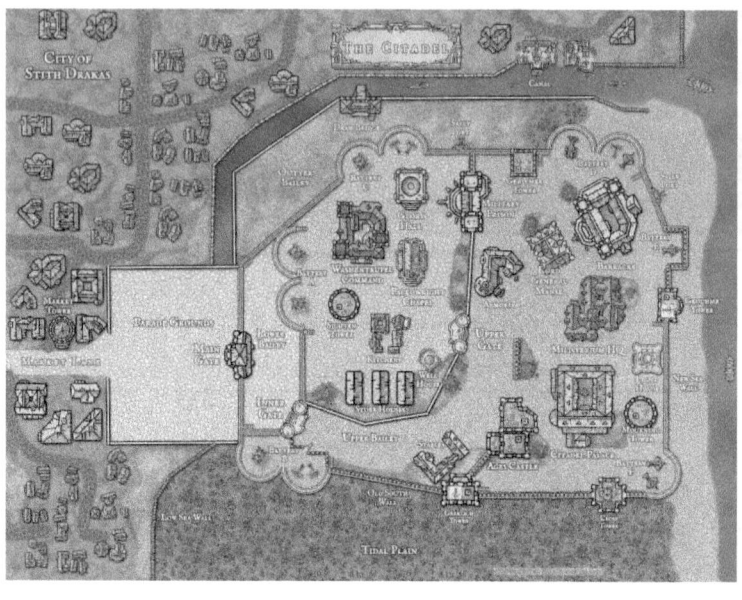

# History of Humankind in the Milky Way Galaxy

Humans first appeared in the Milky Way galaxy as the Loch Norim, Humanity's progenitors. The Loch Norim built colonies in an ever-expanding sphere from their hub at the galactic core. A mystery thrives, from what galaxy they first migrated from is unknown. It is postulated, however, that where the Loch Norim went, Nemesis, their eons-old enemy followed.

A millennium after Loch Norim society collapsed and retreated to the core, the Turboii-human war rages across the Milky Way. With billions dead, the humans have halted Turboii advances and those of their Sizar minions. The conflict is deadlocked with both sides seeking advantage. For humans it entails expanding their acquisition of aquamarine-5, a strategic resource needed by Field generators that, amongst other technologies, allows instantaneous travel across light years.

There are many sentient species in the galaxy. Some, including the humans in the Avarian Federation, have come together to enact ULUP, the Universal Law of Unclaimed Planets. Prior to the Turboii War, the predation of primitive worlds and the harvesting of both beings and resources had reached such a level, and the atrocities so rampant, that the more enlightened and self-sustaining societies were compelled to act. They created a classification and policing system whereby planets of certain classes were afforded levels of protection dependent on their technological and societal abilities to defend themselves. Class E planets, of which Dianis is one, were assigned extrasolar quarantine. No external galactic presence was allowed to interact and interfere with the natural self-development of the world.

Class E planets were to thrive or wither as their own indigenous cultures determined.

Arrival of the Turboii into human space changed everything, and yet the human-controlled worlds were still bound by ULUP. Resource extraction and military recruiting focused on planets, moons, and asteroids that either held no sentient life or were classified above "E) exploitive prone, protected" and allowed extrasolar interaction.

Aquamarine-5, plentiful on Dianis, is a rare commodity in the galaxy.

The signatories of ULUP formed their own contingents of the IDB, Interspecies Development Branch. The men and women of the Avarian IDB enforce ULUP in Avarian-controlled space.

No police force is perfect. No nation adheres to or administers all laws equally. In war, *human* rights can conflict with wartime imperatives. The needs of the war machine, in the service of a society's survival, can trample, if not averted, the goodwill afforded by peace.

# *Prologue*

*In space, the Margel Damansk System*

Krch wiped frost from the shuttle console with her glove. She sat in her space suit in the pilot's chair, stained with Sysreq's blood. The former pilot lay on the floor behind her, frozen solid. The shuttle's cockpit was open to the environment, in this case, the hard vacuum of space. The windshield had been shot out by the plasma-armed indigen back on Dianis at a mine near a town called Wedgewood.

It wasn't quite the catastrophe it could have been, yet. At least she was alive, had a working shuttle, and two tons of aquamarine-5 ore in the shuttle's cargo bay. Now, if only Bleep Nuts would answer her A-wave call. He was a day late for the rendezvous, and she was drifting in space out beyond Lonely Soul, Dianis's moon.

The crew berthing compartment with a tiny kitchenette, really just an autoserv, still retained environmental integrity, so she didn't have to sleep in her suit, but the ship controls were on the shattered command deck.

Her suit's A-wave receiver pinged an incoming call. "Damns," she slurred, her mouth tubes writhing in agitation. It was Junko calling, not Bleep Nuts. Not having much else to do other than fret about her contract delivery, she accepted the call from her former employer.

"You sleaze sucking Twik. Get back here now or I'll have you black-listed with the miners, and when I catch you, you are dead!" Junko's image, relayed to the shuttle's console hologrid, showed him haggard, deadly pale, almost gray. Sweat ran down his cheek.

"Yass," she slurred. "I told you not to call me that."

"Twik? You don't want me to call you a Twik! You are a Twik! Twik, Twik—" The signal cut off with a push of her finger. Tweeunar are humanoid in appearance with notable exceptions: They have no teeth or a moveable lower jaw.

Instead, their mouth was a group of tubes adapted for sucking sap ooze from plants native to their home world, Tweeunar, long overrun by Sizars.

*Blacklist me! Ha!* She mentally scoffed. Trying to blacklist her in the contract mining community when she had a two-ton cargo of aquamarine was a fool's jest. The going rate for sorted aqua ore, according to Junko's contract, was five hundred credits per *ounce*. That did not include the harvest and delivery bonuses that doubled the base rate. Trying to blacklist a person with that much aqua five was like refusing water when dying of thirst. Her problem was not getting outed in the process of selling it. Bleep Nuts was a friend, but he was a miner too, a competitor of Junko's, whose cargo she'd absconded with. Contract miners frequently operated in space where laws were non-existent or vaguely enforced, and the ethics of contract miners matched the territory. The fact she had poisoned Junko and stolen his shuttle with its ultra-precious cargo attested to her own morals. *Although,* she admitted to herself, *I'm relieved he is still alive, unlike Sysreq.* She pondered the grisly corpse. A friend of hers, who, until a day ago, was alive and screaming at the controls. *Junko is the one who should be dead,* she mused, *not Sysreq.*

There was still the remote possibility she could work out a deal with Junko and arrange to drop the cargo with Junko's contract agent. Her share of the sale would still be huge, and his wouldn't be zero, but she didn't like the end customer, who they suspected was Nordarken Mining. *They* suspected, her breath caught, the shock of what she had gone through just now sinking in. Not only was Sysreq dead, but so was Geezer and Gof. The entire Bad Crew were gone except for her.

Remembering Junko's haggard face from the A-wave call, she took cold solace: The bastard was probably dying too, still holed up at the aquamarine mine on Dianis. Unless he sought treatment for the fecal bacteria she'd poisoned him with, a cure easily administered if the pathogen was known, he might die. But the boss was too dumb, too stubborn, and too mean to do something that intelligent.

Lieutenant Hearter's voice came over the ship's intercom. "AI tells me Krch broke transmission silence."

"Yes, sir," replied Sergeant Mears, watch commander on the *IDBS Shields*. "It was an A-wave broadcast. Encoded, but not tight beam."

"She must be desperate," said Hearter, the captain of the IDB enforcement cutter currently in EMCON Silent, as they stalked the damaged shuttle.

"Well, it's not like she left the planet in stealth mode, sir. Anyone with a pair of eyeballs would have seen her leave."

"Yes, but who else other than Junko is listening? Anyone can be out here. And with two tons of aquamarine on board, she'll be attracting a lot of attention. Has the AI decoded the first message? Before Junko's. We need to know where the response came from."

"It was an acknowledgment from someone called Bleep. They confirmed their arrival time, but the location was not specified. However, the arrival time was yesterday, if our AI decrypted it correctly."

"Hmm, I doubt it was Junko's end customer or even an intermediate," said Hearter, which was why he and the *Shields* were tailing, not boarding the shuttle. The larger goal, beyond apprehending and prosecuting the Class E corsair for a dozen ULUP violations, including the murder of provincials, was to find the end customer who contracted the operation. Arresting Krch or Junko for the murders of the village elders whom Junko blew holes through with a plasma pistol was secondary to catching the party responsible for chartering the fiasco. Dianis, before it was newly classified as F: *Highly Protected,* was a Class E world, protected, and therefore off limits to all extrasolar activity.

"Someone is going to show up," offered Mears. "And we know it's not Junko," he sniffed. The mining boss was stranded on Dianis, made so when his foreman shifted off the planet in their Field generator, which subsequently exploded either by sabotage or equipment failure.

"All right. Let's maintain distance and stay in stealth. When we get a visitor we'll inform Clienen. He and Counselor Margret can take it from there. We're not to leave the system."

Bleep Nuts, in his space suit, jetted across the gap between his ship and the shuttle. He landed in the open cargo hold with a magnetic click of his boots on the deck. "Shiren, Krch. Your boat's a wreck. How'd you get *this* far?"

Krch waggled her helmet. "Shears determinations. Wasn't gonna let Junks beat me," she slurred.

Bleep Nuts shook his helmet. "Never knew why you signed up with him. Such a pig."

"You's didn't have a slot for a geologist," she reminded him.

He shrugged, though you couldn't tell with his space suit. "Yeah, well. I still don't have a billet. Life is tough. Ship's maintenance is shit. Which is why I'm late. The crew I *do* have is grumbling they haven't been paid, and the fuel-cell plant in the Hole is out of carbon."

"Smokes, Bleep. Carbon's cheap."

Again, he gave an invisible shrug. "Still takes credits."

She pointed at two pallets of wire-bound ore in the back of the hold. "That'll pay for carbon."

Bleep Nuts turned his headlamp up to high and peered at the ore pallets. "What is it? Copper. Cobalt? Copper's good. The cobalt is better. The 'balt shortage is really driving prices. You told me it would be good. Worth my skin to get you. We're out here in the middle of no—"

"Aqua."

"Huh?" He said, not thinking he heard right. "What is it?"

"Aqua five."

He spun and nearly blinded her, but her suit's sun visor shaded in. "No, nah, Krch. No one has aqua."

"Yes, Bleeps. Two tons."

# Chapter 1
## Achelous the Trader

*Vaal, Planet Dianis*

The warm desert wind ushered in the heat of the day. "Khajeet, you have word?"

Khajeet sent the sailor on his way and closed the door. "Yes, Major. The captain is ready to leave when you say. All is prepared."

Major Startoren stood watching the point of land around which all ships from the northwest coast would have to pass as they came into port. The Warkenvaal city of Vaal spread out behind him. From the veranda of the Pier Point Inn and the comfort of their accommodations, they could conduct surveillance on the harbor.

"Sir, the lookout will send a rider when the ship is seen. We will know an hour before they round the cape."

The major half turned to his Warkenvaal aide. "All rests on careful planning. The emperor must not be disappointed."

Khajeet bowed his cream-white turban. Even in the heat, he wore his iron-plated doublet. The black leather dark against his brown flesh.

"How can you wear that armor in this heat?" The major waved a hand at his own face, feigning to cool himself.

Khajeet smiled at his superior. "You Nakish," he paused, "wilt like the kudu bloom at first light. The desert sciroccos are a blessing."

"Ha." The major returned his gaze to the cape. "Palm trees, sand." He motioned his black hand dismissively. His Nakish skin darker than that of his Warkenvaal subordinate. "You are soft. I should bring you to Nak Drakas. Our frozen gales will toughen you." In the days they waited for the ship and the churchmen, they'd kept up a running banter.

"Ah, but alas, two hundred and fifty leagues! A week's sailing with fair winds, sir. So far, and your needs of me are so many. How could I be gone so long?"

Startoren turned and squinted at his aide. "Excuses. I should take you with me so you can suffer too! Ha!" He smiled as he watched a dark skin lovely stroll past the veranda carrying a basket of some tropical fruit. "I do hope the viscount finds our arranged entertainment to his liking. Do we know if he likes men or women?"

A knock sounded at the door.

"That would be the captain of the *Progulvaal*," said Khajeet.

"Ah, good. Send him in. With Gumeric, too."

"Captain, so good to see you," the major offered their visitor a warm handshake, whether he felt it or not. As chief of the southernmost Nak Drakas intelligence station, the major made it his business to know all the ships and sea captains who frequented Vaal.

Another man, a Nakish dressed in a Drakan infantry uniform, followed the captain into the room.

"Yes, Major, and what is it that I can do for the Washentrufel today? I have time. We can chat."

"Ach, Washentrufel. Why you so suspicious? Khajeet and I, we are of the Foreign Service."

"What's the difference?" The captain found a chair and slouched in it.

Startoren rocked his head. "For you, all the way down here, maybe it does not matter." He took the chair across from the shipmaster. "I understand you are bound for Bareen. I have a message, a very important message," he glanced at the infantry officer, "for General Lord Orn Blannach. Do you know the general?"

The captain shrugged. "You Nakish and your generals. Yes, I have heard of him."

"Good, the message I have for him is of the utmost importance. He must receive it in nine days. Sooner is better."

Another shrug. "You have your ship, the *Tutagrapf*. Use that."

"Ah, alas, I would, but it is not a fast packet like yours, and the captain says it will be three more days before the new pump is built and mounted. A second pump is clogged and needs an overhaul, and the third pump leaks. The captain does not want to leave port."

The master shook his head. "You Drakans, how can you compete with the Sea Haven League if you kick your ships like eenu turds?"

It was the major's turn to give a disgruntled sniff. "I am, how do you say, a land lover. I know not of ships and sea things, but I know this message must get to Blannach. If it does not...."

"You can book passage on the *Progulvaal* for your messenger, but I can't leave for two or three days. My other passengers have not yet arrived."

"Ah, yes. The viscount, from Tivor, though what is such an esteemed bishop is doing in Tivor?"

The captain shook his head in a firm no. "I do not know who my passengers are and where they are from, just that I am to receive a Paleowright dignitary and his party and transport them to Bareen."

"Ya? Then it appears I know more than you. Viscount Helprig and I, well, between you and me," he glanced at Khajeet, "not many like him, but I tolerate him; we have common goals."

The captain said, "I see."

"I have a bargain for you. You take our messenger here, Gumeric, with best speed to Stith Drakas, and I will guarantee passage to Bareen for your Paleowright dignitary. And," he went on before the captain could gainsay him, "I will double what the Church is paying you, and I will charge the viscount half. Everyone wins, especially you. Your ship will not sit here idle, you will earn double, and you will not have to bear the viscount's constant haranguing. He lives to complain. It makes him feel superior to all us grovelers. He will do it for the entire voyage."

It was well-known ship captains had a uniform distaste for haughty, demagogical passengers, especially clergy constantly preaching conversion to Diunesis Antiquaria, the Paleowright's faith. "The Church is paying forty gold. Not silver, but gold."

"Ha. And is that Hebert gold?" the major asked slyly.

The captain's visage clouded. The Paleowright church in Hebert minted their own gold sovereigns and pawned them off as equals to the other gold currencies. Unlike other nations, Hebert smelted the gold with lead to give it the same weight but half the value. "You would pay in Drakan gold?"

Startoren pointed to Khajeet, who went to a chest and withdrew a leather pouch. It clinked when he handed it to the captain. "Has the Church paid you yet?" It was another point the Church was infamous: Late payments and haggling over previously negotiated prices.

"No." The captain hefted the heavy pouch.

Easing back into his chair, the major said, "You would have to leave today, soon. I will welcome the viscount and see that he is taken care of."

Heaving a sigh, the captain stood. "Then we will leave now. I do not want to see your Paleowright churchmen entering the harbor as I am departing."

When the captain and Gumeric were gone, Khajeet said, "Your Ancient smiles on you."

"Ach, Thomas does not care about the trials of his followers; you would know that if you had your own."

Khajeet bowed. He was not a Paleowright; he was a Warkenvaal, and Warkenvaal was a nation of fervent doubters. They had a saying: *If it didn't sway the palms, it was hot air.*

The major gave a nod in return. "Now we wait for our good viscount. And I *will* beseech Thomas, my Ancient, to watch over Helprig's prisoner. It is worth praying the man is still alive."

Three days later, Startoren, through his telescope on the veranda, watched the pirate sloop dock directly across the quay from the *Tutagrapf*. Khajeet had paid an incentive to the harbor master to ensure the viscount's ship was docked so.

Through the telescope, the tableau unfolded. Startoren had indeed met Viscount Helprig once before and was loath to renew the acquaintance, but in the emperor's service he must. As prearranged, Khajeet posted himself near the gangway of the *Tutagrapf*. He would wait there for just the right moment.

Soon enough, after the longshoremen and pirates had started unloading cargo, a party of four churchmen walked down the brow of the sloop. There were four Scarlet Saviors, obvious in their yellow and crimson enameled armor, a docent, judging by his drab missionary tunic, and a bishop wearing a ruby-red miter, gold and white robes, and a red sash.

Curious, the major swept the telescope to the right and scanned the sloop. Where is the predicant? Bishops always had one or more predicants leading the way as they were loath to converse with commoners and certainly not the non-devoted. However, against Church decorum, there was the viscount, in all his gesticulating glory, ranting at any dock man with the ill luck to catch his attention. When he'd run out of dock men, he fixated on Khajeet. Startoren chuckled to himself; haranguing Khajeet was like railing at a palm tree. The distaste he had for the upcoming meeting was mollified by the spectacle.

As the viscount was winding down, dissipating his abundant hot air, Khajeet, as seen through the telescope, professed his sympathies and then offered their solution to the viscount's problem. That launched Helprig into more gesticulating. Startoren smiled to himself. *Ah, well, you are earning your pay today,* he thought. *Better you than me, Khajeet.* Eventually, there was head nodding, and the docent went back aboard the pirate vessel. *Was this ... the moment?* Startoren wondered.

On the sloop, the docent reappeared at the edge of the telescope's circular frame. Adjusting the view, Startoren saw a Scarlet Savior behind the docent with a shackled and hooded prisoner. A second Scarlet Savior, limping, goaded the prisoner forward, down to the quay. Sweeping the glass the length of the craft, Startoren saw no more Scarlet Saviors, and yet he was certain the viscount had departed for Tivor with over twenty of the vaunted paladins.

The telescope slewed to Helprig. There was something wrong with the viscount's left arm; he kept it close to his side, but under the voluminous robes anything, bandages, splints, weapons, could be concealed. The docent and prisoner entered the view, and the prisoner stumbled. The Scarlet Savior in the lead cuffed him on his hooded head and dragged him towards the *Tutagrapf*. The prisoner, clearly injured, hobbled on a bad right leg.

Startoren watched closely, holding his breath as the prisoner was dragged up the brow to the quarterdeck, whereupon the ship's captain interceded. Four crewmen were summoned and lifted the prisoner, carrying him down the midships hatch. All the while, the Scarlet Savior stood in the captain's face, adamant on some point. Startoren knew the *Tutagrapf's* captain and the stony look on his face. The confrontation broke off when the paladin gave up on the captain and went to find his prisoner.

Startoren lowered the telescope, satisfied. Warkenvaal, for Nak Drakas, was foreign territory. Whereas the *Tutagrapf*, even in port, was Drakan sovereign territory. The captain had his orders.

He waited as Helprig, walking as if he were on a church parade, left the quay with Khajeet and was lost from view. Khajeet was to bring him here for their meeting.

Time, too much time, passed. Startoren began to pace. *Where is Khajeet? Where is Helprig?*

A knock sounded at the door. The major composed himself, then opened the door. Khajeet entered abruptly and closed the door behind himself. "The viscount demanded I take him straight to his rooms at the hostel. I have left him in the care of Harrien and her ladies."

Stunned, Startoren began to form a question when Khajeet said, "He said if you must see him, you should do so after he has refreshed himself," the aide smirked.

"Ah."

"Yes," added Khajeet, "I think his intent is to snub you. To show a mere Drakan major must wait at his lord's pleasure."

"Ha!" Startoren breathed a sigh of relief. "And the docent and the four Savior's in Helprig's guard, can they see the harbor?"

"No, they are in the rear rooms that look upon the city, not the harbor. One is with the prisoner."

"Are there more Saviors on the pirate ship?"

"No, their Captain Irons said that was all they needed for an escort."

"Ach, then we go."

When they left the major's apartments, Khajeet turned right and the major left. "Sir," Khajeet called, "Helprig is this way."

"Ya, ya. It's time for us to go."

Startled, Khajeet hurried after the major, who was walking briskly. "Is there something you should say to the viscount?"

"Is Harrien safe?"

"Yes. The sultan's guard commander is her brother. Her establishment is protected. She has bravos of her own."

"Then everything is set," Startoren kept up the pace all the way to the *Tutagrapf.*

The captain stood ready on the quarterdeck. "We are ready."

"Good, then cast off, make way," he waved a hand flippantly, "do whatever it is you do, captain."

Bowing, the captain ordered the topsails unfurled, the rudder shifted, and lines cast off. The first mate ran to the seaward side and signaled the longboat to tow the bow away from the pier. A deckhand made to close the bulwark where the brow had been pulled aboard.

"Nach," the captain waved the sailor away and nodded to the second mate, who moved the cargo boom into position. The mate stood at the ready. Four Drakan soldiers stood at attention on either side of the quarterdeck.

Slowly, the bow of the *Tutagrapf* swung seaward. As sails caught wind, and the ship gained steerage, the longboat pulled alongside and was hoisted aboard.

When the first low swell moved the deck, a Scarlet Savior, the one who had threatened the captain, came charging up the ladder. A Drakan soldier, his hand on the hilt of his cutlass, met the Savior where the brow lay secured on the deck.

"What are we doing?" The Scarlet Savior, to Khajeet's amusement, appeared befuddled. "Where are we going? The viscount is not onboard," the man fumed. "I checked!"

"Ach, no worries, my Scarlet friend," the captain chided, "we are merely shifting berths."

The paladin looked and then pointed at the ocean. "Where? What berth?"

At a nod from the captain, the second mate let the cargo boom swing free under tension from its cables.

The soldier stepped back, and the boom hit the Scarlet Savior in the shoulder and tumbled him over the side, accompanied by a feminine scream and splash. Startoren hurried to the gunwale. "Can he swim?"

The captain didn't bother to look. "Not in that armor."

"Ha! The Scarlet Savior has met his match: The sea." Startoren turned to the captain. "Shall we see what we have caught?"

The first mate took them to a cabin, and Startoren waited for a guard to open the door. The prisoner sat on a bench, his hands tied behind him. What Startoren could not see through the telescope, he could see now. The churchmen had pulled off three toenails on the swollen and bloody foot.

Startoren looked to the captain and shook his head; the distaste of the deed repelled him.

Untying the drawstring, the major removed the hood. The man blinked and blinked again; then, his grey eyes focused on the major.

"Well, that's a start. They left you with both eyes." Startoren slid a small brandy cask over and sat. "Are you Achelous the Trader?"

The man's intelligent eyes analyzed him, but he didn't answer.

"Ach, come, come. You must tell me who you are or-- Khajeet?"

"Yes, sir," the aide stepped from behind the captain. "What did Helprig say he was going to do with our guest here?"

Khajeet grimaced. "It wasn't pretty."

"Tell us."

"They were to transfer ships in Vaal, sail for Bareen, then travel overland to Hebert where the prisoner was to be tried and hanged before the archbishop for his pleasure."

"What?" Startoren feigned surprise. "Tried and hanged? What about findings of guilt or innocence?"

"They don't usually bother with that."

Startoren looked closely at the prisoner. "Hanged after they had more fun with you, ya? You are now in the custody of the Empire of Nak Drakas." He sat straight to let the import take effect. "The Church of Diunesis Antiquaria's claim on you is void, by decree of the emperor, as enacted by Commandant Fritach of the Washentrufel. You are therefore under the emperor's protection. Do you understand?"

Finally, the prisoner gave a single nod.

"Good. Now the next question is important as my Church brothers, and I say that with some reluctance given their treatment of you—"

The first mate interrupted, "Sir, you haven't seen what they did to his hand."

The pained expression on the major's face when he saw the bloody bandages offered a glimmer of hope to the prisoner. The Drakan was not here to kill or torture him, and he was certainly Washentrufel: The Drakan secret service.

"I'm sorry," the major said to him, the silver orbs on the uniform's epaulets signifying his rank, "but I'd rather not see your hand. Captain, you will have the ship's doctor do what he can."

"Of course." Then the captain asked the prisoner, "The Scarlet Savior, the corporal, did he do any of this?"

The prisoner grimaced, then nodded.

A sniff, and the captain said, "We gave him a swimming test. He failed."

Startoren edged his cask closer. "Alas, I have duties," and he asked the next question with a pause in between words, "one-- more—time. Who are you?"

"A trader." The voice came as a hoarse croak.

"Ach, give this man some water!" Startoren tapped his heel on the deck. He watched the prisoner drink half a skin without stopping, his anger rising. *If the Church had killed this man ... such a grave disservice to the empire!*

When the prisoner rested the flask in his lap, Startoren pressed, "Your name?"

Their eyes met. The prisoner showed no fear, which would have infuriated the churchmen. He seemed to measure, analyze the major, calculating outcomes. Finally, one word, "Achelous."

With a nod, the major rose from his cask. "Then Trader Achelous, you are under my care, and the protection of the emperor. If you had not been that man, well.... The captain here and I take our duties seriously." He turned and motioned they were leaving, but then asked, "Helprig left Hebert with over twenty Scarlet Saviors and his predicant Nuritt. This we know. We know they went to Tivor to arrest you, and it was Helprig's secret, not communicated to the archbishop, to take your woman as well. The Lady Marisa Pontifract. She is the mother of your child, is she not?"

Achelous had given up on the notion that safe guarding Marisa's relationship with him would spare her. Their life together in Tivor was widely known. "Yes."

"Where are the other Saviors? And understand trader, the empire did not have a role in your abduction. It is not the emperor's desire to stoke war with the Aorolmin of Tivor. But if there are more Scarlet Saviors following, then the captain and I should know it. Where is his predicant?"

"I know one is dead."

"One?" Startoren blinked. "What of the others? Ten, maybe twenty others?"

This was news to Achelous. In truth, he could account for five Scarlet Saviors and the predicant Nuritt. Nuritt had died from a defense bot vectored from the rafters of Marinda Hall. Four other defense bots had descended on the Paleowright attackers as they invaded the Hall. He himself had killed one with the laser in his handbolt. What happened after that he knew not, knocked unconscious. Regardless, he desperately needed to know what happened to Marisa, Boyd, and Baryy. He was sorely tempted to ask their fate, but he knew through torture survival training you never gave your interrogators a handle, a lever to use against you. The churchmen, during his torture, thinking he was unconscious, repeatedly cursed Marisa. The fact she had not been abducted indicated she, Spirits prevail, survived the attack. Boyd and Baryy, though, he had no clue.

He decided to offer something, hoping to gain something in return. "Nuritt is dead. He died in the hall."

An eyebrow went up. Startoren mused, "Helprig could not have been happy. Was he there?"

"I didn't see him."

"Ach, that would be Helprig. Let others do the dirty work." He glanced at Khajeet. "We leave. Rest, Trader Achelous. You have a long journey ahead of you."

# Chapter 2
# The Crevice

## Wedgewood

"That's new. What's in there?" Outish asked, surveying a new building behind the Special Mill.

Agent Meridia, formerly Senior Corporal Illian Meridia, Avarian Assault Marines, trudged up a path behind the old sawmill. The mill everyone had now come to call the Special Mill, named after the Avarian Special Forces troopers who had taken up residence in improved it during the matriarch's brief visit to Dianis. Meridia unlocked the door with a metal key, distinctly provincial. "Come in and look."

The shed, actually a small barn, smelled of newly sawn timber. The wood, a virgin yellow, undimmed by age. "Lights," called Meridia.

"Whoa. Are you allowed to do that?" Outish, an IDB astrobiologist, exclaimed. "We're Class E!"

"Class F, now," remarked the Ready Reaction IDB Agent. "The news came down from Clienen today. ULUP wants the planet locked down. That gives the IDB more latitude for protective measures. Including *planet-side discretionary improvements to protect indigenous life forms, societies, cultural norms, etc., etc. as deemed necessary by the IDB and their agents in-country.*" Meridia winked at Outish. "And if hidden AI capabilities in IDB in-country structures aid in that prime directive, we're good."

Outish blinked. "Artificial lighting instead of lanterns will help protect Wedgewood?" he asked.

Meridia smiled. "If I don't have to waste time fumbling to light a lantern, then yes."

While Meridia was only two years older than Outish's twenty-one standard, it always struck Outish how *much* older the ex-Marine looked. Outish knew life was hard in the assault Marines, but that only went so far to explain the agent's weathered hard looks.

Outish let it go when Meridia pulled a tarp aside and exposed a dual-o-pellar.

"Whaaat?" If he was alarmed by the automatic lighting, he was stunned by the anti-grav sled. "What's that for?"

"You and me, buddy. You and me."

"What?"

"Yep. We're going for a ride."

"A ride? Where?"

"To the top! You didn't think we were going to *hike* all the way to the top of Mount Mars?"

"Well ...."

Meridia, his close-cropped hair, Marine regulation, and shaven face were distinctly at odds with Outish, who'd gone native, looking like a typical Wedgewood townie. Most of Clan Mearsbirch, however, knew Illian Meridia, Illy to many, as an Ancient; they just didn't talk about it. It was the clan's secret, and they were fine with it. They also knew Outish was an Avarian, or rather an Ancient, but Outish was a local hero, having fought against the Scarlet Saviors in the Battle of Wedgewood. So, the clan was happy with keeping his heritage a secret as well. In truth, Outish had a deeper secret thanks to IDB Field Outfitting: He was not an Avarian human, he was a Halorite transmuted to appear human. It had been his choice, otherwise Chief Achelous Forushen would not have allowed him in-country to conduct his astrobiologist internship.

"Outy, I've humped my ass across too many deserts, through too many swamps, for me to slog it up that mountain if I can ride."

The astrobiologist still looked uncertain, so Meridia called up the *Shields* using his A-wave ear implant.

On the team net, Outish heard, "*Shields* here." It was Sergeant Mears. Outish would never forget that voice. It was Mears who locked him into a powered armor suit and then depowered it so Outish could not fight against extrasolars who attacked the aquamarine mine. He was still sore about that. Outish was crucial to the success of uplifting Dianis and had his own Ready Reaction agent as a bodyguard: Meridia.

"Ready to make our way up to the top, Mears. Is the way clear?" Meridia looked at Outish, "Of any curious provincials?"

"Go out the back doors, take a course of two-seven-zero for three miles, and then you can go straight up."

"Roger that, *Shields*." Still early in the recommissioning of Central Station, the *IDBS Shields* was the only IDB ship, a cutter, in orbit over Dianis and in the Margel system. There were times when, in-country on Dianis, as a former Marine accustomed to operating in an assault battalion, Illian felt very alone. There were other times when it was exhilarating to be out on the edge. Just him, his plasma, and the belief in what he was doing.

"Okay, Outy. I have all the gear we need in the cargo pods. Hop on."

Outish gripped the handrails, and Meridia fastened the sled buckles, which only increased Outish's disquiet.

They whizzed out the back doors; the antigrav spewing pine needles in its wake. Having cleared the *provincial zone*, Meridia mashed the power button, and the dual-o-pellar jolted Outish against the restraining belt; his grip on the rails turned sweaty. They zoomed up the steepening slope. Meridia paid no heed to the blur of passing Ungerngerist pines. To Outish, it seemed the ex-Marine picked the steepest route possible. The snow cover began and deepened as they neared the top. Outish, foolishly, dared look behind him and immediately regretted it: A trough in the white expanse followed them at breathtaking speed up the mountain, jinking around outcroppings, leaving the town of Wedgewood far, far below. Above the tree line, a plume of snow billowed in their wake right up and onto the flattened cornice.

The sled's GPS target indicator pinged, *At Destination*.

Illian raised his goggles and surveyed the site. "So, this is it." He settled the 'pellar on a patch of wind-swept granite. Unbuckling, he stepped off the sled. The air, at that altitude, cold and thin. Glorious sunshine sparkled off the snow. The sky was an amazing royal blue. Meridia felt alive, renewed. He always cherished the adventure when he pulled duty on primitive, pristine worlds. Especially those devoid of Turboii or Sizars, which was a rarity. His former job as an assault Marine had been the tip of the spear. The spear rarely went where there were no Sizars.

Outish, unsteady, disoriented, and perhaps motion sick, unbuckled his harness and slid off the sled, his heart beating, lungs gulping air.

Meridia noticed his friend struggling and helped steady him. "There, that better?"

"What, you couldn't go any slower?" A wave of nausea passed, and feeling better, he pulled out his multi-func and marked where the survey scans from the *Shields* indicated densities of plasto-concrete and albaminia.

Scoured clear by gales, the nearby area was bare of snow.

"That's it. That's the decking that Atch, er, chief, thought was a big hatch cover," said Outish, pointing.

At the spot, Meridia said, "Yep," not bothering to look down on the bare metal he was standing on. A metal whose invention was attributed to the Loch Norim. He pulled a scanner from his pack and held it to his face like a pair of binoculars.

"That's not disguised for in-country," complained Outish. As an astrobiologist, his job was to evaluate planetary sentient life *without* extrasolar influence. *Any* influence.

"You seen any provincials?" Meridia asked, as he turned in a three-hundred-sixty-degree circle.

"No," Outish turned away.

"Did you get that upload, Mears?" Meridia queried the ship.

Mears answered over the team net. "Affirmative. Analyzing and correlating with the recon bot data."

Meridia lowered the scanner and looked at Outish. "You were right."

Outish squinted in the sparkling light reflected from the snow. "About?"

"Airburst for certain. Probably a low-yield neutron missile to take out air defenses." He referred to Outish's extraordinary posting in the *Loch Norim Historical Registry,* where he posited the Mount Mars site was *confirmed* to be Loch Norim and had been partially destroyed in an attack. "Why did you think it was followed by direct bombing?"

"Well, it was really Baryy and the chief who thought that. I just wrote it down and posted it."

Meridia's experienced eye looked for more clues. "Any idea why they thought that?"

Mears, listening in on the team net, answered, "Could it be the depression to the north of your position, at the head of the valley?"

"It's over there," Outish pointed. "It has snowed more since we were last up here, but Atch, er, chief, and Baryy examined rock samples from the crater. Baryy's multi-func registered chemical residues related to hydrazine explosives."

Meridia raised the scanner, making several adjustments. "You know, you can call Atch by his name. He's not your chief anymore. However, we may have to call him counselor instead, the next time we see him."

"*If* we see him." Outish kicked at the snow.

Meridia lowered his scanner. An Avarian in his early twenties, the ex-Marine's care-worn face was understanding but firm. "You'll see him again. I've never met him, so it will be a first for me," he grinned.

Meandering about the wind-swept clearing, they came to a precipice and gazed to the south, the farms in the parks below Wedgewood lost in the distant haze. Standing there, taking in the view, Meridia said, "I have work to do."

"Yeah, we have to survey the site."

Meridia brooded. "That, too."

"What, what else do you have to do?" asked Outish.

The scanner dangled in Meridia's hand. "Payback, Outish. No one kidnaps and murders IDB agents on Dianis without us coming down on them. I promised Lettern that the Church would pay for Baryy's blood in Merinda Hall. We'll find the Scarlet Bastards that did it. They're too arrogant to keep Marinda Hall a secret. We spam enough recon bots across Isuelt, we'll find out who they are."

"They're coming," Lettern said, checking the disguised multi-func in her vambrace.

The mining foreman tried to get a peek at the Ancient technology strapped to her forearm, but the armor shutter had slid into place, concealing the multi-func interface.

"No, no, no." She smiled. Her brown eyes twinkled in the lamplight. "No peeking. You know how the Ancients are about that." Standing inside the entrance to the Crevice, Lettern was silhouetted by the daylight. Her brown hair done up in a bun, the way Illy liked it. *Marisa's bun* is what she called it. The hairstyle was Lettern's only feminine touch to her appearance. Buckskin leather britches, a short sword, and a handbolt were her standard accoutrements.

The foreman looked disappointed. "Why is the Crevice important? All the aquamarine is that way," he pointed down at his feet. "The Crevice goes that way," he waved his arm at the dark cleft. "A slight rise into the mountain, and that's *solid* granite. The fractures with the aquamarine pegmatites are down deep, near the gold seams."

She shrugged. "Outish says there might be Loch Norim in the mountain. This could be the easiest way in. Clienen, I mean Director Hor, I have to remember to call him director; you know those Ancients," she smiled mischievously. "He says it's no coincidence that the Loch Norim built on top of an aquamarine formation."

Lettern was not an Ancient. She was a Timberkeep, a Dianis provincial. As such, she was the only Dianis provincial in the service of the Avarian IDB. There would be more as Director Hor rebuilt the Margel Damansk organization, but for now, she was unique. Clienen had agreed to accept her into the service not only because he needed Civilization Monitoring (CivMon) agents experienced in Dianis society, but because the matriarch recommended her. A month ago, Lettern and been a branch warden in command of Ogden's archers in the Second Ward of the Wedgewood Militia. Then, on a fateful spring day, Agent Illian Meridia had unlawfully given her an IDB plasma rifle with which she immediately found an affinity. She'd carried it into battle against an armed shuttle crewed by corsairs, as they sought to loot the Wedgewood aquamarine mine. Word of her exploit had been carried into space by the extrasolar miners she had thwarted. Krch, one of the miners, had posted a video from the shuttle's cockpit camera to the Fednet Interconn, and hence across a host of human worlds. In the backrooms and bars of the freelance mining community, miners had complained bitterly of the IDB arming Class E provincials with plasma rifles in violation of ULUP. The video had gone viral, and the resource extraction lobby accused the IDB of violating its own charter, but that's not what alarmed the miners most: It was the damage that a single, determined, unarmored provincial could do with a plasma. Lettern Stouttree's face would be seen by a billion viewers as she ducked under a stream of laser pulses, her lithe form rolling away, coming to a crouch, firing, and taking out the cockpit plexiglass. Shockwaves still rippled across planets striving for their own uplift equality.

Lettern, by any measure, was a junior agent in training, but the chaos the extrasolars had wreaked had forced Director Hor to trust her in-country. The irony was, junior agent or not, Lettern's natural home was *in-country* Dianis.

"Loch Norim?" asked the foreman. "Never heard of that. What's a Loch Norim?"

"Really old Ancients," Lettern said, then paused, hearing Meridia and Outish talking outside the entrance. "You know, the ancestors of the Ancients?"

A slow nod showed the foreman struggled with the notion. Lettern, having just completed injection learning for human and Galactic History, understood the leap he had to make. It was all so confusing she opted to concentrate on what she needed *that* day and ignored all the other *stuff.*

Meridia and Outish came, holding oil lanterns.

"You lads ready to go caving?" asked the foreman.

"Oi," answered Meridia, practicing his Doroman. He was Ready Reaction, Lettern was Civilization Monitoring, as was Outish. They were all members of the IDB, but Meridia's responsibility was agent protection and enforcement, whereas Lettern was everything else except for astrobiology, which was Outish's turf. That is the way it would remain until the hundred new IDB agents were recruited, trained, and assigned to the Margel, the IDB quadrant jurisdiction, named after the Margel Damansk asteriod cloud notorious for unscrupulous freelance mining outfits.

"The foreman was explaining the mine to me," she said. "The director suspects there is a shaft in the center of the mountain, going through the Loch Norim site you guys were at the top of. He thinks it goes straight down into the aquamarine deposits."

"Ula," declared the foreman. "The gold seams lead south and down. Not north and up. We follow the gold. Oi, we did find aquamarine, but there's no gold up here, so we stopped digging. Could be a shaft, as you say, down the center of the mountain, but I wouldn't know."

Lettern didn't know much about geology, but saw a whole raft of injection learning courses on it in the Dianis catalog. She would rather trust the director to know what he was doing than literally *dig* through all those courses herself.

"Besides," the foreman continued, "The shaft nearest here, the one with the aquamarine, is closed. We collapsed the aquamarine diggings when the churchmen attacked."

"That can be fixed," Meridia offered.

"Ula, if you want to spend years digging! We burned the timbers, and a massive cave-in buried it."

"Okay," she peered at the darkness of the tunnel before them, "I assume the Crevice goes that way?"

The mining foreman grinned. "That be a good guess."

She gave him a wag of her head, "I'm not afraid of the dark," but she was claustrophobic.

As they made their way to the Crevice, the foreman in the lead, Lettern asked, "Outy, what did you guys bring in those packs?" The satchels appeared heavy the way he and Illy shouldered the loads.

"Gear," answered Meridia.

"Water, food, shovels, and some sort of driller," said Outish.

"It is a hike to the end. Done it twice myself," said foreman as he stopped to hold his lantern high.

After the foreman resumed his pace, Outish said to Lettern, who took up the rear of the expedition, "It's a thousand meters."

Lettern did the conversion to Dianis feet and said, "Oh." She activated her new A-wave audio implant in her ear and whispered to Jeremy, the CivMon AI in Central Station. She loved talking to Jeremy via A-wave. As a Dianis provincial and new to Avarian technology, she was fascinated to have such a smart person in her head ready to answer any question she had. "Jeremy, how far do we have to go from here?"

"Nine hundred and thirty-two meters," came the instant reply. Jeremy was tracking the expedition's progress via the Aura scanner on board the *Shields* in orbit. The deeper into the mountain they went, the more the rock attenuated their aura emanations. That's why, in her pack, Lettern carried an aura beacon boosted to the max. The IDB prescribed a curriculum of injection learning courses for new CivMon agents. Being a Class E, now F provincial, Jeremy had augmented Lettern's own curriculum with what seemed like months more of additional injection lessons. One, which she took on Jeremy's advice, was *Basics of Auras, Emanations, and Shielding*.

At six hundred meters, they came to the end of the Timberkeep diggings where the miners had discovered the cave and named it the Crevice. They gave it that title because no other cave like it existed on the mountain.

"It's not hard," said the foreman. "Just a wee bit tight in places."

The IDB agents just nodded. They'd reviewed the recon bot video and laser image scan. Jeremy's analysis gave it an eighty-eight percent probability that the Crevice was a *sentient-made artifact.*

"There's no side tunnels or caverns for you to get lost in. Strange, that." The foreman settled his frame pack on his shoulders and resumed the march.

After an hour slogging and scraping around protrusions in the dark, the blackness only randomly punctuated by the light of her lantern, Lettern collided with Outish's back. They had come to an end. She was feeling a subtle but rising sense of oppression; the surrounding inky blackness and the immovability of the rock around and above literally weighed on her. Her imagination conjured up an image of the whole massive mountain above shifting just a little bit and squishing them like fleas. Shaking her head, she tried to dispel the creeping panic before it spiraled down to hysteria. In front of of Outish and the foreman that would be an awkward reaction, in the least.

They shined their lanterns at a rubble wall.

"That looks real." Outish sweated in the cool, damp air.

"Oi, cave in. Look at the fractured rock. Could have been a quake. Though we don't get many of those." The foreman picked up a chunk of granite, examining it with the detachment of an grizzled miner. "Hate to dig through that."

Meridia eased his pack off his shoulders and set it down with a thump. Sitting on a boulder, he said, "Roger that."

They waited in the silence that gradually became more awkward. Finally, the foreman said, "Tis a pity to come all the way here just to turn around and go back. But I told you it was a dead end."

Outish nodded. "Yep, you did."

Then Meridia stood and asked the foreman, "I gather you can get out on your own?"

Surprised, the foreman said slowly, "Oi."

"Then go ahead. Lettern will go with you. Outish and I need to figure out what to do from here."

The foreman tilted his head. It dawned on him that his job was over, and he wasn't needed or wanted anymore. He shrugged. "Be fine with me. We've an ore load coming up from the Pit shaft, and I need to make sure the sluice run is ready."

After the foreman's lantern started its clink-clank back down the tunnel, Lettern said, "I'll be back in ten." Though the thought of going, and then having to come back alone, filled her with dread, she took a step, then another, and steeled herself.

Meridia watched her go. "She'll make sure he doesn't have a sudden change of mind and decide to come back."

Outish nodded sagely as Meridia reached into one of their packs and removed the contents, sorting them on the cave floor. The first device was a halon float light. This time, Outish didn't squawk about the use of galactic technology. Meridia set the device to float just below the ceiling. Its bright-white glow exposed the entire tunnel and cave-in. He handed Outish a headlamp and pulled out the next device. Outish recognized it as a geologic sonar transponder.

Setting it on the ground, Meridia actuated it. A low-pitched thrum, just at the edge of human hearing, pulsed from the device. "We'll let that do its work while Jeremy analyzes the readings."

The next contraption Meridia retrieved, this time out of Outish's pack, the astrobiologist didn't recognize.

The ex-Marine exchanged his in-country boots with a pair of insulated wire-braided miner boots, strapped a scanner on his head, and donned a respirator. "There's two respirators in my pack," he said in a muffled voice. "Put one on. There will be some out gassing."

Outish frowned. He'd not been included in this part of the expedition planning. Clienen just said Meridia would take care of the cave-in.

Unpacking a thing that looked like a snub-nosed rifle attached via an armored hose to a small backpack, Meridia strapped on the cable pack and asked Outish, "You see that expeller funnel?" he pointed over his shoulder behind his back. "Make sure it is pointed to the right and directly at the wall."

"You mean this snorkel thing that comes off the top of the pack?"

"Yes."

Outish twisted the expeller nozzle so that, as Meridia stood facing the cave-in, the nozzle pointed at the wall to the right. "Okaaay."

Mears came on the team net. "Meridia, you sure you want to do this without power armor?"

The nearest suit was at the Special Mill. You couldn't stuff them in packs; you wore them. Meridia took a deep breath through the respirator and let it out slowly. He thought about Marisa and her hurry to put the rescue team together and the frenzied activity in Tivor and New Ungern to get the troops and rifles ready for what they were sure would be an assault. "No time to fuss with subterfuge, Sarge. We have to get this done. If we wait until after the mission...." *The rescue might fail, and I might be dead,* he thought.

"Yeah," was the sergeant's slow, grudging agreement. "ULUP wants into the site bad. If we don't do it now, who knows what screwy plans they'll come up with."

"I've analyzed the sonar scan results," said Jeremy. "The tunnel collapse is forty-eight meters in length. Beyond it, the way is clear to the facility. Scan results indicate a substantial facility extending both upwards and downwards from your elevation."

The radar imaging from the *Shields* could penetrate only so far into the rock. Placing an actual sonar transmitter inside the mountain gave better data.

"Well, there you go, Sarge. I've enough energy packs for a hundred meters. And the heat build-up shouldn't be too bad."

"You're the miner. I've never done it before."

Outish watched Meridia's mask bob up and down in agreement. "Illian," he asked, "You've done this before?"

Lieutenant Hearter entered the bridge of the *Shields* as Outish asked the question. "Meridia ready to use the matter atomizer?"

Mears muted the bridge microphone. "Yes, I told him he should have powered armor on."

Hearter sat down in the commander's chair. "That atomizer is an expensive gadget. ULUP paid for it, not us. Probably better than the ones the Marines use for excavating their underground bases."

"You just have to stay clear of the expeller spray and the plasma wall. It will be hot." Meridia told Outish.

Hearter and Mears looked at each other. "That's an understatement," Hearter said.

Peering through the scanner, Meridia connected the control interface to the matter atomizer. The unit came preconfigured as a terrain manipulator. "Send me the course, Jeremy."

A red grid appeared on his scanner's head-up display that superimposed, virtually, the excavation frame on the rockslide to his front. "Stand back, Outish, way back."

"Right!" Outish hustled down the tunnel just as Lettern came up. He handed her a respirator and headlight. "He's going to use the expeller thing."

"Oooh, I wanted to see that," she said, incredibly relieved to be amongst people and the bright halon glow.

"No, you don't. Not up close. Stay back." From Hearter, it was more of an order than a suggestion.

Meridia aimed the plasma emitter, and the atomizer grid in his scanner turned green.

Lettern saw a bright flash in front of Meridia. At first, she thought something had gone wrong, but then it flashed again and again.

"It's working," Meridia said on the team net. He took another small step forward and triggered the gun. Each time, he was careful to keep both the targeting grid green and his shoulders oriented straight at the rubble blockage. He could feel the heat from the expeller nozzle as it sprayed the atomized granite against the wall to the right. Each step took him further into the collapse, and the tunnel grew warmer.

"Wow, Outy. He's eating his way into the mountain!" said Lettern. Jeremy had configured the size of the target grid tall enough so the miner could walk upright and wide enough, so the expeller spray solidified far enough to the right to reduce the risk of a burn to the miner. The floor, ceiling, and left wall of the new tunnel were warm to the touch, but not hot. The expeller wall, though, glowed a dull orange, cooling to black.

After twenty meters, Meridia felt sweat dribbling down his sides; the cold, dank air of the tunnel replaced by a sauna. His feet in the fluid-cooled mining boots were warm. A few more meters, he stopped and backed out of the tunnel, careful to not touch the wall of cooling expeller granite.

He pulled off the scanner and wiped a rivulet of sweat from his eyes. He went to pull his respirator off, but Lettern motioned to keep it in place. "It stinks in here now. You need to keep that on." The noxious gas began to water his eyes, and he put the scanner back on.

Lettern's voice was serious, "Don't burn yourself, Illy."

He shook his head. "Halfway through. We'll let it cool a bit more. I brought lunch." He went and rummaged in a pack, retrieving three foil packages.

"What's in those? Outish asked.

"Roast berga sandwiches and spun toi tubers." He went to the tunnel and set the foil packages in an indentation in the expeller wall. When he came back, he said, "Lunch will be ready in a few."

"Did you make that divot in the wall on purpose?" Lettern asked, impressed.

"Yep. Old Marine trick."

"How does that work?" She asked, pointing at the odd-looking gun.

He knew what she was thinking. Weapons were her thing. "It is a plasma gun, but not like your rifle. These energy packs," he patted the fuel cell clipped to the bottom of the gun, "have sand in them instead of bolt particles. The gun sprays the plasma sand, which atomizes the rock. This," he pointed at a funnel positioned beneath the flared gun muzzle, "is a gravity inducer. It sucks in the matter vapor through this tube, where it is condensed and ejected as a stream out of the expeller snorkel on the pack. The stream lands wherever the snorkel is pointed and solidifies. Just don't let it land on you. *It's hot.*"

She looked disappointed. "Oh."

Meridia chuckled. "Yeah, not much of a weapon, but it's good for smoking rats and tunnel-toads."

When the gas haze cooled and settled around their feet, he retrieved their lunch.

"That's good berga," Lettern said, devouring her sandwich.

"From the Sea Haven League," supplied Outish.

Meridian nodded. "Only the best for the IDB."

"What happened to all the granite?" Outish asked. "Did all the granite get expelled on that wall?"

Meridia shrugged. "That rubble isn't as solid as you think. Some gets flattened into the floor, some is vaporized, a lot is disintegrated, and the expelled rock is dense. It forms tunnel support to prevent another cave-in."

Resuming the work, Lettern and Outish backed way down the Crevice. Several times, Meridia had to stop and retreat from the rising temperature.

Nearing the sonar-mapped end of the cave-in, Meridia took a step, and the top of the expeller grid turned red. He gave the gun another pulse. The heat was nearly unbearable. "You've broken through," said Jeremy on the team net. "Enlarge the opening, and the heat should drop." Two more pulses and Meridia could feel cold air flow into the tunnel.

Shrinking the rubble pile to knee-high, he stopped. "Should I be feeling an air current? It must be open to the outside for me to get an airflow?"

"Potentially," answered Jeremy. "Proceed with caution."

Meridia climbed over the rubble pile and doffed the atomizer gun and cable pack. Lettern and Outish hurried through the new tunnel.

"You got your pack?" Meridia asked Lettern, staring into the cleared darkness.

"Yes."

"Get them out."

She turned her back to Outish, "Get the plasmas out, will you?"

He handed her one of them. She checked the weapon's charge and holstered it, but kept her hand on the grip.

They eased along the Crevice until they came to a wide and tall chamber. The rock was cut clean and smooth. "We're the first humans here in hundreds of years." Meridia scuffed the floor dust with his boot. "Not a track."

"Fifteen hundred and sixty-seven," said Jeremy.

Outish moved his head and lamp around like he was searching for ghosts.

Lettern asked, "What's fifteen hundred and sixty-seven?"

Outish stopped searching the dark recesses and said breathlessly, "Years. Galactic standard. That's how long this site has been abandoned. Maybe it wasn't abandoned." His headlamp started probing the darkness. "Maybe they died in the attack."

Lettern wanted to chide him for being morbid, but the brooding silence stilled her tongue.

They walked a short distance until the floating halon light illuminated a portal, a large door, albaminia by its dull ocher hue. It was open. They stood there, staring at the formidable armored door.

"It's open?" Meridia asked himself.

"It's a tomb," breathed Outish. "Waiting for us to go in. The ghosts. They are."

"Oh, that's creepy," said Lettern. Unconsciously, she moved closer to Illian, her hand tight on the grip of the plasma pistol.

"You believe in ghosts?" Meridia asked.

Outish croaked, "Yes."

"Good. It will keep you honest."

Lettern swallowed audibly. Her plasma was a comfort, but she didn't know what it would do to an unearthly spirit. "Do ghosts live fifteen hundred years?"

Unsure, Meridia replied, "That's a long time."

Hearter unmuted the mic. "Okay, team. I see what you see. It's been a long day. Shall we wrap it up now and pull out, or forge ahead? Ivan and backup are a long way off."

Meridia waited for Outish or Lettern to say something, but when he turned to look at them, he found them staring at him. "Jeremy, what's your threat analysis?"

"Low. The open portal indicates the occupants fled the facility, not caring who would enter after they left."

"Roger," Meridia said, glancing between Outish and Lettern. "No spirits, they boogied." He gave a head waggle. "There's nothing stopping us. Let's go make history."

# Chapter 3
## The Galleries of Norim

*Mount Mars*

Lettern deployed the recon bots. There were ten bots in the kit: Four recon bumble bees, four defense, a control, and an analytic. "Running a recon bot a hundred meters out and another at fifty," she quoted from the ops plan. "The control bot is aloft. A defender is pulling up the rear."

With the halon floating light following above and behind them, they entered through the open door. The portal, more like an armored hangar bay, was albaminia and ferroconcrete, both a dull grey. Lettern fed the video feed of the bot flying out fifty meters to her optic nerve overlay. Meridia took the bot hovering at a hundred meters. The optic nerve implant still gave Lettern occasional bouts of vertigo, but she was growing accustomed to seeing the view of a camera interposed with her own. Two blinks turned the feed off, and three turned it on. Outish had a third bot slaved to a hologrid he projected from his multi-func. He complained the optic nerve was too distracting.

The bots went through an open door at the end of the antechamber. Jeremy called out the recon data, "Recon Alpha is in position, as is Beta. No aura signatures, unusual energy sources, or hazardous gases detected. The path is clear."

Meridia began to move. "Jeremy, send Delta bot to roam ahead. Outy, what are you doing with Charlie?" He saw the third bot hovering at what appeared to be an access panel.

"Uh?"

Lettern looked over at Outish's hologrid. "What ya doing, Outy?"

"Uh, oh. I'm trying to read Loch Norim."

Then Hearter offered, "Jeremy can decipher that for you."

"Yeah, I know," and with a swipe of a finger on the hologrid, the bumble bee bot whisked down the passage.

Delta ranged ahead and marked two side corridors, each leading to stairs going down. At the end of the long corridor, two hundred thirty meters from the party's current position, it came to another door; this one closed. When the bot came within scanner range of the control panel, it winked to life. "The facility has power," said Jeremy. That gave the team pause.

"After fifteen hundred years?" Outish asked.

No one spoke, including Jeremy on the net.

Lettern's hand strayed to the hilt of her gun.

"Lights aren't on," noted Meridia. "Jeremy, watch the bot feeds. Maybe there's a circuit breaker that's been tripped."

"Will do. There is a double-slide door that you will come to that has power at its access panel. The scanner in the panel is operational."

"Can the bot interact with the panel?" Meridia asked.

"Negative. The panel is not responding to any of our near-radio or A-wave protocols."

"Have Alpha and Beta backtrack and search for surveillance devices."

They'd walked a minute when Jeremy reported, "Probable surveillance devices located in ceiling panels. No measurable electrical or other energy patterns discernable. The devices appear to be inoperative."

"Or purposely powered off," said Meridia. "We would do that: Switch off the power relays so the Turboii thought the base was completely down. Then power up at the last second."

They walked a few more paces when Lettern said, "It's been hundreds of years, Illy. Do you think they're still waiting?"

He waggled his head. "The paranoid live longer."

When they reached the double-slide door, they found Tic, the analytic bot, perched on the biometrics input plate with its proboscis glued to the glass.

"Oh—" Lettern blanched, "what's it doing?"

"We've been running protocol permutations to open the door," replied Jeremy. "I've enlisted the assistance of the Central Station server core."

She gave a blank look to Meridia.

"They're trying to crack the code and access the facility's computer systems." He removed a glove and reached out a finger. "Can I try it?" he asked of Jeremy.

"Uploading your aura signature and fingerprint to the panel's local data store."

Meridia touched a icon he assumed was Loch Norim for *Open.* The two doors slid open partway then caught. Alpha and Beta whizzed through the opening.

"Lights coming on," said Jeremy. The corridor beyond the door bloomed into an off-yellow hue. "Those are emergency lights. Central Station hacking programs are attempting to gain access to a local computer grid. Power for your section of the facility is low current only. I am composing a schematic diagram of the base as we identify circuits. There are auxiliary energy coils in maintenance mode."

Meridia cocked his head.

"What?" asked Lettern.

"I know this," bragged Outish. "It means there's power coming from somewhere to keep the batteries charged."

Meridia nodded. "Aux coils last a long time. They don't age. This place has some engineering in it."

They followed behind the path of Delta. Beyond the double-slider, the facility was markedly different. The dull grey of ferroconcrete replaced with pristine white passages whose walls were some form of resin. There were rooms and corridors along the way.

Lettern peeked through the glass window of a door, standing on her tiptoes. She caught Illian admiring her form.

She looked back into the chamber beyond, smiling. "Oooh, what *is* all that stuff?"

Meridia came over and put his head next to hers, an arm around her waist. Something inside caught his eye. "Jeremy, have the recon bots scanned all these rooms?"

A bumble bee buzzed near, and he stood aside to let the bot scan through the window. After a time, Jeremy answered, "Medical bay. Those are cryostasis pods."

"Open the door." Meridia eased Lettern aside and drew his weapon. "Clear the door," he told her, and he himself stood to the right of the opening. They waited.

"Locating the door in the object database. Apologies," said Jeremy, "the dialect of Loch Norim used in the facility has unusual nuances." Then the door slid open. "Assuming the translation is correct, this is *Cryo Berth Three*. It is listed as having fifty cryostasis pods and a medical response station."

Meridia explained it to Lettern, "The medical response station is in case someone comes out of cryo in bad shape."

"What's cryo?" she mouthed.

Meridia rolled his eyes. He slid around the door, weapon up.

"All pods are listed as unoccupied," Jeremy offered.

"Yeah," answered Meridia, "but some hatches are open."

Beta vectored to an open pod.

Meridia waited as the bot hummed around the edge of the coffin-like appliance, then it went inside and backed out when Tic took its place.

Outish stood beside Meridia. His curiosity peaked; he ventured closer to look inside.

"Careful," said Hearter on the net, "we don't know what stasis chemicals they used."

Lettern tried whispering to Jeremy over the team net.

"There's a side channel for you to communicate directly with a single team member," Mears offered.

"Oh," she said, surprised.

Meridia answered for Jeremy, "Basically, a cryopod is a bed, an enclosed bed, that you lay in. You close the hatch and put a breather tube in your mouth. Then cryo fluids fill the pod. The breather tube puts you to sleep. You stay that way until the pod wakes you up." He looked at the pod. The longest he'd ever been in cryo was a week, and that was part of his Marine basic training. "Could be a year, ten, or even a hundred."

"A hundred years?!" She grimaced, stunned. "How do you know you will wake up?"

"The machine is programmed before you go in. You set a timer."

"I have been able to age the fluid degeneration from dried samples in the bottom of the pod," said Jeremy. "The chemicals are similar but different from Avarian."

"Fluid degeneration ...," mused Meridia. "You can determine when the pod was last used?"

"Verifying my findings with IDB Headquarters."

They waited.

"Confirmed. There is a ninety-three percent probability the pod was last used forty-one years ago."

Outish didn't think he heard that right.

Meridia cocked his head. "Say what?"

But Lettern put a voice to what they were all thinking. "Nuts and twigs. Forty-one years? That's almost like yesterday."

"The data and estimation has been verified with IDB Headquarters on Avaria."

Meridia eyed the other tubes in the chamber. "Jeremy, check the other ones." He started walking around the room looking for more clues. "Lieutenant?"

"Yes?" answered Hearter.

Meridia composed his thoughts. "You need to inform Clienen."

"Yes."

"The Matrincy will need to know." He left it unsaid that at fifty-four years, there was the distinct possibility that a live Loch Norim was on Dianis, not just their ghostly ruins.

"Yes."

"They can decide what to tell ULUP." Meridia looked at Outish, "And not you. No posting of this on the Fednet Interconn, or you'll find yourself in a depowered armor suit."

"But I was the first one to look in a pod that held a Loch Norim!"

Lettern shook her head, "Yeah, but I was the one to find the cryostasis, whatever," she waggled her head.

"Outish," said Hearter, "Jeremy will report any attempt to communicate these findings to anyone beyond immediate Central Station staff. Matter of fact, I'm locking down all information dissemination on this mission until Clienen and I have a chance to confer."

"But," Outish stammered, "who gets the finding credits? The galaxy should know!"

Meridia laughed, and Outish turned to fume at him.

"You will. You and your team will all get equal credit, but not until the Matrincy can prepare for the ULUP interrogation." Hearter realized the import of this mission was now way above his pay grade. "ULUP will want to vet this before you ever publish your findings. We learned our lessons from your previous news scoop."

Outish scowled and turned red at the memory.

Jeremy chimed in. "Central Station has accessed the control block memory for each of the pods. All memory cubes for the bay were wiped in 2440 AGS." The AI gave the humans a moment to consume the data. "That matches the fifteen hundred and sixty-seven years ago, our estimates of when the site was attacked and abandoned. Only five of the pods have data entries since then."

Meridia elaborated on it. "When the facility was attacked, the Loch Norim did a system-wide data wipe, at least for cryo-stations and probably all other critical systems, like research, defense, and any other systems that contained personnel and force information. Anything could be useful to the enemy."

Hearter built upon it. "They thought they would be captured and went into shutdown."

"Oh," said Lettern, her face clouding over.

Outish was confused at her reaction.

"They're her relatives, Outy," Meridia spelled it out for him, "think about it. She's a direct descendant of the Loch Norim who lived here. How would you feel if you suddenly learned the demise of your ancestors?"

She waggled her head. "Did they have a chance to fight?"

Silence on the net.

"We'll figure that out," Meridia said. Then to Jeremy, "Read off the data for the other pods."

"This pod, oddly, has thirty-three blank entries. Each entry was manually cleared after exit, however, the record was not deleted."

They puzzled over that until Mears offered an opinion: "Whoever was in that pod came out thirty-three times, and each time they didn't want their presence, or maybe existence, logged. For whatever reason though, they did want a count of exits."

"A long-timer," said Hearter. "Someone who was going in and out fairly often, and for security wanted it anonymous."

"That's a lot of trips." Meridia shook his head in empathy at Lettern.

"The next pod twenty-three," announced Jeremy.

The team went to inspect it. "Has been evacuated and reenergized nine times, each occupation occurring one hundred years apart, starting fourteen hundred and forty years ago. It ceases the cycle five hundred and forty years ago."

"That would be another sentinel or caretaker person," commented Hearter. "I'm looking at the translated data: It says *actuated by programmed event.* That means on a schedule or triggered by an extraneous input. There's a name here, in each of the entries: *Maxailia Terp.*"

"Like a bear in wintertime," said Outish. "He came out of his hole, looked around, didn't like what he saw, and went back to bed."

Hearter agreed. "Right, only the schedule ceased five hundred years ago. Either they liked what they saw, or ...."

"Never came back," Meridia filled in the blank.

"Pod forty-eight was medical-emergency-evacuated four hundred thirty years ago."

"Ula," said Lettern. "For being abandoned, this place has been busy."

They went to find the pod. "No signs of disturbance," said Meridia.

"Tic has found evidence of site cleaning and disinfecting," Jeremy supplied. "There are two entries with names logged in the tube's control block: *Jer Ti,* who made the latest entry, and *Uggula Co Du-R,* who is listed as the deceased occupant. Three hundred and fifty years separate the two entries. The first entry was system generated at the time of the medical emergency."

"Hmm," Meridia glanced at Lettern, "Co Du didn't make it through cryostasis. Something happened, and the tube rejected them. Then Jer Ti—" he stopped. "What tube did Jer Ti come from?"

"Ten."

Walking there, he asked, "Jer Ti evacuated eighty years ago?"

"Correct," responded Jeremy.

"Ugh," Outish, not wanting to be gruesome, but, "Jer Ti came out of cryo to find Co Du rotting in their tube?"

Lettern's eyes widened, and Jeremy responded, "The body would have ceased decomposition a year after the hatch opened and the stasis fluid drained. The body would have been dried and desiccated."

"Mummified," said Mears.

Something bothered Meridia. "Why wasn't one of the other pods evac'ed with Co Du? That's *our* standard emergency medical protocol."

"There are no emergency medical protocols in the bay's control node. Only local programming remains in the pods."

"Ah," said Hearter to Jeremy's response. "When they did the system wipe, they took out the system programming."

"For the cryostasis bays," injected Jeremy. "We are finding other systems with intact programming."

There was one open hatch remaining, and it was close by. "What about this one?" Outish asked.

"Thirteen, it was evac'ed twenty years ago by external user intervention. Someone, in person, potentially the person from the first pod you inspected, manually triggered the pod evac sequence."

"Shiren," exclaimed Outish. "That *is* like yesterday. How many Loch Norim are there?"

"We are still building the facility schematic and so far have found four cryostasis bays. All are empty. No recorded activities since system wipe."

"How many pods each?" asked Hearter.

"This is the small one. The others have two hundred tubes each."

Meridia bobbed his head, thinking. "Six hundred fifty tubes so far. Where'd all the people go?"

Outish didn't seem to care. "That wasn't my question. By my count, there are *two,* maybe *three* 'Norim that could be walking around and talking!"

Lettern laughed at the image of three Loch Norim sitting in Murali's drinking Bash Me Brains. Then Jeremy applied a dose of cold reality, "Given the harsh and hostile conditions of the surrounding environs, compared to what the Loch Norim were accustomed to when they went into stasis, the probabilities, though not reliable, are still low they are alive today if they remained on Dianis. We have yet to find any systems accessed in the past twenty years, but we have no idea how big the facility is. We are encountering proforma cyber security firewalls where there are intact systems."

"But only twenty years," Outish persisted, and Lettern looked hopeful.

Then Hearter came on the net. "The director wants to speak with me. Mears will monitor your progress. And Meridia, keep the team safe. No risks. Backup and rescue is six hours away, minimum."

After the lieutenant signed off the net, Lettern said, "Actually, Ivan could send a drone to Sedge. Sedge would send a rescue."

Mears audibly groaned. "Uh, that would be last resort. Having provincials enter a Loch Norim site to rescue an IDB team would be recipe for a ULUP fiasco."

Lettern shrugged. "It's our site. Our planet."

Meridia gave her a warning glance and a subtle shake of his head he hoped was not seen by any of the bot cameras.

"Well," Mears hedged, "part of that is true, but there is no point in stirring ULUP into a premature frenzy."

Meridia snorted. "And frenzy they will, when they hear about the pods. But, Mears, we both know the real risk to the site is not the Timberkeeps."

"Yes," Mears said slowly.

"Who?" Lettern demanded.

"The Paleowrights," he said with inflection. "And, oh, how about corsairs? Think they wouldn't want to raid this site? And, oh, wasn't it on the Federation Interconn, galaxy-wide news that a Lettern Stouttree, Dianis provincial, fought off a corsair shuttle, not a click from here." He gave her the eye.

She simmered, stewing on his point.

Delta bot, in the meantime, had been scouting ahead.

Mears took control of Outish's multi-func holo projection and showed the expanding bot-exposed floor plan of the facility. He highlighted several new zones of interest.

They left the mysteries of the cryo bay behind, following the path of Delta, only to encounter new intrigues.

At the first zone, Meridia took a guess at what the large chamber had been, wrecked as it was, but waited for the chemical analysis taken by Tic.

Jeremy read off the chemicals involved, the blast-damage direction, and the centers of the explosions. Hearing the evidence, Meridia walked through the rubble, turning over pieces of wreckage. At a far corner, he prodded with his boot a familiar object.

"That's a rifle!" Lettern said.

"Hmm," mused Meridia. "Looks like a large caliber chemical-projectile weapon."

"I concur," offered Jeremy.

"Mears, what do you think? This was an armory?"

Though Meridia couldn't see Mears nod his head, he heard the response: "Yes. The bot has captured images of what were probably weapons racks, armor forms, armor suits, and the total destruction goes beyond what demolition charges would have done. They probably blew up some sort of energy or projectile cache that caused numerous powerful secondary explosions. Fire did the rest."

"Who, who did it?" asked Lettern.

"Probably the Loch Norim," said Meridia. "They didn't want the weapons to fall into enemy hands."

"Which tells you something," said Mears. "If the weapons were average, commodity arms that anyone could get in that era, why bother to blow it? Maybe throw in a few hand grenades, mess things up a bit, but no. They took great care, judging by the charge locations, to ensure the armory was destroyed. Whatever was in there, and it looks to be the whole armory, they wanted it reduced to slag."

"Yeah," Meridia said, looking at it differently. "The Turboii never slagged their stuff before they retreated."

"They knew it was junk." Mears echoed the common refrain about Turboii military technology. Without the hordes of Sizars, the Turboii soldiers themselves were average at best.

The next zone, at least for Outish, was far more interesting.

They followed the indicated track on Outish's hologrid past a bank of what Jeremy said were elevators. "We have not been able to actuate the lifts," he said, "There appears to be a malfunction in the equipment space below."

"Jeremy, who's we?" Lettern asked, wondering if he included his little friends.

"I have enlisted Central Station server core to perform assigned processing tasks. Director Hor has agreed to the tasking."

Outish whispered to her, "That's computer talk. They are playing nice with each other."

Her mouth formed an "Oh."

They found stairs and began climbing.

"The tread is the same," remarked Outish. "They had the same gait as us."

Lettern smirked. "They weren't bugs, Outy. Look at me. I came from them."

Illian stopped to look at Lettern, eyeing her up and down. "There's more like you?"

She huffed but smiled and crowded him as she climbed past, taking the lead.

Climbing, they rounded more landings than Lettern cared to count. Breathing heavily up another flight of stairs, Jeremy signaled, "There is a large chamber beyond the next set of double doors on the landing. That is your zone of investigation."

Lettern stopped. The doors were closed.

"The doors should now respond to your aura signature. Wave your hand. They should open."

She did as Jeremy instructed, and the doors slid apart. She wagged her head, "Now that's top-tree."

Intrigued, she went ahead as Meridia started to advise caution. She halted, her mouth open. She just stared.

"What is it?" called Outish. "Oh, stars--"

"I believe I have found the illumination controls. Shall I try them?" Jeremy asked.

"Yeah, yeah," Lettern mumbled.

A long concourse blossomed under diffused ceiling lights.

She stepped aside to let the others in. "What is this?"

Galleries, equally spaced, branched off to the right and left the length of the long concourse. At the distant far end was a sort of floor-to-ceiling mural.

As if reading her mind, Jeremy said, "Delta's measurements show the chamber is two hundred meters long by twenty high. A court in the center is your first zone of inspection."

Lettern tried to absorb it all. The ceiling was domed, and the entrances to the galleries were framed by stone arches, not ferroconcrete. It was all stone and gleaming marble. "It's like Lycelia! Only underground."

"Oi," breathed Outish.

Caution forgotten, she ran to the first gallery, Outish on her heels. "What is this?"

Inside the gallery stood a single stone monolith as tall as a human and a half meter thick. The monolith was of a dark grey stone with veins and swirls of gold shot through it. Mounted on the monolith were three bronze -- what Outish assumed was bronze -- bas-reliefs, one positioned above the other.

"Tic is performing radiation dating on the monoliths," announced Jeremy. "We are confirming the measurements."

Outish frowned at that. Radiation dating was a simple process for an analytic bot.

Meridia reached out to touch it, but paused. He glanced at Outish. "Can I? This is your turf—"

"He's an astro-b," Lettern interjected, "I say yes. What's it made of?"

"This is an unknown metal, an alloy, not registered in Federation Minerals and Formulas," answered Jeremy.

They stared at the reliefs. The upper depicted humans. Men were sculpted on the right side of the artifact, a single man on the left, and in between them was a structure, a factory potentially. The relief was weathered and tarnished, as if standing outside for a millennium. Whether that was from actual wear or artistic design was indeterminant. The middle relief showed more humans, all from shoulders up. These appeared to be in strife. A number, potentially a date, was welded in the lower corner. The bottom relief, though it was spaced apart from the middle, continued the theme and changed to three flags whose emblems were arcane.

"Where did this come from?" Lettern asked.

"Hmm, go look in the other arches," Mears suggested.

Galleries lined both sides of the concourse. Lettern chose the cloister across the aisle. Here, there were two monoliths positioned side by side. Comparing the joining edges of the two fractured monuments, it appeared they were once one. The bas-reliefs on these slabs bore no resemblance to the first gallery. Lettern ran her fingertips gently over a raised image. She cocked her head. "A spirit," she whispered. "It's a spirit, floating it's flying ...." The image was of a woman in a long flowing robe, appearing to hover, looking down on water, waves, and incongruously, there were stringed musical instruments placed randomly above. The other relief Lettern could make no sense of composed of strange symbols and icons. "That's weird."

"Jeremy, posit, please." Mears had taken control of Delta and was moving the bot ahead. "I think these monoliths, and the others in Delta's video, have been removed or excavated from a variety of sites."

"Analysis of the granular structure of the block edges indicates two methods of separation: Direct mechanical force and laser cutting. Tic's chemical photoscopic scan provides evidence the blocks were mechanically fractured by both environmental effects and artificial force. This would support your supposition that the monoliths were extracted and moved here."

"Like a museum," said Meridia. "This place is an exhibition of some sort."

"Or a shrine," said Outish. "A memorial."

Lettern viewed the stones in a different light.

"What's an environmental effect or an artificial force?" she asked.

"Earthquake and volcanic activity," answered Jeremy, "are the probable environmental effects. There is volcanic residue on some surfaces. There is also residue of manufactured explosives on the monuments leading to the assertion of artificial force."

The monument with the arcane symbols disturbed her, so she left the gallery, proceeding from archway to archway, stopping long enough to ponder the aspect of the artifacts within. Some were statues, and few offered a ready meaning.

Meridia caught up with her at one where her face was twisted in a dark scowl. "What?" He asked. She pointed at an axe and a block.

"Oh," he said, "that's a head lying there."

"And the people lined up across the back?"

He pursed his lips. "The jury?"

She turned away.

Peering across the mall, her gaze found something totally different. As she neared the gallery, twice maybe thrice the size of the other galleries, she stared at the huge circular arch. The metal structure barely fit in the chamber. There was a platform with a podium off to the right. The inside of the arch was embedded in equal spaces with-- She went closer.

"Aquamarine Field transducers," said Jeremy, following her progress with Alpha. "We have determined, with high certainty, that this was a shift zone."

"A Field generator shift bay?" Mears asked to be certain.

"Correct."

"Well, that's an odd design," Mears complained. "They put the aqua inducers directly in a walk-through ring?"

"Not odd if you want it to be ceremonial," said Clienen, who had joined the team net.

"Is it functional?" asked Meridia, even though he knew it would be the first system wiped *after* all personnel had evacuated.

"No," Jeremy answered. "We cannot locate any programming nodes, coordinate data stores, or energy modulation processors for any shift capabilities in the facility."

Meridia nodded. "It's been reduced to a big, expensive museum piece."

"Yes, well, I've communicated with IDB headquarters," Clienen said. "We've taken this mission as far as we need at the moment. Gaining access to the facility is a major accomplishment. You can pull out now."

"What?" Both Outish and Lettern exclaimed at the same moment, but Meridia looked at them, unsurprised.

Lettern knew that expression. Illian had something he wanted to tell her, off camera, off net.

There was one more thing she wanted to see for certain: The remaining zone of interest.

While Outish complained to Clienen and the director explained team priorities, Lettern left the 'Norim Arc' as she thought of it and strode purposely toward the end of the concourse. More galleries branched left and right, but she was focused on the end of the mall.

"Headquarters is expediting an archive restoration and protection team to Dianis," Clienen explained to Outish. "A site of this import and magnitude has to be protected. Now that you have cleared the entrance and found the blast doors wide open, anyone can get in. And, well, ULUP would demand my Avarian IDB authority be revoked if that happened."

Following Lettern, Meridia doubted ULUP would do that, but they could certainly threaten and pontificate, making life miserable at headquarters.

"Well, can I be on the archive team?" Outish was not backing down.

More team-priority speak from Clienen as Lettern neared the end. Outish responded with, "What is more important to Dianis than this!" and he waved both arms in all directions.

"Sir," it was Lieutenant Heater this time. "Lettern has discovered something."

"What—" Outish squawked in mid-arm swing and saw Lettern all the way down the concourse. "Shiren." He ran after her.

She knew instinctively what the sphere on the pedestal was for. "Jeremy, actuate, please."

The sphere glowed a pearlescent white. Lights came on, illuminating the wall before her. A floor-to-ceiling, twenty-meter-high mural decorated the wall. It was a map of the continent of Isuelt. She swept her hand across the sphere, and miraculously, the ceramic mural changed to another map.

"Interesting," said Mears.

"Electro-conductive ceramic," supplied Jeremy. "I did not suspect that. Nor has the control surface responded to my commands. Apparently, it needed a human authenticator to trigger it."

"That's Linkoralis," said Clienen.

Lettern swept the sphere. Another map.

"That's Urgan." He said.

She swept the sphere back to Isuelt. The map was largely the same as what she understood from injection learning, but there were additions and omissions. Curious, she lightly double-tapped the sphere. At the edge of her consciousness, something was reaching out, guiding her. Her hand stuck to the sphere; it would not pull away. At once, she was astonished, afraid, and exhilarated. "Illy, what's it doing?! It's in my head!"

Meridia approached, alarmed, but dared not touch her.

"Tic has detected high sixthsense emission from the sphere," Jeremy said quickly, "telepathic in nature."

"Oh, spirits," Outish gasped, coming to her side. "Let it talk! Let it talk."

She was about to say, *sure, Outish, it's not in your head*—When an image shaded in. She saw it in her mind without her eyes.

The image beckoned, shouldering away her other thoughts. It wanted to say something. It began to look human.

*Yes?* she thought to the image.

More thoughts came back.

*Yessss, I am, well sort of,* she thought to the image. Her brain was in a fog. The image drifted in and out, but she could hear a woman's voice. Nothing existed around her.

*Why, how?* she asked.

*No, I'm not,* she answered the apparition's assertion. When the image, now resolved to that of a woman, flaxen hair, dressed in a burgundy uniform, failed to respond as she expected, Lettern realized the dream was a recording, a message.

*Okay,* she emitted, and the recording continued. The person shifted, or perhaps the camera recording the video moved. Lettern could see the woman clearer. Her gaze went to the medallion pinned to the woman's uniform above a row of medal ribbons.

Finally, Lettern said, "Oh," sadness drawing it out. The globe freed her hand, and she stumbled backward.

Meridia took hold of her. She swayed; her eyes distant.

"Lettern? Let'!? Let'? You there?"

She blinked and blinked again. Finally, she shook her head. "Whoa, that was rude."

Illian hugged her.

"A telepathic transference can be a shocking experience your first time," soothed Clienen.

"Yeah," she pressed her cheek into Illian's neck. "I'm gonna have *her* in my head a long time."

"Who was it? What did she say? Is she here?" Outish bombarded her with questions.

"Eh? What? No, Outy, she's not here, well, at least not *here*," Lettern pointed at her feet. "It was a message, a recording, I guess, for anyone. For the Loch Norim, if they came back. She said they still had hope."

When Outish looked confused, she said, "It was sad, Outy. She spoke to me like I was from Core, whatever that is. From a Loch Norim rescue mission."

# Chapter 4
# Marinda Hall

*Tivor*

"Your visitor is here, my Lady."

"Thank you, Simon," Marisa called as she wiped Boyd's gooey hand; he was slung on her hip as she navigated the busy office, the office of Marinda Merchants.

Elliot, watching his mistress manage three tasks simultaneously, would have directed Boyd's nanny to take the boy, but Marisa would have refused. Instead, he chose a different tack. "Lady, I can confirm the manifest for *Island Dream*. She's bound for Herodd with tea, correct?"

"Would you, Elliot?" Marisa peered past Boyd's little nose. "That would be Ivan."

Elliot, ever the huntsman-diplomat, refrained from comment. He and Ivan, the chief of Dianis Ready Reaction, clashed when the IDB agent had last visited Marinda Hall.

Marissa left the room in a wake of clerks, ship captains, and buyers all wanting attention.

"Enough!" She heard Elliot bark as she followed Simon through the door. "In the Lady's absence, I will answer your questions, but you must line up. One at a time. I will not have anarchy!"

Buzz Too flew past her and landed on its perch in the great room.

"Birdie, mamma. Birdie, go!" Boyd pointed a finger at the bot.

"Yes, I know," she said breathlessly. "You can play with Buzz when we are done."

Ivan Darinarishcan, IDB Chief of Ready Reaction for the Margel Damansk system, in which Dianis was one of fourteen worlds, stood at the threshold. A wiry man whose close-cropped hair, grey stubble beard, and ruddy, weathered complexion marked him as a no-nonsense in-country agent, one responsible for the security of IDB agents across all the Class E and now a Class F world in the Margel.

"My Lady," Ivan reached out a hand Timberkeep fashion. It was their own private signal, recognition of a common goal, the defense of Dianis.

She settled Boyd into his highchair and approached the chief. She grasped his hand, "Ivan."

Saying nothing else, she left her smile to convey the warmth and empathy she felt for the man.

He inclined his head, then looked at Boyd.

"You've never met him?" she asked.

"No, Lady. I have not."

She gave a slow nod. "Then let me introduce you." She said it with the gravity of introducing a state leader.

The three-year-old boy was playing with bot energy pellets, throwing them at Buzz Too. Finally, to appease the boy, the bot, in the camouflage of a Seasheel Parrot, squawked, "Beaks and eeks, always making a mess." It flew to the floor and snagged a pellet, then fluttered to a chair arm. It munched on the fuel pellet. "If I keep eating and eating and eating, I will become a flying pig."

The boy giggled and flung another pellet.

"I see he's made a friend," said Ivan.

"Buzz is teaching him new words. Everything is a *boondoggle*. It's cute when he says it."

Ivan looked to her, then back to the boy. He crouched in front of the highchair.

Marisa made the introduction. "Boyd, meet Ivan. Ivan, meet Boyd. Ivan is one of daddy's friends. He's here to help," she said it as a not-so-subtle hint. "He's known daddy for a long time. Even longer than mamma."

"Daddy come home!" the boy said excited.

"Soon, baby, soon." She reached down and hugged his head close to her.

When Marisa stood and sorted herself, Ivan said, "I see the resemblance," and he said it with a sort of admiration, which surprised her. Boyd, in a way, was the source of all their problems, maybe not for Wedgewood's war with the

Paleowrights, but certainly for Ivan's and Clienen's problems with her, Outish, and Baryy. The boy symbolized the one thing that would confound the IDB and ULUP from now through eternity: The love of one for another and the consummation of that love.

"Ivan, take a seat, please," she indicated the far end of the long dining table. She strode in that direction. "Simon, the Marish Fjiord, please."

When they were seated, and the nanny was fussing over Boyd, Simon carried in a crystal decanter and two glasses.

"I'm sorry, my Lady, but I'm here on business." Ivan waved away the proffered goblet.

"Of course you are, Ivan. You're all business. But, today, you will have a glass with me." She nodded for Simon to pour. "Besides, Ivan, you'd be a fool to refuse a glass of Marish Fjiord. It is arguably the best wine from northern Isuelt. Certainly the most expensive, and I have the only barrel that I know of, to be smuggled, dare I say it, stolen from the Bishop of Taldamir's private stock." She gave a devilish smile.

His eyes widened, "From a bishop's own stock?"

She waggled her head. "They're not the only ones who can be pirates. When you fight pirates, you learn their tricks, and I know all their tricks." She raised the glass, critically judging the maroon sheeting as she tilted the vessel. "And who better to pirate from? But my old friends the *Paleowrights*." The last word came as a snarl.

He nodded solemnly. He refrained from looking in the vestibule where Baryy, an IDB sociologist and CivMon agent, had died, hacked to death by Paleowright Scarlet Saviors.

"A toast, Ivan. To--" her voice cracked, and she lowered her glass. A tear leaked from the corner of her eye, and she looked away, but she managed to say, "Better times."

Even in her pain, she was beautiful. Ivan could see, could always see, why Achelous, his friend, rogue, former chief inspector of IDB Dianis, now exonerated by ULUP decree, had fallen in love with this woman. Her olive skin, ebon eyes, and raven hair compared not to her grace, iron determination, and piercing intellect. And yet, softening what could be a steel edifice was her love and empathy for all things honorable on Dianis. The matriarch had seen it. ULUP had been convinced of it. It was why they accepted her as the first planetary representative of Dianis to the Avarian Federation. Yet, she cared not for the Federation. Her thoughts, he was sure, were elsewhere.

He clinked her glass, accepting the toast. "To better times," he said, raising the goblet. "They will come. I promise you, if you don't rescue Atch, I *will*." His glare was not meant for her, she knew, but for the Drakans and their Paleowright instigators.

"Will you?" she challenged, an edge of bitterness tainting her features.

He took a deep breath, sitting straight, then stared into the burgundy wine. "We are all tied and bound by ULUP in our own ways." He looked up, seeking her understanding, the understanding of a woman whose lover and father of her child had been abducted and was now, most likely, being tortured. "It is enough, they say, that we have helped you this far and exposed so much to you."

"But Atch is one of yours!" she put her glass down. "He's IDB or was. He's an Avarian! An Ancient, and the Paleowrights stole him, captured him, and killed Baryy in the effort," she pointed to the corner of the foyer. "What does ULUP want? Are they to allow all IDB agents to be abducted by unscrupulous provincials and do nothing to save them?"

Ivan shook his head slowly. "ULUP does not care, not really, about the fortunes of IDB agents."

Her eyes narrowed. "Of course, it's all about Class E, Class F, whatever, protect the poor little provincials from the mean off-worlders, but when it comes to saving one of the defenders," she said derisively, "not their problem. ULUP sits in their high and mighty committees making laws, passing decrees, while men like you and Atch have to do your jobs in shackles."

He'd agree with her, but avoided inflaming her further. That she, as a Dianis provincial, a presumably backward, ignorant, non-galactic, had such a fine sense for ULUP politics spoke volumes of what she had learned through her own means. "ULUP," he didn't want to use the word for fear of angering her, "has agreed to the Federation's request that they aid you in the rescue of Achelous, but to a point." He saw her preparing another fusillade, "but, I promise, we will interpret the ULUP constraints liberally. You know Meridia."

A bare smile flickered. "You should get more like him."

Ivan shook his head firmly. "No, Lady. I should not."

She nudged her wineglass back and forth, then asked, "How? How are you going to help?"

He swallowed, and she saw it. "Jeremy," he called over his audio implant to the IDB AI in Central Station.

"Yes, Chief," came the immediate reply.

"Shut down Buzz Too."

The bird-bot gave a startled half squawk as Jeremy turned the bot off. "Done, Chief."

"Thank you, Jeremy. No recordings, please, until I say otherwise."

"Understood."

Then, to Marisa, he said, "Since you have been given a perpetual promise of no memscans or mindwipes, I can say this."

She stopped nudging her glass.

"If I have to, Meridia, myself, and a chosen few of my team, those who have already demanded that they be the ones to rescue Atch, will, in full chameleon armor, plasmas, whatever I need. We'd shift into the heart of Stith Drakas: The Citadel and find him. Nothing would stop us."

Time slowed.

The hustle of activity echoed in the hall, but Simon kept would-be petitioners well away from the giant table. He cleared everyone, even Boyd and his nanny, from the great room.

Wagons and carriages clattered by outside, dimly heard beyond the new, tall curtain wall going up round the Marinda grounds.

She picked up her glass. Her appetite for wine gone, she sat it back down. "It's something," she grudged.

"It's a lot," urged Ivan. "But you must first be seen to attempt your own rescue. For me to go first would irreparably damage our cause here, Lady. Many of the ULUP governing committee are not sympathetic to Achelous. They are to you, but not to him. They say he got himself into this mess by going rogue. By doing that, he broke the contract and trust of ULUP."

Without softening, she said, "For you to rescue Atch, it would mean the end of your career and those who went with you. Maybe a mind wipe."

He pursed his lips, "If they caught us."

The crinkles of a smile teased at her eyes. "You'd know something about how to do that, avoid capture." She waggled her head and opted to dig a bit more, "Perhaps you have learned a thing or two from Atch." This time, the smile spread to her lips.

A frown, but friendly, settled on him. She referred to, of course, that despite Ivan and the IDB's efforts, Atch had eluded detection until the Church kidnapped him.

"To that point," he said, "we come to the reason for my visit."

She cocked her head. "Do tell." She took a sip from her glass.

"I came to ask for Atch's multi-func. I understand that you have it."

When she didn't respond, he said, "It *is* IDB property."

Marisa looked at Buzz Too, perched, depowered, on its stand. She rose and walked to the den and pointed at the bird-bot as she passed. "That you can't have."

"That's Clienen's call," Ivan responded.

Returning, she handed Ivan Achelous's in-country purse. "What about this?" She held his handbolt.

"That you can keep. Do you know how to use it?"

Eyeing the weapon like it was the first time she'd seen it, she went back to the den.

Ivan unfolded the leather purse and swiped the masked control surface; the interface panel of the multi-func flickered to life. What appeared to be berga hide was more of Federation chameleon technology.

He tried a series of master codes as Marisa returned with a pair of quarrels. She slotted one, pulled the handbolt cocking lever back, aimed at the wood paneling where Baryy had died, and fired.

"It works," she said, sitting down.

An eyebrow arched, "Can you actuate the laser?"

Now she appeared interested. "How do you do that?"

"Jeremy will show you. He'll also provide a method for charging." Normally, under Class E rules, he just made a grievous offense against ULUP subject to contract termination and mind wipe. The *provincial* handbolt concealed a seventy-shot laser in the fore stock whose camouflaged aperture opened upon actuation. However, as Dianis' planetary representative, she was afforded Federation privileges as administered by the IDB. Giving her a modern weapon, Clienen had judged a prudent move. The IDB, the Federation, and ULUP all needed this woman alive.

Ivan's face turned to a frown and then a scowl as he manipulated the multi-func. "Jeremy, try the IDB master unlock. I'm having no success."

"Negative response," answered Jeremy, "the account owner's profile appears to have been hacked."

Ivan shook his head and tossed the purse on the table. "Atch, you and your paranoia." He almost said, *may get you killed. It did Baryy.* But Marisa had suffered enough.

"What are you trying to do?" she asked.

"Baryy, Outish, and Atch all swallowed aura signature neutralizers. The devices attach to the lining of the stomach. While they function, they shunt your aura signature, the energy that your body emits, into the air rather than the ether. It plays havoc with the skills of a sixthsense adept, but none of them were sensitives. They didn't care. The problem for us, you, me, is our IDB scans for aura signatures can't find them." That was the team's goal, to not be found. "We suspected the use of neutralizers when we found Baryy's grave. The devices stop working when their host dies. We confirmed it when we questioned Outish. He was told to expel his." Ivan pointed at the multi-func, "You need that to connect to the device and issue the command. And since Atch's multi-func is sitting *here,* he has no way to issue the expel command. Which, I'm sure he would have."

Marisa swallowed, staring at the device. So close, yet so far.

"Yes," Ivan said, "if we could get into the multi-func--poof, Achelous would appear on the scans from the *Shields,* and we could get him. Send in bots to at least protect him."

"Why don't you send bots into the Citadel and search for him?" she reasoned, then pleaded.

"We will, again. He's not there." When he saw the alarm on her face, he quickly added, "Yet. He's not there yet. At best possible speed, the Church can't get him there for another week, probably longer. Maybe two. Cordelei Greenleaf's record, from what we know of her, is as good as the matriarch's."

Marisa let out a breath. She and Outish had gone to visit the Timberkeep voyant in her isolated Wedgewood cabin right at Witching Hour, just when full dark set. The myriad of candles in the hut burned like sprites though they were not to ward off spirits but to attract them, for it was through spirits, good or evil, that Cordelei augured her visions. Baryy and Atch had also gone to Cordelei's cabin, but in the full light of day, and their intent had been to discern if the voyant could scry their real identities. She could.

Rumor and hearsay in Wedgewood was Cordelei's visions never lied, but only the brave should ask for them.

Ivan continued. "What bothers me is Cordelei has been quite clear. That *you,* not us, not the IDB, will find him. Why is that?"

She looked confounded and shook her head.

More to himself, Ivan mused, "Why is it if we flood the Citadel with recon bots we still won't find him? Even when he does get there?" Ivan took a sip of the wine. "Clienen submitted a request to the Matrincy asking the matriarch or any of their voyants for their own viewing of Atch's fate. Their response was immediate and simple. Once a person's future has been seen, it can't be seen by another. The energy, cosmic or whatever, has been consumed. There is nothing with which to divine."

Marisa peered at the handbolt. There was no point in pressing Ivan further. Cordelei's word was final. Thinking counter was like sailing against a flood tide. It would be Marisa to find Achelous, and into the Citadel she must go. Such a monumental undertaking she dared not think about in its entirety, but instead the single pieces, steps, needed along the way. Only by the small tasks could she retain, entertain, any hope. The prospect of achieving the goal gave her no joy, only dread. Cordelei would not, perhaps could not, answer whether they would find Achelous alive.

A dread gnawed at Marisa, compounded by a fear of how many of the brave souls who followed her to the Citadel would die. Every day she struggled with risking so many lives for the rescue of one. When she openly spoke of stopping the endeavor, the aorolmin, Rayamars, and Eliot refused to back down. It was like she was a ship, storm-tossed, blown before a gale, and the most she could do was steer clear of shoals and suffer where the wind took her. Fate was a wild river where the only bounds were the banks of death and destruction. Eventually, everyone came to rest upon those banks.

She picked up the handbolt. The cocking lever worn a dull silver, and the hilt stained dark by grime and oil. The varnish on the fore stock discolored by heat. Gripping the hilt firmly, she said, "Thank you, Ivan. I will carry it with pride. It's mine now."

# Chapter 5
# *Extrasolar*

## *Tivor*

"We need Ogden's help," Lettern said. She was sitting up on her bed at the inn nearest Marinda Hall. Next to her, Meridia was on his multi-func. Outish paced like an agitated cat. They'd only arrived that morning in Tivor from Wedgewood using a hastily excavated shift zone on the slopes of Mount Mars. The IDB engineers had just connected the power cables and balked when Meridia demanded to use the machine without installation testing. A call from Ivan absolved the engineers of any risk. To assuage Outish, however, they sent the eenus through first.

Lettern and Meridia, disappointed as they were to curtail the exploration of Mount Mars, agreed rescuing the former chief inspector was the highest urgency. Outish, though, said he should stay behind to *supervise* the archivists when they arrived. Privately, Meridia suspected Clienen wanted Outish out of the site if Meridia was not there to chaperone him.

A challenge they faced, among many, in rescuing Achelous was timing. Cordelei could not say when Achelous, the new Matrincy Planetary Councilor to Dianis, would be in the Drakan capital, Stith Drakas, at its very center, the greatest bastion in Isuelt: The Citadel.

Marisa leaned against a vanity, staring, not seeing out the second-floor balcony. A ship, one of hers, the *Sunsprit,* under fluttering top gallants, made its way out of the harbor.

"Marisa," Lettern said, "Og would know what to do. The clan wants to help. Woodwern said so."

Meridia set his vambrace multi-func down on the bed. "The sticky part with the clan is Sedge."

"Why?" Lettern looked at him.

Meridia nodded at Outish, who stopped his pacing.

"Baryy and the chief think Sedge is a corsair."

Lettern blinked while Marisa felt a pang in her heart. Outish still referred to Baryy and Atch in the present tense. One was dead, and the other....

"Does it say that?" Lettern asked Meridia, looking at the vambrace.

He shook his head. "They were off the net when they became suspicious. Nothing in Sedge's file hints at that, except maybe his sudden appearance in the service of the King of Mestrich."

"A corsair? If he is, he's a good one," she scoffed. "He beat the Church in the battle. He's the one who called Christina. He's no Quorat," she shook her head. "I stuck *him* with an arrow."

When she didn't get a reaction from anyone, Lettern persisted, "Look at what Junko did. He slaughtered all those villagers. Corsairs are evil. Sedge is not!"

Meridia took a deep breath and let it out slowly. He wasn't used to being the calm, thoughtful one. It was more his role to grab a rifle, shoot, and then sort things out later. Such was the life of a Marine: Point them at a target, fire, and forget. In the Sizar War it was easy to tell who was good and bad. Not so on Dianis.

"We've no evidence--" said Outish.

"We can get a DNA sample and settle it," Meridia offered. "You're the astro-b. But Lettern is right. Sedge, as the warlord of the clan's militia, fought a brilliant battle," Meridia sat shoulder to shoulder with Lettern on the bed. He looked at her. "Those were grim days. If he was a corsair, he would have run when the Troglodytes scaled the wall."

"The problem," Marisa summed up, "is we need Avarian help, Ancient help, to get us into Stith Drakas. Ivan said the Federation is willing to help, but I don't know what to ask for. I can fight pirates, but Nak Drakas.... We need a strategist, an operational commander. Sedge should be with us now. Atch told me extrasolars always came to Dianis with nefarious motives. We don't know why Sedge is here or what he did as a galactic. If he is a galactic he's broken the law and should be arrested by the IDB."

Meridia nodded. "If he is a corsair, he will have broken so many laws to get here that he'd be sentenced to a mindwipe. Assuming he *is* extrasolar, I'm surprised he hasn't run yet. He knows the Marines were here, and the IDB is active. He probably recognized the matriarch. Her face is pasted all over the Interconn." Meridia frowned. "Something's odd. Sedge just doesn't act like an extrasolar. He's certainly not afraid of the IDB or getting arrested. I wonder if Achelous was right."

"Arrange the DNA test," Marisa said. "Until then, I'm not going to worry about him." Reflecting on Meridia, "Do I need anyone other than you, and Og, and Sedge to help plan the rescue? The aorolmin and Lieutenant Rayamars are already in."

"Christina," Lettern said.

Marisa nodded slowly. "If she were here, she's the one I would ask to take charge of the whole rescue."

"Chief," added Meridia. "This rescue is going nowhere with Lettern and me if we don't get chief's approval."

"I'll confirm with Ivan," said Marisa, finality in her voice. "We have an understanding. Buzz Too will make it so." She smiled.

"Braak," Buzz squawked from its perch on an open door, "Work, work, work. Now I'm a messenger pigeon. Do I *look* like a pigeon?"

Lettern snickered and elbowed Meridia. "Marisa is Tall Tree."

# Chapter 6
## Rifles

Two belt-driven milling lathes were busy at work. A pair of apprentice Timberkeeps fussed over each machine. Marisa stood in the doorway, a huge sliding double door, and took in the scene. Carpenters were hammering on the roof of the cavernous building. A young Timberkeep led her eenu to the half-built stables. Everything in New Ungern was half-built. Two of her Marinda-liveried soldiers, members of her personal guard, now that she needed one, loitered nearby. The soldiers were at ease; New Ungern was friendly territory. It was a three-hour eenu ride from Marinda Hall to New Ungern, the fledgling Timberkeep enclave at the foot of volcanic Mount Epratis. The walls of the new foundry weren't finished, and yet the work within: Rifle manufacturing progressed. The craftsmen and women seemingly unconcerned with rain dripping through gaps in the shingles.

Marisa carefully followed the maze of leather drive belts, pulleys, and shafts, keeping her hands safely in her pockets. A wide drive belt went through a large hole in the floor. In the hole, she could see the belt was wrapped around a wheel attached to a wooden shaft. It looked new, the Ungerngerist timber a bright yellow. The scent of sawn Ungerngerist strong, but pleasant in the air. A substantial portion of the Wedgewood population had relocated to Mt Epratis because of the Ungerngerist forest. Fires set by the Scarlet Saviors during the battle for the town had destroyed a third of the businesses, and the raids on the farms by the Troglodytes ruined scores of farms. That, and the promise of a mutual defense pact offered by the aorolmin of Tivor, compelled Clan Mearsbirch to send a third of their members south as settlers.

Marisa stepped to an open wall and noticed the water wheel. "You directed the Bindle Creek via sluices?" she called to Ogden, awed. Indeed, water from the upper part of the river had been diverted via a wooden aqueduct to flow gushing over the water wheel, coruscating down to the rocky river bottom below. The sound and spume reminded her of the sea.

"Oi," Ogden came over, wiping his soot-grimed hands on this leather apron to little effect. "The aorolmin did that. Saved us so much work. That be his workers on the roof. Thought we'd have to do this all ourselves, but no! Tivor has come to help."

"I can see that." She was stunned. She came to ask Ogden if he'd be able to supply any rifles for the rescue mission, assuming his answer would be two or three, but already ten, she counted them. Ten rifles in varying states of finish stood in the gun rack.

"Does Rayamars know this?" She turned from the water wheel.

"Oi. He's training his sergeants on the first two rifles. Those are handmade, mind you. Not from the mill. But they work well enough."

Marisa laughed. "Og." She beamed at him. "You are amazing. Work *well enough*." She laughed again.

He looked down, fidgeting at the praise. "Well, they do."

She shook her head. "Og, was that a hand-made rifle that Rayamars carried on the *Far Shore*?"

"Oi. It was."

"Work well enough indeed," she said and turned to gaze past the river. "Tell that to the pirate captain, and he'll accuse you of devil spawn."

Ogden attempted to demur, but she wasn't listening. *Achelous, we're coming,* she thought. "How many, Og? How many rifles?"

He knew what she meant. "Forty, maybe more. Depending on when we leave."

She turned sharply. "Forty?"

"Oi. Maybe more. We need to keep testing and improving. Not all of them will be the best."

Her gaze narrowed. "What do you mean when *we* leave. Who's we?"

The master smith stiffened. He'd had this argument with the others. The aorolmin, Woodwern, and now her. "I'm going." He did not want to be cross with her. His respect for her was boundless, but on this subject, he was firm. Firm as the iron barrels in his rifles. "If you go. I go. Nothing will stop me."

His rising anger cooled hers. He had a point. Few of the mission planners, none to be exact, were happy with her going on the mission. She couldn't fault him or them. She felt as strong about going as he did.

Moving away from the unguarded opening in the floor, she showed him her back. Stopping, she said over her shoulder, "Okay, Og. We go together."

He was quiet. When he didn't move or speak, she faced him. They stared at each other. Finally, she asked, "What?"

"I'll not say what the Drakans or Parrots will do to you if they capture you."

Her face quavered, but she stood like an Ungerngerist. "They killed Baryy in my house, Og. In my very house with me in the kitchen!" The workers at the lathes stopped the drive belts.

"And Boyd? What of your son? To lose both his ma and da?"

Her composure cracked, but then she gave a very untypical Avarian head roll, the one the matriarch used on her. "He won't lose either of his parents. He'll be getting one back."

# Chapter 7
## For Tweeunar

*Margel Asteroid Belt*

"We are partners!" Krch tried one last time, flinging the plea at Bleep Nuts as he reached for the airlock control.

His hand stopped, a finger touch away. "No, nah." He shook his head and turned to face her. "I'm done, Krch. I'm going to find me another Hole," he looked around at the subterranean chamber they used for their operations center. Next door was the equipment cavern, where they stored and maintained the outfit's mining equipment. "And not this Hole. Nordarken probably knows about this place." A pang of sentimentality overcame him, but he let it pass.

"This is yours home," she slurred. "The Holes is yours! You built it!" Krch's mouth tubes sprayed creep acid when she was agitated.

"Ya, ya, I know what you are trying to do, Krch. But it won't work. I'm leaving while I can still spend my credits." He peered wistfully at the new tunnel they'd excavated and, beyond it, the new fusion reactor they'd installed to replace the decrepit fuel cell plant.

"Bah. I should never have paid you your money," she moaned, and rose from the desk, her slight, wiry frame, moved like an agitated snake, starting and stopping in quick jerks. Trying to brush her lank brown hair away from her face, she gave up Aside from sucking tubes, the most visible genetic variance from humans, Tweeunar's hands were adapted to gripping slimy sap canes. Those same grip pads made their hands poor devices for arranging hair.

He gave her a sad smile. "You're a good Tweeunar. Greedy, but good. I knew you would pay me."

"Two million credits, and now you leave!"

"Ya, but alive. And you should leave too. Nordarken will come here. They know that Dash-5 was theirs."

"They can't prove it! It wasn't stained."

"Nah. They don't have to prove nothing. They just have to think it. Why did you have to sell to Celestial Nav?" He almost pleaded, but they'd had this argument before. Krch was stubborn. "It was bad enough you killed Junko and took the ore, but then you sold it to their biggest rival, Celestial Navigations! Why Krch? You spit in their face when you did that."

She gave him a flat stare, her mouth tubes still. "They paid more."

"Bah. Not by much. And why are *you* staying? You got eight million credits! Give Nordarken the last ton and run."

"I can't," she said. "I need it for Tweeunar."

Bleep Nuts blinked. He took a deep breath, letting it out slow. He knew her history. She'd fought against the Turboii and their Sizar minions when the Sizars overran her home world, Tweeunar. "Sorry, Krch, but the Sizars have it now, and—" he let it drop. There was no good in reminding her that Sizars roaming freely meant every sentient being on the planet was probably dead, hunted, and eaten by the clone-vat, eenu-size arachnids.

"The Fed is going back. And when they do, I will go with them. I'll needs lots of credits. There aren't many Tweeunar left. We can't let someone else take our world, like Nordarken Mining." She spit creep acid.

He peered down at the deck, avoiding her gaze. Unlike her, he didn't have any great aspirations other than just making lots of credits, which he just did, and then living a safe, risk-free life, which he was about to do. "Ya—" he turned and punched open the inner airlock door.

In the tunnel, on his way to the landing bay and his new ship, he didn't see the recon bot hidden in a crack recording his departure.

Krch reached for her multi-func and punched in an A-wave identifier. She waited for the receiver to pick up.

The receiver panel opened, and a Matrincy AI avatar appeared. "Hello, Krch. I will inform Councilor Margret that you are calling. Do you wish to speak with her or leave a message?

"Speak."

"Wait." A long pause, then, "She has accepted the request. No indication for a response time."

Krch didn't respond. She didn't have patience for computer programs feigning sentience. They didn't merit reciprocal courtesy.

While she waited, the avatar on the hologrid appeared to make itself busy. Krch grumbled to herself on how she'd gotten into this predicament. It started with the sudden, uncomfortable appearance at the Brena airfield of two IDB agents, a Fed warrant officer, and Margret. Bleep had just lifted off in his new ship, and Krch had been walking to her own. The warrant server had handed her a tablet showing a depressing list of Federation charges against her. Already the final outcome -- sentencing -- of seven of the charges were already assigned. An IDB agent held a neural suppressor collar, and the other a plasma. According to the sentencing sheet, once they put the suppressor collar on, the Krch she knew would no longer exist. That was when Margret, who she later learned was a Matrincy Counselor and Special Envoy to the planet Dianis, had offered Krch a simple deal. "The suppressor collar or full cooperation in an IDB investigation."

The neural suppressor collar by itself would just incapacitate her. It's where they would take her immobile, but conscious that scared the willies out of her.

The avatar's image faded, and a different one came into view. "Hello, Krch." It was Councilor Margett with her perfect blonde Avarian coiffe, full red human lips, pale skin, and the nauseating attributes went on. Krch wanted to gag.

"Bleep Nuts is leaving. He's sure the Nordarks are coming to get us," she omitted any preamble.

The councilor expected no less from the corsair mining geologist. "Yes. We hope they do. That's part of the plan."

"Can you protect me? Bleep is running. He's scared."

"We can and are protecting you. It will be harder to protect your partner if *he* runs."

"He's not my partner, not anymores. And he doesn't know about the IDB nor the Matrincicess. And how are you protecting me nows? The Hole is an asteroid field. Too much gravity flux for shifting in. And we have sensors all around. We'd know if you were in the belt, even in stealth mode."

The counselor weighed her response. "It's true shifting in a ship, even a small one in freemitt, is a-- problem." She grinned at the understatement. "But not so for armored agents with jet packs. And you are correct: We have not stationed assets in your immediate area. We can't risk the mining contract holder, whoever it is, learning we are baiting them. But we are positioned to intercept and intervene on your behalf should an attack on the Hole appear imminent. We must be cautious, otherwise our little game of dangle the diamond will collapse."

"Like it did on Dianis!" Krch spewed.

"Thanks to you," rebutted Margret. "We were one step, one shipment away from learning who the true customer ultimate was until *you*," Margret pointed at the hologrid camera, "stole the shipment, attacked Wedgewood, and killed Junko."

Krch did the Avarian head waggle, which was uncharacteristic of her and caused Margret to think the Tweeunar was mocking her.

"Junko gots what he deserved."

Margret eased in her chair. "That may be. Did you know the mouse feces in his oatmeal would kill him?"

Krch's mouth tubes flapped in the way Tweeunars laugh. "No. He made me mad. AI says he could have gotten treated for it; he was too dumb to use the autodoc for diagnosis."

"Well, if true, and a truth analytic on your memscan will confirm, it still qualifies as involuntary manslaughter." Margret didn't mention the other charges against Krch, like attempted murder of a Class E provincial with an armed shuttle. The offenses were part of a clemency deal where Krch was to act as bait to lure the Dianis customer-ultimate into the open.

The cumulative sentence for all the violations was lifetime memwipe and personality-base adjustment. All memories since childhood erased, and her personality behavioral profile flattened to that of, essentially, a sheep.

"What about Bleeps," she asked, "will he get to keep his credits?"

Margret pursed her lips. "Potentially," she said slowly. "He's guilty of receiving money from you, money sourced from the legal sale of a *knowingly* illegally mined commodity. That stacks as a minor offense for Bleep that we will probably not prosecute, at least not until we have the customer ultimate, who must believe it is safe to buy and sell your remaining ton of aquamarine. That's why we are letting the Celestial Navigation's processing and distribution of the first ton proceed without interference. In the end, Bleep probably will not be prosecuted."

"And the Federation needs the aquamarine," Krch sneered; with mouth tubes, it was particularly effective.

Margret shrugged. "There are winners, and there are losers."

# Chapter 8
## Conclave

*Tivor*

Marisa met him at the front door of Marinda Hall. "Clienen Hor, at last, so good to meet you." She shook his hand Timberkeep fashion. She was wearing a white chiffon blouse with a sapphire pendant about her neck. The gem was the color of the Angraris Ocean.

"Thank you for inviting me, Lady."

To a servant hovering nearby, Marisa said, "Simon, please take Director Hor's coat." To the director, she said, "The other guests have arrived. You'll know most of them, except perhaps Captain Rayamars and the aorolmin."

"It will be excellent to meet them," he said, taking in the chamber he'd heard so much of and seen through recon-bot vids.

After introductions and all the parties were seated, Clienen began, "If you allow me, Lady, I will brief you on the results of Sedge's DNA testing. They are relevant to our mission." Collecting Sedge's DNA had been a simple matter for an analytic bot: Samples abounded on the Command Deck in Wedgewood.

She glanced at Ivan and Meridia. "You've heard?" she asked the pair.

Ivan nodded, not alluding to his thoughts. "We have."

She arched an eyebrow. "So you recruited the director to deliver the message?" She cocked her head at Meridia.

The ex-Marine leaned back in his chair. "Yes, Ma'am. This is way above my pay grade."

Her eyebrow stayed raised. She looked to Clienen, then to the aorolmin. "The ship has docked."

"So it would appear." Ropert, the aorolmin, spoke to Clienen, "Please proceed."

"Very well. Marisa has an explanation of what DNA testing is. I assume she has told you?" Clienen asked.

"She has," Ropert answered, "and the precarious position we are all in if Sedge is indeed a corsair. And," he paused for emphasis, "a wanted criminal."

Clienen reached into his jacket pocket and withdrew a plain, non-disguised multi-func. He sat it on the table. Swiping a series of commands, a large holo projection appeared in the air above the device.

The startled reaction by Ropert and Rayamars amused Meridia. The two provincials were not prepared for a three dimensional cinematic appearing out of thin air.

Marisa was gentle, motioning for those in-the-know to not laugh. "Yes, sire, it is amazing, yet it is how the Avarians do business. We must adjust."

Ropert swallowed audibly and then stuttered, "Is that so?"

Then Buzz Too squawked, "Wait till pigs fly."

Meridia, Lettern, and Ogden burst out at the surreal scene: A talking parrot and a floating image. And so followed Ropert and Rayamars.

When the hubbub in the room settled, Clienen rotated through the images on the grid. "As a point of reference, we have the DNA tests for others in this room. So you can understand the data identifying Sedge."

The room was still. Even Buzz Too sat motionless.

"Nothing that I am about to show you is confidential. All parties have agreed to be tested and have their results exposed to the rescue planning group. That's us. First up. Outish. As you can see, by this number here," and a highlighted number appeared on the hologrid. "He is ninety-seven percent Halorite." Clienen nodded at his planetary astrobiologist, who immediately turned a deep shade of red. "Halorite is a planet in the Avarian Federation whose species evolution diverged from the human genome some thousands of years ago."

"Next up," the 3D cube rotated, "Ivan Darinarishcan. Now these following scores, unlike Outish, are all subgroups of the human Genome. In other words," and he looked at Marisa, "the people that follow are one-hundred percent human. The differentiators are from what planets and what races. Ivan is eighty-five percent Avarian and twelve percent Gorfl Qu."

"Gorfl Qu is my home world," Ivan offered in explanation. "The highest score, with this particular test, that you can receive for race genetic purity is ninety-seven percent, such as with Outish. There are genes that are not unique to the human species or planets and are not included in the percentages. My twelve percent Gorfl Qu dilution of the Avarian gene pool is due to expected genetic variations caused by Gorfl Qu environmental factors."

Ropert nodded slowly, then sped up.

Clienen explained further, "It's important to understand that while the baseline we are using is Avaria, from which so many other planets were colonized, the Avarians originally, in the dim past, were Loch Norim. Our sub-species mutated, to a small but important extent, for unknown reasons, when Loch Norim civilization degraded and ceased to exist in this arm of the galaxy. It is still a great mystery where the Loch Norim went and why, but within their departure, they abandoned nearly a thousand sites and colonies across the arm. And that list is growing." Seeing the expression on Ropert's face, the aorolmin was lost in the significance of human galactic history, but Clienen had to start somewhere. The important part was coming up.

"Next up," Clienen rotated the cube, "Agent Illian Meridia, sixty-five percent Avarian, twenty-two percent Terran, and nine percent Nerev Weklar."

Lettern looked at him out of the corner of her eye, then whispered, "Does that mean you're a mutt?"

Illian rolled his eyes. "Just because you're Loch Norim."

"Ah yes," Clienen rotated the cube, "Lettern Stouttree." They could read the results. Eighty-nine percent Loch Norim, eight percent Dianis.

Lettern felt a surge of pride at the word *Dianis*. This was her home, her world. Marisa, sitting next to her, reached out and grasped her hand. Lettern responded with the grip of an archer. They were sisters, not by parents, but by blood and planetary DNA. And in galactic terms, that meant they were nearly identical.

"We have a theory," Clienen said, "the reason the orb pedestal in the Hall of Norim responded to Lettern the way it did was because of two things: Her genetic makeup and her emotional ties and intentions towards the planet."

When the room turned in her direction, and she shifted uncomfortably in her chair, Ivan said, "It's a theory, but I'm pretty sure that if Outish had touched the orb first, it would have stayed dormant."

Outish scowled at the implication: A Loch Norim would be required to fully explore Mount Mars. A Halorite would not do.

"Marisa Pontifract," Clienen rotated the cube.

They read the results. Ninety percent Loch Norim, seven percent Dianis.

"Whoa," said Outish. "Those are high scores for both Lettern *and Marisa*. What happened to the ITA engineers? Their interbreeding should have diluted the Loch Norim genes to some measurable extent, registering as Avarian."

"We were surprised, too," answered Clienen. "So we sent our results to ULUP and ITA." He spelled out ITA for Ropert, "The Intergalactic Transportation Authority. Their engineers were what you call the Ancients. They came to Dianis to build out a node, a hub," he looked for a word Ropert could grasp, "an intersection of roads if you will, in a complex, far-reaching road network, complete with way stop, inn, paddocks, etc." He smiled at his metaphor, as ludicrous as it was, but Ropert immediately grasped the concept and nodded vigorously. Surprised at his success, Clienen continued, "ITA's records, history of that time, three hundred and fifty years ago, show there were no ITA projects or engineers working near either Tivor or the Great Latitudes, hence little interaction with your forebears. Also, the environmental influences of Dianis on human DNA are particularly strong. Strong enough to be classified as its own, eclipsing other more subtle indicators. The DNA test needs more Dianis samples to improve its differentiation calculus."

Clienen gave the audience time to gather and sort through their thoughts.

"And now for Sedge the Warlord." The cube rotated.

Ivan watched Marisa and Lettern's reaction.

Outish, who'd not seen the results, scowled, "What?"

Ivan said, "Exactly."

"Is that right?" Marisa asked. "I'm only learning about DNA, but how can that be?"

"Ninety-seven percent Loch Norim," Lettern feigned a pout. "His parents didn't sleep around at all?"

Meridia laughed.

Ivan rose. "May I?" he asked Clienen, who then stepped back.

"These results have caused quite a stir, particularly at ULUP. The debate has coalesced into three differing perspectives. The first is that Sedge is a corsair; that he has no Dianis DNA and should, therefore, be arrested, completely ignoring the import of his ancestry." Ivan let his audience cogitate on that for a moment. "The second position members of ULUP have taken is the DNA results are flawed; that Sedge has manipulated his DNA."

Outish shook his head firmly.

Ivan gave a sneer. "I agree. He could have manipulated his DNA, but to reflect Loch Norim and this well? Our tests have double redundant smearing to check for just that sort of manipulation. We call that ULUP group the *denial group*."

"And the third position?" asked Ropert.

"For that, let us walk through the known career of Sedge." Ivan pulled up a timeline from a larger presentation made to the Matrincy to the matriarch herself just last night.

"Fifteen years ago, Sedge appeared in the service of the Kingdom of Mestrich. Remember, Dianis is a big planet. There are four other continents on Dianis. If he was a corsair, he could have chosen any of them. Mestrich, at the time of Sedge's appearance, was the closest formal government to," he looked around the room, "Mount Mars. What's inside Mount Mars? A Loch Norim site, now confirmed."

While the listeners squirmed, he waited. "Then five years ago, he left the employ of the king and came to--"

Lettern spoke, "Wedgewood. He came to Wedgewood. We had struck gold in the mine and were building our militia. We live on Mount Mars."

"*And,*" Clienen said emphatically, "you found aquamarine in the mine. It's no coincidence the Mount Mars facility sits on top of that deposit."

"He's a Loch Norim." A chill shivered Marisa. "A real one."

"Spirits," said Outish.

"Circumstantial evidence would appear to support it," offered Ivan. "His behavior in Wedgewood does not fit the profile of an extrasolar seeking personal fortune. The man lives simply in a tree house and has accumulated no real wealth."

Lettern's brown eyes were as wide as they would go. Gripping Marisa's hand, "He came from Mount Mars!" Then to Meridia, "From one of the cryopods!"

Everyone began to speak at once.

Clienen waved his hands to restore calm.

Ivan smiled. Smiled like a teacher when their lesson was received with excitement.

"Which cryostasis bed?" Meridia mused, then peered at Buzz Too as a cue for Jeremy to process.

Lettern's enthusiasm flooded the hall. "That's where he came from. He's a real live walking, talking Loch Norim! We have the Loch Norim on our side!"

"So," Ivan said, looking directly at Marisa. "If you ascribe to that perspective, we have a decision to make."

"Yes?" Marisa angled her head.

"Confront Sedge or sit tight. Engage him on the facts, or just watch."

Marisa immediately thought of a third alternative.

Then Outish said, "We need to go back to Mount Mars and take DNA samples from the cryostasis beds. We'd know for certain he was in one, and when he came out."

Lettern's joy turned to a pout, and she sat down.

"What?" asked Meridia.

"What if we can't find a pod that matches him?"

"And why do you imply that I get to make this decision?" Marisa asked Ivan.

"Because, if we are right," said Clienen, "Sedge has more right to be here than all of us, except you and Lettern, who were born here and potentially a direct descendent of *his*. And you, as the appointed Dianis representative to the Matrincy for both Tivor and Clan Mearsbirch, are the closest thing to a planetary representative that we have."

She glanced around the room making eye contact with each person. Uniformly, they all gave her the notion they would respect her decision.

"Given we are right," Ivan said, "the IDB has no jurisdiction over him, and neither does ULUP, though they might like to think otherwise."

Marisa made up her mind. "Then I say we let the man be. Accept him for who he is, a Dianis native like us. Without him, what would have been the fate of Wedgewood? I trust him. He fought the Paleowrights, and he'll have to fight them again." She thought about the matriarch's warning to defend Mount Mars at all costs. *Perhaps that's what Sedge is doing,* she thought. *Is he already defending the mountain?* "The question I ask is, does he trust us?"

# Chapter 9
# The Carriage

*Tivor*

At the aorolmin's insistence, Clienen accepted an invitation to join him and Marisa for a private dinner at Tivor Palace.

The aorolmin's spacious carriage wound its way through busy Tivor, following in the wake of the House Guards escort.

"Director," said Ropert, "I assume you are satisfied with our preparations? I know we are not Ancients with unbelievable weapons, but Ogden's new rifles are impressive, at least to us. Rayamars, who, by the way, has been promoted to captain, is doing a splendid job training his men how to use them. Some of them are quite good shots. They can hit a tea saucer at a hundred long paces. That's astounding."

Clienen withheld comment, careful not to offend either the aorolmin or Marisa. Only because of Achelous' violation of numerous laws could the aorolmin brag about his rifles. The violation of those laws had caused a political storm between the Federation, ULUP, the IDB, and the Matrincy. Each casting blame on the other.

Clienen sought something neutral. "Rayamars is talented. A true professional. I noticed, and I think I have this right: All the men under his command are veterans?"

Ropert laughed. "The Crown's Archers. The very best we have."

Marisa sensed Clienen's discomfort. Even with the loosening of communication protocols between Dianis and the Avarian Federation, Clienen should probably not be dining with a Dianis head of state. There could be no favoritism between the IDB and any Dianis nation. However, the current situation forced the IDB and, hence, ULUP into working with the Timberkeeps and Tivor. An opposing nation had killed one IDB agent and taken another prisoner.

Normally, the IDB had the capacity to rectify the situation without provincial assistance, but the inability to find Achelous and now the confirmation of Loch Norim ruins confounded all attempts at maintaining the no-provincial-contact protocol. Adding more complexity was the revelation a living Loch Norim may actually be working for and aiding the Timberkeeps. *That* news had split the ULUP committee in two: The purists and zealots who didn't care who was who, just that all laws be strictly enforced, and the pragmatists who believed a live Loch Norim could answer grave questions pressing upon all of Humanity.

"Clienen," Marisa used his first name on purpose, "what Atch did was wrong. I know that. And I am sorry he, your trusted lieutenant, deceived you in the process."

Clienen met her gaze.

"Ultimate Cause, Clienen. He was protecting the planet, and yes, Boyd and myself, the best way he knew."

Clienen had read, more times than he could remember, the Federation award that pardoned his former chief inspector of all charges. A formal declaration of Ultimate Cause, requested by the Federation, driven by the Matrincy, approved by the ULUP Board of Control, and signed by himself. He still couldn't quite believe it, but here he was, riding in a coach on a Class F planet, discussing, in the open, cooperation between Dianis and Avaria. A situation that had never occurred in the three hundred and fifty years since the last ITA engineer left Dianis.

Finally, in the uncomfortable silence, punctuated by voices on the street, eenu hooves clattering, and the creak of the coach springs, Clienen said, "Ivan and I talked it over. Neither he nor I think we would have done what Atch did." He looked away; then he said to Ropert, "There is a part of me that is thankful for Atch and his courage. But he's not the only one who broke or bent laws. Baryy, Outish, even Illian Meridia did." He shook his head once. "Agent Meridia gave a plasma rifle to a provincial." He looked at them both with a mock expression of shock.

A slow smile formed on Marisa's lips. Not mocking, but pleased.

Seeing the expression, he sat back. There was no doubt what Marisa thought of Meridia.

"So many people, people in authority who should do better," Clienen grumbled. "Even the matriarch wants to fight for this or that cause on Dianis. I am coming to believe that ULUP is for enforcement on the do-gooders and *not* corsairs."

Ropert folded his hands. "I can see your struggles, Mr. Hor. I, as the one ultimately responsible for enforcing the laws of Tivor and the protection of her citizens, would have a hard time accepting Ultimate Cause, but as this cause benefited me, I am not an impartial judge. I know Achelous. He is honorable. However, I now know why he seemed a bit of a rogue. Always disappearing, coming and going with the strangest news," the last he said more to Marisa. "And rogue he was! Literally!" Ropert laughed at his own joke.

The aorolmin turned serious. "We've a short distance left to the castle, and I have a question that is burning in my mind and has been all day."

Clienen could only guess at what bothered the lord the most amongst so many revelations.

"For Achelous, time is of the essence," said Ropert. "Not to be indelicate, but-- if we don't rescue Achelous soon," he hesitated, "the man is doomed."

Marisa knew the facts all too well.

"Assuming we are ready to leave in two days, maybe a week," Ropert said, and Marisa's eye twitched, "how, director, will the Ancients, uh, the Avarians," he tried using the new word, "get the mission to Stith Drakas? It is six weeks, over three hundred leagues from here. Marisa says that you, the Avarians, can arrange travel, er, transport. How long will that take? How will it be done?"

"Well, I am not the person," Clienen averred, as he looked at Marisa, "to make such arrangements--"

Ropert shook his head. "That's fine, director. I know what we, what Marisa has asked for, is beyond what your

ULUP considered acceptable, but let us assume, for the moment, that if you were such a person to make those arrangements, how long would it take to get our force from Tivor to Stith Drakas? I need to know, director, because I don't see how it can be done." He sat back in the deep cushions of the coach and looked at Marisa with resigned sadness. "We'd have to fight our way through the Empire of Nak Drakas!"

Clienen gave an Avarian head waggle, which confounded Ropert. "Lord, there are a myriad of assumptions and *ifs* in what you ask, *but,* supposing they are all resolved, there are still a few key challenges to overcome."

"Hmm, enlighten me." Ropert saw they were nearing the castle gates.

"First, you'd need a ship, a big ship."

Marisa noted he said *you* rather than *we*.

The aorolmin blinked. "A ship?"

"Yes, an assault carrier, one of our newest. Only a ship of that capability can do a freemitt of a force of one hundred and twenty soldiers in the time you need."

"Freemitt?" Marisa asked.

"What's the time we need?" asked Ropert. He didn't care about the technical details; he was the lord of the realm, but he cared for Marisa and wanted to ensure they were not being misled.

"Twenty minutes," said Clienen.

Ropert blinked, not understanding. "Twenty minutes? What's twenty minutes?"

Clienen's tone leaked frustration, "The time you need to transport that many troops from Tivor to Stith Drakas."

"What?" Ropert's confusion complete. "Twenty minutes for what?"

Clienen saw the gap between their two understandings was insurmountable, at least for the time they had in the carriage. "The time it would take to shift, teleport, using Ancient technology, to pick up over a hundred personnel and deposit them, safely, inside the Citadel."

"Twenty minutes?" The lord's face drained of color. His mouth moved. Finally, he managed, "You can do that? In twenty minutes?"

With a nod, Clienen said, "I can't, but the Federation Navy can. Which is part of the challenge. The navy is responsible only to the Federation Senate."

"Why do you need a ship?" asked Marisa. "Why can't you do it from Central Station?"

Ropert eyed her like she was a transformed being.

"Because we don't have the equipment, power, or trained staff to do a freemitt from Central Station. We've always relied on terrestrial shift stations."

Ropert looked out the window. The carriage had stopped, and a footman opened the door. "Henry," the aorolmin said to the attendant, "please close the door and give us space. We'll let ourselves out."

After the door closed, Marisa could hear the footman giving instructions to clear an area around the coach.

"You absolutely cannot do it from Central Station?" she pressed.

"No. Even if the IDB were to build up Central Station staff to do it, it would be weeks, maybe a month, and that *if* is far from any current plans." He saw the creases around her eyes.

She sensed the rescue plans beginning to unwind. Marisa was sanguine enough to understand nation-state politics. Fleet admirals, which she assumed was the person Clienen refused to name, were a touchy, proprietary sort. They had their own priorities, and rescuing Atch was not one of them.

Regardless of Ropert's confoundment, Clienen gave Marisa the details. "Those ships have the necessary Field generators. They are built around the power plants and shift platforms needed to transport multiple assault teams, one after the other, in quick succession. Those new assault carriers are equipped with an entirely different generator AI and focus processing suite. You see, we don't know where, exactly, in Stith Drakas you want to land your troops." He held up a hand when she was about to say they had maps. "Not good enough. "We need millimeter precision, and a millimeter is the thickness of parchment."

It was Marisa's turn to be surprised. "Why?"

Clienen was prepared for this line of questions, just not with a lord of Dianis present. "Because humans are fragile things. We don't take well to being transmitted into solid rock."

She blanched.

"That can't happen with fixed, point-to-point shifts that the IDB uses here, planet-side." He let that settle with her. "It can happen with a bad freemitt where the end point is not permanently fixed, and the transmitting platform, the ship, is constantly moving. Moreover, it takes a superluminal generator to both shift an object into the ether and then drop it out to an entirely different location. Here on Isuelt, we use two fixed Field generators, one at the entry shift zone and a second at the exit. Simple, fixed point-to-point, no complex calculations needed. Whereas superluminals can simultaneously handle both sides but need millimeter target precision. That's why we need a big ship, an assault carrier because those are the ones that have superluminal generators big enough to deploy an assault force of a hundred and some people in twenty minutes. And you want it done in twenty minutes because every second after the first squad shifts in gives your enemy, the Drakans, more time to recover and attack the landing zone."

Going back to Ropert's original question, Clienen said, "Assuming you get the services of an assault carrier and not the obsolete *Spirit's Fury,* the IDB will need to deploy a package of recon drones and bots to thoroughly map the landing zones. We can do that from the *Shields.*" He waited for Marisa to show an understanding. "Consider the ramifications of getting the shift just a little wrong. Say, shifting in a bit low, putting the bottom of each boot, maybe just the epidermal layer of the foot into the dirt."

"What, what would happen?" Ropert asked carefully.

"I've seen it," said Clienen. "At a target site, there had been an earthquake that went unrecorded. The shift engineers relied on a previous site survey. Bad thing." He shook his head. "Site surveys are done within minutes, if not seconds, of the shift. You need bots at the site watching for transients. Regardless, the ground had risen, and two people lost portions of both feet. Their soles merged with the atoms of the pavement. The results are ghastly."

Ropert swallowed.

Marisa was quiet.

Clienen waited for either of them to ask a question.

Finally, Clienen said, "My Lady, teams that do combat shifts know the risks. I would suggest, if we go through with this, that Ivan has Meridia brief the mission force on the dangers. He's done freemitt assaults."

Marisa took a deep breath and let it out. She'd heard enough. A conversation with Meridia, without the aorolmin or the director, was in order. Reaching for the door latch, she said to the aorolmin, "Sire, we've heard much, both here *and* at the conclave." Her smile eased Ropert's concern at being overwhelmed. "Is now a good time to adjourn for dinner?"

"Uh, yes, yes, certainly!"

About to turn the latch, she asked Clienen, "And who do I have to speak to, to ensure we can get the right ship?"

If the director hoped he'd scared her off, those hopes were dashed. "Anyone less than the matriarch won't do. I certainly don't have the power. Neither does my boss or the executive director of the IDB. Even the matriarch can't order the deployment, but she can request one. It won't be easy. All those ships, I'm sure, are deployed. There's never enough of them. And they don't come by themselves. Usually, they are the center of a battlegroup."

She clicked the handle and opened the door. "Very well. Can you arrange a meeting or a holo-call between Andy and me?"

Clienen frowned and then asked, as Marisa stepped from the coach, "Who's Andy?"

"Oh," Marisa said, letting the footman hold the door for the aorolmin. "I'm sorry." She smiled. "Adrianola, the matriarch."

# Chapter 10
# Fednet Interconn

## Central Station

Andromeda, the matriarch's AI assistant, inquired of Boyd's welfare, how the building at New Ungern progressed, and even how the Marinda ships had fared in the Tivor gale the previous day. If Marisa had not known Andromeda was a *computer program*, she would have assumed she was a genuine, caring human. Marisa grasped, vaguely, what a computer was and that a program *ran* on it, but for her, it wasn't unimportant. So treated Andromeda like Jeremy: A real human.

"Dianis has been on the Interconn recently," Andromeda said.

Watching Andromeda speak, Marisa began to wonder at the resemblance to the matriarch: Fair skin, burgundy lips, dark, thin eyebrows, and, of course, jet black, shoulder-length hair, though Andromeda wore hers straight, not in dread locks.

"You were as well. Do you want to see the article?" asked Andromeda

She had Marisa's attention. "Uh, article?"

"Yes. It was prompted by a report released by the Senate's committee on ULUP Affairs. I'll show you a translated version." And there, in a split grid view, was Marisa's face, apparently taken by a bot when the matriarch had handed her Achelous's pardon. A second picture showed her and the matriarch strolling arm in arm-in the idyllic Ungerngerist forest. She was stunned.

"Those are flattering camera angles. You truly do look the role of a resourceful trader princess and pirate nemesis, who pins her hair with a stiletto. I must say that is a nice accessory."

Marisa rejoined while reading the article, "Accessory? That stiletto is not an accessory. And I wasn't posturing."

"Yes, Lady. The Senate information briefs are scrupulously scrubbed for accuracy. They must be."

"First Dianis government representative to the Federation," Marisa read. "Gatekeeper of access to aquamarine deposits and now a validated Loch Norim site. The site is the principal facility of a Loch Norim research and religious retreat colony over two thousand years old." Marisa glanced at Andromeda. "Research and religious retreat colony?"

"That's what it says. And the matriarch is ready for you now."

The AI's image shrank to a dot, and the matriarch's expanded to full grid.

"Hello, and how are we today?"

Marisa couldn't help but stare.

The matriarch laughed, refined and humorful. "Yes, you caught me in transcendental regalia. I've just come from séance with two hundred adepts, and *I* was their host! Spirits, Mari," she stopped. Surprised at what she said. "May I call you Mari?"

Marisa cocked her head, absorbing the matriarch's jewelry. Across her brow was a jeweled band with a silver ring in the center. From the ring hung an aquamarine pendant centered on an inverted U. The U was silver and diamond studded, each leg touching an eyebrow, narrow and richly black eyebrows. The matriarch's eyes were done in a deep purple eyeshadow that matched the hood of the cloak she wore. Her black dreadlocks glossy in an oiled sheen. Marisa's attention fixated on the nose piercing: A delicate silver chain draped from the piercing across her perfect cheek to her left ear concealed by dreadlocks. From the chain, tiny silver spears dangled. One twitched at the corner of her lip when she spoke. "Uh," Marisa hesitated. She had a sense the jewelry was incredibly old, ancient. "I love your jewelry and makeup."

"Do you? Good. I shall have you here to NvaGira as my guest. We shall dress up together. The Matrincy will be all a buzz." And so, too, would the capital, but she didn't say that.

A premonition struck Marisa: A vision of her on NvaGira.

The matriarch was waiting patiently; her grey eyes were watching closely.

When Marisa realized time had passed, "Sorry, did you say something?"

A smile ghosted across the matriarch's lips. "No. I'm enjoying our time. Are there other things you want to reminisce?"

Marisa shook her head. Premonitions were unusual for her and quite discomforting.

"All to the good. We've been expecting you to call."

"I suppose you have," Marisa surfaced from the distraction. "Meridia, Ivan, and Clienen, they've all been most helpful in planning the rescue. Clienen tells me the IDB is committed to rescuing Atch, and they are ready to go as soon as the Federation has made the arrangements."

The matriarch inclined her head. "The ULUP board considers this an embarrassment and a major obstruction to the formalization of relationships with the Dianis governments. And for us, the Matrincy, we would so like to have our planetary counselor in place."

Marisa thought, *if Atch accepts the position. If he wants to marry me. If he is still alive. If we can find him. If we can rescue him. So many ifs*. Their marriage was a precondition the matriarch herself had applied to terms of the planetary councilor offer. Marisa had come to learn that without the marriage stipulation, the IDB would have refused Achelous to stay on the planet, Ultimate Cause or not. He was a known provincial fraternizer, but somehow, if he married the provincial in question, the IDB would accept his further presence. While she was catching on to the political nuances between the galactic agencies, there were so many more she could only guess at. Interwoven in all of these concerns was her constant dread of what was happening to him.

The matriarch picked up on Marisa's melancholy. "You'll find him. And then you'll get him back." She said it with such certainty that Marisa raised her head, yet she wondered how the matriarch could have such faith. Or was it knowledge? The threads of fate that the matriarch could purportedly construe were capricious, and to interpret them, predicting their outcomes, was an art, not a science.

"Director Hor briefed me on your plans," the matriarch said. "The uncertainty of Counselor Forushen being in the Citadel, when he arrives there, heightens the potential for collateral provincial casualties."

At a planning session that morning, Lettern had shown Marisa pictures, amazing pictures taken by the crew of the *Shields* of the Citadel. She'd never seen a fortress the likes of that, not even Taldamire Castle compared. Assaulting the bastion guaranteed *collateral casualties*. Again, she considered calling off the mission, but Ivan had been firm: "You must go, Lady," he had said. "To not go is to risk a catastrophe on all Isuelt. Consider what the Church can learn, what they can find, and what they can use against all of you if Atch divulges our secrets. Either we rescue him, or ULUP will demand we terminate him. In past extrasolar cases, termination has been used as the most expeditious solution."

The matriarch was talking. "If there is to be armed conflict in the attempt to rescue Achelous, the ULUP board is quite clear: It must be provincials who do the fighting. The Avarian Federation certainly has a justified obligation to rescue their IDB chief inspector, rogue or not. The Federation can aid in the rescue attempt, but its assistance must be limited to logistical and not be the direct cause of injury." She let that point settle in. "Even that is a major exception and temporary." The matriarch's lips shifted to a subtle smirk. "There are other ways to affect the rescue, of course, but ULUP is heaping criticism on the Federation and the IDB for letting this happen in the first place, so having you and your allies be the ones to clean up the mess is the most amenable outcome. At least to the ULUP board."

Marisa seized on the matriarch's tone. "You don't agree with them?"

The matriarch gave a short head waggle. "I'm not the military expert. But I know the Assault Marines offered to do a smash-and-grab. Then, Special Forces heard of the Marines's potential involvement, and they offered their own plan." The matriarch gave a humorous snort. "Your future husband has certainly garnered the support of public opinion on the Interconn once his plight became known. Outish," she sighed, "did more than anyone to aid your cause. Publishing the finding of an intact Loch Norim site on Dianis spawned so many heritage groups to demand his rescue it is hard to follow them all. They give Achelous sole credit for finding the site."

She saw the matriarch look away from the holocamera. The audio switched to mute. The matriarch was speaking with someone out of the grid view.

"Sorry," the matriarch said, "I have many advisors, and some are more persistent than others." She rolled her eyes in the direction of the off-grid advisor.

"I know," said Marisa. "A crucial part of our plan, of course, is gaining access to the Citadel. We have the people, and you have the means."

"Ah, yes. Insertion. Assault lander? Shift?"

"Shift."

Nodding slowly, the matriarch gave a subtle twitch of her shoulder as a clue that the person off-grid was particularly interested in this subject. "How many people are in your operation? The ones that need to be shifted in."

"Could be upwards of a hundred and sixty."

Even the matriarch's eyes widened at the number. When she didn't say anything, Marissa continued. "That's what I've been told is the safe number. Anything smaller, and there would not be enough boots to search the Citadel."

"And the hundred and sixty? They would be prepared to fight?"

"Yes."

The matriarch looked off-grid but didn't mute the mic, "Yes, captain? You want to say something?" The matriarch looked annoyed, but the holocam was allowed to pivot in his direction, encompassing both of them.

"Hello, Lady, I was the Special Forces captain in charge of the matriarch's guard when she was in-country on Dianis. Am I to understand you intend to assault the Citadel with a hundred and sixty provincials?"

By the captain's abrupt manner and the way he said *provincials,* Marisa suspected the soldier's attitude. She gave him her best 'motherly' look. "Not necessarily, captain. We have several contingency plans. One of them includes holding, if necessary, the upper bastion of the Citadel, a relatively small area, should we be forced to search the catacombs beneath." Then she said to the matriarch. "You've met Christina, our Al Suri Ascalon Defender. She is already in Nak Drakas and has new information regarding the Citadel. We expect her to learn more."

"And what is *she* doing there?" the captain injected.

Marisa rewarded the captain with a patient smile. "She is searching for six Timberkeep sensitives that were kidnapped by the Washentroufel from Wedgewood. There is reason to suspect that they and Achelous are in close proximity to each other."

"Andromeda," The matriarch called out, "please ask Admiral Feall, if he's available, to join us on our conference."

Andromeda appeared in a corner of the hologrid. "Yes, your Matrincy. Sending now."

"Marisa, if the admiral is able to join, please update him on your plan. He already has an overview. Give particular attention to your shift requirements." There was a muffled comment from the Special Forces captain, and the matriarch answered, "You are not the one doing the shifting. Fleet is."

After an interim, the admiral's visage joined the hologrid. "Your Matrincy. Your AI has asked that I join you. To what do I attribute this honor?"

"Admiral, you do so flatter me. On our grid is the Lady Marisa Pontifract from Dianis. You remember Dianis?" She asked with a twinkle.

"Yes, I do. And how is Chief-- I believe his name was Darin—"

"—Arishcan, the matriarch completed for him. I assume he is well, though I've not heard. Marisa?"

Ivan's rough handling of the matriarch at the Auro Na conclave was now encased in Interconn social lore. There were even reenactments of it on the leading comedy shows. Admiral Feall, who had been on the shift deck of *Spirit's Fury* when Ivan unceremoniously tossed the matriarch into an actualizing shift sphere in Terabac fi Sur, was taking the singular opportunity to tease the matriarch.

"I spoke with Ivan yesterday," responded Marisa. "Chief is the Ivan we all know and love."

The matriarch laughed. "He is indeed."

The Special Forces captain's face was stony.

"Marisa, dear, please explain your rescue plan of Counselor Forushen, what you believe is Fleet's role, and specifically how you intend to get in and out of Stith Drakas, where it has been divined Forushen will be held."

Marisa plumbed the meaning of *dear*. It was a cue, but for what? She outlined the rescue plan to Feall. When done, she asked, "Can you do that?"

The admiral pursed his lips. "I spoke to our Fleet Admiral when the Matrincy forwarded me a draft of your planning. Assault landers would be unnecessarily," he paused for a word and chose two, "attention-getting." Then, he said, "Wait," and muted the hologrid and opened a private channel to the matriarch.

"Yes, admiral?"

"The lady is asking me to expose top-secret capabilities of the fleet. How do you expect me to respond?"

"Well, admiral, how about telling me if you can do what she asks, and we'll go from there."

"The *Spirits Fury* is old and cannot do what she needs, certainly not with the degree of precision required. Dropping in two companies of troops is possible, but not within the required shift window. Regardless, we'd have to scan the Citadel in advance and take precise measurements, including Field readings throughout that mountain. Otherwise, we could not guarantee a safe shift of the infiltrators."

The last thing anyone wanted was a catastrophic freemitt, atomizing a human into the ground. Even a small miscalculation would cause grievous casualties.

"The *Tempest Dare* and ships of her class could do it," he noted. "They have the energy to shift two companies in less than the required twenty minutes, assuming the teams cleared the shift zone fast enough. But the *Tempest Dare* is a front-line vessel above my command rating."

The matriarch pondered the problem. "And if I spoke to the Fleet Admiral? Would he loan me one?"

The admiral laughed, but then apologized. "Your Matrincy, you would have to ask *him*. I couldn't tell you if they would *loan* you one."

The matriarch cocked her head and said, "Okay." She unmuted the audio of the conference holo channel. "Marisa, when do you need the shift? When do you expect to launch the mission?"

Marisa, along with others, had debated the timeline. She was worried. "Three days, maybe five." It killed her to say five days because it may kill Achelous.

The admiral's eyebrow arched. He glanced at the Special Forces captain. "And how long would you need them on station? That is, there in Dianis orbit, committed to the mission? Let me be more precise. Unable to move the battlegroup and not strand the mission force in hostile territory?"

Sedge, Rayamars, and Ogden had agreed on this: If it came to a battle, combat lasting anything longer than six hours, the rescue force would be overwhelmed by Drakan reinforcements. Much depended on the success of the advance team, as she called them. In total, the rescue force would need to be on the ground for twelve, perhaps eighteen hours, if they got in without attention. So she hedged, "Twenty-four hours."

"And does that include any time for practice?" The captain demanded. "Have any of you provincials been through a shift zone?"

It was Marisa's turn to arch an eyebrow. "Yes. As you know, captain, there's nothing to it."

"But have you moved a hundred and sixty men in an hour? Per your requirements," pressed the admiral. "The combat shift you are proposing requires we first shift or lift your entire force aboard the carrier, and then, when the operation begins, we shift them down in two platoon order, and the platoons are able to clear the drop zone for the next shift. Aerial reconnaissance has to be in place to confirm the zone is clear. This is not an operation you want to conduct without practice." The admiral looked at the matriarch, who passed the glance back to Marisa.

Thinking fast, she asked, "Is a day enough time to practice?"

The captain attempted to interrupt, but the admiral cut him off with a wave. Feall considered Marisa thoughtfully. "What is the level of professionalism of your forces?"

The captain snorted.

Marisa's gaze narrowed, pinning the captain like he was a bug. "They're veterans. And captain, I hear it told that you can measure the courage of a warrior by the length of their weapon. The shorter, the braver. Swords are very short compared to plasmas." And before the captain rebutted, "Not that we have anything against plasmas. One of the infiltrators is Lettern Stouttree. Perhaps you've heard of her? The galactic mining industry certainly has, so I'm told."

"Lady, I'm sure the captain meant no offense. As you said, conducting the shift is simple. But it's the timing and coordination between units, veteran or not, that can derail an operation. We would need to practice the coordination between provincial and Avarian commands. Do you expect to bring eenus?"

"No." She shook her head. Noticing the matriarch's wistful frown, she asked, "You miss Boomsha?"

The matriarch brightened, her black dreadlocks shimmering in the hologrid. "You've found my weakness." Amongst the other legends and rumors growing out of the matriarch's visit to Dianis were the memscan images of Special Forces troopers racing to catch the matriarch as she rode Boomsha, a bull eenu, pell-mell through an Isuelt forest, stopping only to dismount and place a finger into a dried patch of blood at the scene of a human-Troglodyte battle. The blood had been Marisa's.

"This is all preliminary, of course," said Feall. "I do not have the resources nor the authorization to pursue this mission. Obtaining those is up to the matriarch, and madam, you have scant time to accomplish it."

"Then I have my marching orders," the matriarch quipped. "I can't wait for the Interconn pundits to hear I am taking direction from a Class F provincial." She laughed. "No worries. I'll arrange for your air taxi service. Marisa, make sure your force is ready. I would think your Assault Marine can show them how to practice doing the shifts without actually using a ship. Good luck."

# Chapter 11
# NvaGira

*Avaria Federation Capital, Planet Avaria*

The matriarch struggled awake, drifting, swimming, clawing her way to the surface. Conscious and in a cold sweat, the cool air was shocking. She threw off the covers; the sheets were wet.

Rolling over and setting her feet on the floor, she held her aching head in her hands. The pounding would not stop.

"Madam Matriarch, are you in distress?" asked Andromeda through her audio implant.

Concentrating, the matriarch tried willing the pain away.

"Madam, may I be of assistance?"

She stood in a huff. The pain would not abate. Her dreams, the images, were all a jumble. The more she tried to make sense of them, the more her head hurt. They swirled around in her skull like angry hornets. Her eardrums ached. Mumbling, she staggered to the bedroom door. The couch loomed in the distance. Though the room was dark and the night deep, her eyes squinted in the blinding glare.

"I have summoned Councilor Margret. She will be there soon. Shall I summon the medical team?"

She flapped at the air. "Go away!" More noises and voices in her skull didn't help.

Making for the couch, she fell to her knees. She had to get the facets of the augury out of her head. The scenes, the people, their deaths, they kept coming, playing over and over.

Crawling along the floor, she collapsed and felt the cold hardness. It soothed her, chilled her. The shock on her wet skin kept her mind away from the dreams.

"Andy?"

Time seemed to have passed. People were standing over her. "Andy." There was a breath on her forehead. She could feel Margret's warmth, the familiar smell of her hair. She curled up in Margret's arms.

Sitting on the floor, holding the matriarch close, Margret handed the neural manipulator back to the on-duty doctor.

"Better. You better?" Margret whispered in her ear.

She rubbed her head against Margret's chin.

"Okay. How are the life signs?" Margret asked the doctor.

"Back in the yellow. Moving to green. Psychic anxiety and aura disruption are still red."

Margret shifted the matriarch's weight against her. The floor hard and chill against her bottom. "Help me up with her. Let's put her on the divan."

Resting together, Margret looked to the security supervisor. "You can dismiss your people. We need to lower the local aura stimulus."

The security team left, but the security head stayed.

"Was it a vision?" Margret asked.

"Yes." Feeling her strength return, the matriarch forced Margret's arms away. "Ugh," she sat up. "They just won't stop."

"Heart rate rising again," said the doctor.

"What won't stop?" asked Margret.

"The augury. The people. They are spinning around like a flock of insane birds."

"Andromeda," Margret asked, "are you recording?"

"No, councilor. I do not have permission."

"Granted, granted," groaned the matriarch.

"Okay. Let's do this right. Let's get that dream out of your psyche so you can rest."

Sitting bent over, the matriarch nodded numbly.

"Set the neural to aura stimulation," Margret told the doctor.

"No," the matriarch commanded. "No, no stimulation."

"Okaaay," Margret leaned back, giving her lover space. "How about a periendorphin shot?"

"Noo, no, that's ghastly."

Margret sighed. "Well, we need to do something. You know how it is. The premonition will haunt you till you render it."

"Yes. Believe me, I know."

Margret had an idea. She stood and went to the audience reception room. When she returned, she had a crystal glass with two fingers of a clear liquid in it.

The matriarch looked up. In the dim light, she squinted at the glass. "What is it?"

Margret approached and swept the glass under the matriarch's nose.

"Oh," she sat back. "I don't think so."

The security chief approached, "What is it?"

Margret smiled, a mischievous little smirk. "Her favorite."

"No, it's not my favorite."

"You can try denying it, but I know different." Margret held the glass out for the matriarch to take.

"I need to sample it." The agent pulled out his multi-func and activated the
sampling synthesizer.

Margret brought the glass within his reach, not breaking her smile while she watched the matriarch.

"This will take a moment," the man said, lifting the synthesizer probe from the glass.

Resigned, the matriarch stood. At first wobbly, then her legs firmed. She shooed the doctor away. "I'm fine."

She walked to the window and motioned for the blinds to open.

All of NvaGira spread out beneath her. Seventeen million souls. The view from the Matrincy Tower, two hundred and twelve stories high, devolved the largest city in the Federation to silver dust on a carpet of black velvet.

The life force, the aura energy of the souls in those specs of light, filled her. This view, from this place, at this time in the still dark night, always comforted her: It reminded her of why she suffered.

Stretching, she reached her arms way back and then twisted her fists. The strain reached her shoulder blades. She held it there, feeling the tense muscles slowly stretch and then her biceps burn. Opening her fists, she flexed her fingers hard, brutally, working every joint, rolling each finger from pinky to thumb and then back. After more stretching, she turned. Hand on hips, she rocked left, then right. She may look like a twenty-year-old holovid model, but gene therapy went only so far. Her seventy-year-old hips still creaked when stretched just right.

Taking a deep breath, she held out her hand.

"Results aren't ready yet," said the security head.

"It's all right, Torrin. I know what it is. I have my own barrel."

Margret handed her the glass.

The matriarch gave a grudging smile. "Where's yours? We need a toast. You said we were going to do this right."

Margret left, and when she returned, the security head said, "Results are in." He read them off his multi-func. "This liquid has been tested before, but on *Dianis?*" He showed the results to the doctor.

Margret raised her glass. "A toast."

"A toast to Wedgewood."

Margret smiled. "To Murali's."

As the two downed their double shots, the doctor asked, "*Rakia?* What is *marsediminium?*"

Margret quickly set her glass aside and took the matriarch's. "Torrin, help me catch her."

Alarmed, the security head went to the matriarch's side. She looked at him, her pupils wide. He could see to the back of her retina. It unnerved him.

She started to sway.

"She usually just sips it," Margret said, "but when we want to draw a vision out, she'll down a double shot."

Abruptly, the matriarch slumped. The security head caught her and helped Margret carry her to the divan.

"Andromeda, are you recording?" Margret settled the matriarch beside her on the couch.

"Affirmative."

"Life signs going to yellow," called the doctor.

Suddenly, the matriarch spasmed, arching her back. Gritting her teeth, a thrash left, then right. Her eyes rolled beneath their lids.

Listening to her seemingly random mumblings, Margret tried to gauge the progress of the dream. "Easy," she whispered, "let it flow. Don't fight it. We have it. You don't have to parse it. Just let it flow. Water. Down a creek. Draining away and away. Over the rocks, smooth and bubbling."

The tension in her limbs eased, still hard but not rigid iron. Another twitch, more mumblings, some clearer. "Ivan!"

"Oh dear, that's not good," said Margret. When the matriarch threatened to cramp, Margret pleaded, "No, no, that's okay, let it come. It will go."

"Why?" the matriarch moaned, and her head thrashed back and forth.

"Is it usually this bad?" The doctor was readying an injection.

"No," Margret's concern reflected in her attempts to soothe the matriarch. "No, this is extreme."

"Where? Why? Oh, Marisa." A  wracking sob choked her.

"We're finished," exclaimed the doctor.

Before Margret could stop him, he said, "We're done with this," and stabbed the injector into the matriarch's neck. "I'll not have the Grand Counselor of the Matrincy die from cerebral hemorrhage," he hissed angrily at Margret.

At a loss for words, Margret stared blankly as the doctor withdrew the injector.

He stood glaring at her.

The matriarch was crying. A sob came, followed by another. She rolled over and buried her face in Margret's neck. "They're dead. They all died."

Margret leaned back to look at the matriarch's face. The pain she saw made her pull away from the matriarch's grasp. Settling her on the couch, Margret ran for her multi-func. "Andromeda."

"Yes, councilor."

"Send the recording to my device." Flustered, Margret swiped and double-swiped through control screens. "Sometimes she's wrong. Her visions, her divinations are subject to interpretation." Margret said it to quell her fears rather than inform anyone.

Watching the recorded, layered stream on four separate panes, Margret sat at the autoserv counter. The doctor and security head, knowing it was a violation of privacy and security protocol, couldn't help but look over the councilor's shoulder to see what had caused the most powerful leader in the Federation such distress.

The doctor pointed to a number in the bottom left corner of the flat display. "There are six threads."

"I see that," replied Margret. "I'm trying to make sense of these first four. They should be related. Just different layers, senses of the same event."

"They don't look that way," said the security head.

"Well," she equivocated, "yes, and maybe no. Andromeda, we'll need you to dissemble and correlate, then recompose the threads. This is too much—" she froze the screen. Looking at one of the panels, she pressed the slow-play icon.

"Oh." The security head looked at the doctor and back to the screen. "Do we know her?"

Margret barely nodded. She closed the display and sat her multi-func flat. Standing, she said, "You, gentlemen, need to go. We are done."

After much complaining, Margret had them moving towards the door when the doctor halted and wouldn't budge until he got a reply. "The marsediminium. What is it?"

When he saw her eyes flicker away and she made to push him to the door, he refused. "No. I can have Torrin arrest you for poisoning the matriarch if you don't answer my question."

She arched an eyebrow at the head of security and then back to the doctor. "Now would not be the time—"

"I don't care."

She gave a slight head waggle. "Fine. Andromeda, grant the doctor permission to review the marsediminium data."

"Yes, councilor."

"And, doctor. That data is classified well above your security clearance. Only because you are responsible for the health of the matriarch do I condone releasing it to you. Dissemination of what you find in that data, in any event, to any extent, is subject to immediate mindwipe." She gave him her own glare. "Immediate, doctor."

He hedged. "I ask because of its obvious hallucinogenic properties. The alcohol and other residual chemicals in that *rakia* should not have caused her near-death reaction."

She pointed at the door. "It's not hallucinogenic. Read the data." She pushed him at the door.

When they were finally alone, Margret sat next to the matriarch, the multi-func in her lap. The matriarch was pale but awake, even cognizant. "You better?" Margret hugged her.

"Yes," she answered weakly, "the vision is gone."

Sitting together silently, they stared at the blank screen of the multi-func.

Eventually, the matriarch said, "I can rest-- now."

"I'm sorry, but before you do, I need to tell you something."

"What?"

The fear in the matriarch's voice disturbed Margret. "One of the people you saw, the man with the grey hair in a ponytail and beard. The one who died."

The matriarch nodded.

"Do you know him?"

The matriarch shook her head. "But I saw him in Wedgewood."

Margret opened her multi-func, "Clienen Hor filed this Federation Ultimate Secrecy Order yesterday. It was approved by the IDB executive director. ULUP is complying."

The matriarch read the order. "Spirits, Margret, it's confirmed?"

She nodded. "They sent in a bot. It recovered a DNA sample from the open cryostasis chamber. That man, Sedge, is the only known living Loch Norim in the galaxy."

"Spirits and fate." The matriarch stared blankly at the wall. "He dies rescuing Achelous Forushen, rogue IDB chief."

They sat there, both numb.

After a time, Margret enabled the multi-func to show the vision. She skipped past events, stopping at one. Marisa and Christina stood, paused, in action beside each other.

A slight nod by the matriarch, and she looked away. "So many."

Hopping through the confusing array of threads, Margett stopped at one, "Is this the fork?"

The matriarch looked back at the screen. "Yes."

"Then she is the one who triggers it." Margret focused and normalized the raster scan, so the face of a teenage girl honed into clarity. She was in action, her arm outstretched, her hand seeming to push at the air. "Rachael. Their telekinesis master."

The matriarch took the multi-func and looked at the girl. "She is in one fork but not the other. Something happens. She goes on the mission, or she doesn't. Marisa and Christina live to that point in one fork but not the other." She handed the tablet back, drained, devoid of feeling. "That's as far as my vision goes."

Margret swiped through the threads and then closed the display. Rising, she smoothed her blouse. "We need to get Andromeda's corollary. There's too much in there for us to unpack."

Margret went to the window, watching the first purple hues of dawn grow on the horizon.

A hollow feeling settled in the matriarch's stomach. "They didn't find Achelous."

"No. The doctor's injection terminated the vision. The augury broke as you followed the Rachael fork. She was lowering something into a hole. She screeched and fell back. That was the end."

"Margret," the matriarch whispered. "We have to do something."

"We stop the mission."

"Then they'll just die a different way."

Margret pursed her lips. After a long while, she said, "We have to force the fork."

Walking towards the bedroom, the matriarch said, "We have to. It's the only way to save at least some of them for a while. Spirits save us."

"And Rachael, the fork trigger, I'll make sure nothing happens to her and that she is standing next to Marisa and Christina at the inflection."

The matriarch turned back to look at her. "Fate, Margrett," she warned. "You play with Fate."

# Chapter 12
# Retribution

"Do all of the armor pieces fit?" the armorer asked Meridia.

Sampling the edge of the sword she gave him, Meridia answered. "Yes," admiring the new blade. It was modeled after a Bareen marauder cutlass, but the steel alloy far exceeded anything the metalsmiths in Isuelt, even Ogden, could produce. "You can't make this in a fabricator," he said. Clienen's recruiting to fill the open IDB Central Station billets was paying off. The new Field Outfitting armorer knew her stuff.

"No, it can't," she said proudly, sliding the rest of his in-country weapons and Bareen merc gear across the counter. "Dented and weathered looking, as specified. That sword, though, is strictly a hand-forged item. Our fabricators can use titanium and vanadium, but not here. Those materials are strictly off limits to Class E and F."

"That's okay. If you don't mind doing the work, this will hold an edge better than titanium."

"Don't mind," said the armorer. "Running a forge is an art. You can only charge so many plasma packs before you want to scream." The woman was one of the many former Dianis staff that had applied to return from Dominicus, back to their old duty station. "And that is a flicker panel shield," she said, handing him the shield. "It's not exactly ULUP approved but not prohibited either. I like to give in-country the best where I can. You activate it with a multi-func. All it does is change the heraldry on the boss face. Could be helpful for switching sides."

Meridia examined the shield. It looked like steel to him. If he held at just the right angle, he could discern some sort of coating. "I do have a question about the fabricator. I have a couple of sacks of provincial black powder and a sack of forty-four caliber bullets. New Ungern made them for me, you know, for realism," he said as an apology.

"No worries, genuine provincial is good. We *are* Class F."

"Right. I was fiddling with the settings for the brass casings, but the machine jams on the bullets. I don't think they have the precision the machine expects." He explained the problem, telling her he was trying to duplicate ammo Ogden was making, and she offered him instructions on how to tune the fabricator AI to adjust for bullet imperfections. In truth, Ogden had never made cartridge ammunition, at least not yet. But he would. Soon. Stuffing paper charges down the barrel just wasn't working for Meridia.

"Gonna be busy around here," he said, leaving In-country Outfitting.

"Good," she shot back as he left.

Clienen met him in the hall on his way to the Field Gen station. "Ivan says you are on a solo mission to Hebert?"

"I am. It's a quick one. Outish is here," meaning since his primary responsibility was in a secure facility and he could go off on other duties.

"A-ah." The director waited for more.

"Yeah," Meridia slipped into evasive-noncom mode. "The recon drone we have pinned to Marisa's Lizardman has followed him to Hebert. He's marking targets."

"Oh? What targets?"

"Marisa paid him to find the men who attacked Marinda Hall. The Wedgewood voyant said Achelous is in the Citadel or will be, but there are still things we can learn from the kidnappers."

Clienen thought about it. "I know you're new to the service." He hadn't had a chance yet to sit down with the ex-Marine. Clienen had only recently been reinstated as IDB director for the Margel, and Meridia had been in-country since then. "It's highly irregular for trainees to go out on their own, especially into fervent religious zones. It can be easy to offend the populace and not know it."

"I'll remember that. Though, you know, sir, since I've been in Ready Reaction, I've only been on solo missions. The Timmies, er, Timberkeeps, have told me much about the Paleowrights, so I know what *some* of their issues are. Injection learning has filled in the gaps."

Clienen refrained from commenting that Meridia's love interest was a Timberkeep. "Yes. That's what I'm afraid of. The view of victimized people towards their aggressors will be biased. You shouldn't believe everything they tell you. *And,*" he emphasized, "what is a Lizardman going to do when he finds the Scarlet Saviors who attacked the Hall? A toad sings more than he talks."

Meridia shrugged. "I was going to ask him that. Jeremy gave it a high probability, judging by Fire Eye's behavior, that he's marked at least two different individuals."

"And when was this?"

"Two hours ago." Meridia started toward the gen station. "The reptile was at Marinda Hall the night of the attack. He has their scent. I'm told reptiles never forget a smell like we never forget a face."

As Meridia moved further away, Clienen asked, "And what are you going to do? Hebert can be a sticky place for agents."

"I'm going to find Fire Eye and offer my communication skills. I only have eight hours before I need to be back." He waved and hurried on.

Taking his place on the shift platform and holding the reins to his eenu, Meridia called to the operator, fearing the director would appear and ask more questions, "Ready to punch out. Don't want Trickster here to get fussy." Trickster, his eenu, he was told, was accustomed to shifts and was not fussing.

The look the operator gave Meridia made him feel like a noob.

What he didn't tell the director was Marisa had asked the Lizardman for a *kurchka* against the *ruregurir* she was now in with the Paleowrights. Loosely translated from Dianis *reptili,* it meant she had asked Fire Eye to commit retribution upon those who had defiled her den. Since Fire Eye had been at the Hall when Achelous was kidnapped and Zil, a Silver Cup compatriot, had died fighting beside Fire Eye, a blood bond existed between Marisa and the Lizardman. The kinship between she and the prince had started when he helped rescue one of her ships, the *Far Shore,* from Warkenvaal pirates. Like Marisa, Fire Eye was a princeling, though a banished prince.

There would be no intention of trying to learn something from the villains because, as Clienen had so adroitly observed, the communication gulf made a reptile a poor interrogator of a human. Fire Eye had gone to kill.

After the shift, Trickster steadied in the zone. They were three miles south of Hebert, on the edge of the Great Latitude Swamp. Not entirely comfortable on eenu-back, Meridia tentatively nudged the gelding into a trot.

Via his multi-func vambrace, he routed the drone coordinate data to his optic nerve implant. The prince was loitering near a reptile *catchscraw* market just inside a rear gate to the city wall.

After the bumpy ride, Meridia, wondering if he could get a padded saddle, was glad to dismount.

Wearing Bareen marauder armor and gear, the Church pikemen guards paid him little attention as he led his eenu into the city. Inside, he was struck and unnerved by the difference between Hebert and Wedgewood, even Tivor. The city was all stone and old, what he thought of as gothic. The streets were cramped, nothing like the wide-open avenues of Tivor or the pine-shrouded lanes of Wedgewood.

He found the stables in a gritty corner under the parapet walls and paid the stable hand a fee in silver sheqels, as suggested by Jeremy. "I hope Trickster will be there when I get back," he murmured.

"We have him on the aura scan," Jeremy assured him. "He has a breakaway halter and is trained to come at the call of his name."

"Oh. Eenus will do that?"

"They don't, normally. Ours have their own injection learning programs."

Meridia laughed, belatedly aware that others may wonder why. He thought, *it figures the IDB would enhance eenus.*

In his naïve galactic way, he'd assumed it would be simple to find the Lizardman, and there would be only one. He wasn't trained for in-country CivMon work, as Clienen had insinuated. Ready Reaction was chartered for the *defense* and rescue of in-country CivMon agents and interdiction and apprehension of extrasolars. It was the defense and rescue role of the job that Meridia had left the assault Marines. Well, indirectly. He'd transferred out of the Marines to be near Lettern, and Dianis Ready Reaction was his ticket.

Not having done more injection learning on Herbert beyond available services, infrastructure, security, and food purveyors, he was surprised. There were reptiles everywhere of all shapes. Finding a quiet corner, he called up Jeremy. "You connected to my optic implant?"

"Connecting now."

"The drone feed has Fire Eye a hundred meters from here. When I locate him, flag him for me, will you?"

"Yes, Agent. Are you aware that sunset submissions begin in twenty-three minutes?"

"What are those?"

"It's when Paleowright followers submit to their predicant a token of their faithfulness. If they do not have a token, they may request a penance to perform."

"Ah, gotcha. Well, I don't have a predicant." Meridia left the cul-de-sac, and a small, short-horned reptile, half his height, scuttled by towing a rat on a leash. "What was that?" he whispered.

"An Earlking. They are rare in Isuelt. When seen in cities, they are usually in the service of a Troglodyte chieftain."

"Nuts and feathers," he breathed.

"Agent, it is best you refrain from Timberkeep jargon. It does not fit to your Bareen cover."

"Oh boy."

"Neither does Marine slang."

Meridia rolled his eyes, then wondered if that was safe to do.

He moved on. Troglodytes were everywhere. In this quadrant of Hebert, they outnumbered humans. It was strange for him to see loglards, as the Timberkeeps called them, in the flesh and not trying to kill him. Instead, they cohabitated with humans, counter to their reputation in Wedgewood.

"Fire Eye is moving," reported Jeremy. "If you are approached by a predicant or their docent, you may be asked to submit."

Meridia snorted. "Not likely."

"They will accept a parish token but are known to prefer national currency of any denomination."

"And how do I get a token?"

"You buy it from a Church representative, usually a token counter. It is the Church's method of ensuring that collected submissions arrive in Church collection boxes."

"I see," he said as he made his way past a row of stalls, some of them closed, others were closing. "The predicants accept national currency because it is off the token books."

Passersby, the human ones, were making for their homes. Some looked at him, saw his time-worn Bareen mercenary armor, and gave him a wide berth. Bareen was a lawless coastal city south of Hebert, where from the Church hierarchy hired merciless raiders for tasks too dirty for Scarlet Saviors.

He noticed more doors were closing and heard the bolts thrown as he walked by. Shutters were drawn tight and barred.

"How long until dark?"

"Astronomical twilight begins in forty-seven minutes."

He was closing on the prince, but then Meridia slowed his pace. His combat-sense twitched, and he always trusted his combat-sense. There were no humans in the street now, just the random Troglodyte, most carrying the tools of servants: Brooms, mops, and buckets.

"Jeremy, where is everyone going?"

"Analyzing for possible societal phenomena."

"Okaaay." He kept walking, but slower. Fire Eye should be around the next corner to the left and then another corner on the right.

"Tokens for Torrence! Tokens for Torrence. Followers of Torrence. Torrence the Ancient calls."

The sing-song chant drew closer, coming from the next street.

"My analysis postulates that the local populace has retreated to their homes to avoid paying the submission."

"Oh. What about me?"

"You can pay in silver sheqels, or the drone shows a courtyard ahead; on your right, the gate is ajar."

"Got it."

He found the gate and ducked in, closing it behind him.

"Tokens for Torrence! Tokens for Torrence." The voice was loud, just outside. "Followers of Torrence. Torrence the Ancient calls."

Meridia waited, listening to the chant recede. The courtyard behind him was empty, though he heard voices from a stucco apartment it fronted.

"What Ancient was Torrence?"

"CivMon has drawn a correlation to a Torrence that was an ITA heavy lift crane operator who worked on the Vaal geothermal plant."

"Oh. How long ago was that?"

"Three hundred and thirty-two years."

Meridia moved to open the gate when Jeremy called, "Two Troglodytes are coming, fast. They are warrior class."

He let them run by.

"Alms! Alms. All who love her, Alms for Arietta, Arietta the Ancient."

Meridia sniffed. Arietta was a common female name on Avaria. He'd never heard it used on Dianis.

Waiting while the chanters came and went, "How long does this go on for?"

"Drone coverage detects no more solicitors working your area."

"Just in case, can I choose what Ancient I want, or would I have to pay for all of them?"

"The projected psychological profile of a Paleowright predicant predicts each predicant would want you to submit to their own Ancient."

"Ah, well. Pity the poor bastard who can't find an open gate."

Turning at the next street, he headed to an intersection where Fire Eye, according to the position icon, was stationary.

A door opened, and a young woman, wrapped in a headscarf, peeked out, looking left and right. She saw him and immediately discounted him as a threat. He didn't know how to take that.

"No alms needed here," he said to her. "My Ancient has their own money." He gave her an Avarian head waggle.

She stared, aghast, then slammed the door.

"I guess that's what Clienen meant by inadvertently offending the populace."

Jeremy did not reply.

Approaching the intersection, more people, humans, were emerging. Some storefronts reopened. The keeper of a tobacco shop eyed him suspiciously as he lit the torches on either side of the shop awning. "Smoke? Do you smoke? We have Bareen hash," the merchant said.

"No," he replied. "That shit will kill you."

The shopkeeper stalked away in a huff.

"Agent, a word of caution. The wise—"

"Jeremy. Save your processing. I'm leaving soon."

He turned right at the intersection. There was an emporium just across the lane, a reptilian sage rose emporium, judging by the clientele. The cramped lane essentially an alley. More and more people were out, and it seemed many of them were coming in his direction. Two boutiques past the emporium, he saw what he assumed was a human brothel, judging by both the dress and cosmetics of the men and women who lingered outside soliciting passersby. Beyond that was another brothel. Further yet, there were more shops of what he could only guess.

On his retinal overlay, the prince's icon was stationary outside the second brothel. Meridia scanned the crowd, but no Lizardmen were highlighted. "Anything, Jeremy?"

"Negative. Positioning data has the prince forty yards to your front, but there are no clear street-level visuals."

Scowling, Meridia walked past the emporium.

"Take great care, Agent. I have determined that is a sage rose dispensary. Beware, Troglodytes under the influence of sage rose can become belligerent, exceedingly hostile.

"Hmm. What are those trogs, the big spikes, with the reed arm rings?" For once, he used the correct IDB term for an entity: *Spike* for male Troglodyte.

"Those are guards. The Church requires all reptile businesses within Hebert to provide their own guards to keep peace."

"Hmm. They pick the big ones. I didn't know they smelled so-- so strong. Lettern said they did."

"That would be reptilian musk oil they secrete to lubricate their leather hides. Some reptiles will roll in vats of distilled muskeg, fish entrails, and urine to alleviate dry scales. It will have its own odor."

Nearing the first brothel, he caught a purple flash on his retinal overlay.

"Prince Fire Eye is now within your optical range. Turn your head right. You will see him—"

"Got him."

Next came the part he'd not really planned for. Up to now, he assumed he could introduce himself in private. He'd never communicated with a Dianis reptile, so he was not sure how to begin. On a busy street in a hostile city, Fire Eye might react untoward. "Jeremy, how should I say hello? How will he know me?"

"Approach him from the front so only he can see your shield boss. Activate the flicker graphic and show him the Silver Cup coat of arms. He will understand the signal."

"Silver Cup?"

"Yes. Prince Fire Eye is a bravo of the Silver Cup Courier's Guild. They specialize in security services and delivering important messages across Isuelt."

"Okaaay."

Meridia got his first real-life look at a Lizardman, one of the three sentient species of reptiles on Dianis and the true original inhabitants of the planet. The prince was taller and thinner than his Troglodyte cousins. He didn't have horns, and his snout was longer and thinner. Instead of hard ridge vanes on the side of his head protecting the aural cavities, he had what looked like flat ears.

Meridia saw the hilts of two swords in shoulder sheaths. No shield. He paused, then turned to look at the emporium's Troglodyte guards. They carried maces, spike clubs, and even a flail. They all had shields. Crude iron plates were attached to hip-long tunics as body armor.

Fire Eye, he noted, wore a sleeveless chain mail hauberk, and his tail was longer by half. Troglodyte tails didn't reach the ground.

He had the prince's attention. He supposed he was probably gawking. Out of eye angle for everyone except the Lizardman, Meridia unshielded the multi-func display on his vambrace and brought up the flicker icon set.

"That's the one," said Jeremy, "the picture of the silver chalice."

He pressed *Activate*.

Meridia's shield face turned black. A large silver chalice with a silver wreath along the bottom appeared. Even for a Lizardman, Fire Eye's reaction was demonstrative.

"Tell him Marisa sent you. You are *kurchka orgum Baryy*."

Meridia deciphered what that meant. And he was. He was, indeed.

He approached the Lizardman, who was a good foot taller than him. Fire Eye's tongue flickered in the air, and the tip of his tail thwacked the cobblestones.

"He's agitated," noted Jeremy.

"So am I." Then, to the prince, he growled, "*Kurchka orgum Baryy.*"

The tail settled, and the tongue slurped instead of flicking.

They stared at each other. Fire Eye's yellow, black-slitted eyes were inscrutable in their examination of the human.

"We together," came guttural words from Fire Eye.

"That's a question," said Jeremy.

"Yes. We are together."

Two slurps of the tongue.

"That means yes, or he agrees, depending on the context. One slurp means no."

Meridia nodded. It was going to be weird having a conversation with a reptile while an AI server at Central Station jabbered in his head.

He deactivated the shield insignia. "Are the targets in there?" He angled his head in the direction of the second brothel.

Two slurps.

"Hmm. Let me guess. You can't go in there."

Two slurps.

"The whole male, human female thing. Can't be letting male reptiles in with naked human females."

Two slurps.

Meridia considered the problem. "Do you know who Ancients are?"

Two slurps.

"Well, I'm an Ancient. So while it may appear I'm talking to myself, I'm not."

No slurps.

"I can speak to other Ancients, far away, that you can't see. So, I'm going to start doing that now."

No slurps, then he got two slow ones.

"Jeremy, you understand our situation?"

"I do. We have the genetic materials that Seargeant Horalznick sampled from Marinda Hall. Recon bots from the drone are inbound to the target location. They can compare the uploaded DNA profile to samples they find in the human pleasure establishment. Please wait for execution."

*Human pleasure establishment, that's what an AI calls it,* thinking to himself. He grinned at Fire Eye. "My friend, another Ancient, far away," he tapped the side of his head, "has bugs and birds in the air up there."

Fire Eye did not deign to look up, but his reptilian eyes darted to the opening of the brothel when the three bumblebee recon bots buzzed inside.

"Yep. Those would be the little ones," Meridia said. "Bees. Bumble bees. But different."

Fire Eye's tail tip began to thump again.

Meridia stretched his shoulders. "Relax. We'll find them. Those recon bots are relentless."

"Agent, it is not appropriate to discuss extrasolar information with provincials."

"Ha." Meridia laughed.

Fire Eye's golden orbs refocused on him.

"Sorry, prince. But I'm getting lectured by an AI that I shouldn't tell you things when I was the one who landed in an Avarian assault ship in Wedgewood. Seriously, Jeremy. The big guy and I are about to get into some shit, and you want me to be coy?"

"Agent, what are your plans?"

"Get me those DNA hits and I'll show you."

There was a commotion at the sage rose emporium. Meridia watched as three spike guards dragged a thrashing Troglodyte out and onto the street. They dumped it there, a spike, and let him flail about until he finally subsided, unconscious.

"Overdose," said Jeremy, "sometimes fatal. This one appears to not be. They would spasm into a death arch if it was."

Meridia let out a long sigh. An overdose was never pretty, no matter the species.

A woman, half-naked, ran screaming and cursing from the first brothel. A churchman, an officer of pikes judging by his uniform pants, followed her. He was shirtless. "Come here, you worthless whore. You'll do what I want."

"Not if you don't pay me double," she spat at him and fled down the street.

His friends, in various states of drunken stupor, followed him outside. "Bah, Nercherl, go get her. We'll pay. We want to watch." At their encouragement, the brothel patron staggered after her.

"Lively place," Meridia said to no one in particular.

"It will become more so as the evening progresses," came Jeremy's response.

The longer they waited for the recon bot results, the more Meridia began to worry he and the Lizardman would attract attention. He motioned for Fire Eye to follow him. They moved down the street and stopped short of a hookah den, the smell of marshcat and other aromatics wafting out. Across the street was a paraphernalia vendor, and beside it, a wine merchant. Both doing a brisk business. The vendors on the lane were ready for the evening, wall sconces lit, streetlamps guttering, and alms to the Ancients paid.

"Recon bots have finished their search," Jeremy sounded at last. "Two human subjects matching DNA samples from Marinda Hall have been identified. Will send a map overlay to your optical implant."

"One of our *orgums* is upstairs, and the other *orgum* is downstairs," Meridia said to Fire Eye. "Jeremy, add aura indicators for other sentients."

Red dots appeared on his optic nerve overlay.

"Hmm, any way to tell who their friends are?" He shook his head at the prince and tapped his ear.

Jeremy responded, "Given psychic profiles and visual evidence, other possible Church personnel are now highlighted in bright red."

"Ouch," Meridia said out loud. Then to Fire Eye, "There's twelve churchmen in there. A popular place for the devoted. Let's hope they're all drunk or have their pants around their ankles."

Two slurps from Fire Eye.

Meridia had the sense it meant *okay* rather than *yes*.

"Jeremy, zoom out the overlay and show the best evac route to the stables."

Nodding to himself, Meridia said to Fire Eye, "I'll lure the targets outside, then I'll take them around that corner there," he pointed to a lane leading off to the right, "and you meet me there."

"Meridia, what are you doing?" It was Ivan on the team net.

A single slurp came from Fire Eye.

"Uh?" Meridia wondered if he missed a slurp.

"I said, what are you planning to do?" Ivan pressed.

"You's know where they's are?" Fire Eye rasped.

"Hang on, Chief, I'm talking to a Lizardman. And, yes, I know where they are."

Two slurps and Fire Eye started for the brothel.

"Whoa. Where you going?" Meridia asked.

"Meridia," it was chief again.

Fire Eye slowed, "Show's me." Then kept going, his tail sweeping the cobbles.

"Uh, Chief, I'm following the big guy here."

"Don't go in there, Meridia."

"Uh--"

"Shiren," Ivan cursed, sitting at a console in central Station. He saw the *Shields* was on the team net. "*Shields*, you copy?"

"Affirmative," Mears answered. "There's a defense bot package at hover. Want them to follow Meridia? I can arm the 'twenty."

"What? The particle cannon?" Ivan watched the drone aura and visual feeds. Fire Eye was at the entrance of the brothel.

"Affirmative."

"We're not at war."

"Vectoring the defense bots. Assigning to Meridia. Agent protection protocol."

Ivan flinched. Meridia, an in-country agent, was alone and in potential danger. Mears had made the right call.

Fire Eye's icon was now inside the building. Ivan felt completely helpless, a feeling he hated. He hit the Ready Reaction alert button and ran for the Field Gen station.

A human bouncer made to stop the prince, and a scaled, meaty forearm caught him under the jaw and cracked the bouncer's head against a wall.

"Whaaat!?" The bartender yelled. "What you doing in here rep-tile!" The man vaulted the bar with an iron baton.

That was a mistake.

Fire Eye's two scimitars came out, and blood sprayed.

Two patrons or bouncers charged with batons drawn.

Meridia fired the handbolt, reloaded, and fired again.

Chaos reigned as Fire Eye's tail swept into the sitting room parlor.

"Where?" rasped the prince.

Meridia jammed the handbolt into the holster and drew his cutlass.

A half-clothed Scarlet Savior emerged from a side hall. He drew a rachier from the bouncer's weapons rack.

Meridia parried, stepped inside, shield bashed, and swept the cutlass down. The man grasped his neck. "Arggg." He fell to the deck.

Following in Fire Eye's wake, Meridia rushed forward. The superimposed target icon was across the lounge, through a hallway, and in a room to the left.

Screams; women and boys were scattering. A female bar server cowered at the bar, staring aghast at Fire Eye, whose twin swords were dripping blood. The bartender was on the floor, mewling.

A churchman came at Meridia snarling. "Bareen dog!"

Meridia saw the defense bot, a new Type Three Dragonfly vectoring for the paralysis.

Throwing his shield up, he deflected a thrown crockery and jabbed with the cutlass. The point plunged deep. He had to twist it to pull the blade free. The dragonfly veered off.

"Mears!" he yelled. "Save them for my back."

He charged across the lounge. Everything was upholstered in red: The rugs, tapestry, leather cushions. Ornate gold candelabras decorated the tables, those that were left upright. Crystal decanters sat on the sideboards.

A whore hurled a dagger at Fire Eye. A flick of his sword sent it *twanging* away.

Another crock came his way. It *thunked* against his upraised shield. "Mears—get the whore at the upstairs railing."

He made it to the hallway; two churchmen stood there, one naked, both confused.

Pulling the cutlass back, he brought the hilt around in a swing, and the bronze crossguard knocked the naked churchman flat. The second squealed like a girl and fled down the hallway.

With a swift, hard kick, he smashed in the door to target icon's room.

Standing in the opening, Meridia saw a young male in the bed and another older man standing, reaching for his pants. The optic overlay identified the standing Scarlet Savior's DNA as coming from the den at Marinda Hall.

Meridia gave a smirk. "You know Achelous Forushen?"

The man's eyes first widened, then narrowed.

"I am Agent Illian Meridia of the IDB. I am serving a Federation Warrant. You are wanted for a memory scan to confirm or refute your participation in the assault on Marinda Hall, the Aorol of Tivor—" Meridia had the neural suppressor collar in his shield hand. He was about to activate it when the target growled an Ancient obscenity threatening something about balls and entrails and grabbed for a rachier that hung on the wall.

"Forushen, the heathen blasphemer and his Tivor slum whore?! I serve the Ancient's will!" he railed and dragged the sword-axe from the scabbard.

"Okay," Meridia said aloud to anyone on the team net, "this is--"

"I have a defense bot in stunner mode ready," Mears offered, "I can—"

Meridia back-stepped the rachier's wild swing and cleaved down with his cutlass, connecting with the hilt. The Scarlet Savior dropped the weapon but came in low and fast with a dirk in his left hand.

Meridia didn't see the blade, but saw the shoulder dip and surge forward. He stepped inside the weapon's arc, driving an elbow into the man's jaw.

The boy-man on the bed had risen from the bed and leapt on Meridia with a berserker scream.

Spinning around, Meridia tried to tear the kid's claw-like grip from his face. He ran backwards full tilt, slamming them both into the wall. The door frame cracked, and they fell through.

Rolling over and coming up cat-ready, Meridia heard Mears say, "Got him with a stunner."

The Scarlet Savior burst through the wrecked door and had three swipes at Meridia before Mears said, "Vectoring—"

"Too late," Meridia gritted. Face to face with the paladin, he swept his shield up, blocking the view of his cutlass jabbing up from below. The bot arrived as Meridia heaved the man off the blade. It came sliding out with a sucking sound. The churchman staggered back and toppled over the prone form of his sex partner.

"You!" bellowed from behind him.

Meridia glanced over his shoulder, and a fully armored Scarlet Savior launched into a charge. "Mears--"

He heard a commotion upstairs.

Curious how the dragonfly would deal with the Scarlet Savior's armor, he left it for the after-action replay and bolted for where he was sure Fire Eye was wreaking mayhem.

Screams from above merged with the gargled cry and metallic crash that came from behind.

"Got him," said Mears.

Bodies littered the lounge area. Meridia jumped two prone figures and headed for the stairs. Ichor was splattered on the pink walls heading up.

Regaining a semblance of resolve, the bar server had crept from behind the bar. She slotted a bolt into a crossbow. Rising to take aim at Meridia, she heard a buzzing. Bot Four latched on with its tarsus grapplers, raised its abdomen, and jabbed down.

"*Arr!*" The server felt a burn at the back of her neck; her face met the bar with a solid *thwack.*

At the top of the stairs, the balustrade was missing. The crock-throwing whore lay slumped against the pink wall, drooling. A crash came from the hallway. A patron, knocked flat by a reptilian tail protruding from a doorway, scrambled to get up. Meridia drew and slotted his handbolt. He assumed Fire Eye was attached to the swinging tail.

The man scrambled for a dropped dirk.

Meridia jammed the handbolt cocking lever down and aimed. The man glared at him and charged, dodging left and right.

Holding fire until the last moment, Meridia shot the bolt square into the assailant's forehead. Hopping left, Meridia watched the attacker's forward motion carry him past, through the missing balustrade, and down.

Snatching another bolt, he started checking each room as he went.

Then he came to the one with Fire Eye. The Lizardman had a sack and was tying it to his belt.

"You okay, big guy?" he asked.

The prince gave two slurps. He was covered in blood, and impossible to tell if any was his. The room was a wreck. Not a piece of furniture remained whole. A rachier protruded from a closet jamb buried deep. Meridia saw a body. "Uh, where's the head?"

Fire Eye patted the sack. "*Kurchka pffgeat.*"

Oddly, Meridia found himself stunned by the casual brutality. He wondered why. Sizars ate humans. He'd seen many partially devoured corpses. Was his discomfort because he expected more from a sentient on his side?

"*Pffgeat* means proof that the *Kurchka* has been fulfilled," offered Jeremy.

"Ah." Meridia drew his bloody cutlass and showed the blade to Fire Eye. "My target wouldn't cooperate. *Pffgeat,* the DNA will prove it."

Fire Eye gave a very human sign of doubt by cocking his head.

Meridia laughed. "Don't worry, big guy. Marisa will understand."

"Surveillance drone has video of multiple probable hostiles inbound to your location," reported Jeremy. "Suggest you leave by the rear entrance."

"Right." Meridia tapped his ear for the prince's benefit. "Directions, please."

"Meridia, we are three minutes from the front gate." It was Ivan.

"Roger that. Egressing now."

Outside, they ran to the first corner, or rather, Fire Eye loped and Meridia pelted.

They turned another corner and waited for a stream of city watch to enter the brothel.

Clearing the street, the pair darted across the lane and fled down the narrow passageways, making turns called out by Jeremy. Night settled over the city. Meridia blessed his genetically enhanced vision. Many of the alleys were narrow, dark tunnels devoid of lamps.

"What's that?" Meridia stopped, Fire Eye's reptile musk right behind him. He listened. A horn sounded from the direction of the brothel. Two short notes, then a long. The horn repeated the series. "It is a city watch alarm trumpet," Jeremy said. "Drone surveillance shows the city gates are being closed. I can reroute you to a low point on the wall. You can access it by stairs. There is a seven-meter drop on the other side. Suggest you remove your armor to reduce the weight of impact."

Meridia took off, then slowed. "Uh--" Dropping from the wall might be a problem, but he didn't like the prospect of being on foot, without armor, so close to the city. "What about Trickster?"

"He will remain in the stables," said Jeremy.

"Hmm, I don't know--" Meridia came to the suggested turn for the low point in the wall. The stables were a hundred meters away. "Big guy," he tapped the side of his head, "they want us to jump the wall. You wanna try the gate? They say it's closed."

Ivan and Mears waited.

Fire Eye rasped, his tongue flicking, "Scout."

Meridia nodded. "Good choice."

They ran to a corner nearest the stables. Peering around the corner, the gate, now closed, was thirty meters away. A squad of pikemen arrayed in front.

"What do you think?" Meridia asked the prince.

"We go," came the raspy response.

"Whoa, Big Guy," he said, grabbing an arm, "I have to get Trickster. He's in there."

"I get."

The Lizardman pulled away and walked across the cobbles, his tail loosely swinging.

"Agent, the guards do not know why they were ordered to close the gate, but they will interrogate anyone who approaches."

"Makes sense," acknowledged Meridia. "How's Trickster gonna react when a reptile gets close?"

"No problem," answered Ivan, "as long as Fire Eye doesn't act hostile."

"Uh, Chief, what will the gate guards do when they see a reptile leading an eenu," asked Mears.

Ivan sniffed. "Yeah, that'll be suspicious."

Lieutenant Hearter, sitting beside Mears at the command console, muted the mic. He pointed at the threat overlay of the city on their hologrid. A phalanx of ten pikemen, with red-triangle icons superimposed on them, were marching to the gate. "They're gonna have trouble."

Mears showed a wild, brain-flash expression.

"What?" asked Hearter.

"We can blow the gate! Look!" He zoomed the display at the massive gate doors, and the targeting AI for the twenty-millimeter ion cannon circled the four impact points necessary to drop the gate.

Hearter arched an eyebrow.

"They're screwed if we don't."

Unmuting the mic, "Chief—" Hearter signaled.

"I'm ordering Mears to engage with the twenty. He will destroy the gate to aid in the safe egress of ground assets from a hostile zone. He will not target provincial life forms."

Trickster emerged from the stables at a trot.

"Trickster!"

The eenu spotted Meridia and came to him. Fire Eye followed behind. He waved a claw at the agent and loped toward the gate.

"Particle cannon charging," Mears informed the net.

"Are you sure you can do it without killing anyone?" Ivan asked.

Mears and Hearter were fans of Meridia. Space-bound, their hands were often tied when trying to help provincials against corsairs.

"Affirmative," replied Hearter. What happened when the gate fell was a different matter.

Meridia got his feet in Trickster's stirrups. The gelding was side-stepping and throwing its head. "Big Guy is going for the gate! Yeeha!" He kicked the eenu, and it sprang away.

"Charging, charging," called Mears. "Charged."

A burst of ionized particles emitted from the *Shield's* twenty-millimeter cannon. The bolt streaked from the heavens and blew away the upper hinge of a gate door. The guards cowered from the sudden, mystifying explosion.

"Yaa, yaa," Meridia dug his heels into Trickster and managed to direct the eenu at the gate. "The Ancients come!" he bellowed. "Alms for Arietta, The Ancient's wrath is doom!"

"Charging," Mears sounded on the net. "Two seconds."

Trickster galloped, and Meridia hung on. "Wrath, wrath! The Ancients come! They blast with fire!"

The *Shields* fired. A streak of light blew away the bottom hinge. The guards scattered in horror. The Ancients had come. A third bolt disintegrated the locking bar, and the fourth bolt struck the remaining hinge. With a huge creak and then a grinding, the gate fell. The resulting *boom* echoed down the street.

"Yaa, yaa. The Ancients are angry! They come!" Meridia yelled at a squad of city watch, staring at the destroyed gate. They dropped their swords and fled.

Trickster jumped onto the flattened gate door, clattered across, and galloped into the night.

"I see him," said Ivan. He spurred his mount, and Horalznick and another trooper galloped to intercept Meridia and Fire Eye.

"Disarming the twenty," Mears called out.

Hearter sniffed, forgetting to mute the mic, "You've been wanting to use that cannon ever since you came aboard."

"Aye, sir. Needed to test it."

# Chapter 13
## Commandant Fritach

*Empire of Nak Drakas*

The hood came off; the light blinding. Achelous' augmented vision quickly adjusted. He took stock. The smell of tar and hemp mixed with sea air told him he was still near the water; the carriage ride from the ship had not taken him far. His hands were bound behind him, but he was not tied to the chair in which he sat, nor were his feet shackled.

"So, you are what the fuss is all about? Ya?"

Achelous focused on the man seated in front of him.

"My Paleowright friends are upset!"

The man, in a Drakan uniform with two fleurs-de-lis on each shoulder board, was a general, a commandant general, if he remembered his Drakan ranks correctly.

The commandant laughed. "They are not happy with us, their Drakan hosts. We, well, there was a *little* confusion in Vaal. We thought the viscount was staying, having fun with his new friends, and we so wanted to meet you, and so, vie-la-da, here you are."

Achelous peered at him. He was Nakish, bald, as was the style of their aristocrats. A short, black goatee hung below gaunt cheeks. His dark, almost black skin contrasted with the light grey of the uniform.

"Good for you too! Ya? Trader Achelous?"

It was a question. To this point, per his IDB captive training, he remained mostly mute. The complex training regime stressed how to behave dependent on the parameters and variables of their captivity, and particularly who their captors were.

The commandant looked at Achelous' heavily bandaged right hand. "Otherwise, our Scarlet brothers would have done far worse. Ya? They are pigs, those churchmen. So impatient. Kill, kill, kill. If you blaspheme one of the Ancients, Nickola, Arden, or Thomas, they kill you. Bah, such animals." The commandant studied him. Every one of the trader's fingers on his right hand had been smashed with a hammer; several of his toenails were removed, all before their ship had docked in Vaal. And yet this man, this captive, had not broken.

"We are all Paleowrights here, friend Achelous. We have no complaints with your Mother. She is, how do we say, a Mother. Who can fault that?" The commandant's patient smile never waned. "Is true our Church brothers from Hebert are zealots, but you need that to protect the faith."

Achelous measured his breathing and triggered a reduction in adrenaline. Without his multi-func he could only issue rudimentary commands to his embeds, the hormone stimulator at the top of the list.

"I am a patient man, Trader. There are so many paths to accomplish things. The Church, the bishops, that fool Helprig, they are so hasty, so quick to offense." The commandant leaned forward in his chair. "We have so many options. So many things we can do!" The commandant threw his arms up in the air. Standing, he began to pace.

"So many choices. I can," he spoke as he paced, contemplating the floor, "of course, give you back to the Church."

That simple admission of power confirmed what Achelous suspected: His latest interrogator was none other than Commandant Fritach, head of the Washentrufel, the Drakan Empire's secret service.

"But then what good would that be?" Fritach went on. "You'd be dead, and your Tivorian woman, the Landy Marisa, of House Pontifract, and your son," the commandant paused in his pacing and looked quizzically to Achelous, "what was it Larech said? Ah, Boyd, your son's name is Boyd. Ah, sad, Boyd, your son would be fatherless."

Real fear, real pain gripped Achelous' chest. He willed it under control, bound the turmoil, and shoved it away. His chest eased.

"Then, we could go the other path. We could release you now and send you home. Though how you would get there through the League blockade ... but maybe that is not much issue. Our ships manage." A few steps and the commandant turned and paced back along his track. "And there are so many things in between. Setting you free now, well, the emperor would not be happy with that. He is certain you know things the archbishop does not want us to hear. Helprig, alas, he is greedy, so selfish. If he cannot have your information, he will kill you before you share it with us."

The commandant stopped pacing. "So, trader, shall we start there? Ya?" He signaled to one of the guards, "Untie him. How can he rest bound like that?"

Fritach grabbed his chair, turned it around so the back faced Achelous, and sat on it, crossing his arms on the back of the chair. "So, let us start with things we know, things you have done well. Things even I admire." He waved to a guard, "Get Larech."

The soldier left, and soon, a Washentrufel agent entered.

Through the open door, Achelous saw more clues. They were in a building beside a busy street. The windows were high on the walls with bars in them. This was a jail, or perhaps a barracks, but not high-security detention. The Washentrufel agent he recognized from bot and drone surveillance files taken in Wedgewood before the Paleowright attack.

"The drawing."

Larech reached into the satchel he carried and showed Achelous a drawing.

The commandant studied him. "We can be friends, or we can be enemies." He continued his introspection, watching the pupils of Achelous' eyes. "Or, we can be neither. Something in between. You help me, I help you. Ya? You tell me what you want, and I tell you what I want. We trade. Of course, you will want to go home. And maybe we can do that. A partnership!" The commandant brightened. Then he feigned sadness. "Alas. There is a problem." He waited for a reaction. Apparently, he saw something in how Achelous' eyes narrowed, for he continued. "The Church. Helprig. How can we be certain our new partner won't be kidnapped again? Bah!" He looked away, shaking his head. They are so much trouble."

Achelous knew he was being played. The commandant was setting him up for bargaining by, ironically, acting good versus evil. The situation presented him with a dilemma, and not just one. Self-preservation at the top of the list.

He considered answering Fritach, smooth as he was, and Fritach saw that, so he paused in his monolog and waited.

If he were to escape, he needed greater freedom. Baryy and Outish were certainly fretting over his capture, and, thank the Spirits, the commandant had confirmed that Marisa was alive; at least, Fritach wanted him to think so. Marisa, with the help of Baryy and Outish, and perhaps Ogden, would plan something. Though how they would find and rescue him without IDB help, he could only guess.

His hands free, he rubbed his wrists. Looking askance at the drawing, he took it from the agent. It was a hand-drawn sketch, and judging by the familiar grain and color of the parchment, it came from a Timberkeep press in Wedgewood. "It's a handbolt. Who drew it?"

"He speaks!" the commandant leaned back in the chair and said to Larech, "There, see. What the Church fools could not do in three weeks with torture, we did in five minutes with respect." He turned to Achelous and resumed his inscrutable examination. "Who drew it is not important. That we have it *is*. A partnership, Trader. You are a trader? Ya?"

Achelous tilted his head, not enthusiastic about conversation.

"Then you know how to trade, how to deal." The commandant pointed to the special cocking mechanism on the drawing. The mechanism that made the weapon fast-loading and simple to operate even on eenu-back. "Where? Where did you find that?"

"Lamar."

Sitting back, Fritach arched an eye. "Where in Lamar?"

"Saphinus."

"Ach. I have never been to Saphinus. Where?"

"The bazaar. I traded for one."

The commandant pursed his lips.

If Achelous could control the narrative, stick to the CivMon-crafted plots, he would be safe using the cover story he lived for the twenty years as a Dianis in-country operative. The cover and pretend events now affirmed by two decades of real history.

"And your blacksmith friend. The burly axeman. He is a good fighter? No?"

Achelous blinked and regretted it.

"Ya, ya. We know of Ogden the mighty." Fritach stood, turned his chair around, and slouched in it. "Uloch. Decurion Uloch. Do you know him?"

This was new. "No."

"Ha!" Fritach slapped his knee. "He fought you in Wedgewood. You and that Defender, your vaunted Al Suri." He looked at Achelous with respect. "I know all about her. *Sublime Knight* is what it means in the tongue of the Lamarans. Ach, the torch-bearer for all Defenders. Ya. She is good. Uloch is better, but she fooled him. Nah, nah, it was not Uloch's fault. Larech has told me all. Uloch had to save our Church allies from Helprig's folly. Ach." The commandant shook his head. "Such a fool. He wants your woman. More! More than he wants you. You were consolation. But that Lizardman." Fritach scowled. "That Lizardman. And what was it the Tivor troops used when they came to your Lady's rescue? The same, ya, in Wedgewood? That night, in the foundry. Ha." He slapped a knee. "It terrorized the churchmen. The stories—" Fritach raised his hands. "You would think the Ancients came forth and smote the world with lightning."

A warning bell started to ding in the corners of his conscious. Something about the way the commandant pursued the line of questions.

Fritach slowly straightened from his slouch. "Did they, Trader Achelous? Hmm? Did the Ancients come forth that night?"

By the commandant's smile, Achelous began to suspect he was after something more important than the origins of the handbolt. "Tell me of that night. What happened in the foundry?"

He thought through probable alternatives, but the commandant said, "Nah, nah. Don't tell me. Better you should hear first what some of our Wedgewood friends tell us. That way, maybe you won't lie. You wouldn't lie to me, would you Trader? I so want to be a valued *customer.*" Fritach rubbed two fingers together in the universal sign for money. "Larech, tell him."

He listened to Larech recount, in surprising detail, the night in the foundry during the Battle of Wedgewood when Baryy had used a rifle for the first time in combat on the planet.

Achelous had not been there, but the story told by Larech was nearly as accurate as Baryy's version. He'd planned for this moment, but not with the Drakans. "Rockets."

"Eh?" said Fritach.

"We were making rockets," he told the tale, most of which was true, of a king in Urgan who used a primitive form of gunpowder to thrill his children, adding chemicals to make colored explosions and smoke. "You trade with Urgan," Achelous added to the crafted cover. "Their alchemists make fireworks for celebrations. We put a cone on the back of the reed tube and attach it to a stick and shoot it from a crossbow." He didn't worry that he was giving away any real idea. Rockets shot from crossbows were, of course, impractical and dangerous.

"Hmm." Fritach rubbed his goatee. "Explosives? From Urgan?" He brightened. "Larech, look into it."

He wondered how long it would take the Drakans to find the formula, gather the materials: The charcoal, saltpeter, and sulfur, and begin testing. He hoped he was not around when it literally blew up in their faces.

"And the day the Ancient was killed. Tell me about that."

"Ancient?" He was at a loss.

"Yes, the Ancient, named Quorat."

Achelous kept his gaze steady. *How did they know that name?* "I wasn't there."

"Ya, ya, you weren't there. We know. But this Quorat, who was he? And who were the others? And the ship that flew through the air. Tell me about that."

*How much do the Drakans know?* He was out of cover stories.

The commandant watched him. "Ha. Ya, ya, you know!" He leaned in Achelous' face. "Was this man, this Ancient, was he a friend of yours?"

He shook his head, "No."

"And the others, what of them?"

"Lettern? She's a warder for the clan. Alex, he's a Life Defender--"

"Ach," Fritach waved his hand dismissively. "Tell me of the ship that flies. What is it? And who came in it?"

Achelous shook his head.

"No? No! Is that *no*, you don't know, or *no*, you won't tell me?"

"I don't know." It was a lie, but the commandant couldn't prove it. If Fritach caught him in an overt falsehood, he'd lose his nascent power to negotiate.

Fritach scowled. He held out a hand to Larech and snapped his fingers. The agent pulled the device from his satchel. Achelous' consternation was too late to conceal.

"Ya, you know what this is." The commandant rolled the device in his hands, then handed it to Achelous. "Try it."

He refused, shaking his head. Now he realized, perhaps too late, what the commandant's true purpose was, and it was *not* gaining information about Ancient technology. Where the commandant had acquired the commercial night vision goggles, he had no idea, but that the commandant should choose to show such a random device told him it had been a chance event that landed it in his possession.

"Ach, of course, you have one of your own? Ya?" Their eyes locked. This was a new game. Not the game Achelous had come prepared to play, but the one Fritach did. A game of learning Achelous' real identity, his origins, and what that portended for the empire.

"So." The commandant stood. "We are done for the day, ya?"

Achelous guessed, again perhaps too late, why the commandant had watched him so minutely as he did now. Conversely, the Church — Helprig -- had not cared who he was, just that he be punished for blasphemy.

"We will speak again soon. You rest, Trader. You have been through much." Fritach strolled to the door. "Think, Trader. The empire can be of much-- assistance. There is no need to suffer."

As they passed through the guardroom, Fritach handed the night vision goggles to Larech to conceal. There were too many prying eyes, too many Church spies, even amongst the Washentrufel.

In the privacy of the coach, on their return to the Citadel, Larech asked, "Do you agree?"

Fritach, not wanting to give the agent too much credit, averred. "You know what this trader did not do?"

Larech shook his head. "What?"

"Gold. Ask for gold. If he is a trader, traveling hard roads across Isuelt and even Urgan, why did he not ask for silver?" The coach turned a corner onto a cobblestone road. "Because he is not interested. I offered to be a customer, and a real trader would have bargained. This Achelous did not. And do you know why he did not bargain?" The commandant didn't wait for an answer. "Because we have nothing he wants." He deigned to give Larech a smirk. "Imagine, Larech, the Empire of Nak Drakas has nothing this man wants. And, ya, I watched his eyes. You are right, his pupils, they are not normal."

Larech sniffed. "The difference is slight, but I saw it when I woke him. They are not ... human."

"Hmm, ya." Then, a thought struck him, and he slapped a knee. "Ha!"

"What?" asked Larech.

"Those churchmen, such idiots. They give us Paleowrights a bad name." His grin faded as he watched the countryside roll by. "An Ancient, Larech. Helprig wants to hang an Ancient."

# Chapter 14
# Contractor Haven

*Margel Damansk Asteroid Belt*

"Desperate deeds," Bleep Nuts had once said to Krch, "never go as expected, and rarely end well."

And yet here she was, in Contractor Haven, never one to follow another's sound advice. With her precious cargo safely ensconced in shipment escrow, all Krch had to do was wait.

The human waitress served her a bowl of Avarian stewed and mashed roots and vegetables. It wasn't tree sap or vitubinum nectar; those were a rarity out here in the belt. Human and sentient species workers were the norm in the habitable and business zones of Contractor Haven, as bots and drones were not allowed. Out beyond the docking gates and shipping warehouses, areas open to vacuum, bots were the norm. On Contractor Haven, client anonymity was a key feature, and hence the appeal of the hollowed-out trade asteroid. No sneaky recon, surveillance, or assassination bots were allowed past the quarantine sensors and doors. Aura signature dampeners were installed throughout. No signatures could be logged and tracked inside the habitable zone of the rock.

Krch was about to immerse her sucking tubes in the bowl when the waitress, unsure of how Tweeunars ate, asked, "Can I get you a drink with that?"

Krch thought about it. She needed to stay sober, at least until boredom became unbearable. "Nosss."

Sucking down the pureed vegetable gruel, she watched the pricing on the electronic menu fluctuate, keeping pace with current market prices. The most expensive beneric and trium drinks bounced as much as ten percent a minute. On the *Cargos for Sale* hologrid, the most recent cargo bids were displayed at the top. No seller or bidder names were attributed to the bids, just cargo type, quality, mass, and deadline time counter. Amongst thirty-odd commodities and equipments for sale, Krch's aquamarine-5, all two thousand pounds, was at the very top.

Slurping her soup, she listened to the other patrons of the tavern. According to their rampant speculations, the aquamarine-5 cargo was the topic du jour, with everyone wondering what the final bid price would be, who the seller was, and if they were on the rock.

It was Krch's idea to bring the shipment to Contractor's Haven. Celestial Navigations had the interest and the money to buy the remaining ton, but Internal Security had eliminated them as a potential suspect, and so Krch had been instructed to refuse to sell to them. While waiting in the Hole, she had a few lukewarm offers come through back channels, but no one wanted the whole ton, and none were willing to pay anywhere near what Celestial did. Nordarken Mining, apparently, had gone dark.

Her mouth tubes sucking the bowl clean, Krch suspected Councilor Magret acquiesced to the need to get the Dash-5 in the Fed supply chain. Whereupon Krch's value to the Federation and Matrincy would drop to zero. She had clemency for killing Junko and raiding Dianis, but not for being complicit in Sysreq's attempted murder of the now famous Interconn star Lettern Stouttree. Margret had told her the Fed would be lenient given her cooperation. Krch didn't believe it. Councilor Margret, with her perfect blonde hair and genetically sculptured body, was greasy as a pond slug.

Desperation at her plight clawed at Krch. Trapped between a certain mind-wipe and personality reset, Krch, now out of the Hole, had a plan. She hadn't quite figured out how to launder the proceeds from the second ton of aqua, but almost half of the proceeds from the first ton were safely loaded in a stealth drone rocket bound for Asteroid 12390-99, Margel Damansk.

The waitress returned with a drink. Krch, surprised, hadn't ordered a drink *and* it didn't come from the autoserv's ejection chute. She called the waitress back. The woman waved, "Paid for."

Eyeing it suspiciously, Krch sniffed the drink with her tubes and looked up at the drink board. An Austrium Black Hole made of trium was going for seventy-eight credits, way out of her penurious price range. She looked around the tavern, but there were no obvious admirers taking credit for their extravagance. Whoever had ordered it knew something about Tweeunars: They couldn't tolerate alcohol, beneric caused vicious hangovers, but  they could consume trium just fine. Lifting the glass to take a wary sip, she saw there was writing on the napkin underneath: *Geocontract, fourteen hundred hrs, C gate.* Natural enzymes in her breath caused the nano dissemblers in the ink to actuate, and the writing faded. She was tempted to ask the waitress who the patron was, but they'd probably tipped her to have a bad memory.

Staring at the chilling rocks in the drink, Krch frowned. This was not her plan. Her ship was ready. She'd give them, the IDB and Matrincy, a run for their trouble, for her memories. Her soul was at stake. Desperate deeds.

Fourteen hundred hours was three hours away.

# Chapter 15
# Command Loft

*Wedgewood*

The lift operator cranked the winch as the pawl click-clicked with each foot of rise. Lifting the passenger fifty feet to the first deck of the Command Loft was no simple feat, but the burly Timberkeep managed it with ease.

Sedge, on the second deck above the lift station, heard the pawl snap into the final gear. Arrayed before him on the planning table was a large, table-size, hand-drawn map of the Citadel, the best they could do between what the clan voyants could discern from their insights and the smaller maps provided by Meridia. The loft map had been updated several times with crucial details from drone over-flights. Arrayed on the map were wax figurines depicting the various units they were deploying and those they expected to encounter.

The stairs coming up from the first level creaked. His visitor had arrived.

*The first gate, the Main gate, that's the critical objective,* Sedge mused. *If we don't take that, well, we'll be trapped. Unless the Avarians can manage an emergency extraction.* With so many personnel and movements, such an extraction would be-- challenging.

"I brought you a gift."

He set down the figurine representing the Drakan pikemen they'd seen in the recon photos patrolling on the wall above the gate.

Ivan Darinarishcan stood there holding a two-gallon cask of Octavian De No ale.

Sedge raised an eyebrow. His grey hair tied back in a ponytail, the same shade as his short beard and the hair on his chest. He always wore his tunic unbuttoned.

Ivan approached unbidden.

Not saying a word, Sedge reached for the cask. With both hands, he held it up to the late afternoon light, the sun sinking behind Mount Mars. He read the gold filigree label; it was printed in Galactic Standard. "Hmph, is this in return for the Bash Me Brains?"

"It is," Ivan answered.

"Then we should open it? Noi?"

"Oi, we should."

Sedge searched for the spout release, found the snap, and pulled. A satisfying hiss came from the flagon as the charging tablet volatilized the dormant carbonation.

"Have you been there? Octavia?" Ivan asked, pulling a chair from the planning table and sitting.

Sedge appeared thoughtful, then set the cask down on a table as he went in search of mugs. "Doesn't sound familiar. Where is it?"

"About forty-two million light years into the Tenfinetty Arm." He used the Loch Norim name for the Orion Arm of the galaxy, the Milky Way.

"Tenfinetty? You say?"

"Yes," Ivan watched Sedge's face as he brought the two mugs. "The matriarch owed me a favor. This is it. She had it shifted in this morning. Do you know who the matriarch is? Do you follow our Fednet Interconn?"

"Yes and no," he answered as he filled the mugs from the cask. The metal of the cask already frosting over from the activated chilling. "I'm not much for staying up on current events. Except," he handed Ivan a mug whose thin, perfect froth stopped just at the rim, "those of Clan Mearsbirch." Sitting, he relaxed his muscular frame in the chair. "I do know who the matriarch is, however. I was pleased to see her here in person. She understands the importance, the significance of this planet, this mountain, to the human race. That is good." A wry smile filled in where more could be said.

Ivan searched Sedge's face, waiting, but the warlord took a long pull from the tankard.

"To what do I owe the honor of receiving such an excellent gift? We can order up another pitcher of Bash Me Brains from Murali's, just down there," he leaned in his chair to look through the railing. "But this, forty-million light years?"

Ivan gave a head waggle and avoided eye contact.

Sedge smirked, though not unfriendly. "And, yes, I know who you are."

Ivan met his gaze.

"So, Chief of IDB Ready Reaction, are you here on business, or is this a purely social visit?

Ivan felt his chest constrict as he said, "Purely social."

The warlord cocked his head. "Oh, come. You're as dour as Cordelei Greenleaf. If you came to socialize with that expression, you can hop an eenu and head for the lowlands. Octavia or not."

Ivan sat back and raised his chin. "The mission."

Looking across the rim of the tankard, Sedge asked, "What of it?"

Ivan's Adam's Apple bobbed. "You will die."

Sedge finished the sip and rested the tankard on this crossed leg. His expression hadn't changed. "An execution?"

Ivan snorted. "Spirits no. Not if I or everyone I know could help it." He rubbed a thumb on his mug. "Which, evidently, we can't."

"Ah. I see. Friendly fire or hostile action?"

Ivan peered closely at the warlord, wondering if he was being taken seriously. "Hostile fire."

Finally, a subtle reaction told Ivan that Sedge was indeed listening.

"And this revelation, it came from the matriarch," he raised his mug, "or someone else?"

Ivan nodded once. "The matriarch."

"Hmm," he peered into his mug. "I understand she is usually right."

"She is," answered Ivan.

"And you came to me, why?"

Ivan looked to the cask to say he came to deliver the matriarch's farewell gift. For recognition of his service to Loch Norim Humanity, but that wouldn't be the truth. Instead, he'd come to tell a doomed soul his life was about to end. He came because that is how he would want to be treated. But now—

"Ivan, do you know how old I am?"

"I can guess."

"Okay." Sedge stared out from grey brows. "Guess."

"A thousand years, give or take."

"Hmm. You're a little light. Sixteen hundred and fifty-five, Galactic Standard. How many of those years do you think I spent awake, outside of a cryostasis tube?"

Ivan pursed his lips, noting Sedge's grey hair and carelines, and factored in what he supposed was superior Loch Norim age management. "Three Hundred."

Sedge laughed. "Souls and saints no. Gaea forbid I'd be that *old*. *I* would ask to be executed. No. Two hundred and ten, and believe me, that is long enough when you are one of two remaining members of your family, and most all your friends, except the new ones here in Wedgewood, died fifteen hundred years ago. We're social animals, Ivan. Very few of us do well as hermits. I certainly don't."

Behind Mount Mars the sun settled, and the loft eased into shadow.

"Ivan, in the past millennium, I have been in and out of cryostasis thirty-three times, each time emerging from the tube hoping Core had come back, and each time finding only silent, dusty hallways." He shook his head and, for the first time, appeared bitter as he stared out past the south wall to the farms in the distant plains below. "I was a younger man when Nemesis attacked. We had just finished Lycelia. I was overseer for it."

A chill air current flooded down the mountain, ushered by dusk.

"I stayed here in the mountain when we evacuated. I stayed with those who didn't shift back because Dianis had become my home, not Core. Those of us who stayed, and you see their sons and daughters below," he motioned with the mug, "decided we'd rather fight and endure Nemesis here, hoping they would forget us. I was an architect. I had a goal to see all we had built survive."

Ivan listened.

"And Nemesis never returned. Their first attack their the only, though it succeeded in destroying our infrastructure. Without aid from Core, we could not repair the systems. Too many of our specialists, scientists, and senior engineers had fled back to Core. Understand, Dianis was originally a small research station and then, later, an agricultural facility. Later still, it became home to expatriates, what you would call religious separatists, each forming their own conclave on a fertile distant world where they could go and live a utopian life."

Sedge may have sneered at the last, but Ivan wasn't sure.

"The planet was never militarized." Sedge sighed. "We had few defenses."

The lift operator called from the top of the stairs, "Sir, do you want me to light the lamps?"

"Noi, I'll do it," he answered. When the man had gone back down below, Sedge said, "I learned all my family, except my sister, had perished on our home world, Focri, between here and Core. Soon after, we implemented emergency isolation procedures, ensuring our Field generators could not be used against us. All A-wave beacon channels were erased. Then, I, and a few others, decided to go into cryostasis. Rather than age and wait for Core to return, we opted to sleep and wait in turns, tours of duty." He let out a long breath, "We were the caretakers of that facility," he tilted towards Mount Mars. "Each time I came out, the world had changed. Our population had changed, evolved, and devolved through the loss of genomic maintenance therapies." He paused, working his jaw. "It wasn't long, the second, third time out, that I realized everyone I ever knew, except those in cryo with me, were dead."

Ivan saw the water in Sedge's eyes, but the tears didn't come.

"After the twentieth or thirtieth time," Sedge waved dismissively, "I knew it was hopeless. Core was dead. If they weren't dead, they had no interest or capability to come back. By then, I was just going in and out of cryo because that is what I did. It was my job." A deep breath. "Finally, two sleeps ago, I came out, and someone had returned and left! It was you, Avarians, your ITA engineers, and they were worshipped like gods by our descendants who had no real notion of who they were or where they'd come from, so complete was the degeneration.

"The Church helped with that," said Ivan.

Sedge arched an eyebrow, the one that had a natural tilt. "Hmm, by finding and hoarding  all our books and charts and diagrams. Anything that could educate Dianis as to what it really was, and lift these souls out of ignorance."

"And propogating the myth of the Ancients were someone greater than the common Diesian."

A nod, and Sedge said, "That was the greatest disservice. By doing that, the Church stole the truth, the hope, and the prospect of Dianis reseeding itself as a Loch Norim colony. It's true the Nemesis attack destroyed too much of our modern society to survive as it was, but the Church made sure of it. Dianis had to pull back upon itself, find the primitive basics, and regrow." He smirked. "This a long way for me to explain, that I'm not going back into cryostasis. These people here, Ivan, they are my friends now. The sons and daughters of all those I knew fifteen hundred years ago. Fifteen hundred years," he stressed. "All that time weighs on you. Humans are not meant to span fifteen hundred years, not alone."

"You don't have to go into cryostasis. Just don't go on the mission," Ivan said.

Sedge snorted. "Stay behind and cower? Not likely." The grey eyes, from beneath bushy brows, showed like the steel of a sword. "Do you Avarians know anything about multi-dimensional thread calculus?"

"We know of the multi-verse and how quantum mechanics works."

Sedge shook his head. "No. But I suppose if you haven't built a decent quin-layered quantum computer, you can't do the calculus. Have you?"

Ivan's frown showed the answer was no.

"You see, what your matriarch and Cordelei do, being the savants they are, is tease out of the ether the endpoints of a multi-dimensional thread. What they call Fate."

Raising his chin, Ivan scratched his neck in understanding.

"A good quantum computer with the calculus and layering can run the equation." Sedge leaned forward, holding his mug between two hands, "This close to the matriarch's predicted event horizon the equation is immutable."

"Im-mutable?"

"Well, there are enough opportunities in a two-hundred-and-ten-year lifespan to influence some of the variables in one's own equation, but at this point, it's too late."

Ivan frowned, "Too late?"

Sedge nodded, "Yes, when your number is up. It is time to go." He sat back and took a long pull at the ale. "I could *not* go on the mission and try to foil the prediction, but I'd just die some other way. Fifteen hundred years, Ivan. It's about time."

Ivan shook his head. "There is free will. You have free will."

The warlord burst out laughing, almost spilling his ale. He wiped a hand across his mouth. "Oi. There is. And we practice it all the time." He nodded in agreement. "But, just like gravity and cosmic force, dimensional chains cannot be broken. Certainly not by Man."

Sedge read Ivan's puzzlement but ignored it. There were things the Avarians would just have to learn on their own: Every life was a long mathematical equation, with the parameters filled in at birth, even before. The exact day and time of death was just a rounding error. He peered into the empty depths of the tankard. At last, he stood to pour a refill. "More?" He asked.

Ivan handed him his tankard and saw the Citadel map. "You've been busy."

"Oi, the bastard Drakans haven't changed. They never leave the gate open."

"The Main Gate?"

"Yes. They always were obsessive about security. They use this pocket door here," he pointed to the map, "to send a guard out to inspect papers and cargo. Once cleared, they open the gate."

"What do you mean they were always obsessive ?"

Sedge shifted, picking up the pikeman figurine. "In the old days, the really old days," he chuckled, "the Unionists were notoriously secretive."

When Ivan looked to ask, Sedge answered, "The Drakans. Their forebears are from the Unionist Souls faction." He worked his jaw. "Bastards. So they are finally going to get me."

Ivan waited for more.

"I never got along with them." He placed the pikeman at the wall above the gate. "We need to do something about these, a diversion...."

"I've been wondering about that myself. We can shift in scaling ladders with the lead team, but the wall patrol," Ivan pointed at the pikeman, "will probably see them coming."

"Could try to overwhelm them. Our archers are good. Swing the ladders up and pick off the guards as they try to throw the ladders down."

Ivan slowly shook his head. "We could, but it would be risky. We'd only get one try before reinforcements arrive." He bent low to look at the wall facing the marsh. "Is this map accurate in all distances?"

"Why? I believe so." Sedge bent beside Ivan to examine the map, like two boys working on a miniature starship.

"I have an idea," said Ivan, "what were you thinking about a diversion?"

"Ah." The warlord reached across the other side of the map and put his finger on a gatehouse. "There. Can your bots scan a lock?"

"And then we cut the key?"

"Oi." He straightened. Walking to the railing, he peered down on the town, the people he'd come to care for, deeply. He was, after all, their ancestor. "When Cordelei delivered her vision of Achelous in the Citadel, she said it would be my end."

Ivan, in the peace and silence of the command deck, heard the town sounds from below. They beckoned with the assurance of a millennium of human history.

"So I was not entirely surprised you came." Sedge contemplated the lives below. "I am honored that you came to pay me your respect, but I dare say my death is not the only ill omen the matriarch delivered."

Sedge turned from the rail. "Does anyone else know you are here?"

"The matriarch, but no one else."

"Good. It's for the best."

# Chapter 16
## Gate C

*Contractor Haven, Margel Damansk Asteroid Belt*

At thirteen-thirty hours, the bid on the aqua cargo was up to four million credits, still below what they expected a whale like Nordarken Mining to pay. Margret had messaged that maybe Krch should put a deadline stop on the bidding.

Krch's tubes twisted in anger. The human was in a hurry. Margret didn't care about the money or Krch's memories. In the past two hours, while she watched the bidding on her cargo, Krch reminisced on all her favorite things, places she loved, the faces of her parents, all the memories she would lose. They would not be archived in some deep data store but permanently wiped. Memories of friends and family now dead, killed on Tweeunar by the Sizars, gone, as if they had never lived, never existed because their last surviving relative didn't remember them. It hit her like a punch to the stomach. A person's identity was the culmination, the quilted blanket, of all their experiences.

However, if she and her past friends were to avoid that fate, she had a more immediate problem: How to shake her tail. She was sure she had one or more followers, but she couldn't pick them out from the throng of miners, stevedores, and hub workers. There were at least four different sentient species roaming the market deck; telling one of them apart from another was like telling one rat from another. Without sucking tubes, humans, Halorites, and whatever all looked the same. Stopping at an info kiosk, she downloaded the hub map to her multi-func. Paging through the decks, from top to bottom, she looked for a route to Gate C less used and easier to spot a tail.

In the end, the problem was solved for her. On her way, outside of the fuel cell recharge station, the hydrogen gas alarm blared. A steam valve hissed, and an oxygen recycler vented into the corridor. A warning light for emergency depressurization started flashing, and the air-tight doors for the passageway segment swooshed closed. She was trapped in the gas contamination zone. The three other people in the zone began to panic, whipping out their multi-funcs, but then the alarms and lights ceased wailing and flashing, and a depressurization-safety door at the far end slid open. A worker in a hazmat suit, but with his helmet off, ushered the scared pedestrians out of the containment area. When Krch made to scurry past he caught her by the arm and whispered, "Fourteen hundred Gate C." The other people were running to clear the area before the doors closed again.

The hazmat man pulled her toward a side door. "In here. Hurry."

Through the door, down a passage, through another door, and around a corner, Krch was now lost without looking at her multi-func. Fearing she was being abducted, she stopped and yanked her arm free. "Thisss isn't the way to C Gate," she guessed.

"No, it isn't," the man said.

When he didn't make a move to grab her, she asked, "Where'ss are's we going?"

"B-K Gates."

Looking at the hub map on her multi-func, "Those are the heavy lift gates."

"Correct. We should go. You are being followed."

Hustling her along, Krch, exasperated, said, "The aura sig damperss's don't reach out there."

"They don't have to."

That bothered her. Her abductor wouldn't need aura damping if he were going to kill her. She stopped.

The man accepted Krch was very afraid. "We'll use hazmat suits. No signature, no infrared, and the cameras have been disabled. We'll be invisible."

"If I go with you," she challenged.

"Do you have a choice?"

Her tubes froze still. "Yass, yeass, I do."

"Fine," the man said, "but you need to decide because I'm leaving."

Her mind was spinning furiously. She spat, "Why you need me?"

"We need a geo, and you know the planet for our contract."

"Whats Outfit?"

"You never heard of us. We're new."

Not particularly reassured, new outfits were notorious for their low rates of success and hence payment to their contractors; she asked, "Whats planet? I know lots."

The man looked like he might answer, and he might not.

She cocked her head. "Protected?"

Judging by the man's hedging, she figured the planet was indeed ULUP-protected. That reduced the list to four that she'd been to. Tossing the names at him, she hissed, spewing creep acid, "Dianis."

He sort of inclined his head.

They wanted her for her aquamarine knowledge and, more, her knowledge of the planet. Oddly, the idea didn't scare her, not as much as it should. *Vengeance.* The emotion kindled her spirit. Vengeance against all the waiting, against the worry about the mind-wipe, against Bleep Nuts for leaving her, against Junko for killing those people, and against Margret and her threat of destroying everything Krch loved.

She could've, should've asked a thousand more questions, but hazmat man was growing impatient. The fake containment leak, she guessed, wouldn't keep her pursuers at bay for long. "My ship, I'll need it."

He shook his head. "We handle all transportation. The IDB will impound the ship as soon as they think they've lost you."

"My cargo. My eight million credits."

"My outfit will buy it. Legally. You just have to authorize payment to a non-Fed space account. The hub will get its cut, though."

Wondering about the financial mechanics of making the transaction work, hazmat man interrupted her thoughts by grabbing her sleeve. "We have to go. I have a hazmat suit for you. You need to put it on, and then we'll hitch a ride on a fueling tug out to B-K."

"They'll know what ships left port," she asserted.

Dragging her with him, he acknowledged, "That's good,"

# Chapter 17
# Toll Haven

*Toll Haven, Sea Haven League*

"It's rough today, Alon."

Christina could see that. Whitecaps splashed over the breakwater.

The first mate of the Haven Directorate ship, the *Black Gull,* led Christina, Alex, Mitchern, and their five Zursh mercenaries below deck.

"But even with this blow, we'll still have you at the coast around midnight. It's only eleven leagues from here." Making their way down the steep stairs, ship odors assailed them: Tar, varnish, wet canvas, and moldy hemp line. The officer showed them their temporary quarters. Docked in Toll Haven harbor, the capital of the Haven Directorate, the *Black Gull* rocked, straining against its mooring lines. Between the Directorate and the Sea Lords, the two republics formed the Sea Haven League, a cornerstone nation in the Western Alliance.

"If any of you start feeling sick, there's buckets in the corner," the mate said, holding the cabin door open. "Best to call for a deckhand if you need it dumped."

Alex asked, "And if we want fresh air, can we go on deck?"

The mate considered it, not wanting to refuse the Life Defender. "It'll be dark. The seas will be steep and rolling. We'll be running with no lanterns. If you were to fall overboard, we'd never find you."

After the officer left, one of their Zursh mercs said, "Yeah, I'm taking my armor off now. I don't want to sink like a stone down to the deep and darkest."

"Alon, why the change of plans?" another merc asked. "Why rescue this adept first? If word of their rescue reaches

Stith Drakas, then the other three might be moved, or they could be waiting for us."

That had indeed been their plan. Of the six Timberkeep adepts kidnapped by the Washentrufel before the Battle of Wedgewood, two had been killed and one severely wounded by vengeful churchmen. When the archbishop in Hebert had learned of the Drakan's plans to interrogate and conduct experiments with the adepts in an attempt to establish their own sixthsense cadre, the archbishop had ordered them killed. Anything threatening Drakan dependence on the Church for Ancient knowledge was hypocrisy and dealt with, given Hebert could not be seen overtly impeding Drakan goals.

In an ironic twist, the coaches carrying the six adepts were guarded by both Washentrufel agents and Scarlet Saviors. When the mock highwaymen ambushed the carriages in the Central Plains, they were forced to fight their fellow churchmen. The attack partially succeeded.

When the reduced Washentrufel party had reached the safety of Drakan territory, a wounded Timberkeep, too ill to travel, had been left at an infirmary in Pontif, eleven leagues off the *Black Gull's* bow. With the few remaining adepts, the Drakan agents had pushed on to a Washentrufel barracks near Stith Drakas.

"Mitchern, tell us what you have heard." Christina unbuckled her armor. She doffed her helm and shook out her flaxen hair wound into a braid. She'd been to sea and was not enamored of it. There were no pastures, forests, or Believers, just endless expanse of water.

Mitchern, their telepath, recounted, "Oi. My sister, who I am in *touch* with, has passed word that the clan has contact -- Mother bless us -- with the captive pathic. They are waiting in a town called Pred, just south of Stith Drakas, though they know not what for. There is more news. The clan agreed to support the rescue of Achelous, the trader."

The Zursh mercenaries looked among themselves. "How was he taken? When was he taken? Why? By whom?"

"Much has transpired since we've been gone," said Alex. "Mitchern only received word this morning." The Alon and her party had been on expedition since after the Battle of Wedgewood as part of a cavalry force pursuing the shattered Church battalions east.

Mitchern recounted more news from the West.

"Stith Drakas!" the Zursh sergeant exclaimed. "Alon, do not question my resolve. The Drakans are my life-long foes, but to go to Stith Drakas and rescue this man, is that not folly? Our mission to Pred is fraught. I expect the Drakans in Pred to be alert, wary. With Mother's Light and her Will, we will prevail. But for Tivor and the Clan to go to the Citadel? How," he stuttered, "is that not...." His words found no voice.

The other Lamaran troopers were silent in the face of their sergeant's entreaty.

Christina unbuckled her sword belt, sitting it beside her on the bench. Her leaf-green eyes, tall frame, and flaxen hair were always a welcome sight amongst Life Believers. The scars over an eye and one on her cheek did not detract from her striking image, but accentuated it. Those features in Nak Drakas, however, were a liability. She could not pass for Nakish. Many thought she was Lamaran, but her tan skin and green eyes put that also in doubt. "Mitchern, how does Sedge propose the rescuers get in and out of the Citadel without fighting the whole of Stith Drakas?"

Mitchern, in all his seventeen years, had never thought he would say this: "The Ancients will deliver them."

Their mouths dropped.

Alex let them ponder that in stunned consternation. Then he sealed it by announcing, "Achelous is an Ancient."

"Whaaa—" the sergeant exclaimed.

"I was there when Lettern killed the Ancient Quorat. I saw the Ancient's Assault Marines materialize out of thin air. I rode with them in one of their ships. Ivan, the mercenary guard captain for the High Priestess of the Auro Na, he is an Ancient. As is she."

"Mother, help us," a trooper whispered.

"So many," said another.

"Where do they come from?" asked the sergeant.

With no inflection, Alex said, "I think Mother has sent them."

The ship trembled, a premonition, as the sails were hoisted and the lines cast off.

"They were here before us, and now they have returned. Mother has called them," said Alex. "The Ancient, Ivan, told me as we rode in their lander that all the world, what he calls the *galaxy,* is at war, far beyond here. The war has come to Dianis, and here we are to fight, to save one man who has secrets to help win the war."

"This one man," Mitchern whispered to the mercs, "is more important than you, or all of us."

"Mother's Blessing," intoned a merc. "We are bound for Stith Drakas, and the Ancients will deliver us."

Christina offered him solace: "Fear not the deliverance. The *Black Gull* will bear us. It is those in Wedgewood, who we shall meet in Stith Drakas, that will be carried by the Ancients."

No stars shown in the dark night. The *Black Gull,* navigating by compass only, heeled to port, but the pitching eased as the waves fell off. They were closing on Pontif. Christina held to a lifeline, having come on deck at a request from the captain. He stood beside her and warned her to brace against a steepening crest. "Soon, we should see the lights of the town. We'll be looking for a set of three lanterns. A single light, then a half mile to the west, two more lights, and then a half mile further, three lanterns stacked vertically."

"That's the signal?" she asked.

"It is. Nak Drakas may be Paleowright, but there are Believers even here."

"Mother, keep them," she invoked.

He looked at her. The ship was running dark, no lights. The midshipman, casting the sounding lead, called findings in a whisper that sounded harsh against the splash of waves. "Alon, you bless them by coming here."

She chilled at the risk they placed Mother's children in.

The ship's deck settled to level as it came within the lee shore. Turning to starboard, the '*Gull* sailed, stirring no more sound than her namesake. A messenger, a young squeaker, relayed soundings to the captain.

"Ten fathoms and steady," the captain said to her. "That means we're on the shelf. It will stay at this depth until a half mile from the shore. We'll launch the longboat there." The plan was for Christina and her men, for she was the only woman on this mission, to be rowed ashore. Their guide would meet them there.

Paddles dipping in water and the creak of oarlocks were the harbinger of their coming. Stars began to peek and hide behind low, scudding clouds. A crewman jumped from the bow of the longboat and splashed into knee-deep water. Another crewman helped pull the craft ashore, crunching on the tide pebbles. Christina slung her broadsword into its shoulder sling; she conferred with the second mate. "At dawn, first light, we will see you here."

"Aye. And it be good if it was just you." He grinned. "We've no room for churchmen."

She took his meaning. "And if not at first light, then tonight, an hour after full dark, two miles south. We'll hold two lanterns side by side."

"Aye."

She made for the bow of the boat and eased into the low, cold surf.

Splashing through the tidal ebb, she met the party gathered around their guide, a young Nakish female wrapped in a hooded leather slicker. The teen stared at Christina as she approached. She bowed, "Al Suri Ascalon. Mother holds you dear."

"Rise, child." Christina offered her hand. "You may call me Alon."

"Her name is Bera," supplied the sergeant.

Bera smiled tentatively. "It is rare that we say Mother's blessing in the open. Paleowright inquisitors are everywhere. It is not safe for Life Believers. If we are found out…"

"You're safe with us," said Alex.

"She says the adept is at the infirmary inside the Drakan Auxiliary hostel," said the sergeant. "There's only two guards at present, along with the doctor and the other nurse. The doctor and nurse live in the rear apartments. Bera, here, is the other nurse. The town watch are all auxiliaries and are at their homes, not on duty. It's a small town, more of a village."

Christina peered at the Nakish teenager who cast her eyes down. The Alon reached out and gently lifted her face. "I am nothing to fear or to hold in such regard that you dare not look at me." She offered an encouraging smile. "Can the adept walk?"

"Yes, Alon. She can walk, but I think not far. She has lost much blood. Her arm—"

"I know." Christina had heard the grisly outcome of the ambush. "Take us there."

"There is more," Bera said, anxious. "There are Scarlet Saviors in the town. They do not wear their gaudy armor, but the doctor says he is sure they are. They came to our clinic last night before dinner. There was a predicant. He demanded to see the sensitive. He said she had committed crimes against the Church and was to be punished. He demanded the doctor release her."

"What did the doctor do?" asked Christina.

"He refused. He said the Westerner, for that is clearly what she is, was too ill to travel. And that our emperor's men, the Washentrufel, had entrusted her to him until they returned."

"And how did they take that?" asked Alex.

"Not well, I'm afraid. They threatened the doctor with excommunication if he did not comply. He threatened to have his men take the woman. The doctor told me to run and fetch the Watch. Which I did." She looked around the group to see if they believed her. "When I came back, the predicant and his men had left, but they are still in town. They stay at an inquisitor's house. The night sentry of the Watch told me the Watch is nervous. There might be trouble."

Christina glanced to Alex. "We should hurry."

"Yes. It's a fine night for foul deeds," he answered.

Bera led them along the beach through a swale in the dunes. Beyond, bracken tidal pools devolved into a marsh. The girl followed a track of sand through the reeds to the town and an outlying building, a fish salting plant. Arranged around the packing house were tarp-covered salt piles and barrels.

Creeping across a sandy lane, past a few nondescript buildings, Bera pointed. "There, that's the infirmary."

The party crouched, stacked in a line beside a row of old derelict fishing boats; any passerby could have seen them.

"What? What, lass? What's wrong?" the sergeant sensed her consternation.

"The door. The side door is open. It was closed and bolted for the night."

The sergeant's sword scraped from its sheath, followed by four others.

Alex whispered. "We need to go."

A nod of his helmet, the sergeant made a set of hand signals, then started in a crouch across the intervening space. Halfway to the infirmary, he paused, scanning in all directions. Satisfied, the sergeant moved to the building and stood beside the open door. Peering in, he pulled back and pumped his gauntlet fist up and down.

One by one, the team rushed the door.

Entering a dark hallway, Alex ran, his boots thumping on wooden boards. To the right, another hallway opened, and a light showed at the end. A sound, the clash of steel, came. He motioned the others in that direction and went to the left. Lamp glow came from an open door.

Christina followed with Mitchern and Bera.

Running to catch Alex, Christina heard a woman scream from beyond.

At the open door emitting lamp light, Alex sorted friend from foe. A man had a dagger raised, but another, pinned to a bed, held the attacker's arm with both hands. Noting the crimson robes, he guessed the dagger wielder to be a Church clergy. The churchman's free hand, in a fist, bashed the victim about the face. Alex's sword came up. A swift chop at the neck stopped the fist. Alex pulled the clergyman free as blood sprayed the man underneath.

Running down the passage in what seemed an eternity, Christina came to the room and the source of the scream. She banged into the door frame, took a quick glance in, and drew her long sword. A man, holding a rag, wiping his bloody rachier clean, looked up.

"You!" She held the sword point at him. Though her shield boss was covered, the man saw her amulet, a white lily, hanging on a chain about her neck, resting on her brass breastplate.

"What? You dare!" he tossed the rag and raised the sword-axe.

She attacked.

Christina's fury blazed.

The rachier tried to parry and block as the Scarlet Savior staggered against a wall.

Christina closed hard and fast, ramming an armored knee into his groin; her elbow came across the chin, and the sword came up from below and sank deep.

At the door, Mitchern, at full draw, kept aim.

Christina heaved a gasp and went to the adept. The Timberkeep's eyes stared like pale opals. "Arggg!" She held the woman's shoulders and pressed her face into her neck, willing her to stay. Praying, pleading for Mother to return her.

Pounding steps thundered in the hall, coming closer.

Alex and a merc collided as they halted at the door. "The doctor and nurse are alive. The others are—"

Mitchern turned away. "That's Judith. She was seamstress, as gentle a flower that Mother ever bloomed."

On the beach, in the approaching dawn, they waited for the *Black Gull's* longboat pulling steadily to shore.

"I say we should go for the predicant and his guard," one of the mercs argued. "They can't be let off."

After saving the doctor's life, the doctor confided with Alex that the predicant and another Scarlet Savior stayed behind at the inquisitor's home while the other three Paleowrights came for the adept.

"No," said Alex. "The doctor promised he'd not call the Watch until after dawn. If we go after the predicant, we'd face the Watch as well. They didn't kill Judith."

"Alex is right," said Christina, looking at the shrouded form on the stretcher of the adept they failed to save. "We're not here to wage war against the Church." Though she knew that's exactly what the Zursh mercs wanted. "There will be more fighting. Now, we need speed. From here, the captain says, with a fair wind, it is a half day's sail to Stith Drakas. A full day if the wind is foul. We can beat any messengers the Watch sends east, but we can't tarry."

"If we don't meet any Drakans," mused Alex.

"There's that," she said, "when word reaches Stith Drakas, the Washentrufel will be on the alert for more Church treachery."

# Chapter 18
## The Bait

*Nva Gira, Planet Avaria*

Margret accepted the A-wave call from the Internal Security agent at Contractor Haven.

"She's definitely not here. We spent the day going over every inch of this rock. Krch got out."

"So our mouse is in play," said Margret.

"Appears so. She had help, too. Pretty sophisticated. They hacked the hub's emergency systems and sealed a section with Krch in it. By the time the false alerts were cleared, Krch was gone. Someone took her."

"By force?"

Hedging, the agent answered, "We don't think so. Witnesses reported seeing her talking to a man in a hazmat suit and that she went willingly with him. But she did leave her ship behind. Probably doesn't matter to her; Nordarken Mining bought her entire cargo and paid eight million for it."

An eyebrow went up.

The agent snorted. "Yeah. They bought it through a two-step intermediary. Took a bit of digging, but it was them. They didn't really go far to hide the purchase."

"Did you confiscate the funds?"

"Couldn't. They were deposited in an out-of-Fed account. The only funds we could seize are the fees Krch paid the hub for storage and commission: Four hundred thousand credits," he sniffed. "That's a lot. We could go after that." He let the suggestion hang. When Margret didn't bite, he said, "Yeah, better to let them keep their money. It was a legal sale."

Margret stewed over a notion she entertained. There was the downside of not labeling the shipment as ULUPcontraband. Nordarken Mining had bought it on the open market, fair and square, albeit at a premium. "If Krch's ship is still there, how did she get off?"

"Ah, that's the interesting part. We tracked all vessels leaving the hub from the time she disappeared to the time we forced the hub into lockdown. All five ships have been boarded and searched in Fed space. No Krch."

"She shifted out?" Margret asked, surprised.

"Yep, has to be a military-grade shift generator, too."

Her surprise turned to a deep frown.

"We haven't found it yet. We think it may have been dismantled and shipped out while we were boarding vessels in the Margel. Our cutters and surveillance drones registered a low energy ether anomaly thirty-three minutes after the hub's false environmental alarm actuated. At first, the ether anomaly was ignored, as they usually are in non-combat zones. But then we went back and cross-analyzed the readings. We added other Field measurements from other sources and are convinced it was a low-energy, shield-fused shift. Just one. Those types of shifts are for stealth insertions of one or two people, max. The energy profile goes logarithmic with the mass shifted, and we would have caught it."

"Not everyone has mil-grade Field generators," complained Margret. "The Matrincy certainly doesn't."

Nodding, the agent said, "That's because you don't run clandestine ops."

"Are they even licensed? Don't they need to be registered on the network and all those other regulations? They're mil-spec for a reason."

"So you come to our quandary. Krch's new sponsors are considerably more upmarket than Junko."

"And Nordarken Mining bought her cargo." Margret saw her carefully laid sting thoroughly unravel. "They are either desperate, have nothing to hide, or want to flaunt it in our face."

"Who?" asked the agent. "Nordarken, or her new partners? They may not be the same. We know from the recon bot surveillance between her and Bleep Nuts that she hates Nordarken Mining. And why would the 'Darkens want to rescue Krch after they bought her Dash-5?"

"They want to get their money back?" Margret gave a derisive head waggle. "But you're right. The way Nordarken is acting, or whoever it is, a new party or not, are sure we can't catch them." And that notion troubled Margret. Access to military-grade equipment, particularly Field generators, put their adversary in an entirely different league, one on par with the Federation itself.

The hologram was silent as they both ruminated on implications.

"Okay," she said, "let's stay focused on Krch. We know where her money went, even if we can't seize it. She'll need to surface to spend it."

"If she wants to spend it in Fed space."

"Tweeunar is in Fed space. She lives to go back there," Marget said. Then a thought struck her. "We need Krch more than ever. Her patrons, as you said, are bigger and more sophisticated than we'd thought. More brazen than Nordarken Mining, though who that would be, I don't know. It's important we learn who they are." She paused. "They went through a lot of work to get her, even at the risk of exposing themselves. Who or why would someone want Krch that bad?"

Thinking, the agent slowly shook his head. "Who?"

Margret's perpetual smirk was back in place. "I can't tell you the who, but I can tell you what Krch is."

The agent waited for illumination.

Margret spelled it out: "She is the lone extrasolar geologist with in-depth knowledge of Dianis and its aquamarine-5. What's in her head is all you need. No risky survey scans necessary. Now that the IDB is back on Class F Dianis, the ability of corsairs to secretly land planet-side go way down."

"Dianis? You think they want her for a Dianis op?"

Margret gave a head waggle.

Still skeptical, the agent said, "Go back to Dianis after Junko and Quorat? Okay, but they had better be real good or real stupid."

Margret arched an eye. "Aren't they all? Real stupid, that is."

The agent shook his head.

"What?" she asked.

"People with mil-grade generators are not stupid. Have you considered that Dianis may no longer be just about Dash-5?"

A question, then a concern crossed Margret's countenance. "What else?"

"Mount Mars, and the Loch Norim. Krch has been there."

# Chapter 19
## Port of Pred

*Empire of Nak Drakas*

The *Black Gull* hoisted the Hawk's Claw pendant. In the wan dusk-light the black on red claw fluttered fitfully.

"Pred is a smuggler's harbor," the captain told Christina as the quay loomed before the darkening town. "The Hawk's Claw signals that we are a blockade runner and have cargo to sell. The dock quartermaster is in a hut at the foot of the pier."

They discussed the details of the plan now that the captain saw the best berth for a quick departure was open.

"When quartermaster sees the Claw, he'll send a runner when we dock, asking what we have. The master will want the port's fee for landing the cargo, which is usually five percent. Mari, my second mate, will go to the master's shack and negotiate. Mari is part Nakish and has done this before. If the quartermaster wants more than five percent, which he might, Mari will haggle." The captain looked to Alex. "If you don't haggle, the master will get suspicious.

"When the carts are here, Alon, you should wait until all the cotton is loaded and then slip into the last cart or wagon; it will be dark by then. I'll have Mari get something covered, like a dory. He'll tell the carters you have sacks of flour that can't get wet."

"Will they try to board and search?" Alex asked.

The captain shrugged a shoulder. "They could always try, but they haven't yet, and we wouldn't let them. The lines will be singled up, and the wind is offing so we could clear the quay. Boarding blockade runners is bad for business. The way the Drakans see it, any cargo snuck past the League is good cargo. Cotton and gritcorn flour are hard to get in Nak Drakas this time of year. They'll let it through and leave us be. This isn't a Drakan navy yard. Pred is for profiteers." He grinned.

"What do we owe you for the cargo?" asked Christina.

The captain chuckled. "Nothing. We'll make a profit. Mari will see to that. The admiralty encourages us privateers. If we can make money scalping the Drakans in trade rather than boarding, fighting, and looting, the better for me and the crew. What we learn from the Drakans in the process is invaluable."

Tied to the quay but with the crew at the ready, the second mate and three mercs, dressed as sailors, headed for the quartermaster's shack. None of the mercs looked Nakish, that is, slanted eyes, dark skin, and black hair, but none of them appeared Doromen or Eldred either.

Mari returned with three covered wagons clattering on the pier planks. Night had fully settled, and a longshoreman walked the quay lighting lantern posts.

"How'd it go?" Alex asked, carrying a bale of cotton down the brow.

"He was itchy about us not wanting his carters, but I paid for it with a higher rental for the wagons. I let his five-and-a-half percent commission go, but with a lot of grumbling. He complained about doing business at night, which is when most pirates sneak in here; he knows that. We need the wagons back by noon tomorrow; otherwise, he'll send the constables after us." Mari heaved a bale into the wagon. "Have you seen the nags that came with these termite traps? I wonder if we can get off the pier?"

Christina, wearing a peasant's tunic covering her armor and a home-spun cap with earflaps, carried a bale of cotton down the gangway. She tossed it in the last dory and climbed in after it.

"All loaded," called the sergeant. He and his men were the drivers of the other two dories.

Alex snapped the reigns on the pair of sway-backed eenus, and the wagon creaked into motion.

At the master's shack, the quartermaster blocked the gate. "Need to inspect your cargo. Gots to make sure you didn't overpay me." A cynical grin split a mouth missing most of its teeth.

"Ain't' no more haggling, Gurfgor. You got your five and high in advance," Mari growled. "You want more? The captain has a stop in Stith for passenger pickup. We'll take the cargo there."

When the master scowled but didn't move, Mari told Alex to turn the wagon around.

"Bah." The master spat on the planking. "I better not be hear'n you sold more than what you told me. I know all the buyers. I'll find out."

"Then you'll know we dealt you square. Go," said Mari.

Alex snapped the reins.

As the last wagon rolled past the dock master, Mari said to Alex, "That's why we keep the backs open: So the workers can peek in and act like they are doing their job. Keeps their suspicions in place."

Clip-clopping at a crawl through the warehouse district, Alex felt the hair at the back of his neck rise. He resisted the urge to look over his shoulder for couriers from Pontif. Surely, they were on the road by now.

"The Washentrufel compound is two blocks east of our last stop," said Mari. "You'll know it by the Drakan flag and blue tile roof. All the warehouses are on this lane. When we get to the first, I'll bang on the door and roust the buyer. You and the others will head to the compound. Leave two mercs to drive the dories. I'll take my time haggling for prices on my way through town. When I get to the last warehouse, I can only wait so long. The captain plans to slip the lines at three bells, and *I will* be onboard." Mari glanced at him.

"Aye." Alex thought through their plan: Free the adepts, get them to the ship, and then continue on foot to the outskirts of Stith Drakas, three leagues distant.

At the first stop, Mari banged on the door. It opened promptly. Businesses in Pred were accustomed to blockade runners coming at all hours. Two mercs stayed with the lorries, while Alex and the others slipped off into the night. Alex could hear Mari banter back and forth with the storekeeper. The wall sconces, at either side of the wide double doors, guttered, flaring acrid smoke. The keeper was interested in the flour, but Mari wasn't prepared to sell it yet. When the keeper offered his best price for both the cotton and gritcorn, Mari said, "Ya, ya. You can have the cotton now. If that be the best price for flour, then I'll be back."

In an alley, Christina asked, "All set?"

"Let's get the adepts," he replied.

The Washentrufel compound was a group of three buildings. The first, the sergeant judged by peeking in a shuttered window with broken slats, was some sort of unoccupied library or storehouse. The second was a barracks. A candle burned in a room adjoining a larger bunkroom. An adjutant was sitting at a desk bent over, reading a scroll. The bunk room, except for a dozen or so empty beds without bedding, was also unoccupied. The third building was a detention center. The windows in the back of the building were high on the wall and barred. Lantern light illuminated the entry, and a fire burned in the hearth of the front room.

Peering carefully through a barred window beside the door, the sergeant spied a guard sitting in front of a pot-bellied stove feeding it kindling. Another guard was coming from a hallway that bisected the building.

"I'll feed the eenus," he heard one of the guards say. "And get our dinner."

"More fish, I suppose," said the other guard.

"Hopes not," said the first. "Saw Warrecth smoking a swinelet. Could be that."

The sergeant ducked from the window and made his way back to the team. "A guard's leaving now to feed their mounts. We should follow him. Take him out there. There's at least one more guard in the building. There looks to be cells in the back, but don't know if they are occupied."

"Alex," Christina said, "take a merc and follow the guard. Count the eenus. We can use them. The rest of us will subdue the other guard and search the building."

At the detention center, Christina's group readied themselves at the double entry doors. She made a signal, and the sergeant knocked on a door and pushed it open.

"Ya?" said the guard, looking over his shoulder from his seat in front of the stove.

"You the duty watch? I have a message from Pontif."

The guard slowly rose. "What sort of message? The agent is in the barracks."

"There's been an attack on the hostel. Scarlet Saviors. They killed the adept."

The guard blinked. "Scarlet Saviors?"

"Aye. I'm from the town watch. There was a fight. The head watch thinks they may be coming here next."

"You don't look like town watch."

"I'm not. I'm a merc. I work for the Trufel. We were called to support the watch. They took a beating."

"Oh." The guard's face lit up. "I'll reckon they were. The agent should know."

"Have you moved the other adepts? We'll need to double the guard."

"Double? Nah, nah. Triple."

"Are they back there?" the sergeant pointed down the hall.

"Ya."

"Go tell the agent. I'll stand guard. And be quick. If they come, we want to be ready."

The guard hurried out the door, and a *smack-twack* sounded, and then a heavy *thump*.

Mitchern and a merc dragged the unconscious guard in. Christina followed them. "Quick, grab the wall sconce, let's see who's here."

They found a jail block at the very back of the building. Mitchern held the lamp high, looking through the bars. A Doroman held her hand up, shielding her eyes.

"Peek? Peek, is that you?" Mitchern asked.

"Oi?"

He handed the lamp off and fumbled with the keys he'd taken from the guard. Finding the right one, he turned the lock, threw open the door, and rushed in. She stood, and he hugged her.

Christina used the keys to open another cell.

The sergeant held the light behind her.

Christina stood in the cell door, her face and armor cast in shadow, but her profile, to a Timberkeep, unmistakable.

"I knew you would come. I told them," the female voice said. "I saw you, Alon. I never gave up hope—" A wracking cough choked her.

Christina entered. Bending low, she helped the young woman rise. "You're Twenti. I have dreamed of you. You called to me." Embracing the girl, her frail body against the brass breastplate, "Mother sent me. I am here."

"I told them. I told them."

Mitchern called out, "Torerre is here, our pathic. He is well!"

"It's true, Alon," Torerre offered, "Twenti said you were coming, but after, after the Church attacked the Washentrufel I began to give up. Then Mitchern and I touched. You were in Toll Haven. It was like spring come to the mountain. And Judith? What of Judith?"

Mitchern shook his head and looked away.

"We were too late," Christina bit off the words.

Peek turned pale, then slumped.

A merc grabbed her as she fainted.

"We must go," urged the sergeant.

Outside, they met the merc who'd gone with Alex to the stables. "This compound is a waystation. Curriers come through with messages for the Citadel. The stable is full of mounts."

"And Alex?" Christina asked.

"He's saddling eenu's. We can ride to Stith Drakas."

"Stith Drakas?" exclaimed Torerre.

"Not you," Christina said in a soothing tone. "You'll take a ship for Toll Haven."

"A-- Alon," Twenti was uncertain.

Something passed between her and Christina. "Yes?"

Twenti bowed her head and mumbled.

"We have to go," the sergeant hissed.

They found Alex at the stables. Five eenus were saddled. He was cinching up a sixth.

"Mitchern," Christina said, "we need another eenu. Help Alex. Sergeant, set the other eenus free. "

The duty agent for the station finished penning the last missive. Sealing the scroll with the blue wax of the Washentrufel, the agent stamped it with the station's imprint. The daily currier from Pontif was due by the turn of the glass. He'd meet him at the stables with the station's packet, then go to bed. In the meantime, he'd make the night rounds.

Strapping on his dirk, lantern in hand, and satchel on his shoulder, the agent went out. His first stop was the transfer barracks to say good night to the guards.

A shadow loomed large in the dark. Pausing, the agent raised the lantern. "Huh?"

Walking closer, it was an eenu, loose, grazing in the station's garden. "Hey, go!" He shooed the animal away, then stopped. So the animal wouldn't spook, he approached more casually. The mount didn't have a halter, but it had a brand, a Washentrufel brand. Alarm filled him. It could have come from only one place: The stables. He hustled to the barracks. The door slightly ajar. Drawing his dirk, he pushed the door open. The room looked normal, but neither guard was present. He searched the building and found one of the guards bound and gagged in a cell. The man was unconscious, a large swelling brewing on his head. "Blast! Ancients and fire!" Checking the other cells, the prisoners were gone. "Damn, damn." He ran from the post, calling for the second guard. The night was eerily silent.

At the stables, he confirmed all the eenu's were gone. "Damn. Thomas the Driver, save us." There was a constabulary a short distance; he went to roust them.

"They're on the move," the *Trilonair's* sensor's officer reported. The Avarian screening frigate was the advance guard of the inbound task force. The vessel's mission was to scan, collect, and track the aura signatures of the mission's members and then chart the disposition of enemy forces. Using the IDB Dianis database, they had finally gotten a hit on the Al Suri Ascalon's signature and that of Alex, a Life Defender. A recon drone, dispatched from the frigate, loitered overhead, providing real-time visuals and threat detection data to the ship's AI.

The *Trilonair's* captain, in the captain's chair, routed the ground action to his hologrid. Seven green triangles, indicating the targets were on eenu back, were galloping along a gravel road, leaving a town labeled *Pred.* The initials *CT – Christina Tara* -- followed a triangle. Numerous grey dots, triangles, and squares reflected the presence of other humans. Grey meant they were human and non-hostile. "Are they in trouble?"

"No threats above the warning threshold," answered the AI.

The executive officer, acting as IDB liaison, said, "IDB reports provincials in mission leadership are in touch with a pathic in their party." The exec flagged Mitchern's icon, so it pulsed. "They have received and acknowledged their orders and are proceeding to the rendezvous."

# Chapter 20
## Way Stop

*Stith Drakas*

Two guards, Drakan Cuirassiers and the Washentrufel Agent Larech, escorted Achelous to the carriage. He bore manacles but no shackles. The carriage was an armored coach with iron-bound sides, steel window shutters, and hub spikes protruding from the wheels. So heavy, the wagon needed a team of six eenus. The driver sat in an armored enclosure forward of the coach box. Six mounted Cuirassiers stationed themselves in front of the wagon and another six took up position behind.

"All this for me?" Achelous asked as he climbed into the padded compartment and sat on surprisingly comfortable seats. "This your typical jailer's wagon?"

The two Cuirassier guards ignored his question as they climbed into the wagon behind him. One sitting beside him, another across from him.

Larech took a birdcage from a carriage attendant and then climbed in himself. A Cuirassier pulled the door closed and bolted it from the inside.

Settling in, Larech noticed the trader's interest in the pidgeon in the cage. "Ah. A messenger. Should we experience any difficulties on the way, I will release it."

Achelous wanted to quip, saying he was not much of a threat for one guard, let alone the twelve outside, but something in the flat stare of the guard across from him said this was serious business. Instead, he asked, "Where are we going?"

Surprisingly, Larech answered him. "Fritach. The Commandant wishes to renew your acquaintance. So we go to the Citadel, in the city. Have you been there?"

"The Citadel or the city?"

"Either."

"The city." Though he had been a much younger agent, not a chief.

"Were you *trading?*" Larech said it with a smirk.

Achelous gave his best smile. "I was. Just starting out, though. Drakas isn't much of an armor market. Too many of your own armorers, but spices you buy. Lots of."

The wagon was moving now. Through the slatted windows, he could see they had rolled onto a road, heading into a forest.

"Ah," said Larech. "The city is known for its fine armorers, but spices ...."

Sergeant Mears entered the command deck on the *Shields*. "What do you have?" he asked the duty officer.

"The AI on the *Trilonair* is querying our Dianis database and is coming up with negative hits," the duty officer answered.

"For what?"

"A breed of dog?" she looked at him quizzically.

Mears frowned. "Show me."

A live recon drone feed popped on the hologrid. "Who's drone is this?" he asked.

"Theirs. It's pinned to a possible threat."

"Where?"

In response, she added a geo display cube to the hologrid. The bird was in Nak Drakas, nearing Stith Drakas.

"Oh. Christina's party."

"Affirmative," she said. "The *Tril's* AI flagged this group," and she highlighted eight pink triangles and one oval four miles behind Christina's party. "The aura signatures originated in Pred. Originally, there were sixteen, but they split. One group vectored to the south, towards the harbor, and this group to the northeast, following the same track as Christina. Both groups have the same type of dog."

"Hmm." Mears watched as the duty officer zoomed in the drone feed and focused it on the dog. It was definitely leading the eight riders, who were all armed and looked to be

Drakan constabulary. The dog was long-bodied, had shaggy black fur, and a pronounced nose. "I don't recognize it, but I'm not a dog or fauna expert. Ping Ivan."

They watched the feed while waiting for Ivan to come on the grid. The dog was loping in miles-eating motion. It held its nose low to the ground.

Ivan came on, and Mears shared the drone feed. "Have you seen these?"

"Hmm. It's a Kretchmer. A bloodhound. Who's it after?"

"Christina's group."

Ivan's expression changed. "Oh." He watched the feed and skewed to the constables following it. "That bloodhound won't give up. It'll drop dead first."

The *Trilonair's* AI, that was monitoring the comm circuit, escalated the color of the triangles from pink to red.

"If we get any closer," Alex called, "we'll make those dragoons nervous. They'll—"

As if reading his mind, a Cuirassier peeled off from the wagon escort ahead and stopped sideways across the road. In the universal warning, the path ahead was barred: The cavalryman drew his saber and laid it across the pommel.

At fifty yards, Alex brought their party to a halt. They stood there staring down the distant sentinel.

Finally, casually, the Cuirassier sheathed their saber and then cantered after the receding wagon.

"Well, that's that," said the sergeant. "We get any closer, and we'll have to deal with more than just one."

Christina peered into the forest on both sides of the road. "I know of no better way to the city. There may be one, but we'd have to cross through the forest. We'll stay to this track and keep our distance. Perhaps at the next way stop, they'll let us pass."

Ivan briefed Clienen on the evolving situation with Christina.

"She doesn't know about the trackers behind her?" Clienen asked.

"No."

The pair were standing in the Ready Reaction command center in Central Station. "I've called Lettern, but it will take her three hours to get to New Ungern. Ogden then will have to use a pathic to contact Wedgewood. Presumably, they will get word to Christina."

"Drone capsule?" Clienen asked.

Ivan nodded at the suggestion. "I'll have the *Shields* send one to Sedge. But that doesn't really fix our problem."

Clienen waited for Ivan to expound.

"We need comms on the ground. Christina galloping through Nak Drakas on her way to Stith Drakas without attracting attention is problematic. It is one thing to execute a successful seaborne rescue in a sleepy seaside village, but riding to Stith Drakas is pushing her luck."

Clienen offered Ivan his *I'm waiting* pose.

"We send Meridia and the team now," the chief answered. "They rendezvous with Christina, and Meridia takes them to the safe house."

"Is it too early for Meridia to go in? The longer they are in ...," he let the obvious risk of exposure and contact with Drakan patrols go unspoken.

"It *is* too early for Meridia, but the risk to Christina is escalating. If we put the decision to Marisa, I can guess which way she would swing." Saving Clienen more debate, he added his own frustration, "We need someone on the ground, with direct comms to fleet. Relying on provincial pathics is just too slow. Meridia and crew can hold up in the safe house."

The wagon with its cavalry escort pulled off at a wayside. The twelve cavalry were arrayed around the wagon. The way stop, a tavern with a paddock and hay barn, was set back at the edge of the forest.

"Keep your hands on your reigns," Alex called as they neared the verge of the stop. "And keep riding. We're not interested in them. Let's make it obvious."

Achelous peered out the slatted windows of the wagon.

Christina felt her awareness expand; multiple energies vied for attention. She drew her hood up and ensured the scarf was high about her neck and chin. She wanted to look at the wagon. It beckoned. The feeling of a soul in need was all too familiar, one she always answered. The verge was opening; the trees made way for the staging area and paddock. The coach was black, all iron, a rolling fort. She kept her eyes averted but noted the reflection, the glint of sun: The Cuirassiers had drawn their sabers.

Larech commented, peering wistfully at the tavern. "I've stopped here many times. They sell one ale, and only one, a Brixtom mash that will keep you weaving in your saddle all the way to the Citadel."

Achelous decided to be amicable, to a point. His captors were ahead of him in the game of *Who Am I*, and he needed to catch up. "They make it with Darnkilden grain."

One of the guards shifted at the name of their historical enemy, but Larech only laughed. "How do you know that?"

Achelous turned back to the window as the party of riders they had pulled over for, rode into view. "I'm a trader. Brixton only grows in Darnkilden."

"I did not know that," said Larech.

Riding past the inn at a trot, Christina was second in the outside column, her head turned away. Suddenly, a coyote howled, and a rabbit darted right before Christina's mount. The eenu reared.

Christina caught the eenu's muzzle with her right reign and wheeled it about. Rubbing the mane in soothing strokes, the animal calmed. When she looked up, she was facing the wagon.

Achelous saw her green eyes, and that's all he needed. The flash of recognition chilled him to the bone.

Another rider, his shield boss covered, urged the party forward at a canter, but not before Achelous saw his face: Alex.

Life Defenders had come to Stith Drakas, but *for him?*

He'd never met the Al Suri Ascalon in person, but he'd seen her in Wedgewood, and she had seen him. She could wear a hood, a mask, a cloak, but she could not hide those eyes. Her image was posted on the "Persons of Note" gallery at Central Station.

He slouched in the cushions of the wagon.

Larech made a comment, but Achelous wasn't listening. *Are they here for me?* He worried. *Spirits tell me no.* He'd rather be left to find his own way to escape rather than risk the lives of a rescue party. The notion made his stomach turn.

When they were past the way station, Christina spurred her mount to a gallop. They rode hard until Alex finally compelled her to pull over. "What is it, Alon?"

She turned her mount about and let it crow-hop till it settled. She glared, not at him, but at their predicament. "If I tell you, you will demand we act, and in that act, we will meet our end."

He darkened. "How?"

"What did Twenti say?"

He pursed his lips.

"Is she here?" asked Alon.

Mitchern answered for all of them, "Why, no, Alon. Twenti is safe at sea."

Christina faced in the direction of Stith Drakas and prodded her mount.

As the Ascalon trotted off, the sergeant asked, "Why does she ask about Twenti?"

With a sour expression, Alex said, "It wasn't Twenti she asked about."

Puzzled, Mitchern cocked his head, then, "Oh. Twenti's vision."

# Chapter 21
## Mount Trufel

*Stith Drakas*

The coach began to climb, going around one corner and then another. Peering through the slats, Achelous noted the white stucco and beam buildings clustered together, the tighter and more cramped nearer the top. All vying for their place on the Rock.

"We're near the Citadel parade grounds," Larech said. "We'll be there soon."

The entire journey, the agent had kept the bird cage between his feet and seemed anxious to be rid of it.

A watch tower, with burgundy, grey, and black banners hanging from its battlements, hove into view. From the turret's conical roof, a pennon, a black eagle on a grey background with a burgundy border, snapped in the brisk ocean wind. On the huge dome of the rock, Mount Trufel, the bastion of the Citadel, sprawled. At the base of the dome to the east, the Angraris Ocean crashed and spewed in constant irritation. To the south, the approaches were guarded by a broad tidal flat, treacherous bogs, and a prominent sea wall. To the north, a canal hewn from the rock afforded a sheltered waterway for those merchant vessels brave enough to risk the narrow tide channel through the coastal shoals. The canal, wide enough for two small ships to pass abreast, wound its way from the ocean, past docks, wharves, underneath a drawbridge, and ended at a pier a hundred feet below the parade grounds. At the grounds, the armored coach and its escort came to a halt, waiting for admittance through the Main Gate.

Achelous watched as two full companies of pikemen practiced coming to arms, bracing, and then charging. Here, Drakan might was on full display. The pikemen moved with precision. His trader's eye caught the nickel tint to the steel as the afternoon sun slanted off spear points. Those weren't cheap parade weapons. He did a double take; a Scarlet Savior led a band of Troglodytes past the carriage heading to the gate. He turned to Larech.

"What? Troglodytes? Ah, ya, surprised? Why?"

"I would have thought it was too cold for them."

"Ach. They may not like it, but the Church brings them. There's a lodge on the tidal flats. The Church parades them about like pets, bragging they can control them." Larech shook his head, turning to a Cuirassier, "The Church's powerful ally," he sneered the words. Then back to Achelous, "Ah, but you would know all about the reptiles. Helprig and his Wedgewood conquest. Good thing Uloch and our Hoplites were there or—"

The carriage jerked into motion, and the eenu's hooves clattered on the flagstones. A shadow enveloped the wagon, and there was a tight turn to the right and more climbing.

The sound of rumbling coach wheels and eenu hooves echoed off the high wall just outside the slatted windows. It turned to a deeper drumbeat when they passed through another enclosed gate. Achelous tried remembering more of what he knew of the Citadel; his life may depend on it. There was a ring of defenses inside the outer wall of the fortress from what he could recall of a long-ago glance at a hologrid. The Main Gate, Lower Bailey, Inner Gate, Upper Bailey, and Upper Gate comprised the route they followed to Washentrufel Command. He fitted those names to the structures they passed. *There should be a castle and maybe a palace in here somewhere,* he thought. Out the right window, he saw a stable.

Larech watched Achelous' interest with some amusement. "Curious about your new home? Ya? You will know it quite well. The prison? Ya." He feigned a shiver, "For me, it is too cold, too dark, too damp. Maybe your jailor will give you blankets?"

Passing through the shadow of another gate, the coach came to rest on level ground. The Cuirassier next to Achelous unlocked the door and pushed it open. Once outside and standing, Achelous felt like an old man after the cramped, bouncing, daylong carriage ride. A spasm threatened his lower back, but his embeds kicked in and subdued the strained muscles.

To the front, in the last light of day, Washentrufel Command, home of the Drakan Secret Service, hulked, grey and foreboding. Instead of taking him there, the Cuirassiers lead him past the red-tiled roof of a Paleowright chapel conspicuous in its mundane, inauspicious construction so unlike other Church temples. To the left of the chapel was Glory Hall with its green and blue crystal dome, waiting in peace, a memorial to past Drakan emperors.

They hurried him, his manacles clinking, to a squat, two-story building, nearly black with cliff moss that covered the windows. It seemed they hustled to keep him out of view. "What's this?" Achelous asked, not really expecting an answer, but to his surprise, one of the cavalrymen answered, "Military prison."

# Chapter 22
# Shrine

*Stith Drakas*

"Alon," Alex called. He held up a fist.

Mitchern was holding his hand up in the pathic's sign they were *in touch*.

Slowly, he lowered his arm and then rode to her. "Sedge sends word. We're being followed. Seek safe harbor in Union of Souls. Remain ready. Friends in stars will mislead pursuers."

"Union of Souls?"

"That's what he passed. Union of Souls."

She moved her mount to where she could better view the road from the way station.

The party gathered their mounts close.

"How does he know the shrine is safe?" Alex asked.

Christina arched an eye.

"Sergeant," Christina explained the route to their new destination. "Have a soldier hang back and trail us. He's to come fast if he sees the trackers."

"Aye."

Turning about, she spurred to a canter.

"Ground team has changed course and speed," reported *Trilonair's* sensor officer.

The captain adjusted his hologrid. "The timing works."

"Yes, sir," answered the executive officer. The provincials are speeding up their pathic network.

"Deploy the bot," the captain ordered.

The weapons officer smirked. "Okay, sir. Defense bot released." The IDB's Chief of Ready Reaction assured them they were not about to violate ULUP protocols, as their actions were in support of IDB ground operations. No sentient species would be harmed.

The Kretchmer hound loped along, its tongue lolling and its floppy ears riding the breeze.

A dragonfly buzzed past the dog's head and hovered over the bouncing shoulders; its injector armed for stun.

With a swift jab and yelp from the dog, the dragonfly soared away.

Slowing, the hound panted. It took one last baleful gaze to where its quarry ran ahead and collapsed into a slumber.

"How long will it be out?" asked the captain.

"Twenty-four hours, plus or minus," answered the weapons officer.

"Good. Flag it for AI monitoring."

The trail wound through a boreal timber stand and came to a clearing, stopping at a moss-covered stone arch. Mounted atop the arch, an engraved wooded sign, not in harmony with the structure beyond, read in peeling red and yellow paint: *Diunesis Antiquaria*.

Beyond it, in the center of the idyllic clearing, a double-domed temple lay serene in white marble columns. The smaller dome of the two was raised above the other by short columns resembling human hands. The edifice was open through all sides except the rearmost wall.

"A Paleowright shrine?" The sergeant asked.

"It wasn't always," Christina replied. "Alex, confirm it's clear, please."

"Oi."

"We'll ride around back," she said, critically viewing how the structure had aged and what the Church, its current caretakers, had done to it. The temple was three stories high. Made of white and grey marble, the shades of stone were arranged to accentuate the open arches. From most sides, you could see through the arches to the forest on the other side. A stone block, not marble, offering vestibule was erected at the front of the temple. A wooden sign was nailed to the front of the vestibule, listing the required tithing amounts for visiting the shrine.

"It's clear," reported Alex. "There's a priest's hovel in the woods, but it's deserted. Not enough pilgrims," he added cynically.

Christina just nodded, her scowl deepening when she saw engraving on a side arch that did not match the motif of what she knew was inside. The engraving read *All behold the sacred honor. D. Antiquaria preserves the Ancient.* "So they say," she whispered.

The team secured the eenus behind the shrine while Christina entered the shrine. "Stay there," she pointed to the broad steps ascending to the arch. "Don't enter until it's open."

Watching Alon walk away, the sergeant said to Alex, "It is open."

"Not the way she means."

A stone statue occupied the center of the shrine. Christina read the inscription:

*Ancient Knight, Tara the Guardian*

She looked up, and a range of emotions washed her face. Then she laughed. It rose in her and carried outside, echoing in the temple's dome. Laughing, she cleared her eyes, seeing the mix of armor, shield, haughty stare, and halberd the statue held. She laughed again.

Sitting on the stone bench before the statue, she put her head in her hands. The laughter stopped. She began to cry.

The Lamarans sought to comfort her, but Alex held them back.

"What's wrong with Alon?" whispered a merc.

Alex had never been to this shrine, but he'd been to other Ancient sites with Alon that Diunesis Antiquaria had subsumed. Those, too, she behaved differently. The statue, twice the height of a man, was of a woman warrior. The Church's sigil, of water pouring from a chalice portraying the purveyor of knowledge, was embossed on the warrior's shield. Alex could see nothing untoward about the statue, except for the braided ponytail, Lamaran style, that rested on the woman's breastplate. The halberd was of the Ompo style, which, to his discerning eye, conflicted with the Lamaran braid.

At last, she rose. Woodenly, she approached a wall, the only wall in the temple. There were etchings along the cornice of the interior dome. On the wall, the etchings were larger and deeper. From where he stood, Alex could see the engravings were in Old Ancient, which was different from New Ancient that he now understood originated from the Avarians. Old Ancient, which he was learning, predated the Avarians and formed the root of all Isuelt languages.

In the center of the wall, below the largest engravings, a metal plate, albaminia, was embedded. Christina placed a hand on the plate and waited. A *snick* sounded. Then another, and then a sliding noise.

In front of Alex and the Lamarans, the floor slowly folded down, forming steps.

She came to stand beside them. With a pronounced, elegant flourish, though her face impassive, she extended a palm toward the yawning descent. "The Union of Souls grants you safe harbor."

# Chapter 23
## Union of Souls

*Stith Drakas*

The sensor officer swiped the controls on the grid. The recon drone sensor readings displayed on a second grid. The officer spun the grid, confounded.

"What is it?" asked the *Trilonair's* executive officer.

"Uh--"

"What?"

"Uh--"

"Yes?"

"AI confirms. No sensor malfunctions, neither the ship's nor the drone's over the ground team."

The exec frowned, "Why should there—" then he saw the map display. "Where'd they go?"

The sensors officer shook his head. "Gone." More head shaking. "Just gone. I checked the drone feed. From its altitude and angle, you can see them go in that building, come out, get their eenus, then go back in. Then nothing. They disappear, no readings."

"Where's the drone now?"

"On the way down, vectoring." The hologrid with the map display changed to the drone's nose camera. It swooped down to what appeared—"Smokes," vented the officer.

"What?" The captain was out of his chair and huddling over their shoulders.

"Is that Loch Norim?" questioned the sensor's officer.

"How do you know?" asked the captain.

The executive officer, seeing the open columns of the structure, called up the task force link and requested access to Dianis IDB Central Station. "Jeremy, you have access to our drone's feed?"

"Skipper," It was Mears on the *Shield's* ship net. "You better get in here, quick."

"What?" Hearter asked as he hurried through the hatch before it was half open.

"*Trilonair* patched into Central Station. Bypassed us. They want to know if this Paleowright temple," Mears slaved his hologrid display to that of the *Trilonair's* recon drone, "is really Loch Norim? And if it is, why is it not listed in the historical register?"

"*What?*"

Hearter sat in a console chair and watched with Mears as the recon drone slowly flew around the temple at head level.

"In the open," Hearter said.

Mears nodded. "*Right out* in the open."

"Looks the Paleowrights tried to dress it up."

"Yeah," said Mears, "from above, it does look more like a Paleowright archive, but when you get close ...."

"What caused the *Trilonair* to go snooping around there? It's off any roads, in the forest."

Mears glanced at him. "It's where Christina and her team went to ground, waiting for mission start. When they went in there, poof, they disappeared. No visuals, no infrared, no aura signatures."

"What is this place?" the sergeant asked.

"It's Ancient," Alex said simply, leading his eenu down the ramp beside the steps.

"Where does the light come from?" asked a merc gawking at the glowing ceiling panels.

Christina strolled in silence to an underground stable. Securing her mount in a stall, she said, "The feed system is not working, so we'll have to go out after dark and find forage, but I think I can get the waterer to work." She looked at them, and they, including Alex, stared back, dumb.

"It was not my choice to come here," she offered. "But here we are. Find a stall for your eenus. I will be down the corridor to the left."

When she had parted, the mercenaries broke into excited chatter, peppering each other with questions and speculation, especially Alex.

Hanging his saddle on a metal, not wooden, rack embedded in the wall, he said, his own suspicions now grown to certainty, "All will come clear when we need. Until then, appreciate a warm place out of the weather. We rest here until Sedge sends word."

Tracing the marble hall, whose polished floor and walls were a stark contrast to the weathered wear of the temple above, Alex came to an open chamber with a grand staircase of many steps leading down to a wide round platform and altar. Pews were arranged around the platform, enough to seat a thousand souls.

On the altar hulked a burgundy marble sarcophagus, twice the height of a man. Behind it, an enormous marble statue of a winged angel gazed down on the tomb. The woman angel held a wreath in one hand and an hourglass in the other. Evenly spaced around the tomb were eight grey-metal candelabras, their candles burning. An incense smudge smoked behind the statue.

Christina sat at a wide marble table that stretched forty paces. Odd metal chairs were arranged around the table. Some sort of pungent herb smoldered in a small brass bowl in the center of the table. As Alex walked past the tomb, he noticed the etching on the pedestal. He stopped. Squinting, he ran his fingers over the engraved words. Looking up, Christina was watching him.

Relieved, he went to her. "Is that amusement I see?"

The twinkle in her eye pulled at her lips. "Figure it out?"

He sat in one of the chairs. Unbuckling his sword, he put it and his shield on the table. "You lit the candles?"

"I did. It will appease the spirits. The incense is our tithe for entry. They will like that as well."

She rose, pulled his shield closer, and removed the cloth cover, exposing the white lily on a field of green. Settling back, she said, "I see the Church didn't put that on the statue's shield."

He blinked, "What, the one above, in the temple?"

"Yes."

"Why would they?"

She averred her gaze to the angel. "Memories."

"On that tomb," Alex pointed at the sarcophagus, "those words, do those say ...."

"What?" she asked.

"Stith Drakas."

"Yes."

He waited, but she eased back in the metal chair, relaxed, watching him.

Blinking, the smoldering herb in the incense burner was having some sort of effect on him. "What do the words mean?"

"Union -- of --Souls," she answered, emphasizing each word.

"*Stith Drakas,* is that Old Ancient? What the Avarians call Loch Norim?"

"Yes."

"Then the Loch Norim settled Stith Drakas?"

"Hmm, no, that came later, but they certainly built this retreat. The Drakans descended from the Loch Norim. As did you and the Lamarans and even those from Hebert."

"Do the Drakans know that?"

She smiled, shaking her head. "I suspect not."

He pondered the ramifications. "What does *Nak* Drakas mean?"

A crinkle of humor teased at her features. "Garden of Souls."

"Ha!" his laughter echoed amongst the pews.

"I thought you'd think that funny."

"The emperor rules in the Garden of Souls."

His mirth lightened her spirit. "From the Union of Souls."

"Paleowrights don't believe in souls," Alex smirked.

Her humor faded. "They should start."

He watched the candlelight dance across her eyes. The incense whorls caught in the flames and wafted away on an unseen current. A tendril drifted past his nose, pleasant yet alien. "Ancients are men," he mused under her inspection. "Souls are transcendent."

# Chapter 24
## Tempest Dare

*Dianis Orbit*

"Easy girl," Lettern rubbed the neck of her eenu, Moonlight. "You *have* to take a Timberkeep eenu?" Ivan asked. "Let Outfitting at least give it a neural embed. That way—"

"Chief, you know there's no time," Meridia interjected. The available IDB-trained eenus were already assigned to Meridia and his squad of Zursh mercenaries.

The mercenaries, outfitted courtesy of Central Station as Drakan Auxiliaries, watched Lettern and Moonlight with trepidation. This was the squad's first-ever shift. They met it with a mixture of excitement, awe, wonder, and escalating fear. To get to Stith Drakas, they had two shifts to make, the destination of the first shift being a place that no Dianis provincial, including Lettern, had ever been.

"She normally that twitchy?" Meridia asked.

"Noo," Lettern turned Moonlight in a tight circle and kept turning her.

"What's wrong?" asked the Lamaran onorio, a senior sergeant in the Zursh mercenaries. If Lettern couldn't pull this off, then ….

"She knows this is different. Somehow, she knows." Lettern turned the animal about two and three times more before it finally accepted that Lettern meant business. With a gentle prod, the eenu finally pranced into the designated shift zone: A large circle marked by powdered chalk behind the Wedgewood Special Mill.

"Will give you the word," Meridia answered a question from the ground controller on the team net.

"Yeah, tell them to ice their thrusters," Lettern said, trying to calm her own nerves and relax in the saddle. Moonlight begged for a cue to bolt.

"What are thrusters?" asked the onorio.

Meridia laughed. "Things that Lettern uses to get stuff done. They burn gas and blow lots of hot air."

A merc asked in awe, his belief in Ancients supreme, "She uses those?"

"Ready," Lettern breathed.

"Acknowledged," ground control on the *Tempest Dare* answered. "Clear the shift zone. Shift in five, four--"

Meridia kept his eyes on the mercs and their onorio, a senior sergeant. This foray was turning out to be a trial run for the much larger mission.

When Lettern simply vanished, he gave them a grin, their eyes wide. "That's it, folks. Lettern is two hundred miles away." He omitted the part about being above the planet in orbit.

Moonlight reared, the new surroundings just too much for the animal to comprehend. Lettern hung on and leaned into it. Moonlight crow-hopped across the shift platform like only an eenu can. Lettern gripped tight with hands and legs. "No, don't shoot!" she yelled. "I'll get her. She trusts me!"

An IDB veterinarian brought aboard just for this operation stood with a plasma rifle on his shoulder. The rifle set to stun. The captain didn't think tranquilizers worked fast enough.

Moonlight reared high, back-stepping, then dropped to all fours, and before it could rear again, Lettern grabbed its mane hard and said, in a voice that brooked no argument, "Stop." When Moonlight hesitated and tensed, Lettern swung the mare around in a full circle and then again. The animal quieted, staring frightfully at the alien scene in front of it.

Cheers and clapping erupted from the crew members, and rather than spook the eenu further, the human voices seemed to calm it.

Captain Trich, captain of the *Tempest Dare,* a new assault carrier, stood outside the shift zone. He said, "Nicely done, Agent. The IDB says they can ride eenus through shift zones. I had to see it."

The veterinarian remarked, "That's not an IDB eenu. It's provincial."

Lettern picked the voices out of the crowd. Not familiar with the man's rank insignia or military protocol, she said simply, "Yeah? She knows better," and patted the mare, congratulating it for being a good girl.

A Marine corporal asked her lieutenant, "So that's Lettern Stouttree?"

"Yep. That's her."

"Where's her plasma?" asked a sailor.

When the crew had learned of the ship's temporary posting and then who was going to be shifting through using their platform, the off-duty personnel came down to the hanger deck to see the Interconn holovid celebrity in person. Judging by the admiring stares, they were not disappointed.

"Can't take plasmas where they are going," answered the lieutenant. "But that's a spiffy new bow, not the provincial version she was packing when Corporal Meridia and I saw her. She killed a corsair with a bow before we could get him with plasmas. Meridia is coming through as well. We were on the old 'Fury' then."

Lettern dismounted and led Moonlight off the shift platform. Stepping on the alloy deck, she hesitated, then stomped on it. The crew laughed.

With an Avarian head waggle, she said, "Feels real enough."

Another laugh.

The veterinarian, in an IDB uniform Lettern realized, took Moonlight's reigns while another IDB headquarters staffer directed Lettern towards two men.

"Wow, I've never actually seen someone wear the uniform." She pointed at where the veterinarian was leading her eenu and looked the staffer up and down.

The man smiled, patient, almost condescending. "I suppose things are different for agents in the field."

Lettern shrugged. "I don't know." She looked down at her in-country garb, all genuine Timberkeep. "This is me."

"Let me introduce you to the captain and the executive director."

"Captain of?" she asked.

"This ship, the *Tempest Dare*. But more importantly, you are about to meet the executive director of the IDB. He reports to the ULUP Board of Control, and the Senate. He's only here for an hour before he shifts back out. I'm his events manager."

Lettern appeared surprised. "Event?"

The man stopped. He was guiding her gently by the elbow and donned his patronizing smile. "Don't look, but there are three news-vid bots orbiting the platform. They're part of our PR efforts."

"PR?"

"Public Relations. Which are very important. And I dare say you riding that wild eenu onto the Federation's newest assault carrier will be all over the Interconn."

"Moonlight's not wild."

He gave a head waggle she'd never seen.

Having learned the Avarian handshake in IDB-protocol injection learning, Lettern was prepared to clasp hands, Federation style, with Captain Trich and Executive Director Nethenel. Like the events manager, Nethenel was in uniform, but his was different. To Lettern, it looked -- *commanding*.

After introductions and sound bites for the Interconn, the director motioned to have the bots resume monitoring the shift platform. The five Zursh mercenaries were about to come through. The cooperative effort to rescue the Matrincy's Planetary Councilor to Dianis was big news.

"The Federation is taking a lot of risks doing this, Agent," said the captain. "If it goes in a black hole, we'll all look bad."

Lettern blinked. *Black hole? What's that? They'll all go there?*

"Do you think you can pull it off?"

She began to understand why Illy complained about officers, but she wasn't a Marine non-com. She was a *wild* Timberkeep warder. Leveling a stare at him, her dark brown eyes reflected battles past and those to come. "We'll get him. Mother's Will is my arrow."

The captain angled his chin.

"You'll have our support, of course," supplied the director. "To the limits allowed by ULUP."

She turned her stare on him. "I have a friend who says it's boots on dirt that matter."

The director acquiesced. "Ah, Agent Meridia. He'll be useful for when you swap that bow for a plasma."

A look passed between the captain and the director.

The captain saw her frown. "Dianis is not just important to the Federation. Did you know there are humans that collaborate with the Turboii?"

Her frown deepened. "No."

The director said, "They don't care if we are enslaved, or eaten, or wiped away, as long as they make money in the process. They think they are above it, playing with the Turboii. Greed. They forget that they won't be able to spend their money if the Federation dies."

"We are reasonably sure the Turboii know about Dianis." The captain's sad expression spoke volumes.

"That's not what you need to know now," the director hurried on. "The mission at hand is paramount."

"But," the captain said, "When you finish this mission and come back alive, Spirits willing, keep your plasma charged. I'm quite certain an arrow won't kill a Sizar."

# Chapter 25
## Cordelei

### Wedgewood

The mother let Cordelei in. "Daja is in the room just there. She's sleeping, but the nightmares...."

Cordelei ventured a nod, her expression matching her nickname, *Sour Dour*. Her colorful scarf, at odds with her long grey woolen dress, offered no relief from a mouth whose corners were down-turned and a severe nose that brooked no pity. Some said Cordelei's white frock of hair was bleached by the dreams of ghosts that haunted her steps.

Candles burned everywhere in the cozy, well-kept cabin.

"Why are there so many candles?" Cordelei asked.

"Uh, oi, I thought you needed them?" the mother answered.

She gave a quick shake. "No. Spirits come to candlelight. Put them out. A lantern only. We are trying to banish evil dreams," she flippantly waved a hand, "not invite more."

At a chair beside the troubled girl's bed, Cordelei sat and lit a taper from the mother's lantern.

The mother hovered just at her shoulder. "I—" She was loath to ask the voyant questions. No good ever seemed to come from her answers, her readings yet more riddles, or so the townsfolk said, but tonight the mother was desperate. "Can—can you help her?"

"Hold that," Cordelei gave the mother the taper. From a pouch, while she listened to the sleeping girl's mumblings, Cordelei packed a pipe with a pungent aromatic.

"Citadel," the girl's head tossed left and right.

Cordelei cocked an ear, the pipe motionless.

"There, that's what she's been saying. I'm so worried," moaned the mother. "I know not what she speaks. That's why I sent Timory for you."

More mumblings and Cordelei bent close to Daja's lips.

"No, no, run, chains—"

"There—" hissed the mother, but Cordelei shushed her. Taking the taper, Cordelei lit the pipe. Puffing it alive, she inhaled deeply and blew the smoke across the girl's face. She grasped the girl's hand and closed her eyes, waiting for the marshcat to smolder its way through her system. Cordelei's limbs began to tingle; she shuddered.

The girl was there, in the ether, but so was someone else. Another girl pulled at Daja. They ran across a stone wall, high and old. "Let's see, you need to see!"

Cordelei gripped the girl's hand tight. "I see Lute. Go child. Go with Lute. I will go with you."

"Lute—" the mother gasped and stepped back. "She's dead." A victim of the Timberkeep's Curse.

Cordelei was a voyant, not a medium. Spirits -- conduits to mediums -- confused the auguries voyants wanted to see, what Cordelei came to see, but spirits didn't care.

Lute led, dragged Daja by a ghost hand to a tower as Cordelei drifted behind, a wraith in the dream fog.

They went through a closed door without opening it. They floated down stone steps that spiraled their way from the heights of the tower to the dungeons below.

"No, no," Daja pleaded. "We don't belong here. We need to leave."

Lute pulled her through a heavy oaken door that was barred from within. A guard stood before another door. He wore the robes of a Church docent.

Daja squealed, her physical body quaking as Lute went right through the guard and the door beyond. Startled by something, the guard rubbed his arms as if trying to get warm.

Down a long hall, past cells and their iron-bar doors, Cordelei followed the girls. At a cell near the end, the pair stopped. Lute wanted Daja to look. Too afraid, Daja kept an arm in front of her face.

"Fear not, child, I will look for you," Cordelei said as she went to the bars.

She knew the man bound to the iron chair within. He, whom so many sought. A torturer held an orange-hot nail with a pair of blacksmith tongs. A brazier, full to the brim, burned a fiery yellow. Another man, wearing a red sash and red miter, gloated at the bound prisoner's pain. "Ha! No Washentrufel now!" the man exclaimed proudly.

"Go Lute. Go now and leave this girl be. You have delivered your message. Leave her be, or I will show you the light."

Daja heaved up in bed and vomited.

Her mother gasped and scurried to get rags.

When she returned, Cordelei had extinguished her pipe and folded the defiled blanket into a bundle. "Wash this well," Cordelei said, "there are noxious portents on it."

"I'll burn it!" the mother hissed, holding the blanket at arm's length.

"The girl will not be troubled by these dreams again," Cordelei intoned, "but Lute is mischievous. She may show her other things. If she does, summon me."


"Now?" Demanded one of the two warders stationed at the foot of Tall Lofty, the Ungerngerist of the Command Loft.

"It's past Moon High," reasoned the other warder, uneasy at refusing the voyant. He didn't want to be the focus of one of Cordelei's visions.

"Now," she invoked the word as a formal decree.

The two warders looked at each other. The voyant's visits to Sedge were infamous.

A warder pulled the message cord. High above, a gentle tinkling sounded.

With some grumbling from above, a message basket came down on the cord.

Cordelei shoved a ribbon-wrapped reed tube at the warders and waited for them to put it in the basket. She watched it rise as the unseen operator cranked it up the Ungerngerist to the loft high in the branches of the tree.

With the reed tube gone in the night, Cordelei stood there staring up, seeming to regret her actions.

Uneasy, wishing she would leave, one of the warders asked, "Is there more?"

In the dim flicker of a lantern, she directed a malefic glare at him. "Are *you* going *East*?" The word *East* had become the simple code for what many mothers, fathers, wives, and husbands had come to dread: The mission to the Citadel.

The warders shook their heads.

"Be glad you're not."


"Master!"

Dimly, he heard a sound. An urgent force pressed down on his back.

"Master Smith!" The shaking became rude.

His dream of fishing and catching a Golden Eye on the Twisty Nook evaporated. Ogden rolled over and grumbled, throwing an arm over his eyes. A lamp loomed above him. "Oola? What have the wood wisps done now?"

"You have a message from Sedge. Terren says it's important."

"Noi?" He threw off the blankets and sat up.

The messenger, a young forge runner, held out a tiny piece of parchment.

"Oola," Ogden pushed the boy back so he could get off the bed and go to a table. He held out his hand.

"Light the lamp," he said, holding the missive.

While the runner fumbled with the table lamp, Ogden mused, *I don't have to read it. It can wait.*

Unfolding the note, there were two sentences, and it was signed *Sedge*.

Breathing deep, he didn't want the runner to see him shake. "Get me the Tivor Cavalry lieutenant. Tell him we need riders for Tivor." As the boy ran to the door, "And roust the Second! Tell them we march for Tivor at dawn."

The moment he'd been waiting for, not knowing how it would come, finally did. An icy dread had come with it.

Marisa couldn't sleep. She sat at the kitchen table staring at, not seeing, the shipping manifest and tide table for the Marinda ships departing on the morning tide.

Eliot, who'd arrived in the kitchen at his normal predawn hour, puttered about as the morning cook made carva. "You need to rest. The stress--" He put his hands on his hips and launched into a familiar lecture. "You're wearing yourself out. Our dockmaster can do that. You know that."

She wasn't listening, at least not to him. She cocked an ear toward the great room door. Rising slowly, she padded in her slippers to the door and placed a hand on the frame.

Eliot stopped in his harangue. He'd seen that behavior from her before and went to the kitchen armory closet.

Marisa pushed the door open, waiting. The two Marinda Marines snapped to attention, seeing the mistress.

There was a pounding on the Hall outside door. A Marine opened the eye slot. There were words, and Eliot came to stand beside her with a long sword and shield. "This time, I'm prepared."

The Marine shut the eye slot and opened the door. A Tivor Cavalry sergeant came in. He was flushed, his riding cloak spattered with mud.

"Lady," he strode forward, "I come from New Ungern."

"Yes?" They had pathics in New Ungern. She'd been meaning to ask Woodwern if she could billet one or two at the Hall, but there weren't many to spare.

"Sedge sends word. Cordelei has seen him."

By *him,* Marisa knew who the rider meant.

"He's there, in the Citadel. Ogden is coming with the Second and all the rifles and ammunition he has on hand. They left before dawn."

"He ... did Sedge say if Atch is okay?"

The man wrung his gloves. "No, my Lady. He did not."

She nodded. "Simon!" Her butler was lurking somewhere.

"I'm here," he called.

"Please see the riders are taken care of. And Eliot, send word to the aorolmin. We'll meet at the practice yard."

"All of us?" he asked.

"Yes. Everyone. Marines, Rifles, everyone. The hourglass turns."

Ogden led his double line of Timberkeep warders, the Second Ward, Clan Mearsbirch, to the gate. The Tivor City Watch saw the round shields with a black anvil on a green facing. They recognized the troop and waved them through without question or inspection: Twenty axmen, followed by twenty archers and five Riflemen. Behind them trundled three wagons packed with supplies. They marched through the wide portal at a brisk pace, though they had been on the road for three hours.

A Watch stander nudged a fellow. "Rumor is they got the call."

"Aye. The archers are packing triple quivers."

# Chapter 26
## Umpires

*Tivor*

Ivan waited for the Second to arrive at the *practice field,* as it was called. Master at Arms Sifle had found a portion of Tivor Castle that could, with temporary modifications, resemble a small portion of the Citadel, particularly the Main Gate, Lower Bailey, Inner Gate, Upper Bailey, and a mockup of the Upper Gate. To the west of the practice field was Tivor Castle's flower mill, which was made to double as the Market Tower in the Citadel. In between the tower and the Main Gate an area roughly the size of the Citadel's Parade Grounds was roped off.

Ogden settled his ward in with the other troops and made his way to where the mission leadership had gathered. "Oi, you're here too! Faster than your message." Ogden clasped arms with Sedge. The warlord was dressed as always: Loose linen pants, a baggy, open-necked shirt that exposed a mass of grey chest hair, and a long sword. A long sword Ogden now suspected was not made of any Dianis steel. The warlord's long grey hair was tied back in a ponytail, and the white beard meticulously cropped short. All in contrast to his thin black mustache and black, bushy eyebrows. Deep care lines etched his forehead, and crow's feet clawed at the eyes.

"Travel courtesy of our friends there," Sedge tilted a chin at Ivan. "No more whittling for you. Woodwern wants to know if you have his southern sojourn finished."

An Ogden bellows laugh sounded across the practice field. "Whittling, you say? Southern Sojourn?" He feigned surprise as he cast about, "And where is the Wood? You left him behind?" Woodwern, Clan Mearsbirch's Council Chief, was a notorious non-traveler.

Sedge gave Ogden his sly smile, the one Ogden, through many battles, knew so well. "He has other things to worry about. The new mode of transportation would be unsettling."

"Sedge is in command, Og," Marisa said. "The aorolmin and I agreed. "He's the one to lead us against the Church and the Drakans. Captains Rayamars and Enderma will report to him." Both Tivor officers nodded, one the leader of forty Tivor Riflemen and the other the leader of the forty Tivor Marines. Except for Sedge, all four of the men had fought together with Marisa on the *Far Shore*.

"And Christina?" Ogden asked with deference. "It be good to have her with." To the Life Believers, having the Al Suri Ascalon along on a mission as fraught as the Citadel was Mother's Boon.

"She's already there," Sedge said, "waiting for us lazy ones. We're late."

Ivan added, "Outside Stith Drakas. The advanced team with Meridia and Lettern have gone to rendezvous with her."

"All right, listen up and gather round," Sedge called out in a booming voice. He waved at the group of troops gathered with the Second and at an equally large group of soldiers and castle workers wearing burlap tunics dyed in a myriad of colors.

"Ivan, here, is the chief umpire. He has other umpires assisting him. They all wear yellow." At a clue, they raised their hands. "Ivan is running the practice field. He will signal to me and the team leaders when it is clear to move to the next objective." Sedge pointed at a makeshift burgundy, black, and grey flag, the colors of the Drakan Empire. "Wherever you see one of those, that is an objective." He let the gathering see where the flags fluttered in the breeze. "Master at Arms Sifle is running the opposition force, the Drakans. They are wearing dark red tabards. It is *mock* combat. Do not land any killing or wounding strokes. Blunt edge or wooden weapons only. If you are killed or wounded by an opponent, the umpire will call it and put a red or yellow rag on you. Red means dead, yellow means wounded. Do not argue. I don't care if you don't think you should have died. That's not the point." He turned to glare at the nearest of the mission force, who was wearing their real colors and armor of Zursh mercenaries. "Remember. This is mock warfare. No real killing or wounding. You will be issued wooden swords and blunt -tip arrows. You want to capture objectives fast. A prolonged fight with anyone will just delay us. You need to get up to the top, past the Upper Gate, and secure the extraction zone as soon as possible so that you can all leave as soon as you have our target." He let that sink in. "Only when the extraction zone is secure can we start the full search for the target." Through prior briefings by their commanders, the mission members understood who their target was. "The landing and extraction zones are marked by those bales of hay with the red sheet." Sedge made his way through the soldiers and put his foot on a bale of hay. "When you are shifted to the Citadel, you will land here, within a wagon length. I will let Ivan explain what *shift* and *land* mean. Up above," he pivoted and pointed towards the makeshift Sighten Tower, "beyond the Upper Gate is the other bale. You will need to be within the same distance to be *extracted*." He glanced at the Ready Reaction Chief. "I'll let him explain that as well."

Sedge strode to a rope line that bordered the practice field. "Platoon and ward leaders, assemble your teams here in the order on the assault roster. The first team will muster here, and the six other teams will form groups leading that way." He held his arm out. In reality, the area he referenced was onboard the *Tempest Dare*. There were nods all around and some fear. Sedge was sure a good many of the troops didn't believe the operation would actually happen, as fantastic a proposition as it was, but once they were in space on the Avarian carrier, more than a few of them would have weak bowels.

"There is a two-minute time period between teams shifting in. Don't ask me why," Sedge said, "maybe Ivan can explain cycle time to you." He smirked. "For our practice runs, we will have to make do without our real advance team. They are already there. At the Citadel."

There was silence at the news, confirmation they were already committed. They had comrades waiting for them. Sedge made his way through the throng so he could identify the ten members of the City Watch wearing grey and black tabards. "They will be acting as Lettern and Meridia with their mercenaries. We will assume, may Mother bless us all, that the advanced team—" he stepped so he could get a clear view and pointed at the castle's flower mill, where a fake Drakan flag hung from a window, "has captured that, and has positioned themselves in this parade ground, to cover the landing zone."

With his part of the instruction done, he went to stand next to Ivan and Master at Arms Sifle. "Your turn."

"Right," acknowledged Ivan. He laid out the rules of engagement, how to capture an objective, what to say to the umpires, and other details. "These," he held out a hand, palm up. A large dragonfly sat there. "Are your friends. Do not swat them. They are there to help." The crowd pushed in close, trying to get a look. The bot, in this case, a defense bot, slowly lifted off of Ivan's hand and hovered above their heads. It began to slowly circle the audience. People ducked and cringed. Others gaped in awe as the creature buzzed by. "We have three versions of these that you will see in the Citadel. And I repeat, they are friends. When you see one, you should feel good, not fearful. And if you see a Drakan trying to swat one, kill him."

The aorolmin blanched at the Avarian's directness. Ivan was never the one to mince words.

"Horalznick here, one of my umpires, will come to each of your teams and show you the three types of bugs. We call them bots. You can ask more questions then. But the bots will be going on the mission with you and performing reconnaissance. They are how we will know where the enemy is, how the battle, uh, rescue is going, and most importantly, how the Drakans are reacting."

A hand shot up. "How will they do that?" Someone yelled out.

"Telepathy!" Ivan shouted back. "Our bugs are special. They are pathics."

There were *oo's* and *ahs* throughout.

Marisa tried to contain her surprise. The aorolmin sidled a little closer and whispered, "Is that true?"

She had never wondered how the little things communicated. She whispered to him, "It works for me."

# Chapter 27
## Safe House

*Stith Drakas*


Lettern rode point for the squad. She listened to directions relayed to her from the ground controller on board the *Tempest Dare*. The party were all wearing armor of Drakan auxiliary cavalry and posing as a packet-escort from north of the Sea of Lore. To blend in with the Nakish populace, the team applied dark skin bronzer, black hair dye, and ethnic hand and face tattoos from Ompo removable with a Field Outfitting disassembler. Inside the onorio's pack were authentic-looking orders, and a communique destined for the Washentrufel agent on duty at the Citadel. The parchment of the scrolls identical to that of Drakan Empire pressers.

"Fifteen hundred meters, and you will come to a fork. Turn left there," announced the ground controller in her audio implant.

Lettern still struggled with the conversion from hands, feet, and wagon lengths to meters, but she figured fifteen hundred meters was far enough, yet, to not worry.

They were riding through low coastal farmland. The Citadel, atop Mount Trufel, was visible in the hazy distance. A wind blew steadily from the ocean to her right, a half-league away. She'd been to Tivor and gaped at the tall ships in the harbor, but the view of the sea had been obscured. Here, the ocean, in all its immensity, glistened like a vast field of crystal shards. The scale and enormity of the water was staggering. *So much water!*

A Nakish farmer behind two red-speckled oxen pulled a double plow tilling a field. She wanted to gawk at the strange beasts, but forced her attention to stay on the road.

Further along, the road turned from gravel, which she thought was impressive enough to stone blocks, cut and laid tightly. She stopped Moonlight and stared. The stone road ran straight, arrow straight, to Stith Drakas.

Meridia halted the company. "What?"

"I've never seen a road like this. Who did it? Tivor doesn't even have them."

"Aye," said the onorio. "We have them in Zursh. Built in the days of the Lamaran Empire. Those days are done, but the roads, they last forever."

She urged Moonlight, who was unsure of the surface, onto the stone. Soon, the mare was clopping along.

"Five hundred meters to your turn," said the laconic voice in her ear.

"Beware, there is a full-strength, hundred-man, Drakan Hoplite century marching on the road you turn on," announced Jeremy. While the news was worrying, Jeremy's voice was comforting, especially now, so deep in *enemy* territory. As an IDB CivMon agent, she shouldn't look at the Drakans as enemies, but instead as client provincials her purpose to monitor. However, the Battle of Wedgewood was hard to forget. She pulled up and looked at Meridia and the onorio as Meridia explained to the merc what was coming.

"What do you want to do?"

The onorio shrugged. "We've all this bloody makeup on. Nerven looks like he's a Nakish tanner and has the tattoo to prove it." The others laughed. "We have their armor, and damned nice armor it is, better than anything I've ever worn. I say we ride right past them. We're cavalry. They're foot, bastard Hoplites or not. They can bloody well look up to us."

"What about Lettern? They'll see she's a woman." Meridia had rehearsed their cover story, but he wanted to hear the onorio's rendition.

"True. Regular Drakan units have no women. But they'll see we're auxiliaries from the frontier. I've fought more than one Ompo woman scout. And there's horse archers up there that have women in them. But she'll be noticed." The onorio said to her, "Just don't take no lip from them. They'll expect you to be a tough burr-sticker."

Lettern snorted and prodded Moonlight away.

When she was back out front, Meridia said to the onorio in a low tone, "She *is* a tough burr-sticker."

"I heard that."

Meridia sniffed. "Got good ears, too."

Taking a left at the way crossing, they came upon the double rank of a hundred Drakan Hoplites marching at an even, brisk pace. Every step in unison.

Lettern eyed them with cold detachment as they passed each other. They saw her, and she saw them. She glanced at their arms and armor. The Hoplites she'd seen in Wedgewood had been outfitted to look like mercenaries, but these were not hiding anything. They were the real thing, complete with Drakan eagle flag, cedar-wreath guidon, burnished helms, breastplates, and round shields.

The centurion barked a rebuke about being silly boys, never having seen a woman, and Lettern rode past, her first real encounter as an undercover IDB agent over. Her heart was beating, but she felt oddly calm. She had met the enemy and had overcome via subterfuge and bravado. It was a new feeling for her.

An hour later, they arrived at the *safe house*.

Meridia sought out the tenant. It was a modest farm, some hard-scrabble corn, a few hay fields, a garden, and a woodlot.

Meridia found the farmer, a scruffy-looking Nakish, stacking firewood.

The farmer kicked his boot in the sawdust. "I didn't think Horalznick was coming back. He told me to hold the rent. He'd be back to collect, but he didn't say when. That was five months ago."

Meridia smirked, eyeing the wood pile. It was right in the center of the shift zone's pre-set coordinates. Horalznick's in-country cover was a traveling tin man and tinker. Five months matched the time just before Lights Out.

"Oi, er, yeah. Zick said that," Meridia agreed. "That's three silver sheqels a month." The rent was a bargain for the farmer, or so Horalznick had said. It was common practice for the IDB to employ provincials to manage in-country assets, such as farms with a shift zone, buried Field generator chamber, and a secure house. None of that was known to the tenants, except the landowner was wealthy and often away.

The tenant fiddled with a pouch and pulled it open.

"Uh, you hold onto that," Meridia said. There was no way he was going to take the poor peasant's money, fair deal or not. "I may have you go into town and get some ale, but there are some other things I need you to do. The roof on the granary is in rough shape. How much to fix that?"

Jeremy immediately intruded on the net, "Going rates for labor and materials to fix the roof would be four silver sheqels."

The peasant studied the grain shed.

Before the farmer could quote a price, exorbitant or fair, Meridia said, "Take four sheqels of the rent and get that fixed. Either do it yourself or pay someone. I don't care."

The peasant brightened, his eyes wide. Jeremy's estimate appeared to be high.

"And it looks like you are sparse in spreading the corn seed. How can you pay rent if our fields are below yield?"

"Well ...."

"Yeah. I need to see more corn growing there when I come again." He smiled at the peasant.

"Well, I've been cutting wood—"

"I see that." Meridia had been on too many planets ravaged of their natural resources and didn't like it. "Let's try and make more money from the corn and hay. And that wood pile."

The tenant eyed it. "Yeah?" He was expecting to be told to sell it so Meridia could collect the rent.

"I need you to move it."

"What?"

"Yep." It was the reason he and the team had to freemitt with the *Tempest Dare:* The nearest in-country IDB shift zone to Stith Drakas was blocked by a woodpile. "Move it. Clear over there, near your cabin. And the owner's house, anyone been in there? You know the rules."

"No, no. No one has been in there. I followed Horalznick's instructions." Which was true. Jeremy had checked the entry logs.

"Very well. How long to move the wood pile?"

"A day?"

Meridia didn't want the poor guy to kill himself. The pile was head-high and longer than two wagons.

"Take three, but keep it clear. 'Zick is funny about keeping things where they belong."

The man had a question he was fretting over.

"What?"

"When do you want the rest of the rent?"

The cabin door pushed open, and a youngling, maybe six or seven, came out. "Pa, safe to come out? Momma wants to know."

The peasant made a quick hand gesture, and the child scurried back into the cabin, slamming the door.

The man's fear evident.

Meridia studied him, and the peasant began to fidget. "Do people come here and harass you?" He waited for the man to answer. "Because if they do, this is our land. Zick and I are partners. You are under our protection. We're frontier cavalry. No one screws with us."

"I, I, didn't think I — I didn't know who to ask for help."

"Hmm. Yeah. Well, we're back." He waved to the team, signaling they could proceed to the landowner's house. "You see her?" Meridia tilted his chin at Lettern as she rode Moonlight slowly past.

She looked at the peasant and then at the cabin.

"Yes."

"She'll come to your cabin later. To see how your misses and the younglings are doing. You can discuss the balance of the rent with her. She likes ale."

Digging a toe of his worn out boot in the dirt, and snuck a peek at the door to the hovel.

"I'll let you get back to work," Meridia said. "Start with that pile of firewood."

They secured their eenus in the shed behind the safe house, which looked like other Nakish stone farmhouses, albeit on the large side. Indeed, the house was genuine provincial, but its modifications, deep underground, were not. Inside, Meridia brought up the control panel for the facility on his multi-func. He set the proximity sensors to give an audible warning in the building. He let the Lamarans hear it: A male Nakish voice saying he spotted something.

"Now, we wait," Meridia said.

"For?" asked a merc.

"The *go* word. Mission start."

# Chapter 28
## Major Vuulanin

*Tivor*

Observing Blocking Force Alpha move through the practice bailey, Ivan interrupted the major's thoughts. "We can get a better view from up there." He led the Marine major up the steps of a temporary observer's station.

The major was dressed in IDB-supplied provincial clothing suitable for an advisor in the aorolmin's court.

"They haven't fired their rifles yet?" Major Vuulanin asked. An assault Marine lieutenant was with him, similarly dressed; the same lieutenant who commanded the assault lander Corporal Meridia first landed on Dianis during the Quorat operation.

"No," answered Ivan, "and they won't, not in this scenario. This one is what we call *All Stealth*: No loud sounds to attract attention from the city. But the next scenarios we run for you will force the use of rifles as we escalate the Drakan response level. Marisa is trying to conserve gunpowder, but we will run at least two live-fire exercises."

The Federation observers watched Blocking Force Bravo, in staggered starts and stops, sprint past the cargo boxes representing the palace.

"Where are they going?" asked the lieutenant.

"B Force is responsible for clearing and searching the Milisterium HQ. We'll have to move to the next observation post to see that. Once they have cleared the HQ they will take up positions inside at the windows to apply interdiction fire on the barracks. There could be as many as two hundred warriors in the barracks. We want to keep them there."

"You're not going to clear it?" the major asked.

"No," answered Ivan. "In a perfect world, they'll find Atch -- the target -- and shift out without the troops in the barracks ever being alerted."

The lieutenant snorted. "A perfect world does not exist. Count on things going in the shitter at the start."

"Deep, dark, dead." The major referred to an infamous Marine freemitt assault where a platoon had landed in a swamp in a quicksand pool.

The Obsidian ballroom in Tivor Castle had been requisitioned for use as the mission planning center.

The large-scale, three-dimensional map of the Citadel occupied a sizeable portion of the parquet dancefloor. Potters and clay makers were still adding structures. Major Vuulanin and the lieutenant walked around the map as Sedge, using a yard-long pointer, picked out the points of interest. The bulk of the planning team, giving the observers space to move around, gathered behind the map. It was the job of the observers to report back to the captain of the *Tempest Dare*, the battle group admiral, and the IDB Executive Director as to the readiness of the mission team. The readiness would be scored, augmented by AI's analysis. A score of eighty or less out of a hundred was an automatic no-go.

Sedge began the formal briefing. "At 1:00 in the morning, two nights from now, Advanced Team Meridia will have secured and cleared this area." With the pointer, he tapped a circle marked with a red *X* in the parade grounds. "Should Meridia and team fail to accomplish that objective by 1:00, we will, of course, adjust. By then, the entire mission force, except for teams Meridia and Alon, will be onboard the *Tempest Dare*." He expected the two Marine observers to ask questions when they wanted, so he continued.

"Assault Groups One through Seven will cycle through the shift zone in two-minute intervals." As he explained the operation, he motioned to Rachael who lofted the applicable clay figurines, placing them kinetically where Sedge pointed.

Her casual nature at the feat impressed the major. While not uncommon to see on Avaria, her confidence was disarming.

Fourteen figures, each the size of a thumb, floated into place. Each miniature soldier represented ten soldiers, Clan archers, Tivor Riflemen, Clan axemen, Tivor and Marinda Marines, healers, and individual figures for each of the command team: Marisa, Christina, Sedge, Rayamars, Enderma, Ogden, and Meridia.

Sedge took a breath and looked around the table. "Though it looks impressive, we'll not win by strength. Not by far. Surprise, shock, and speed are how we will succeed. Rachael, if you please." She began lofting into place the Drakan units as Sedge continued the briefing.

"What are those?" the lieutenant asked as a figure with a long pole-axe was placed near the barracks.

"Halberdiers," she answered brightly. "They're supposed to be tough."

"Don't be so enthusiastic, child," admonished the aorolmin.

"Yes," agreed Sedge. "Though they only perform ceremonial duties at the Citadel, Ivan says there may be as many as forty in the barracks. They are the heavy, elite infantry of the empire, drawn from the most experienced Hoplites which are the Drakan shock troops. We've faced Hoplites before in Wedgewood. Fortunately, none of *them* are stationed in the Citadel."

"How do you know that the emperor will not be at the Citadel that night?" asked Vuulanin.

It was Clienen's turn to answer. "We've been following the movements of the emperor, his senior courtiers, and the general staff closely. We have their aura signatures. The emperor, out of habit, prefers the palace in the center of Stith Drakas. He only goes to the palace in the Citadel for military events. The same is largely true for Lord Orn Blannach. Rather than stay at the General's Manse, he resides at his manor on the outskirts of the city."

"As long as no dignitaries or courtiers are staying at the Citadel's palace, the guard size is reduced by as much as forty," said Captain Rayamars. "But there is still a sizable number of Drakan pikemen and archers in the barracks."

Sedge tapped the model of the Citadel barracks. Rachael had already placed twenty figurines, counting as two hundred, near that building.

Sedge pointed out other buildings, and the troops housed there, concluding with the Washentrufel HQ. "There will be agents at the Washentrufel Command." Two clay soldiers stood there. "Prison guards here," he tapped the two soldiers at the prison.

"And that's where Achelous will be?" Marisa asked the leading question.

Sedge took a breath. "It is," he hedged, "reasonable to assume that, Lady. Ivan, if you will."

Ivan picked up the cue. "The granite of that mount, along with its underlying magnetic field of iron deposits, is, as we knew it would be, impervious to aura transmission to more than a dozen meters. But we can scan the buildings. Nothing, yet. The drones in orbit above the city and the Citadel have not sighted any unusual activity, especially near the prison, but recon bots have picked up the target's DNA." He saw hope bloom on her countenance for the first time. "Unfortunately, the wind across the mount is persistent, and so precise locations are unreliable. The wind blows from the east. We didn't detect any of his DNA until the bots checked what we call scent traps, such as the underside of stairs facing east. There, we got multiple hits. Enough to confirm he is or was somewhere in Citadel as of this morning. Recon bots have penetrated some of the buildings seeking visual verification, but the problem with the Citadel is the quality of the stonework. There are no ventilation shafts, air intakes, or plumbing vents that the bots usually use for infiltration. The stonework is tight and routinely sealed with batting to keep the mice and vermin out, which we hear is a problem in the city. The bots can and will wait for a door to open to enter a building, but our bots, as good as they are, are substantially bigger than any flies found on the mount, which are not many, again because of the weather. We've lost more than a half dozen to zealous servants and their brooms. When we started picking up on complaints between the Drakans about a sudden infestation of bees and flying beetles, we decided to cease close-intrusion activities, at least until the mission force is ready to go in."

Undaunted, Marisa's hope gave no weight to Ivan's details.

Moving on, Sedge said, "The Main Gate," and tapped the parapet above the gate. A piece of baked clay chipped off. "Oh, sorry about that."

"We should hope it crumbles like that in real life," quipped the aorolmin.

"Hmm, I doubt it will. Nevertheless, the Main Gate," and Sedge described the edifice, the walls, and guard rotations, all information that was observed from the *Trilonair's* recon drone. "It is our primary obstacle. There are others, but this is the first and most challenging."

Ivan interjected, "We scanned for a different assault zone, but the parade grounds offer the only area large enough and clear of transient debris that our advance team can gain control of."

Clienen glanced at the aorolmin and Marisa. They'd heard his explanation of freemitt perils.

"Direct observation and access to assault zone is key. The parade grounds are the closest Team Meridia can secure, clear, and guard, but they are *outside* of the Main Gate."

"What about that?" the lieutenant pointed to a clay structure overlooking the parade grounds. "None of the scenarios we watched included it."

"That's right," said Ivan. "The Market Tower. It's outside the walls of the Citadel, and it *does* have a guard. It is supposed to serve as an observation post overlooking the city, but it really serves as a toll booth for vendors and carters who use the parade grounds on Market Day, which is every third day."

"Lettern and their mercs will need to capture the tower before they can secure the assault zone," supplied Sedge.

"Which means effectively securing the entire parade grounds,." noted the major. It had been a point of contention when they watched the scenarios play out. Just how much of the parade grounds must Meridia and team really control? Just the southwest quadrant or the entire field?

"There are risks," acknowledged Sedge. "Certainly, the Market Tower is one. That's why we have developed four plans for capturing the Main Gate. Two of them do not require control of the Market Tower. We can find no historical record of the Citadel ever being assaulted. Any response plans the Drakans have certainly will not include an enemy suddenly appearing in their midst. Surprise and complacency will dictate their response."

"Until the first shots are fired," said Rayamars.

Sedge grunted. "They won't know what those loud banging noises are, but citizens in the city may be curious and come look. What will definitely get their attention is armed warriors not wearing Drakan grey and burgundy."

"Except for Meridia's team," Marisa noted.

"Yes," agreed Sedge. "As we have rehearsed, Meridia and Lettern and their mercs, outfitted as Drakan auxiliaries, will attempt to gain access through the Main Gate's postern door. "Their claim will be they have an Ancient artifact to be delivered to the Washentrufel HQ. If that ruse should fail, the first assault group, Ogden's, will have a formed charge of gunpowder to blow the gate."

"Oi, I've tested it," Ogden spoke up. "Or one like it. It put a wee big hole in a triple-stacked barn door."

Rachael snickered. "Gone to smithereens. "

Ogden colored. "Well, I may have used too much powder."

There was laughter in the room.

"That option we do not want to use unless Plan Three and Four do not work. But regardless, we *will* get through that gate." Sedge pointed at the portal.

"You've informed our Avarian friends of what Plan Three and Four are?" asked the aorolmin.

Major Vuulanin answered, "He has. And I appreciate the reasons for secrecy, but it's hard for us to include those in the readiness assessment since you can't practice them."

As the meeting broke up, Clienen drew Ivan aside. "No matter what Marisa achieves during the mission, it will stun the emperor and the Drakan high command. The surprise, the audacity of the attack...." The two IDB leaders shared knowing expressions.

"Sedge said there are Doromen in Wedgewood suspected of being too friendly with the Paleowrights," said Ivan. "Word is the story of Baryy and his use of the rifle in the foundry have reached the Washentrufel. We know Tivor is all a buzz with their new Riflemen and Marisa's cannon. Merchants and traders are carrying the news far. To other continents."

Clienen's expression continued to sour. "And suddenly there is an attack using the rumored rifles in the very heart of Stith Drakas."

Ivan shook his head, a reflection of the doom he felt. "The emperor won't stand for it."

"He'll perceive it as an existential threat."

Ivan cocked his head. "Which, given enough time—"

"It will be," completed Clienen.

They stood there, deep in dark thoughts.

Marisa, seeing their gloomy expressions, came over. "Is there something we've missed?"

Ivan peered over his shoulder at her. "Have you thought of how the emperor will react once you've rescued Atch?"

She took a deep breath and nodded tersely.

"And?" Ivan pressed.

A determined edge colored her tone. "Woodwern says the clan is joining the Western Alliance. They've been non-aligned until now, but when Oridia came to their aid without asking.... Darnkilden and Sea Haven are already fighting border skirmishes with the empire. The oligarch has been ringing the alarm bell for a year. The aorolmin asked me to make sure Woodwern had considered the implications of the rescue. So I did." She gave them a sharp frown. "Do you want to know what Margern said, his sister, the town chairwoman?"

Clienen straightened, preparing himself. As Director of IDB Margel Damansk, he had an uncomfortable front-row seat to his principal planet on the verge of war. A war, in part, facilitated by him and the IDB, who were chartered to protect Dianis from outside influence.

Marisa told them, "Margern said Timberkeep funeral pyres have blackened the forest. They are at war, and they wait for the next blow, be it the Church or the Drakans. The clan can fight the Drakans in Wedgewood or in Stith Drakas, but fight them they will. If only it were Hebert."

# Chapter 29
## Helprig

*Stith Drakas*

Christina ascended the steps to the altar dais. The mercs stopped their muted chatter; the honing stones paused on blades; oil rags were set aside. "We've word from Sedge," announced Christina. The electric sense of expectation had charged the air in the altar chamber. "The mission is a go. We leave at sunset."

Without conversation, the men began collecting their gear. Sunset was two hours away.

Alex led his eenu up the ramp in the face of cool, damp air flowing into the subterranean sanctuary. Christina, followed by Mitchern and the line of Zursh-Lamar mercenaries that trailed down the incline; the clomping of the eenu hooves and jingle of harness echoed in the marble stairway.

The last light of day faded. As the sergeant moved to take point, Christina called, "Hold."

She hadn't drawn her sword or appeared alarmed, but she was focused on a bird perched in a tree at the forest edge.

"What is it, Alon?" asked Mitchern.

Alex saw it. He prodded his mount toward it. A stone's throw away, the black crow contemplated him.

"They see our drone," said the *Trilonair's* sensor officer.

"Affirmative," replied Mears on the local ship-net.

"Our friends are here," Alex said as the mercs gathered near.

"How can you tell?" one asked.

Another said, "Looks real enough."

Another merc spit, chewing a bit of honey leather. "Too shiny. The feet are strange."

"We'll be seeing more of it and others," Christina acknowledged. She turned her eenu away. "Remember, any big flies are probably theirs."

A merc shook, feigning a deep shudder. "Oi. What can't they do?"

Alex snorted. "Fight the Drakans. That's what they can't do."

Mears looked at Hearter, who'd been alerted to come to the command deck when the drone started detecting aura signatures. "There's another thing we can't do," Mears gave a frustrated head waggle.

"What?"

"Use Loch Norim sites."

"That hasn't been proven."

Mears looked at him askance. "Okay. We can keep the existence of the shrine in the fleet until after the op. No point in stirring up ULUP even more. But after that...."

True to Christina's foretelling, the party now followed a goshawk attack drone. The model was the best Central Station Outfitting could craft with the limited materials in inventory. The bird flitted from perch to perch, a tree, a post, a rooftop. "Keep it in sight," urged Alex.

"Don't worry," said Christina, "If we lose it, it will come back."

He looked skeptical. Trusting the Avarians was still new to him.

The bird, its three-hundred-kilowatt laser disabled per ULUP, plotted a path through the neighboring countryside and then into Stith Drakas proper, as directed by *Trilonair's* threat AI.

Mitchern halted, holding his hand up, palm open. He was nodding to himself.

In the night stillness, he looked to Christina, her face illuminated by a nearby post lantern. A few Nakish civilians moved along the cobblestone streets. "Meridia and Lettern are approaching the Market Tower. There is a place where they can hold and wait for us to get into position."

"You've met this Meridia?" Christina asked Alex, as she had not.

"Oi," he smiled. "Though not as a Timberkeep." They both grinned at the irony.

"She's paired with him, an Avarian?"

"She is."

Christina studied his expression. "She loves him?"

"I expect she does."

Christina looked away, wistful. "Is he," she looked back pointedly, "loyal?"

"You mean worthy?"

She lifted an eyebrow. "That, too."

Alex shifted in the saddle, tightening the reins. "He is loyal to our cause. Certainly for Wedgewood. Whether he is worthy for Lettern, that's up to her."

Grumbling and complaining, Viscount Helprig climbed the wharf ladder up from the gig bobbing on the evening tide. A Scarlet Savior gave him a hand. Standing on the wharf, Helprig turned to view the fortress. "Like a thief in the night!" he hissed. "I am *not* a common criminal!"

"Yes, Your Excellency," the Savior gave a curt bow.

"It is for the best." Predicant Greglor, the viscount's new assistant, gave a deep bow. Helprig's previous predicant had died in Marinda Hall, not at the hands of guards as it was assumed, but by a defense bot. "The sentries at the Main Gate have been instructed to watch for you. They are to notify the Washentrufel, who will escort you to the emperor's palace. They are allowed—" the predicant reminded Helprig and chose the words carefully, "to use influence." The situation had been explained to the viscount on board the Drakan blockade runner moored offshore.

"Bah! The Washen-fufel. The festering sore of all Drakan Nakish. The archbishop must really have them banished or outlawed. Both! We'll start with Major Startoren, that heathen blasphemer." A sudden gleam came to him.

The Scarlet Savior took a breath.

"What's that?" Helprig swiveled on him.

"Nothing, sire. Captain Irons is waiting for us."

Helprig's eyes narrowed. "Has the prisoner been moved?"

"Uh—"

"What!?" Helprig wheeled on the fawning predicant.

"He has sire, but Captain Irons had to use force."

"*And?*"

"They were forced to kill a guard," the Savior replied.

"Then the stupid jailors should have released the prisoner when we demanded him!" Helprig couldn't decide who he despised more, his new predicant, or the paladin who showed him no obsequience.

"When the guard is changed at midnight, the dead and bound guards will be found. The captain and his squad were seen entering the prison. We can expect they were seen leaving with the prisoner."

"So!?" Helprig was tiring of this debate.

The Savior continued his patient summation. "The guard will be rousted. The barracks alerted, the Citadel sealed, and the prisoner searched for. They will know we killed the guard and took the prisoner."

The predicant added, "They will arrest Captain Irons—"

Helprig turned on him, but the predicant went on quickly, "Unless the captain and the Saviors are not in the Citadel."

His burgundy miter askew, Helprig's lips tightened. "What are you saying?"

"That the captain and all us Saviors must leave the Citadel before midnight, your excellency." The Savior, to forestall more anger, offered a bow. "You should visit the prisoner before then and leave yourself."

"Ha!" A wild look set the viscount's miter further askew. "Visit? I'll do more than visit. I will poke out the gutter-born scum's eyes with a red-hot poker. They have a brazier in the dungeon, do they not?"

"But sire," the predicant dared to reason with the viscount, "they've taken him to the dungeon, the old, closed section. Not the chapel. It was deemed best."

"Best, why is that best?" The viscount made to straighten his miter.

"To keep, or perhaps delay, the Washentrufel from finding the prisoner," supplied the Savior. That section of the dungeon below the old castle had been little used since it was discovered cliff-dwelling Vringis Bats, from sea cliffs below the walls, were able to get into the cells. Vringis Bats were a sub-species of vampire bat attracted to warm-blooded creatures. They carried a virulent pathogen that infected the brain. When a large prey was found, the colony would swarm to attack and suck the victim to a shriveled husk.

"The prisoner will be dead, sire. That was your desire," offered the predicant. "There is no real need to go—"

"No!" Helprig waved an arm, flapping the voluminous sleeve of his robe. "I will say what is the need."

Seeing the viscount would not be dissuaded, the Savior said, "We must go now before the prisoner is dead."

# Chapter 30
# Draw Bridge

### The Citadel

"Sedge said they would deliver the key?"

"Yes, Alon," replied Mitchern.

The goshawk watched from the eave of a wharf warehouse the team huddled beside. Across the canal stood the Citadel's drawbridge, raised. Beyond the bridge was the Outer Bailey, a wide grassy flat that flooded at high tide. At the far edge of the bailey, the rock of Mount Trufel rose an imposing hundred feet. Atop that sheer escarpment, the walls of the Citadel rose another twenty feet.

Out of the night, a pulsing, veering flutter came. It resolved into a buzz. The Mark Two Dragonfly defense bot hovered in front of Christina. In the grasp of its six feet was a key.

"Whoa, you don't see that every day," exclaimed a merc.

She held out her hand, palm up.

The dragonfly alighted, released the key, then veered sharply up and away, lost in the darkness of night.

She arched an eyebrow at Alex.

"Good to their word," he whispered.

"Sedge said there's no one in the bridge house." Mitchern glanced at the goshawk, who stared back impassively.

"I found the skiff," said the sergeant. "It'll take two trips to get us across."

Creeping from lantern shadow to shadow, they came to the ladder leading down to the skiff dock.

Settling in the rocking boat, Alex mused, "Now would not be the time to tip."

With a signal from a merc standing watch on the wharf, they began the paddle across the canal. The channel was wide enough for two barges to pass, and the middle was illuminated by torchlight.

"Easy," Christina admonished the rower. "We'll get there."

"Hope the line is long enough." Alex paid out the return line in the craft's wake.

There was no dock or landing on the far side, on purpose. Bumping against the stone of the canal wall below the raised drawbridge, Alex whirled the grapple about and heaved it, rocking the skiff. The hooks caught on something beyond the low wall that ran the length of the canal. Giving it a solid tug, he said, "Well, here goes." Pulling hard on the grappling line, he jumped out of the boat, causing it to tip dangerously. Christina held onto both sides, keeping her weight low. Alex's feet landed against the fitted rock of the canal wall. Hand over hand, he walked up the wall and, reaching the top, grabbed and pulled himself over, his armor scraping on the stone, harsh and metallic in the night. Any second, they expected to hear a hue and cry from the Citadel's parapet high above.

Nothing.

He reached a hand down and helped Christina over the wall.

Helping the first Lamaran up, she said, "I'll go see if the key works."

"Oi," Alex agreed. "Before we all cross."

Christina drew her sword and crept around the drawbridge keep. The night was moonless. Low scudding clouds blanked and then cleared the stars. If there were wall walkers behind the high parapet, she'd never see them unless they leaned out with a lantern.

Steeling herself, she sprinted across the bailey, the ground firm but rife with the aroma of tidal flat. At the granite face of the mount, she crouched, then hurried west towards the ocean. Looming in the dark, a structure resolved itself into the bulwark guarding the Sally Port. Constructed so an enemy could not bring a battering ram to bear, the heavy concrete structure formed a tight, enclosed space in front of the door. The confines inky black and cloying.

Removing her gauntlets, she felt for the edge of the door frame. Knowing the general premise of how the portal functioned and having found the door frame, she sought the locking bar crank socket. Just above or below the hole would be the lock mechanism.

Time ticked by. She found the crank socket, but the keyhole to engage the locking bar crank eluded her. "Blast. Mother's Spirit, where is it?"

She searched further and began to despair. *The Avarians found it, but where is it? Sedge passed word that Mears had watched off-duty guards use the portal to fish from the bailey. Who is Mears?*

"Alon?"

She yelped, her skin crawling.

Mitchern's hushed voice came from outside the bulwark.

"Yes," she gasped.

The voice came closer. "Are you in there?"

"Yes. I need light. I can't find the keyhole-- if there is one." Logic said that was irrational. The Avarians had found it and made a key for it. She could imagine how they made the key, but where was the lock?

A *snick, snick, snick,* sounded immediately behind her. Taking a deep breath, she tried to calm her nerves, pressing both hands firmly against the door.

Mitchern's torch flickered to life.

"Keep it low," she advised.

In the wan yellow-orange light, she sought the lock that would engage the pawl. Once engaged, a lever placed in the crank socket would release the locking bars binding the door closed.

"There—" Mitchern pointed to a slot above the socket.

Christina retrieved the key and eased it into the lock. Such devices failed to disable the pawl if forced. She tried the key, left, then right. She felt a click. "Give me the torch. Go fetch the crank."

More muffled voices and a scrape of metal on stone sounded from outside.

Mitchern returned with the cranking handle. "Right where Mears said the fishermen hid it."

"Who is Mears?" She fitted the handle in the socket.

"Don't know," Mitchern answered. "An Ancient?"

She looked at him, her green eyes reflecting the torchlight.

"Uh, I mean an Avarian?" After their time in the Union of Souls, he understood the world better.

She nodded. "That's better."

She rotated the crank. It turned easily. *Too easy? Is it engaged? Is the door barred from the inside?*

Alex sensed her fear. He moved Mitchern aside, grabbed the handle, and pulled the door open.

In the glow, he looked at her.

Sheepishly, she smiled. "Thank you."

Drawing his sword, shield at the ready, he said, "Ready."

Christina heaved the door fully open, and Alex led the way in.

Wall sconces lit the steps, hewn from the rock of the mount, going steeply up.

"They're in." Mears breathed a sigh of relief.

Hearter checked the clock. Then back to the hologrid. "They're too late."

# Chapter 31
# Market Tower

### The Citadel

"How do you know Moonlight will be safe?"

They had left the safe house on foot, and now the seven of them waited at an inn at the foot of *Parade Nuar Grand,* the main road winding up the mount and servicing the Citadel. It was the only wheeled access to the fortress. Two hundred meters up and at the top of the slope was the Market Tower.

There were a few patrons at the inn and those sat at the bar, slowly sliding deeper in their cups. The cook and barmaid were glad to have the soldiers for business, ribbing them with jokes of awesome barracks food.

Sitting at two tables in a back corner and the barmaid off to the kitchen, Meridia called on the team net, "Chief, you there?"

Ivan's response immediate. "Yes."

"Let' wants to know if Moonlight will be safe."

"I have three Ready agents just returned from Dominicus. Focun is one of them." Ivan answered. "Stith Drakas was part of his area of responsibility, so he knows the actors. With the shift zone cleared, he'll retrieve your mounts. Moonlight will be well taken care of."

"Thanks, Chief, I raised her from a colt," Lettern responded on the net.

Ivan wanted to say something about using personal property in official IDB business, but instead, "I know this is like asking a squirrel to not chew on a nut, but you should only use that carbine in defense of yourself or a fellow agent in immediate harm."

Her eyes darted to the pack one of the mercs carried. Meridia rolled his eyes at her.

"That does not include provincial personnel."

They'd had that lecture before. Chief was reading them the ULUP party line over the team net, where an AI would record it.

Meridia had tasked Jeremy to find a way around that ULUP clause, and he did. A different section of the IDB's charter read:

> *Provincials engaged in IDB support activities* and *critical to an IDB operation are, therefore, granted physical protection equivalent to their role.*

But Lettern couldn't let it go. She was not a laconic former non-commission officer. "Chief, Ogden says he can make the carbines. That means they're in-country allowed."

Meridia gave her a hand signal to cease.

"Has he? Made them?"

She frowned.

Meridia gave her the *I told you so* look.

"Noo—"

"Until he actually makes one, they are not in-country allowed, and their presence in your packs is granted a temporary exception for this op only. Use only in dire need."

"Nuts and twigs," she whispered off the team net.

Meridia snorted a laugh at her disappointment at not being able to use her newest toy. "Roger that, Chief," he injected before her pout turned into a whining complaint. "Bows and arrows only for Lettern."

"What about *you?*" she shot back.

He shrugged. "I'm getting used to the sword thing."

When they were off the net, he chided her. "Let, no way Og can make those carbines."

The Lamarans were all ears.

"He said he could," she answered defensively.

Meridia dug in his tunic beneath his breastplate. He pulled out a cartridge and sat it on the table, careful the view from the bar was blocked. "The bullet is lead, which Ogden has made many of. The casing is brass, which Ogden has said is simple enough. The powder inside the casing comes from Marisa's alchemist." He tipped the cartridge on its side. "But, you see that little silver disk on the bottom?"

"Yeah," she said.

"That's a primer. It will not pass ULUP inspection. If we get audited for possible unauthorized use, they will catch it."

"What's special about it?"

"Fulminate of mercury. Our armorer told me all about it. That technology is unknown on the planet."

Her brows furrowed. "Fulminate of whatever," she gave a derisive waggle, then eyed the pack. She liked the compact rifle inside. It wasn't big, bad, and bold like her twin-barreled plasma, but it was accurate, effective, and she handled it well, especially in close-quarters drill.

Lettern knocked on the door using the iron door knocker. She waited in the torchlight, a pair of torches mounted on either side of the Market Tower door. Like other keeps, the door was on the second floor and could only be reached by a narrow flight of steps that ended on a small landing. The stairs and landing were designed to collapse when the support pegs were pulled from the inside the tower.

Impatient, she rapped the knocker three times, each time harder, harsh in the night.

The eye-slot snapped open. "What!" said an eye surrounded by black skin.

"Tolls for morrow."

"Too early." The slot snapped shut.

Meridia, standing out of view below the landing, saw the way she twerked her hips and knew what that meant. He smiled inwardly.

*Rap, rap, rap.*

Again, "Whaaat!"

"Tolls for morrow."

"Come tomorrow." *Clunk,* closed the slot.

"I don't want to wait in line!" she yelled in her best Drakan drawl. "And I don't want to get here early!"

For the fourth time, the eye-slot shot open. "Blazes woman. Go away, or we'll come out there and tar you."

"How much?"

"For what?"

"The best spot at the front of the grounds, right on the track."

The eyeball looked her up and down. She'd taken off her armor but carried her bow. Her tunic and blouse were open just enough to get the eyeball's attention.

"What you selling?"

She gave him a smile. "Cloth."

"What kind?"

"Silk, velvet, and some ermine."

"Ermine? From where?"

"Neuland."

Mears and Jeremy were chatting on the team sub-net so it wouldn't distract her. "I know, she's a natural," Meridia responded to one of their comments.

"Uh, she *is* a *provincial*," responded Mears.

"You're not from around here, are you?" asked the eyeball.

Lettern almost gave him the derisive version of an Avarian head waggle, but caught herself. Instead, she put her hands on her hips. "Uh, sorry, but what part of me looks Drakan?"

Mears laughed while Meridia tried to stifle his snort.

"Neuland, huh?"

"Yeah."

"They all look like you up there?"

"Pretty much."

The eyeball turned away. "Eh, got a Neulander out here. She wants to pay for tomorrow. Ermine. Best spot on the lane."

There were different muffled voices behind the door. At least two.

Eyeball turned back. "Three sheqels, plus one for early pay."

Jeremy had told her what to expect as a fair price. "*Three,* plus *one?*" She gave eyeball a wicked smile, "Are you boys worth it?" She raised the crock of corked ale from the tavern, her secret weapon. "Three sheqels and a half, and we have a deal."

Eyeball went from the crock to her bosom and back. "What you want to do with that?"

"Drink it."

More muffled conversation from behind, then one of the other voices drew closer. "Is she a scow or a looker?"

Lettern gave a start.

Mears laughed. Little did the guards know they were graced by the hologram log-on avatar for many Avarian servicemen and women. The video feed from Krch's shuttle of Lettern's lithe form blasting away with her plasma was all the marketing she needed.

"A looker."

The other voice, "Let her in. Let's get a gander at her."

Meridia moved to the bottom of the steps, careful to stay in the shadow. The onorio was on the other side. Meridia signed he would go first.

A bolt and another bolt were *thunked,* and the door opened, flooding the platform with light. Eyeball resolved itself in a burly Nakish wearing leather under-armor. Two more guards were off to the side. A fire burned in the hearth on the far side of the chamber. "Three an'a 'alf." Eyeball held out a hand.

Lettern stepped into the keep, a hand to her hip and smirk to her lips. "Three? Is that it?"

"Huh? You wanna pay more?" asked the second Nakish.

"No, moron, she asked of us," Eyeball hooked a thumb at himself.

The third Nakish went to close the door.

Lettern stopped it with her foot. With the same mischievous smile, she said, "I have friends."

The third Nakish asked, "More like you?"

"Yes. Just like me."

As footsteps pounded up the stairs, she stepped aside, continuing to smile sweetly. "Here they are."

Eyeball looked alarmed and moved back.

Lettern pulled her bow from her shoulder.

Eyeball lunged for the weapon rack beside the door, but the bow came whistling, *smack* beside his head. The hit presaged the next blow. She snapped her wrist, and her archer's forearm *cracked* the bow just above the ear. Eyeball's body crashed into the rack, sending spears and swords clattering across the floor.

The onorio had a sword point at a guard's throat, "Yield."

As much as he could with the point on his jugular, the guard croaked, "Aye."

Meridia had the other guard cornered and unarmed against the stone steps leading to the loft, and above that, the roof.

The last of the Lamarans entered and bolted the door.

"Let', check the roof," said Meridia.

"He says it's just them," called the onorio as Lettern went up, an arrow knocked.

"Are you robbing us?" a guard asked. "You've come too early. No tolls till tomorrow."

"Sit," ordered Meridia. "We'll be gone in an hour. You want to stay alive?"

He took the guard's sullen silence as a yes. "Then be at peace." It was code for what a Marine said to a comrade when they were dying. "I will kill you if you're not."

In the loft, Lettern confirmed it was unoccupied. Climbing a wooden ladder, she emerged on the roof with its surrounding parapet. All around the tower, Stith Drakas slumbered in the deepening night. No alarm was raised. It was a peaceful contrast to the havoc wreaked below.

She moved around to get a better view of the Citadel. It was her first, other than through a drone feed, and this was real, not on a hologrid in Central Station. She was seeing it live and in person. The feeling was exhilarating. The tower was right on the edge of the parade grounds and across the grounds, the Main Gate. She studied the primary objective. Torches burned along the wall parapet above it. Now that she had a visual augmentation embed, she could see so much better at night. Enough where she could pick out a lone pikeman walking the wall.

She peered at their first intermediate objective and blinked. Pursing her lips, she rationalized what she saw. "Uh, Mears," she called on the mission net.

"Go," came his reply.

Conscious that the entire mission force was listening, "Is the assault zone clear?"

There was a pause. It grew longer.

"Negative. I repeat, negative. Assault zone obstructed."

There was a flapping of wings above her. The ladder leading to the roof shifted; someone was coming up.

A buzzing zipped past her, heading for the assault zone.

"What?" asked Meridia, coming to her side, breathless.

She pointed, "That."

Jeremy joined the mission net. "It is a merchant's cart. They have arrived early for Market Day. The stall they are erecting is in the assault zone."

"Whaaa? How'd they get in first? That's not fair," Lettern simpered. "We followed the rules."

"What part?" asked Meridia. "The clubbing or gagging part?"

The matriarch, in the Adept Center in Matrincy Tower in NvaGira, looked past her hologrid, slaved to the drone feed, to Margret, who sat with a group of adepts at their own grid. Nearly every grid in the center was slaved to a drone or bot feed from the mission.

Margret typed a message on her grid.

It popped up on the matriarch's. It read, *So it begins.*

Clienen, on board the *Tempest Dare* with Ivan in Ground Ops Control(GOC) said, "Tell him."

Ivan went on the mission net. "Meridia. You have fifty minutes to clear the zone and get the gate open. Fifty minutes to Go time."

On the hangar deck, Marisa, Sedge, and the mission leadership team watched the drone feeds of Meridia's team. Marisa said, "Go, Meridia, go."

Major Vuulanin, who was their escort on the *Tempest Dare,* said to her, "Push that button. It will put you on the mission net."

She punched the button. "Meridia, go. Lettern, no time to waste."

With news bots hovering in the hangar, the entire mission force, a hundred and eighty Dianis provincials, were neatly organized in their nine assault groups. The *Tempest Dare* and her Riflemen, axemen, archers, and Marines were primed.

"We're going," Lettern called on the net as she ran down the stone steps. At the door, she grabbed a pack and started rifling through it. One of the bound, gagged guards stared at her. Careful that she was off the mission net, she said to him. "Looks like we're leaving early. You can have the place back."

With satisfaction, she withdrew the object of her desire.

Meridia saw it. He shook his head in resignation.

She jacked a round in the chamber, and safe'd it. She slung the carbine beside her quiver, overstuffed with arrows; her hard expression dared him to speak.

Outside, at the base of the tower, Meridia gathered the team. "All right, we'll—"

"Let me handle this," said Lettern. "I'm CivMon."

She strutted over to the two caravanserai who, in the poor lantern light, were setting up their stall for the morning's market.

"What the hell are you doing?" she demanded.

They stopped still.

"Have you paid the toll?" she growled. A non-com she wasn't, but a drill sergeant she could be.

"Well!?"

One of them tentatively shook their head.

"Yeah, I know you haven't. You're trying to jump the line. Aren't you?" She got in the face of the nearest merchant, who tried to back away.

"But, but, we were—"

"Were what? Going to pay in the morning?"

The one started nodding his head.

"Oh no. No, no, no. You pay first, then set up."

"But we are almost finished."

And Lettern could see the pair were brass smiths and most of their urns, plates, and pots were already arrayed for display. "Sergeant!"

Meridia snapped to attention. "Yes, Ma'am!"

"I have need of your squad." She glared at the two line-jumpers. "They will pack your things." She gave a waggle. "Most of it. We'll keep a portion for-- labor."

"No! No!" They both exclaimed in unison, suddenly scurrying about tossing pots and pans into their cart.

With an eagle eye, she watched them. "You have ten turns of a short glass. Anything remaining will be confiscated."

Ivan turned to look at Clienen. "And you made her CivMon?"

"It wasn't my idea, but she came highly recommended."

Turning back to the drone feed, Ivan said, "She makes Meridia look like a camp counselor."

"You will park your cart at the tower door," Lettern pointed. "You will wait there till six hours past. Then, and only then, may you request to pay your toll. *Do, you, understand?*"

"Yes, yes," they called her everything from sir to sire to highness.

Finally, with a contented smile, she called out, "Sergeant! For our other business."

Meridia formed the Lamarans up in two ranks of three. Then quietly said, "Remember the skip step."

"Bloody Drakans," grumbled the onorio.

Lettern took position at the back of the column as Meridia moved them out.

The Lamarans were remarkably good at the odd step-step-skip the Drakans marched to while on parade. Jeremy had picked it up in his analysis of the guard rotation in the

Citadel. All units passing through the parade grounds used the formal parade step.

As the squad marched past the caravanserai, whipping their wagon team into motion, Lettern said, "I'll be watching you. Six past, no sooner!"

# Chapter 32
## Glory Hall

*The Citadel*

The steps took a right turn.

Alex held up a fist. He bent an ear.

Voices sounded distant.

The team listened.

"They're arguing," Christina observed.

Alex inclined his head, parsing the faint words.

"I'll go." He handed her his shield and drew a dirk. Stealing himself, he began treading lightly up the steps.

Christina motioned for the party to stay while she crept to the corner to watch the Defender's progress.

Waiting in the dank stairway, the rough rock cold and musty, the group sweated in their armor. The sconces were guttering low on oil.

Quick steps came back from around the corner.

Christina backed and waited.

Alex appeared. "Oi. They are arguing, and there is no mistaking that pompous bastard's voice."

Christina harkened back to the day in Wedgewood, at Timber Hall when Viscount Helprig had demanded the clan surrender the aquamarine mine. "Helprig? He's here?"

A quick nod. "Captain Irons, too."

Her visage narrowed. "Murali's."

"It's him."

He could sense her decision, the jaw, the eyebrows. "They're at the head of the stairs. Debating to leave or...."

"Or?"

"Or watch the prisoner die."

For Christina, the cold cruelty was a clarion call. She rarely demonstrated anger, though that night, in the Citadel, Alex saw it: Her green eyes alight with Mother's Wrath.

When Christina didn't move, the sergeant asked, "Alon?"

"She's thinking," answered Alex.

Her breathing measured; she gritted. Glancing back to the troopers, "We need to get to the gate. Mother bless us. We're late."

Rising from her crouch, she settled her shield on her arm. "We don't know how many there are."

Alex cocked his head. "Helprig will have a squad of the paladins with him. Irons may have brought more. There's a Church temple up there. Who knows how many are there."

She was hoping for some clue how the assault on the gate faired or even if the attack had commenced. She could be leading her small party into a fruitless battle against an entire garrison. Their retreat option was perilous: Back down the stairs, across the bailey, lower the drawbridge, find their eenus still there, and ride through hostile territory to who knows where. The entire mission, especially the survival of her men, rested on taking the extraction zone, which was in the center of the area bounded by the Washentrufel HQ, the Paleowright chapel, and Sighten Tower. Her team's objective was to first take the tower and then attack either the Inner or Main Gate, depending on the situation.

Her gaze softened; she peered at Alex. "We've no choice."

"Aye."

"I'll lead." She moved around him. The team rose as one, the lanterns guttering in low flickers.

The sergeant whispered back to his men, "For Mother's Life, be quiet."

"When we get to the top of the stairs, we'll rush them. Don't stop." Christina breathed. "Keep running. We'll come out in Glory Hall. From there, we'll make for the Sighten Tower."

"With Mother's Wind," said a merc.

"Oi, Mother's Wind," said another.

Leading up the rough rock steps, she heard the voices steadily grow and then a sudden bark.

"Now!" Helprig's pompous tone unmistakable.

Ascending steps, she stopped.

Cocking her head to listen, the voices had ceased. Waiting for more clues, she clenched her sword hilt, her hand sweaty in the gauntlet.

Nothing.

She waited. Still nothing.

"Now."

They darted up the stairs not caring who heard.

As she came through the landing door, Glory Hall opened around her. Neat, ordered rows of tomb pedestals loomed cold and soulless. From their graves, the emperors of past Drakan glories glared at the Life Defender. How dare she tread in their sanctum.

Her sword ready, she moved further into the mausoleum; the team spread out behind her.

Walking, then trotting, she made for where she expected a door to the outside. Incense burned in the cold air; floral wreaths adorned the tombs.

"Aura signatures of Team Christina have emerged in Glory Hall," the *Tempest Dare's* threat AI posted on the mission net.

Mears skewed his hologrid to show the eight green triangles moving through the hall. "I hate that place. The gravity flux of that rock is a real problem." He and Hearter had waited tensely from the time the team's signatures had faded off the sensor grid, not knowing the extent of the tunnels beneath the mount or if there had been a situation.

Halting by a sarcophagus where they could see the door, the sergeant asked, "Where'd they go?"

"Outside, to the prisoner," Christina answered.

Gathering herself, she sprinted the distance to the door.

The double brass-embossed doors were massive. Scenes of Drakan history were etched in the gleaming metal. There was nothing else she could do; she grabbed one handle and

Alex the other. Mitchern had an arrow notched, and the troopers readied for a sprint.

Heaving his door open a crack, Alex peered outside. The edifice of the Diunesis Antiquaria chapel directly in front. Opening it further, he spied the prison on the left and the walls of Washentrufel HQ to the right.

Running footsteps came.

Alex leaned back, nodding to Mitchern, who aimed at the opening.

Through the bare crack, to the right, past the chapel, and in front of the Washentrufel HQ, he could see a gathering of torches. "Something's afoot," he said to Christina. "At the Trufel HQ. It's clear here."

Heaving the doors open, Christina crept onto the portico. The yellow and crimson-enameled armor plain in the light. *Where is the prisoner? Are they gathered for him or something else? The Main Gate?* Those thoughts counsel caution, patience, but she was out of time. They could charge the churchmen, scatter them, and then go for the Main Gate. They would create a distraction, a diversion, perhaps. It was fraught, but they'd come on a mission. Mother's Voice beckoned.

# Chapter 33
# Ruse

*The Citadel*

It was two hundred paces, give or take, to the Main Gate from the assault zone.

The onorio led the squad, at a skip step, across the dark parade ground. Lit by torches, the gate grew in the distance.

Meridia and a Lamaran split off from the squad and doubled back to the assault zone. True to Lettern's command, the brass tinkers had parked their rig on the other side of the tower.

"Team Meridia approaching primary objective," *Trilonair's* sensor officer reported on the mission net.

On the hangar deck, the shift zone pulsed. Major Vuulanin announced, "Sapper deployed."

Councilor Margret swept her fingers across the holo panel.

A message appeared on the matriarch's grid. *Did you see that coming?*

*No,* came the response. *I rarely see them.*

"Thirty minutes till *go* time," Ivan called on the mission net.

In the tense wait, Meridia decided to give it up. Off the net, he said, "Lysil, let me see your pack."

The merc turned so Meridia could unbuckle the straps. He reached in. "I may get fired for this."

"Not you, sir," Lysil countered.

Meridia snorted. "Yes, me. But if it comes to saving Lettern, there are things a man must do."

He pulled the cover off, inserted a magazine, pulled the slide back, and let it snap forward.

"Shit," said Mears, watching via surveillance bot.

"Yeah," agreed Hearter. "That's not the same model Lettern has.

"Nope."

The squad approached the gate.

"Are we ready to move up *Go Time* if they get in sooner?" asked Captain Trich, standing beside Ivan in ground control.

Ivan switched to the ship net. "Vuulanin, move Group One to the shift zone. Ready them for an early departure."

Team Meridia was close enough to the gate where they had the attention of the two pikemen on duty.

Marching right up to the gate, the onorio called, "Squad, halt." Their boots landed as one. Even Lettern managed it.

The onorio approached one of the Drakans and held up a scroll. "I have orders to report to Washentrufel HQ."

The sentry held out a hand, and the onorio gave him the scroll.

The sentry unrolled it and read. Then he said, "It says you have a second scroll for the Washen Officer in Charge; their eyes only."

The onorio reached beneath his armored breastplate and withdrew a second scroll, showing the burgundy seal still intact. "I am to deliver this directly into the hands of the agent in charge."

The sentry frowned but marched, no skip step, to the postern door and knocked.

While they were waiting, the second sentry said, "The gate is closed at dark. You should have come earlier."

"We have orders," the onorio stated simply. "Once we deliver, we go back home."

"Auxies," the sentry noted the squad's armor. "Cavalry?"

"Aye."

"Where'd you come from?"

"Lamaran frontier," the Lamaran said stiffly.

The pikeman studied him. "That's a long ride."

"It is. My chafed ass hurts more than a whore's bum on payday."

The sentry smiled.

The second sentry returned. "The corporal says you are to wait for the agent to be summoned."

Watching the drone feed, Ivan said to the captain, "We were afraid of that." Jeremy had estimated a fifty-three percent probability the squad would be let through without further challenge.

"Can he demand to be let through?" asked Trich.

Ivan called on the mission net, "Lettern, we'll mark the time, but the onorio may need to escalate. Christina's party is delayed."

Marisa walked over to Ogden, who stood on the shift zone platform with Lettern's sister Rachael and eighteen members of his Second Ward. "Og, be ready with the explosive charge. Christina is delayed, and Lettern is being stalled at the gate. Meridia will let you know when you get on the ground."

The master smith gave a short, tense nod. "Oi."

She could tell he was uncharacteristically nervous. "Og."

"Yes?"

"You are of the rock on which this world was built, so sayeth Mother, and so sayeth me." She stood there. "Let Mother guide your strike."

He gave another nod, this one more determined.


A knock sounded on the door.

"Enter!" he called. Larech, the Washentrufel duty agent, was just about to undress and go to bed. It was well past midnight.

The door opened, and a pikeman leaned in, "I've come from the Main Gate. You have a scroll there."

Larech looked over. "You don't have it?"

"No, the auxies who carry it presented their orders, and it says not to be opened except by the Washen Officer in Charge.

Larech groused, "Well, then, send them through. Escort them up here."

As the pikeman made to close the door and leave, Larech grumbled, "Ach, I'll go with you. No point in waiting; I've an early day tomorrow."

Casually, more out of habit than need, the agent grabbed his rapier and strapped it on.

Walking past the second-floor windows of HQ, Larech caught the light of torches in the Areaum, as the space was called between the chapel and Sighten Tower. Walking to the stairs, he stopped at the next window. It was a group of Scarlet Saviors, a large group, more than the few ceremonial guards posted to the chapel. He squinted in the poor light, then did a double-take at the burgundy headdress of the clergyman in the center of the Saviors.

He spun around, catching the pikeman off guard, "Did you know Viscount Helprig is here?"

Snapping to attention, the pikeman answered, "No, sir."

"Standing orders are to hold the viscount at the gate until he can be escorted to the emperor's palace."

"Yes, sir. Those are the orders."

"Then why is he standing right there." Larech pointed out the window.

The pikeman wanted to go look, but didn't break attention. "Uh, I didn't let him in. I mean, we didn't, not on our watch."

Peering out the window, "Ack. He's here now." The agent figured he would let it go till morning when Fritach arrived for prisoner interrogations— "Damn the Ancients!"

"What?" The pikeman broke attention.

"Helprig, that's what. Here, in the dark of night, with a platoon of his favorite goons. He's up to no bloody good."

Larech hustled down the stairs. Standing before the door leading outside, he said, "The reason he was to be held at the gate was for the safety of the prisoner. And yet, here he is!"

The pikeman was taken aback.

"Quick. Go alert the prison. Tell them to bar the doors. No one in or out without my permission. And go to the barracks, roust the duty officer. Tell him I want a half-century mustered in front of the prison with speed. He's not to dally." Larech moved to open the door, "And," he said slowly, "you better go out the back way. Don't let them see you." With more reflection, he added, "It's probably foolish, but the viscount needs to know this is the Drakan Empire, not his personal sandbox. Find the Halberdier captain and tell him, with his satisfaction, he is requested to form a platoon in front of the pikemen."

"Yes, sir."

"Go."

The agent braced himself. This would not be pleasant. He opened the door and strode into the night.

A black form, a marsh wraith, ascended the moss-covered rock. Rising, the apparition reached the stone of the south wall of the Citadel, ghosted left to a corner, and followed it up. To the left, a clear view showed the lanterns burning beside the Main Gate. Above the marsh wraith were the massive twin ballista mounts of Battery B.

Lettern wanted to look but kept her body at attention, directed at the gate.

Up the shadow moved.

At a wall crenelation, code-name Sapper because of ULUP's sensitivity to potential exploitation of its species, the apparition grabbed the rock, and a forked tongue slithered from its snout, tasting the air. Easing, slithering into the crenelation, Prince Fire Eye spied the wall walker, a pikeman, moving towards the gate. The recon drone had marked a second sentry in the battery.

Sliding down from the crenelation, leaving a smear of tidal mud and slime behind, the lizard man pulled a javelin from his quiver. Creeping, padding as only a reptile could, he spotted the lookout gazing south, out beyond the wall, directly above where he began his climb.

Snapping forward, the javelin impaled the lookout, slumping him against the wall.

Fire Eye was on him; a swipe of his scimitar severed his throat.

*So much for* our *exploitation of them* appeared on the matriarch's grid. She glanced past the grid and saw the adepts around Margret chattering. Margret's own grid was super-sized so the flock of adepts could watch together.

"First blood," said Captain Trich.

Clienen responded, "There'll be more."

Then Ivan quipped, "You should recruit him to CivMon."

"Why? Too soft for Ready?"

Ivan batted back, "You could make him IDB liaison to the Church."

Lettern could see a pikeman on the wall directly above the gate. It was an easy shot for her.

"Shifting Group One in five, four, three--" sounded on the mission net.

Lettern watched the pikeman, ready to unshoulder her bow.

"Group One on the ground in good order," it was Meridia's voice on the mission net. "Clearing the zone."

Fire Eye hefted the gore-covered javelin. He stalked the first pikeman. The walk torches were sparse, affording wide swaths of shadow for a marsh wraith to hunt.

Mears, as did much of the Fleet, watched the unarmored apex predator stalk a fellow human.

Angling for a throw that would drop his prey where it stood and not over the wall, the prince sidled through a light-well and closed the distance.

In the mindless watch routine, the sentry turned to walk back toward Battery B. He stopped. There was something— The javelin took him in the chest through the formal dress tunic of a parade ground sentry.

Lettern saw the man drop from view. Shifting her eyes to the left, she sought the second wall-walker.

One of the sentries standing in front of the squad heard the sentry's spear clatter on the parapet. He looked up. Not able to see to the top, he backed toward the onorio.

Standing at attention, waiting for the Washen officer to appear, the Lamarans were tight as a drawn bow.

"Balen?" the guard called. "You up there?"

No response.

The two guards looked at each other. One shook his head. "I'll tell the corporal."

Lettern watched the onorio. His hand slid to his side as the guard went to the postern door. She willed the onorio to move, and, on his own accord, he did.

The sword sliding free of its scabbard drew the guard's attention.

Lettern broke ranks, grabbed her bow, and pulled an arrow from her quiver.

The sentries froze, befuddled.

The onorio's blade swept up in an arc. Lettern nocked the arrow, drew, and loosed.

Closest to the portal, the guard staggered and crumpled against the door with a Wedgewood green and white fletching in his throat.

The onorio's victim gasped and struggled on the sword, only to fall back in a clump.

Lettern notched another arrow and aimed at the eye slot in the door, half-drawing the bow, her bicep tight against the tension. She thought about dropping it and pulling the carbine.

The eye slot opened. Her arrow zipped through.

"Aaay!" echoed a voice beyond the door.

A different eye appeared in the slot.

This time, she didn't miss.

A scream pronounced her score.

The eye slot snapped shut.

Whirling to face the assault zone, Lettern yelled, "Sis! Sis!"

Rachael came sprinting out of the dark.

"Grapple." Lettern pointed. "Up the wall!"

Rachael unslung her pack and retrieved the grappling line and hook. Swinging it around, she lofted it in the air and, with her mind caught and sent it straight through a wall crenelation.

Lettern made to take the line, ready to scale the wall, but Rachael ran forward, pulling the line tight. Just like when they were kids scaling the massive Ungerngerists, Rachael leaped, line tight. Her feet met the wall, and she literally ran up the block face. A tug and lift with her mind, and she was atop the wall. From her bullet pouch she plucked a rifle bullet and searched for targets.

The matriarch braced herself. Fate threads twisted, converging.

Margret announced on the Adept Center broadcast system, "Master kinetic in action. Dimensional distortion on the planet Dianis, Margel system. Fate fork is nearing. Distortion will cause permutations."

"Racheal scaling the wall was not in the plan," Ivan said.

"No," agreed Clienen. Their hologrid skewed to a recon bot diverted to Rachael. He watched her draw her arm back.

Meridia announced on the mission net, "Group Two on the ground in good order. Clearing the zone."

Rachael ran to the edge of the wall and threw. What her physical skills lacked, her mind made perfect. The projectile zipped past the Inner Gate and curved, catching the messenger running up the Upper Bailey. Knocked forward, the man stumbled and fell, dropping his shield, and his helm went rolling.

A Special Forces officer stood with Captain Trich and the ops staff. Ivan heard the officer comment.

Getting up, the messenger started running again. Rachael's arm came back. She held it, focusing all her energy.

The matriarch felt it; Fate lines were all askew; the wild card she instigated into the future was at work in the present. Gripping the arms of her chair, the matriarch saw Margret and the adepts peering at her. She shook her head: *No, I did not see this.*

Rachael let go. The bullet flew hot, burning with an energy Rachael never dare expose. Embedded in her cells and coursing in her blood, marsediminium energized her kinetic sense and propelled the bullet to a hypersonic crack. The runner went down, half his head gone.

"Shiren," exclaimed the Special Forces captain. "Our kinetics can't do that."

# Chapter 34
## Ovids

*Tempest Dare, Dianis Orbit*

"Major Vuulanin, we need to speak with Sedge, the provincial, before he returns to the planet."

Something about the way the ULUP commissioner spoke caused Vuulanin's combat-sense to flare.

Sedge's own Group Three was on the platform.

"Now?!" he snapped.

"Yes, now." The three ULUP commissioners, serving as special observers for the unique event, stood shoulder to shoulder. In terms of Federation politics, they were an odd group: One from Valcania Six, one from Mara Four Kryzlictin Perseus, and one from Tochman Lower Five Outer. Only one, Valcania, was in the Federation. Lockman was a far outer planet with an opaque society, and Mara Four was a water world of a sentient aquatic species that had appointed a human as their commissioner to ULUP. None of the planets adhered to the same governmental systems, nor did they have the same ULUP objectives.

Vuulanin had been instructed by both Captain Lich and the IDB executive director to show deference to the commissioners, as these were three of the twelve on the oversight committee. "We're ninety seconds from shift!"

"We understand that," said Lower Five's commissioner. "But it can't be helped. We need to speak with him. There are just a few questions we need to ask. You can send him down later. Instructions will be forthcoming from the Governing Board."

Vuulanin's eyes narrowed. Something about how the other two commissioners shifted their stance and looked away?

"We have authority here. Sedge is a provincial." Lower Five noted.

Vuulanin cursed and walked to the shift platform. Sedge and Captain Rayamars, with eighteen Tivor Riflemen, waited. Sedge was at ease, whereas Rayamars tense, expectant.

The major explained the situation to Sedge, who looked over to the three commissioners.

"Mr. Rayamars," Sedge glanced back, "Give the lady my respects and tell her I am delayed."

Rayamars, alarmed, reached for an arm to forestall him.

"Noi. The lady, you, and the others know the plan. Carry on. I will be with you shortly."

Meeting with the three commissioners, Sedge asked, "What is this about? I have an operation to run."

"It's most urgent," said the commissioner from Valcania, looking to Lower Five to complete the plea, who added smoothly, "We need to know, before you go, some things about Nemesis." The commissioner from Kryzlictin jerked.

Sedge's eyes went from him back to Lower Five. Intrigued, he said, "Lead on."

Vuulanin, with sixty seconds before the shift, watched them walk to a crew lift, which bothered him. It all bothered him. *Why take him to a lift?* Vuulanin hustled to the holo terminal and punched in GOC. "IDB, you there?"

"Affirmative," answered Clienen, stepping into view.

"The three ULUP observers, the commissioners, just led Sedge away to ask him questions."

"Why?" Clienen asked as Ivan moved into view.

"They wanted to ask him about Nemesis? What's that?"

"Now?" Clienen's sour expression matched Ivan's headshaking.

"When I challenged them on it, they said Sedge was a provincial, and they had authority over him."

"No!" Ivan snapped.

"No, they do not," Clienen added more calmly, "they have no direct authority over any provincial or any world for that matter. All direct authority over planets flows to the IDB from their funding governments who take *license* from ULUP."

Ivan stepped in front of Clienen. "Dianis may be an unclaimed planet, but it's in Federation space. This is a Federation ship; the captain is in command here."

Trich came over. "What?"

"Did you authorize the commissioners to sequester Sedge?"

The captain blinked. "The mission leader? Hell no."

"Vuulanin," Ivan commanded, "get him back."

The major ran to the platform where Rayamars waited, bewildered. "I'm sending you down without Sedge. Continue the operation. We'll find him and send him shortly." Vuulanin turned, waving his arm in a circle above his head, signaling for the shift to start.

"Sizars and death," Captain Trich cursed. "Security," he called on the security channel. "Locate the Dianis provincial, Sedge. Pipe his signature location to Vuulanin. And send a team to support."

"Aye, sir," responded the Security AI avatar.

"Sedge is to be returned to the hangar deck post haste. The ULUP observers are to be escorted to my cabin. Send a detail there as well."

"Aye, sir."

Vuulanin was at the crew lift the commissioners had taken, waiting for its return. "Delta deck, compartment Fox twenty-one," the security AI told Vuulanin. "A security team will meet you there."

"I see," said Sedge. "What you want to know will take considerably more time—"

Lower Five interrupted, smiling, "We have time."

"But I don't," answered Sedge.

"Your mission, well," Kryzlictin hedged, "is not as imp—
"

Valcania interrupted him. All three commissioners wanted to speak at the same time, "We can't have you dying on the mission."

Sedge gripped his sword hilt, "So that's what this is about?"

A pounding came from behind the locked compartment door. "Open up! Marine Security!"

Lower Five calmly drew an ion pistol from inside his cloak, energized it, and set it to *high stun*. He fired at the door lock, frying the control circuits.

"Unauthorized weapon discharge," immediately sounded in the GOC. "Delta deck, compartment Fox twenty-one."

"Really, commissioner. Is that necessary?" asked Valcania.

Lower Five flipped the power switch to *full pulse*.

Sedge saw the gun arm turning in his direction and drew his sword, too late. The blast caught him in the chest. In quick succession, Lower Five fired twice more.

"Unauthorized ion weapon discharge. Casualties, Delta deck, compartment Fox twenty-one."

"General Quarters, General Quarters. Internal threat alert, *Tempest Dare*," sounded the Combat Command AI.

Captain Trich lunged for the holo grid. "Do not stop the assault," he announced on the All-Hands circuit. "I repeat, this is Captain Trich; do not stop the assault.

"Why?" asked Sedge as Lower Five leaned over him as he lay on the deck.

Lower Five was surprised the Loch Norim was still alive. The others were clearly dead. He probed the wound in Sedge's chest and found the damaged albaminia chain mail. He rose. "You should have been wearing energy armor."

"Why?"

The Marines beyond the door stood back and charged their weapons.

"Ever hear of Annber Octavia OvidSirus?"

Sedge coughed up blood. "OvidSirus? The Ovid sector?"

Lower Five eyed him with a sadistic glare and raised the gun. "Yes, and you know about it. You know where it is, who they are, and how you Norims persecuted them."

"Ovids? You're human." In his dying sight, Sedge saw the man for what he really was. "You're an Ovid sycophant."

"Yes," he sneered, "and we survived Nemesis where you failed."

A Marine fired at the lock once, twice, thrice.

"You allied with Nemesis?" Sedge choked.

Lower Five gave a mocking Avarian head waggle. "Friends. But," he said wistfully, "now it's the Turboii." The wild gleam returned. "We will rid the galaxy of all humans."

A Marine kicked in the door and aimed as Lower Five disintegrated Sedge's head.

The Marine fired.

# Chapter 35
## Areaum

### *The Citadel*

His hand on his rapier hilt, Larech called out to the gathered churchmen. "Viscount Helprig, if you please, a moment of your time."

There was talk amongst the churchmen. Three Scarlet Saviors broke off and came his direction, one holding a torch and the others with their rachiers at the ready.

Larech did not like the look of them. He drew his rapier and pointed it at them. "Upon my authority as Citadel Duty Officer, I order you to halt and bear explanation before the emperor."

The Saviors kept coming.

The agent, smart though he was, hated running from anyone. He stood his ground.

The torch bearer raised the flame higher to cast more light on their target.

Christina and Alex, at the encouragement of the Lamarans, had pulled the covers off their shields. That night, they were there to do Mother's Business.

The agent heard the running steps coming from the direction of the prison and, beyond it, the barracks. It too was soon yet for the pikemen to heed his summons. Perhaps a squad was on an unscheduled round?

Christina saw the lone Drakan officer, his weapon drawn, facing off against three Scarlet Saviors. She went from a run to full tilt.

The pounding feet caused the nearest Savior, in his arrogance, to casually look right. The white lily on a field of green embossed on a shield baffled him. The agent saw it as well, amazed.

Christina crashed, shield-first, full on the befuddled Savior, sending him, arm flailing, rachier flying, hard to the cobbles.

From his angle, unable to see the shield heraldic, Captain Irons yelled, "Washen mercs!"

Alex literally ran over the second Scarlet Savior. In the process, the man managed to trip him, and Alex  went sprawling on the flagstones.

"Team Christina is engaged at the extraction zone," the threat AI announced in Meridia's ear.

With the sixty members of Assault Groups One, Two, and Three, Meridia pelted for the Main Gate postern. He saw Lettern, who scaled the wall after her little sister, open the door and let the onorio and his men in. Meridia skidded to a stop and followed the last merc in.

"Did you hear?" asked Lettern beside the door.

"Yes. Inner Gate?" He asked about their next objective.

"Rachael and Fire Eye are on it."

Mercenaries, Timberkeeps, and Tivorians flooded through the gate.

Group Four materialized, and Marisa started running hard to catch up with Team Meridia.

Larech back-stepped, not knowing who to fight.

A charging Scarlet Savior bowled over a mercenary while another mercenary grappled with and flung down his opponent.

The two opposing sides were even in numbers and evenly matched, which surprised Larech. The Saviors should have easily dominated mercs, but whoever they were, were good. And the two Defenders, there were *two* of them -- *here,* in the *Citadel!*

Captain Irons managed to hack his opponent down with a heavy chop to the pauldron that slid into the neck. A blow landed on Iron's shield rim, and the Lamaran sergeant's sword cracked him on the helmet.

Christina wanted to help Alex, who was wrestling for his sword with a Savior. Her opponent, thinking he was smart, readied a classic sword attack: A Swinging Richy. She saw him tilt his left knee, bring his shield in, and dip the rachier low and behind. She gave him the opening: A clear stab below the breastplate.

The knee pulled back, the shield swung left, and the hidden rachier came in low.

She backed just enough. The rachier swept past her midriff; as the Savior's shield carried to the left, she lunged, stabbing him in the neck.

Blood sprayed. The man staggered back, clenching at his throat, and dropping his rachier.

A Savior, to the man's left, momentarily distracted by the ghastly sight, fell victim to Christina's next blow, one to his helm. He, too, staggered back, but the dented helm saved his life. Christina pursued him as she heard the Drakan officer yell at her, "To your right!"

It was Captain Irons coming for a rematch of that afternoon in Wedgewood. The one where Lettern had been flung through Murali's front window and Christina had forced the Church to yield.

Without seeing him, Christina spun to her left and kept spinning, bringing her sword hard on the boss of Irons' shield, sliding across it, toward his face, along his cheek to lodge between his ear and helmet.

"Go, Go!" Marisa, not knowing where Sedge was or when he would shift in, had taken command. Blocking Force Alpha was forming in the Upper Bailey just before the stables.

Lettern needed no urging. She was running, fleet as a gazelle, up the bailey to the Upper Gate. Meridia and the team followed in hot pursuit.

"Fire Eye!" Marisa called. "Fire Eye! Prince!"

He came loping out of the darkness, Rachael running behind.

"Here, take this." She handed him a shirt. "That belongs to Atch. He wore it the day he was taken."

A forked tongue flicked out, tasting it.

He handed it back to her.

"Is that good?" she asked.

Two slurps. Turning away, he trotted into the gloom.

Rachael waited for an order.

"Go. Follow him. Send word if he finds something."

"Lieutenant," Marisa grabbed the shoulder of a Tivor Marine. "Take a platoon and follow them!"

Christina gave Irons credit; he was as tough as his name. Bleeding from his cheek and severed ear, he kept coming. Theirs had become a personal duel while the others fell wounded around them, and Helprig hurled insults, taunting her from behind his predicant, who stood, shaking, holding a dirk.

Alex, suffering from a rachier thrust that slid inside his back plate, fought on Christina's immediate left. Blood leaked down his side along his thigh. He parried and blocked. They were backing, nearly to the Sighten Tower steps. An arrow whizzed past his shoulder, but the Scarlet Savior, a stout fighter, had his shield up, and Mitchern's shaft hit the face and deflected at the predicant. The clergyman squealed. It gave Alex just enough chance to thrust low, but Irons reached over and drove the sword down with his rachier. Christina shield-bashed Irons, stomped his foot, and hammered her sword hilt into the helmet flap covering the destroyed ear.

Irons staggered, stumbling back.

Christina called, "In the tower!"

Mitchern, frustrated, his arrows thwarted by the superior Savior armor, took careful aim.

Helprig went down with a *"Aiy!"* Hit in the thigh, sure to cause the most pain.

The viscount wailed, horrified by the shaft buried in his leg.

Three of the Saviors moved to shield Helprig. The fourth grappled the merc beside Alex. The merc and Savior went down in a crunching heap of armor, weapons, and flailing feet.

The first of ten pikemen came running.

Alex bent to aid the Lamaran as a pikeman hefted and threw his spear. Christina hit the edge of the spear with her shield, but it still caught Alex in the shoulder below the pauldron. The solid *thud* spun him around.

The Savior made to stab the Lamaran again with a dirk, but Mitchern, just feet away, put an arrow through his neck.

Seeing the Lamaran beneath the dead Savior was gravely wounded, Christina hissed at him, "Stay down. Fake like you're dead."

She went to Alex.

Grabbing Alex by the shoulders, she dragged him up the steps into the tower, and Mitchern slammed the door shut, bolting it.

"Quick, go to the top," she told him. "Look to the Main Gate."

Searching for a back door, Christina came back to help Alex. "No way out."

The circular tower was old, probably an original fortification. Stout, the door nevertheless did not elicit confidence it could withstand a determined attack.

"Get this thing out of me," Alex said.

Christina examined the spear, buried deep. "You may bleed out if I do."

Alex looked at the stairs that wound around the wall going to the top. "No way can I get up there with it stuck in me. And we don't want to fight them here."

"Alon!" Mitchern called from above, through the door leading to the roof. "We've taken the gate. Timberkeep archers are there!"

"Can you get help?"

"I'm trying to touch with them, but there is so much confusion. Everything is a jumble."

"How many arrows do you have left?"

"Two."

"Is there a way down?"

Mitchern went away while Christina gripped the spear. Leaning forward, her resolute gaze held Alex's.

"Do it," he whispered and closed his eyes.

Careful to pull straight back, she eased the shaft out of sucking flesh with a constant determined pull.

"There's a bucket and line used to fill the cistern up here," Mitchern called, "We can use that."

"Not me," Alex breathed as Christina stuffed a poultice pouch in the wound.

"Go, Mitchern. Get help." Then, looking Alex in the eye, she said, "You're going to help me get you up those steps."

"Aye."

# Chapter 36
## Blocking Force Alpha

### The Citadel

"Clear a zone! Clear a zone!" Buzz Too squawked, swooping in and landing on Marisa's shoulder. "Clear a zone."

"Buzz!" she exclaimed, "You're not supposed to be here."

"Clear a zone. Chief wants a zone cleared."

"*Here?*"

"*Brawk,* one-man zone. Chief is coming down."

"Oh dear," she said. "That's not supposed to happen. Okay, Marines," she instructed the seven Marines of the command reserve, "form a circle. A big circle. Keep everyone out of it."

A recon bot circled around the zone, scanning the pavement and sending telemetry data to the *Tempest Dare*.

Even before the Marines had finished expanding the circle, Ivan materialized into existence. "Zone clear in--" he walked out of the circle. "Stay where you are," he instructed the Marines. "Zone clear."

Shifting just one or two humans allowed for a much faster cycle time.

Ready Reaction Agents Horalznick and Focun appeared. "Znick," Ivan said, "Bring down the healers and medics. No point in waiting."

"Ivan, Mother's Breath!?" Marisa exclaimed.

"The mission has been compromised. The ULUP observers are dead. One of them was a spy."

"What!"

"They killed each other. We'll talk later. Right now, Ogden's blocking force has got to move." He brought up a holo display from his multi-func showing the situation.

"Og!" Marisa called to where he was forming Blocking Force Alpha.

He came and peered at the holo display. Ivan pointed, "You see these red triangles moving through the prison and coming out there?"

"Oi."

"Those are pikemen. Go get them. Go through the Upper Gate, to the left of the chapel, and block there." Ivan pointed at the Areaum. "Secure the area, then push them back to the prison, and if you can, take the prison."

"Oi."

"And hurry, Og. That's the extraction zone where all those red triangles are."

Ogden was off, yelling for the force to follow him.

Rayamars, with all of Bravo Blocking Force on the ground, was hovering at Marisa's elbow.

"You," Ivan said to him, "take your force past the Upper Gate, sweep in skirmish order towards the barracks. Set up here," Ivan pointed at the space between the manse and the Milisterium HQ. "Watch your left flank until Og can secure the prison."

Rayamars ordered his force to move out.

"Those green triangles, are those us?" Marisa asked.

"Yes."

"Why are some of the triangles dark?" Dotted across the Citadel were a number of dark red and green triangles. In the Areaum, at the extraction zone, were the most of both colors.

"Dead. The pink and teal are wounded."

"Oh no."

Ivan peered at her, his eyes black against the torchlight. He just nodded.

Mears viewed the same display Ivan showed Marisa. He said to Hearter, "Christina's team got hammered." There was only one green and one teal triangle left amongst a swarm of red.

Lettern ran up to the Drakan guards at the Upper Gate; they were preoccupied watching the fight in the Areaum. "More reinforcements are coming. Let them through." Before they could stop her, she darted in the direction of the kitchens.

Meridia saw Lettern run through the gate unchallenged, so he followed hard and fast, the onorio on his heels.

A guard made to stop him, "Halt!"

Meridia jammed an armored elbow straight to the pikeman's jaw and shield-bashed the next. The Lamarans lay about the three guards, subduing them. "Upper Gate secure. Og can come through," he announced on the mission net.

Lettern was waiting for him at a corner of a kitchen. "There's a group by the tower beating on the door. Another over by the chapel. There's enough bodies out there."

Meridia moved back from the corner so he could show them the holo display. Two green dots, different shades, were inside the tower. A line of red was leaving the prison and marching directly toward him and Lettern. "Shiren." He called on the mission net, "Ivan, you with Og?"

Breathing hard, Ivan answered, "I'm catching up to him."

"There's a line of red gonna come right past the inside of the Upper Gate. Suggest you form up and take them on."

A moment later, "Affirmative."

There was a *crash,* and cracking noises came from the tower.

"They're getting in!" Lettern said, agitated. "I'm going!"

"Shiren—" Meridia cursed again.

Running hard, Lettern pulled her bow, notched an arrow, and paused long enough for a shot.

The pikeman smashing away the last pieces of the tower door took the arrow in the back.

Closer, Lettern shot again. The leather and scale armor no match for her tungsten-tipped arrows.

Closer, she shot again.

The pikemen, seeking their harasser, turned from the tower. They raised their shields, and charged. More pikemen, in loose groups of ones and twos, came from between Washentrufel Command and the chapel.

Lettern stood her ground, shooting arrows. One punched straight through a shield and hit a Drakan in the forehead. Another zipped beneath a shield and struck a knee.

While no news bots were allowed on Dianis, they did, however, use the holo displays on the hangar deck. The hologram slaved to recon bot focused on Lettern was mobbed by news bots. The data feed of her shooting arrows was A-waved across the Federation. The caption at the bottom of the feed read:

*Lettern Stouttree in action against Forushen captors.*

She shot again.

A pikeman was close enough to spear her, but she danced away, feigning a shot at his foot. When he dropped the shield, she shot him in the throat.

Meridia clashed with the next pikeman, and the onorio and his men formed a skirmish line.

The crack of a platoon rifle volley echoed from the Upper Gate, followed by another.

"Reload!" Ogden bellowed as only his barrel chest could. "First platoon rifles, first axemen, form a line here! Branch warden, take them to that building there." He pointed at the dark mass of the prison. "Form up outside. The rest of you, come with me!" In a double line, axemen in the lead, Ogden led the blocking force to the left of the chapel in a sweeping maneuver to clear the Areaum.

"Let's go!" Lettern raced for the tower.

# Chapter 37
## Sighten Tower

### The Citadel

They'd gone to the heart of their enemy, and they were undone.

Christina leaned over the rampart. The battle waged below and around her. Low scudding clouds came ashore, swirling around the grey, forbidding rock of the Citadel. Rifle fire, a strange sound on Dianis, came not from the Main Gate but to the east, at the Upper Gate.

"They're coming," gasped Alex.

Christina whirled, her great two-handed broadsword ready in her hands. She ran to the spiral steps that led into the depths of the keep. The jingle of harnesses, trod of heavy boots, and the grunts of men preceded the Drakans. Alex sat propped against the wall near the step's door. He was dying.

She waited. Braced at the head of the stairs, her shield slung across her back. Holding her sword in both hands, she'd defend the top step, and then when they forced her back around the corner, Alex would stab them from where he sat. They'd have to come at her single file.

A shadow preceded the first Drakan. He came up the steps at a run, shield at the ready, sword pumping up and down.

Christina saw him come. She backed two paces. The black anvil embossed on the green shield stayed her swing.

The soldier landed on the top step and gave her a concerned glance as he searched for an enemy. Though he didn't know her, he recognized her. "Need help?"

"Not here," was her grim reply.

Three Lamarans came behind him, followed by Lettern. "Dearest Mother, Alon," she gasped, "I was afraid we were too late," but then she saw Alex slumped against the wall, his life draining away on the flagstones. Amongst the carnage in the Areaum, she had seen the bodies of Christina's five mercenaries.

"They trapped us here," Christina said.

"Illy, quick, get one of your magic bandages." Lettern bent low over Alex and lifted his chainmail and then the bloodstained leather jerkin underneath.

Christina watched the soldier, clearly not a Timberkeep but carrying a strange Second Ward shield. He pulled out an alien-looking package from a hip pouch.

"I've got one left after this, Lettern, and I'm saving it for you." He stripped off a wrapper, tapped a pair of buttons and the device came to life, lights glowing. He positioned it over the wound and tapped the *Activate* button.

When the man stood, Christina saw he had brown eyes, the same as Lettern. "Who is this?"

He gave her the seasoned smile of a person wholly comfortable amidst mayhem, disaster, or victory.

"That's Illy," answered Lettern. "He's an Avarian."

Christina frowned, "Avarian?"

"Yeah, like Achelous and Outish. You know, Ancients. We've brought more of them with us." Lettern looked to Christina. "I work for them now, Alon. I'm IDB."

"By platoon! Fire!"

Rayamars was marching Bravo Blocking Force in an alternating line abreast past the armory on his left and the Lord General's Manse on his right. The barracks was fully alive and awake, pikemen running to and fro, some attempted mustering out front. His Riflemen had thirty rounds a piece.

"Hold fire!" They marched forward in silence. His ten Marines, as they had drilled, ran to take their place in front, screening the Riflemen behind.

Ogden led his half of Alpha past the east side of Washentrufel Command.

Agent Larech watched the dark figures. He could tell they were not Drakans, but in the black of night, with few torches, it was hard for him to pick out their nationality. He ran to the aviary, penned a message on a tiny scroll, plucked a pigeon from a cage, clasped the message to a leg, and tossed the bird into the dark sky. He penned another tiny missive, same message, and lofted its bird skyward. When he was out of birds, he made his way to the roof.

"Clear the zone!" Marisa ordered. "Place the markers." Her Marines pulled the dead and wounded from the zone and laid the red cloth strip around the perimeter. Torches on poles were driven between the flagstones at the edge. The entire scene, to the uninitiated, appeared like an arcane demon-worship ceremony.

Once cleared and measured by the recon bots, Horalznick signaled on the net, "Extraction zone clear. Placing the wounded." The Fleet corpsmen and Timberkeep healers who had come down in the temporary zone moved the three mercs, still alive from Christina's team, into the zone.

Decurion Uloch was woken by an on-duty Hoplite. "What time is it?"

"Half past the One Hour, sir." The Hoplite was at attention.

"A signal from the Citadel? What sort of signal?"

"A flag semaphore from the roof of Washen HQ."

Fully awake now, the new commander of the Third Hoplite Cohort of the First Hoplite Legion asked, "What flag?"

"Under attack, sir."

Uloch glared and leaned in close to the Hoplite's face, but the man was unflinching. "Yes, sir. Red banner, yellow dot. Under attack."

Uloch had seen the banner before. He knew what it meant. "Show me."

At the observer's post on the roof of the Hoplite barracks, the sentry swiveled the telescope in the Citadel's direction.

Looking through the glass, Uloch held it steady; sure enough, there was a man on the roof, between two torches, waving the giant *Under Attack* flag. Uloch grunted. "How did you know to look there?"

"Noises, sir. The city watch reported popping sounds coming from the mount."

"Popping, you say?"

"Yes, sir. A lot of popping. "

Uloch eased up from the telescope. "Check the aviary. Here and at Legion."

Below, in the officers' quarters, two of his centurions were awake, and one had half his armor on and buckled.

When Uloch looked at him, he stopped buckling. "I thought it was a good idea."

Uloch sniffed. "It is. If that fool up there is signaling a false alarm he will have a full cohort of angry Hoplites to contend with. So, snap to. All centuries are to muster immediately. As they are ready, they are to march to the Citadel drawbridge."

Having armored up with the cohort command baton in hand, Uloch made his way to the drawbridge. The command group, guidons, Halberdier octos, and message runners followed in his wake. A Hoplite messenger came running from Legion HQ, "There was a message there from the Citadel, sir."

Uloch stopped and opened the larger, transcribed version of the pigeon scroll that read:

*Washen Command Duty Officer, Larech, HQ Citadel.*
*Under attack from unknown force. They have taken the*
*Areaum. Fighting at barracks.*

"For the love of Thomas," Uloch swore. He knew Larech. The man was no fool. "At the double. Octo Herdiona, run to the bridge. Get it down, now."

Larech saw the stirring of torch lights in the distance, near the Hoplite barracks to whom he'd been frantically waving the flag. Exhausted from waving the heavy signal, he sat the staff in a holder and pinned the flag open, stretching it to the hangar pole. He ran downstairs. Someone had to open the Sally Port.

"Rider coming."

"I see him." Enderma, in command of the Main Gate Assault Force, watched the rider approach the gate but did not dismount.

"Ho! Main Gate, open up," the rider yelled.

As practiced, a branch warden of the Mearsbirch archers yelled down from the wall-walk. "Gate closes at dark. Opens at dawn."

"I'm the sergeant of the watch for the Fifth Light. Send the gate corporal to open the postern."

Without looking away but staying out of sight from the rider, Enderma told the Marine beside him, "Go down to the postern and amuse him. But do not open it."

Moments passed, and the rider, whose mount was fidgety, yelled up, "Well! Where's the corporal?"

"He's coming," Enderma yelled back. "He was on the shitter."

The Second Ward archers hiding below the parapet made jokes about Drakans using pinecones to wipe their arses.

"What is it?" growled the Marine, snapping open the eye slot.

"Open the door," ordered the sergeant.

"Under whose orders?"

"Mine."

"Not good enough." The eye slot snapped shut.

"Under penalty of a command inquisition, I order you to open the door."

The eye slot snapped open, and the eyeball made a point of looking all around. "You aren't no officer. Go away." The eye slot snapped closed again.

The rider glared at the door, then looked up at the wall. "Where's the sentries?"

An archer raised a hand above the parapet. "I'm here, I'm here."

The archer looked past his fellows to Enderma, who just shrugged. The dance was nearing its end, and the Drakans were stirring at the sound of gunfire.

Scrambling along the wall to where a dead sentry had lost their helm, the archer put it on and peeked above the wall. Pale as autumn wheat, it was plain the archer was not Nakish.

"Who are you!" demanded the sergeant. "Name and unit!"

"Hmm," pondered the archer. "My name is Fillibutt Farthead, and I am a—" he jumped up and drew his bow.

The sergeant's spooky eenu saved his life as the steed twisted when the archer released his Wedgewood arrow. The pair galloped into the night, but not before another arrow came their way.

"You hear that thud?" asked the Timberkeep next to him.

"Yup, I got him."

# Chapter 38
## Rejoined

*The Citadel*

Marisa rushed forward and hugged Christina, "Alon." She cupped the Defender's face in her hands and peered into the leaf-green eyes, overjoyed. She hugged her again. Blood and gore were splattered across the paladin's armor, sweat streaked her face, and her braided hair smelled acrid.

Christina held her back at arm's length. They'd not seen each other since the Battle of Wedgewood in Timber Hall. "You've changed."

Marisa laughed and hugged her again, letting her go. "You have not!"

For the first time, that long day that showed no end, Christina smiled.

"Wounded in the zone," Horalznick ordered.

Christina saw the Lamarans of Meridia's team carrying the stretcher bearing Alex.

Marisa turned to watch Ivan approach the stretcher. He clasped hands with the Defender.

"You've come," said Alex. "You *are* one of us."

Ivan harkened back to the day he'd first met Meridia and gave Alex and Lettern a lift in an assault lander. "I don't know that I'm one of you, but I *am* here to help."

At Horalznick's urging, the stretcher moved into the zone.

"And you are going on another ride." Ivan tilted his head upward.

"Sorry, Chief, I need to check the wound stabilizer," said a Fleet corpsman.

Ivan backed away.

A voice asked, "What about the Drakan wounded?" Corpsmen and healers were treating the wounded all alike.

Ivan said to Marisa, "Your call. Do we send them up as well?"

"Is it safe?" she asked, still not knowing what happened onboard the *Tempest Dare*.

"Yes."

She peered at him for a clue, but he was stone-faced. "Will the captain mind?"

He gave her an odd look she could not fathom. "If you asked him to send down a battalion of Avarian Marines, he would."

She started at that. "Well, then send all the wounded. Everyone."

"What happened?" asked Christina as they gathered Search Team Prime. Ivan was out of earshot.

"I don't know," answered Marisa. "But they didn't send Sedge down. Maybe they know." She pulled Meridia and Lettern aside. "Is Sedge coming or not?"

Lettern shook her head quickly. "I don't think so. The net has gone dark."

When Marisa gave a puzzled frown, Meridia tried to add more context. "There was an internal security breach. Ship security procedures immediately locked down all comms. The only net we have access to is Mission; even the IDB nets are locked out."

It was Marisa's turn to share. "When Ivan landed, he said the mission had been compromised and that a ULUP observer was a spy, and they killed each other. Just now, he volunteered to send down a battalion of you guys."

Meridia's eyes widened. "Assault Marines? That would be a slaughter. That can't happen."

"Don't worry, it won't happen. This is our planet. We may fight each other, but this is *our* struggle." She stopped, the irony not lost on her. "I appreciate your help, Avaria's help in finding Atch, but we need to draw the line." She glanced at the carbine slung on Lettern's shoulder. "That--"

Lettern knew to which Marisa spoke.

"--is pushing it. Let Ogden innovate himself. He's happier."

"Are we ready?" asked the onorio. The search team was gathered. Ogden and Rayamars had the Citadel garrison pinned to the barracks. When the Drakans made a move outside, they were rewarded with another casualty.

"Yes," answered Marisa. "You up for it, Alon? Fire Eye and Rachael are searching the marsh side."

With Alon's ascent, Marisa gave instructions to Meridia. "Og went through the prison already. Atch is not there. Start with the Washentrufel HQ, then the Paleowright Chapel. After that, the manse and Milisterium."

# Chapter 39
## Mears

*The Citadel*

"Damn. Why isn't their threat AI flagging them?"

Hearter waited while Mears manipulated the hologrid.

Mears zoomed in on a column of Drakan infantry marching to the Market Tower.

"Classify it," said Hearter.

Mears isolated the troop and read the threat AI's classification. *Light infantry. Scouting troops. No Threat.*

"Oh. Well, that's a problem," noted Hearter. "Flag it has *high threat* and reclassify for the *Tempest*."

Mears answered, "Can't. Security lockout in place."

"Go to Mission. Broadcast it."

"All units, all units, Drakan infantry force nearing Market Tower," Mears announced on the mission net. He shifted the grid display further west beyond the Market Tower. "Shiren." He went back on the net, "Drakans, battalion strength, entering Citadel sphere of interest. Vector is Main Gate."

Ivan heard the broadcast and listened to Buzz Too relay it to Marisa. "I'll have a corpsman run the extraction zone." He said to her and then to Focun, "Get to the Main Gate. We need comms."

On the mission net, Ivan heard Hearter calling, "*Tempest Dare,* your threat AI is non-functional. I repeat, non-functional. Additional Drakans approaching from the north. Six cohorts, Hoplites, threat level high. That's six hundred of their best, *Dare.* You need to get on the ball."

Captain Trich wheeled on the executive officer. "XO! What the hell!

"Checking," he answered.

The chief security officer, not the AI Avatar, came up on the ship net. "Cyber breach detected by Ops, all AI's are going down. Nope, they're down."

"Damn!" Trich smacked the console. He went on the Fleet net, "All ships, all ships, disconnect A-wave grids from the *Tempest Dare.*" He hated to give the order and never thought he would. "Laser comms only, data systems isolation. All ships run cyber security scans. *Trilonair,* are you operational?"

The captain of the Trilonair responded, "Affirmative. Running cyber scans. Systems isolation in effect."

"Take over ground control of the mission," Captain Trich ordered. "Ready your Field generator for mission extraction. All ships, if you have a Field generator, ramp it up for force extraction."

"Hangar deck has shifted the zone control to manual," reported the XO. "Our Field generator remains operational. Shall I order screening units to move from Overwatch to Aggressive Defense?"

"Yes," answered Trich.


Kicking open a door on the second floor of the Washentrufel HQ, Meridia said to Christina, his optic implant set to highlight human infrared, "They're having big problems upstairs. Someone hacked their systems."

Instead of asking him what *hacked* meant, he was caught off guard when she asked, "Do they know who?"

The room was empty. He looked at her. "Do they know *who?*"

A curt nod. "Your fleet should be secure from that. I still don't know what happened to ...."

Meridia went to the next room. "I know."

Larech met Uloch at the drawbridge. "The Sally Port was open. Someone let them in."

"How many?" asked the decurion. He was waiting for his first century: A hundred Hoplites, their pounding boots, double-timing, presaged their arrival.

"Hundreds."

If Uloch had thought he'd heard the impossible, Larech capped it for him: "The Ascalon, the woman Defender from Wedgewood, she's here." He omitted she saved him from grievous harm.

An eyebrow went up. "She's here? With hundreds?"

"Yes."

Uloch pursed his lips. "Then she'll fight us on *our* land this time." Previously, the two had squared off outside the walls of Wedgewood when Uloch had come to the relief of a Church battalion the Alon, with Lamaran mercenaries, had ambushed and forced to surrender.

"Drakan Hoplites nearing the drawbridge," Mears called on the net, not waiting for an update from the *Trilonair*. "They will cross the bridge in force and enter the Citadel via the Sally Port."

"Can he be certain of that?" asked *Trilonair's* captain.

On the map overlay, the sensors officer plotted the predicted path. "It's likely, sir."

Rachael ran to the top of Ages Castle. "Hey! Hey!" From atop the castle, she could see across the mount into the Areaum where the torches of the extraction zone highlighted Marisa with Ivan and the others. In the dark, she yelled, "Hey! Hey!"

They couldn't hear her.

Scowling, she glared at them. There was something green on Marisa's shoulder. Tiny in the distance, but Rachael knew what it was, and if she could see it....

"We need to do something about those Hoplites," Ivan said to Marisa. "Block them before they get up here."

*Brraawk!*

Buzz Too was yanked off her shoulder and streaked away in a ball of synthetic feathers.

Ivan, stunned, "That bot can't fly that fast."

Marisa gawked. "It wasn't flying."

*"Brraawk,"* Rachael caught the bot in her fist.

Rachael's teenage face, huge blue eyes, hair in a wild tumble, bloomed wall-size on the Adept Center's hologrid. "Listen here, bird brain," she spoke directly into the hologrid, and all the adepts gathered around the matriarch. "Tell Marisa we've found where Achelous is. We just have to get him out."

Looking into the camera, she pivoted, pointed an arm at the Areaum, and drew back. The hologrid view streaked when Rachael heaved the bot. *"Braaaaaaaaawk!"* It tumbled away in the night, the image on the hologrid blurred and whirled dizzily. The adepts in the center awestruck.

"Marsediminium," whispered Margret to the matriarch, having moved to sit beside her. "She was raised on it."

Buzz Too arrived back at Marisa, a frazzled mess of torn and missing feathers. She caught it as it dropped into her hands. *"Brawk,"* it croaked but delivered the message.

"Wahoo!" Marisa raised the bedraggled bird-bot and waved it like a trophy. "Wahoo!" she called to everyone. "They've found him!"

Tight-beaming to Meridia's personal audio implant, Mears said, "Rachael says they have found Achelous. She was atop the Ages Castle when she, uh, sent the message. Suggest you move to that location to establish comms and assist."

Ivan, ever focused on the issue at hand, pressed, "Lady, that is indeed good, no-- great news, but the Hoplites?"

"What? Oh." She sobered. "Who's left?" She cast about, but Ivan was grim. He'd already done a mental tally.

"Ivan, take charge."

Surprised, he'd expected her to pull troops from either Ogden, Rayamars, or both.

Misreading his body language, she said, "Don't worry, Ivan, I, as planetary representative, authorize it. Marines! To me." She started for Glory Hall and then, over her shoulder, "Get Atch back, Ivan. Send help if you can."

He frowned at her back. "Damn." She and seven Marines would not stop six hundred Hoplites.

"Damn," he cursed again. "Damn." He called up a tight beam to Clienen. "I'm going to tell Hearter to ready the twenty."

"The cannon?" asked Clienen.

"Affirmative. We'll need cover fire while we're extracting. Too many Drakans coming."

Clienen looked over to where Trich and the XO were dealing with their problem. "I have a better idea."

"Meridia, where you at?" asked Clienen.

He and the team were running through the Upper Gate.

Meridia came to a stop, listening to Director Hor. Then, "Lettern, take the onorio and find Rachael. Call back with a sitrep." Lettern tilted her head, confused. Then, to Alon, he said, "Marisa is leading seven Marines against six hundred Hoplites." He cracked a fatalistic grin, "Wanna help her?"

Of everyone on the mount that night, she, by far, had done the most fighting, and Meridia knew it.

Christina looked to Lettern. "By Mother's Life, bring Achelous back to us."

Lettern bowed to her. "By Mother's Life." Then she leapt into Meridia's arms and gave him a fierce kiss. Before he could respond, she was running away, tears forming.

"Wow," he said.

Christina gave him an appraising look. "I've asked if you were worthy of her. I have my answer."

Enderma listened to the Drakan commander's ultimatum: "Surrender the gate, and you will be spared. Those are our walls, not yours. Surrender them now or suffer your annihilation."

Enderma peered down at the neat, ordered ranks of Drakans, a battalion, and more.

"There's another mustering in the city," said Agent Focun.

Enderma snorted. "As if that isn't enough." He had thirty troops: Twenty archers and ten Marines.

"No ladders," noted the branch warden.

"Not yet," responded Enderma. "I'm sure they've figured that out."

Focun called on the IDB net Jeremy had restored sans the *Tempest Dare*, "Mears, keep a close watch on the approaches to the Main Gate. Ladders, grapples, wagons, anything they might use to scale the wall. If you see it coming, tell me."

"Roger," answered Mears.

Enderma called down to the waiting Drakan. "I like your keep. You can have it back at dawn."

The officer looked up at him. "You will surrender at dawn?"

"At dawn, you will find us gone. We will leave on the wings of Ancients just as we arrived."

Handbolt at the ready, Marisa led the way down, cautious, stopping to listen for noise from below. Half of the wall sconces had burned out. The others flickered at a low ebb, turning the stairway into a claustrophobic tunnel.

"There," a Marine above her on the steps whispered. "They're coming."

Another Marine, in a hiss, said, "They say Hoplites are the best."

"No," breathed Marisa. "Tivor Marines are. And the Drakans will learn that."

Crouching, she waited in the shadow of a dead lamp. The next two lamps down the steps still burned. She holstered her handbolt, comforting as Atch's weapon was. Holding her shield close, the House Marinda heraldic emblazoned on it, she drew and gripped her cutlass hard.

"Marisa's aura has gone off the grid," Margret said to the matriarch. The number of red triangles entering the tunnel's aura dead zone, compared to green, was breathtaking.

"The fork is coming," the matriarch said.

"It's already different," noted Margret. "Sedge did not die on the planet."

"That's because Kryzlictin extracted him from the mission. But, time-wise, there's only an hour difference between the foretelling and the real event."

Margret sensed the matriarch's sadness at knowing when a person would die, regardless of how the tragedy unfolded.

Ivan was getting nervous, and he hated it. He'd learned long ago to never worry about something beyond his control; to never worry, but act instead. "Znick get to Rayamars and Og. There's too much lag with the pathics. I need A-wave comms. Assess their situation. If you can, send some of them to Glory Hall."

# Chapter 40
## Ages Castle

*The Citadel*

Rachael encountered the body of the dead jailer. She realized it was one thing to kill a person but another to look into their lifeless, accusing eyes that said, *you did this*.

She backpedaled, then ran forward and leapt the corpse. "Ugh," she shuddered.

Timberkeeps burned their dead soon after they departed. Like they had done with her mother. The clan had lit her pyre the night she died of Timber's Curse. It was Mother's Blessing neither her father nor Lettern were sensitives. At least she'd never have to see them die that way. Like her mother, Rachael was kinetic. As she grew into her own skill, she suspected that her mother had hidden her true strength. Her mother never needed to unleash it.

Passing through two more open doors, Rachael came to where the Marines and Fire Eye waited. His tail was twitching erratically, left, right, up, and down. "They still in there?" she whispered.

"Aye," answered the lieutenant. "Haven't come out. Did you get word to the Lady?"

"Oi." Rachael tiptoed to the door and tried to see through the bars in the door, but she was too short.

Fire Eye seized her by the waist and lifted slowly.

Holding onto the edge of the bars, she peered into the room to the left, where a jailer sat with his back to her, snoring. A door on the opposite side of the chamber opened, and she pulled her head back.

"Ay, slacker. Thought you said Viscount Prigness was coming." The second jailer kicked the first's chair.

"Whaaat?"

"Where's Helprig? I want to start business. Coals are burning."

"Dunno."

"Ach. I should start without him."

"Don't do that. Get us both in trouble. Kill him too soon and no Ancient will save us."

"Ach."

"Do you see any bats?"

"Not today."

The second jailer went back through the opposite door. Rachael motioned for Fire Eye to put her down.

"If I could just see the bar," she whispered in his ear, "I could raise it."

The door's cross-bar was on the inside.

"A mirror?" she asked the lieutenant. "I need a mirror." He shook his head. They'd discussed the problem. They could hack their way through the door, but it would take forever with just swords, and in the meantime, the jailers could either kill the prisoner or run out a back way, if there was one, and get help.

Fire Eye drew a scimitar, apparently examining the edge. Then he reached for a Marine's cutlass.

"Ay," hissed the Marine.

The prince eyed the blade critically. Rachael's eyes widened. She nodded profusely.

Marines were famous for polishing their weapons.

Fire Eye handed her the cutlass and lifted her to the window.

Daring the jailer to turn and look, she slid the cutlass between the bars. With her tongue sticking out of her mouth, wiggling back and forth, she angled the sheen on the blade to reflect the locking mechanism. Her tongue quit wiggling, her body braced spring tight as she angled the blade just right.

There was a moment of perfect tension, and then a *thunk-thunk* sounded from beyond the window.

The jailer stood, saw the locking bar on the floor, the cutlass at the window, and Rachael's big blue eyes staring at him. "Hey!"

Fire Eye tossed her at the nearest Marine and shouldered the door open. Claws raked the man across the left of his face, and the other hand got the right. Not waiting, Fire Eye yanked open the opposite door.

Both scimitars out, he advanced on the second jailer.

Turning the yard-long poker in the brazier's coals, expecting to see Helprig or a Scarlet Savior, the torturer casually looked up.

"Wha? You're not a churchman?" he said.

Glancing left and right, slurping the air, Fire Eye resumed his stalk.

Holding the broiling rod at the ready, the jailer took a long look at the Lizardman and thought better of it. Flinging the poker, its yellow-hot tip twirling in the air, he ran.

Fire Eye parried the instrument in flight and watched the torturer run to a door at the far end of the cell block. Sheathing a scimitar, the prince pulled a javelin and flung it straight away.

The man fell hard on the stone floor, rolling in a tumbled heap. "Wow," said Rachael from the door. "You're good."

He gave her a baleful stare.

Proceeding from cell to cell, Fire Eye crouched on all fours, his tongue flickering. The scene gave Rachael the willies. There were no reptiles in Wedgewood, but here, in the castle dungeon, there was a *big one,* hunting about like a badger.

Rusting jail cells lined both sides of the crypt, and the torture chamber occupied the center. Torches burned on the walls black with soot, mold, and lichen. The whole place made Rachael shudder; the horror appalling. She tried not to think of what happened here.

While the prince checked for scent in the cells nearest the jailer's holding room, Rachael and the Marines spread out, looking for clues. Near the body of the torturer, the cells stopped and were replaced by evenly spaced iron grates in the floor, three on each side of the chamber. Four of the iron grates were pulled aside, exposing a square hole in the floor.

She shivered. Creeping up to one, she got on her hands and knees and peeked over the rim. It was a black hole. She could smell ..., "What is that?" she asked herself.

"Sea air."

"Ai!" she leaped back, "Oola, you scared me!" she exclaimed at the Marine behind her.

"Oh, sorry." Then he pointed, "You see that winch and the rail?"

There was a rusting iron rail pinioned into the stone ceiling that ran above the three grates on the other side. From it hung a rope winch and a dolly that rolled along the length of rail.

"Yeah?"

"The one for this side is broken. That one looks like it still works."

"Huh," Rachael offered intelligently. Mechanical apparatus were not her thing.

"My guess is," the Marine offered, "the winch is for lowering and raising prisoners out of the pits."

"Pits?" Her eyes were huge, eyebrows high. "They put *people* in them?"

The Marine gave a solemn nod.

Fire Eye had made his way back and was slurping about the grates on that side.

"Oh dear!" she gasped. Standing up and running to the first of the grates covering a pit, she squinted into the gloom beneath it. "Damn." She tried pulling the grate free, but it wouldn't budge.

"Get back," said the Marine. He grabbed the lift rings for the grate and heaved. It slid off the hole, and he dragged it clear.

"How deep is it?" asked a Marine, peering into the pit Rachael came from.

"Your guess," said another. "Here," he retrieved a torch from the wall.

Waving it over the hole, the Marine said, "Can't see nothing."

"Drop it in," said Rachael. She watched.

"What is that?" asked a Marine peering into the hole. The torch had landed at the bottom of the pit. "Cave in?"

"Could be," said the other. "Something moving down there, though. Rats?"

"Mother, no," hissed Rachael. "Give me a torch."

The Marine fetched her one, and they went to the last grate covering a pit. He pulled the grate clear.

Holding the torch over the center of the hole. She squinted. *What is that?* She dropped the torch.

A face appeared, staring up at her. The torch landed in the man's lap, sitting against the pit wall. His voice croaked, "Don't do that."

Something came streaking up at her, and she screamed, "*Aiii!*"

Falling back, she rolled away from the hole.

"Arg, bats!" hollered a Marine. They backed away. Suddenly, from the hole with the cave-in, bats, clouds of them, exploded out of the depths.

Rachael rolled over, covering her face with her arm, and peeked. To her horror, a mass of bats swirled, circling like agitated hornets.

Lettern stopped. Her sisters' scream unmistakable. She slung her bow and checked the safety on the carbine. When she started running down the steps, caution to the wind, the onorio didn't need an explanation. A recon bot hummed right behind.

Vaulting the stairs, they came to a prone figure. Lettern ran past without comment. They could hear yelling, the sounds of hysteria. Coming to the door Rachael had unbarred, Lettern stepped into the room. Another figure lay there, again, not one of theirs. Lettern approached a half-open door from where the yelling issued and a strange flapping, fluttering noise. She brought her carbine up and flicked the safety off. A nod to the onorio, and he pushed the portal fully open.

Stepping in, Lettern tried to make sense of what she was seeing.

A warm-blooded human opening the door and standing outlined there was a *Come Get Me* invitation to the swarm. As one, they coalesced into a huge amorphous fist and flew straight for Lettern.

"Mother—" Lettern ducked back into the room, "Shut it! Shut it!"

The onorio heaved the door closed. *Eeek, eeek.* A bat was caught in the crack, and the door buffeted by furry bodies and flapping wings.

Lettern backed away and aimed. *Bang!*

The bat's torso exploded in red spray.

Sealing the door, the onorio said, shaking his head, "Oola, that's loud!"

"Vringis Bats," Jeremy announced on the IDB net. "Extreme health risk to humans. Proceed with caution."

"Ya *think!*" Lettern snapped.

When the onorio looked confused, she tapped her ear, the signal for A-wave communications.

"Can we get them some help?" Hearter asked.

Mears slid a finger across the grid, picked Drone Package Three, and tapped release. "Take it, Jeremy."

A large, non-stealth surveillance drone tipped downward from its patrol pattern over the Citadel and plummeted straight at Ages Castle. "No sentient beings involved," offered Mears. "We can use these."

Amazed, Rachael watched Fire Eye stand above her, his twin scimitars whirling in a rhythmic pattern. Apparently, reptiles were not tasty to bats. When a bat came to feed on her, he moved an arm and blade and shooed the bat off. The more persistent threats *eeked* and splashed crimson when hit.

She looked to her left. A Marine was down. They were all either huddled, trying to protect exposed skin, or unconscious. The Marine nearest her lay face up, Fed on by a dozen bats.

"Ugh," she reached a hand out, and though yards away, three bats were swiped off the Marine. "Ugh." She swiped again. They kept coming back. "Ugh!" She netted a half dozen and flung her arm, smashing them into the wall. They hit with a satisfying *eek, eek,* leaving red spots on the wall. "Ooh."

Rachael sat up, careful to stay in between Fire Eye's flickering scimitars. Aiming a grasping hand at the furry mass on the Marine, the bulk of them lifted off and cartwheeled against the wall.

A gleam of vengeance came to her.

"Package in-bound," announced Jeremy.

The drone pulled up at the last moment, dive-bombing the entrance to the castle. Four defense pods were released, and fourty defense bots, under Jeremy's control, buzzed down the steps.

"But there might be hundreds of them," Hearter said.

"The Mk Two's injectors have been calibrated for the size and mass of the bats," answered Jeremy. "I project the injector reservoir has enough venom for five bats."

"Ready, Lettern?" called Mears, "They're coming—open the door!"

The onorio flung the open door, and Lettern entered, swinging her bow. She swept it left and right, snapping her wrist. When the scything arc caught a bat there was a hard thump and an "*Eek*".

The Mk Two Dragonflies entered the fray.

At first, the unsuspecting bats ignored the dragonflies as they were not natural enemies. Vringis Bats were vampires, not flying insect feeders.

Brown, flapping fur balls began to fall. A Mk Two followed the zigging flight of a target, latched onto the heavy host, jabbed its Probuteral injector, detached, and searched for a new target.

"Go to a Marine who's being mobbed," Mears suggested to Lettern. "The bots are centered on you."

She was going to ask which one, but it didn't matter. Some of the Marines were able to huddle, head down on the floor, and fend off the fangs, their armor affording areas of protection.

Coming to a Marine in dire straits, Lettern's bow *whack, whack, and smacked* them from his body.

"Stand clear," Jeremy instructed.

"No!" Lettern yelled. "Get the ones in the air! I'll get these." *Whack, whack, smack.*

Rachael could feel her strength fading, her head hurt. The bats were scattered, piles of their bodies heaped along the nearby walls. She stood back in a corner, resting. Fire Eye had ceased his whirling action and, instead, guarding Rachael in the corner, took careful aim when a bat came near.

Darting, diving, buzzing, flapping, stabbing, and biting, the aerial dogfight quickly evolved, with the bats fighting back.

Lettern and the onorio dragged the unconscious Marines to the jailer's room and urged the others to get up and follow.

Rachael watched the battle unfold. Bats continued to fall, but so did bots when a bat snagged their wings and bit off their heads.

Mears watched the *Defense Bot Deployed* count drop from fourty to ten.

Suddenly, the assault was over as quickly as it started. The remaining bats gathered in a mass and plunged back down the cave-in pit.

"Quick!" Rachael said to Fire Eye, "Block the hole."

They slid a metal grate over the pit and then used rotting blankets and even the dead torturer's body to cover the grate.

Lettern came to her kid-sister, seized Rachael's face in her hands, looked closely for harm, and then hugged her fiercely. "Da would have my skin if anything happened to you."

Rachael sniffed, her nose running, and nodded. "We found him." She pulled an arm free of Lettern's hug and pointed at the hole. "He's in there. Alive."

Lettern reluctantly let her go and rushed to the hole. Crouching, hands on the edge, she peered down.

A face looked up at her. The man was holding a torch. "Achelous?"

"Yes. You woke the bats."

"Uh? Not me! They were feisty when I got here."

Looking up from the bottom of the pit, Achelous saw Rachael's face appear at the rim. "Hi, Atch." She waved.

For the first time since his abduction, his face unaccustomed to it, he smiled. "Hi, Rachael."

# Chapter 41
## Assault

*The Citadel*

"They're not waiting for dawn."

"No," observed Enderma.

Three groups of Drakans came running from the darkness bearing ladders and torches.

The branch warden stood back from the crenelation. "Archers! Ready." He watched Enderma for the signal.

He raised his hand and dropped it.

"Loose!" The branch warden yelled.

As one, the twenty archers rose and fired. The ten Marines waited out of sight to repel the ladders. Across the parade grounds, a thousand Drakans had mustered. They were not doing the skip-skip step.

"It's good they only have three ladders," Hearter grunted.

Mears repositioned the holo display and zoomed the drone's camera at the lane approaching the Market Tower. "Lots more coming."

Marisa parried the spear. She had the height advantage, but the Hoplite had the reach: His spear thrice as long as her cutlass. Two abreast, Marisa and her Marines were backing up the steps in starts and stops. Three Marines had already been pulled back, blood splattering the steps, to be replaced by their fellows.

She swiped, caught a spear on her shield, and the Marine beside her hacked it viciously with his cutlass. When they were able to break a spear, it was quickly replaced. The space on the tunnel steps tight. Her new shield had been one of Ivan's *gifts*. She'd discovered her set of unique women's armor in the kitchen armory in the Hall. Elliot claimed ignorance as to how it got there or why it fit her so well. The titanium alloy, unknown to Dianis, was resilient and light.

A spear point etched a line up the top of her shield and came over. Another angled for her guts. Again, a Marine hacked the spear, and it snapped. The Hoplites wanted her and made a goal of it while her Marines were equally determined to defend her.

Up two more steps they went.

"Marisa!" Meridia called from the top of the stairs. "Get out of there! We'll hold them up here."

"Ready?" she asked the Marine. "On my command—"

From behind, a body shoved them aside, and a two-handed bastard sword swept down in a massive arc, smashing a Hoplite shield, knocking his spear loose, and sparked on the steps. The adjacent Drakan made to recover, and Christina kicked hard and hacked down. "Go!" she said and turned, shoving them both up the stairs.

Meridia waited with his Lamarans arrayed in an arc outside the door at the top of the stairs. As Marisa's Marines came out, he added them to the arc. Finally, Marisa and Christina emerged.

"They're coming," Marisa gasped, gulping down air.

"Shut and bar the door," Meridia ordered.

As the second locking bar fell into place, something hit the other side, thudding into it.

Meridia looked Marisa over.

She limped, exhausted, smeared ichor and rivulets of sweat streaked her face, but she was unbowed.

"Having fun?" he asked in all seriousness.

She tossed her head. "They're not pirates. They don't run."

"They found Atch."

She waited.

"Alive and kicking."

Her relief total, she put an arm on his shoulder and threatened to sag.

He held her up. "We have a problem. They managed to get him and the wounded Marines to the top of Ages Castle and shifted out. But the *Tempest Dare* has been sabotaged."

She regained her footing. "Sabotaged?"

More thudding hammered the door.

"They'll get a battering ram," Christina said. The thudding was replaced by a metallic hacking sound.

"Yeah," said Meridia. "They think one of the ULUP observers seeded a virus into a ship's terminal. All the AIs are down, and the Field generator is being run in manual. That's how they got Atch off the roof of the Castle. But cycle time is way down. Something's wrong with the *Tempest's* power generation. Fleet is scrambling to send reinforcements. All the screening units are on high alert." Meridia held up a hand, "Wait," he said, tapping his ear. "Roger. Moving to the entrance." He looked to Christina. "Ivan needs us to fall back to the entrance of the building. We'll hold them from outside."

Horalznick waited.

Rayamars fired. *Bang!* "They're getting cheeky. Don't mind taking casualties."

"We're falling back. Mission accomplished. You're to hold the Upper Gate." Horalznick went to deliver a similar message to Ogden.

Focun kept his carbine slung, but had his bow ready. Ostensibly, he was there for emergency communications only, but he found it hard to stay out of the fight. A Drakan managed to crawl through a crenelation and made to stab a Marine in the back. Considering it a threat to himself, Focun's IDB arrow pierced the Drakan in the back. Another appeared in the same slot, and Focun waited, holding the bow steady. The man showed more of his torso, and Focun loosed.

"Focun, pull them back. We're falling back. Form up at Battery A." It was Ivan's voice on the mission net.

"Roger. Main Gate Garrison moving to Battery A," he replied. "Enderma! We're going! To the rope ladders!"

Another Drakan appeared in the slot. Focun notched, drew, aimed for the head, and loosed.

"Back! Back" Enderma ordered, and the call was echoed along the wall. Scaling ladders were everywhere. He ran down the wall steps behind Focun. "And no bloody too soon either. Marisa is calling it close!"

"No," Focun said, running for a rope ladder that hung down from the Areaum wall and the Sighten Tower beyond. "Marisa was in the tunnels fighting Hoplites." He started climbing. "Six hundred of them. She's falling back, too."

"Aye." Enderma grabbed a wrung. "That be the Lady's style, pick a fight with the best."

Ogden formed his twenty Riflemen in a line facing Glory Hall. In between each rifleman was a Marine or an axeman.

"How many rounds you got left?" Meridia asked.

"Five, Ten," Og scratched his beard, his cheek blackened with pan smoke. "Depends."

Meridia saw a patch of beard singed from backfire. "It get hot?"

"Oi. Them bastard Halberdiers would not give up. Rifles or no."

Marisa found Ivan by torchlight at the extraction zone. "Meridia says we have a problem."

"Yes, sort of. Group size and cycle time for the Field gen on the *Tempest* is way down."

"To what?"

"Five and three. Trich and team are trying to debug, but the ULUP commissioner from Tochman Lower Five screwed them good."

She didn't know what *Tochman Lower Five* was, but she did know shift group sizes. "Five? Five people only?"

"Yes. Every three minutes."

"Oh, Ivan." Her brows knit, the worry plain. "There's a hundred and—"

"Thirty-seven of us." He finished. "Yes, I know."

She searched his face. "We'll be out of ammo." But somehow Ivan didn't appear as concerned as she expected.

She'd worked with him enough to sense he had a plan. "How?"

He pointed up with his thumb, not looking up himself.

She peered into the night sky. There, burning yellow, was a string of seven glowing orbs, growing larger as she watched. It made an impressive sight. She could only imagine the fear of what it was like to be on the receiving end-- not the rescuing end of the impending assault.

"They don't need an AI," Ivan said as she stared upward. "Those pilots are real space jocks. They live for this. They probably turn off their AIs anyway."

A lone rifle shot came from Glory Hall.

"In order! Right to left!" Ogden's voice boomed.

One of the bronze double doors was pushed fully open, and two more rifles fired. Then more, and Hoplites fell.

Marisa moved to get a better view. "Oh, Ivan, we need to stop this."

"Tell *them*," he answered.

So she decided to do just that. "White! White! Give me something white. I need a white flag!" She ran at Ogden's line.

Someone shoved a white linen at her, and she tied it to her cutlass. "Hold fire! Hold fire!" A recon bot hovered just behind her.

"The fork is nearly here," Margret whispered. "Is it going to happen?"

The matriarch braced herself. "Soon." Fate forks were notoriously fickle. Mankind's arrogance in assuming it could manipulate the cosmic force a folly.

Marisa waved her cutlass and approached the steps of Glory Hall, the Drakan Empire's shrine to victory, and yet, there, at its doors, were a pile of its dead and wounded.

"Parlay." She waved the cutlass. "Parlay."

She waited.

"Drakans approaching the Upper Bailey," Horalznick reported on the mission net. "Permission to open fire."

To Marisa's profound pain, Ivan answered, "Granted."

She could only be in one place at a time.

Uloch, carrying a decurion's baton, strode forth from the hall.

She saw him survey his dead and the line of Riflemen. Gun smoke lingered in the air, acrid. He came down the steps. They met, each sizing up the other. The rumble from overhead caused him to look skyward.

She noted the awareness of assault landers dawning in his gaze.

Returning his attention to her, he shifted right to get a better view of the warrior who had come up behind.

Jutting his chin upward, toward the sky, he said, "You've come for the Ancient."

"We have," answered Marisa. "He's with us now. In the stars. And we are leaving."

He glared at her. "Ancients or no. This is not your place."

She pursed her lips. "I know."

He made a hand motion, and Hoplites came out to retrieve the dead and wounded.

Looking to Christina, he said, "Do you remember me?"

"I do," she answered.

"Then you know, Ancient magic or not, I will sweep you from this mount like dust before a broom."

"Ranger One to Mission Ground. Ranger One coming in hot. Flaring in ten seconds. Clear the landing zone."

Ivan responded to Ranger One's announcement, "Clear the area! Clear the area!"

Neither Marisa nor Christina turned at the commotion but continued to focus on Uloch.

"We are going," Marisa said. "Achelous, the father of my son, is an Ancient, and he is home. To there we go." She turned her back on him, took Christina's hand, and walked away.

Ranger One hit maximum thrust on its six landing thrusters. Flame blasted across Areaum paving stones. As the Marine assault lander touched, the rear ramp lowered, Four fully armored -- energy and kinetic -- Marines exited and formed a perimeter. The lander's guns pointed straight at Glory Hall.

"First twenty! In!" Ivan ordered.

Two Assault Marines took the place of Ogden's Riflemen.

Unflinching, Decurion Uloch stared them down.

A second assault lander flared and hovered a man's height off the ground, facing the Drakan battalion marching up the Upper Bailey. Their march turned into a stalled body of awe.

"Fork is almost--," Margret hissed. She was sitting close beside the matriarch, holding her hand.

"Now, you fools. Before she gets away. Get them both!"

Helprig turned from the stained glass window in the chapel. "Go! Or the Ancients themselves will roast your hearts!"

Irons stared at Helprig. Their ends were at hand. He would die, but that was his cause, to serve the Church.

They hefted their spears, holding their shields tight, and waited for the sea witch and daughter of Mother Spawn to walk past the chapel.

Ranger One lifted in a blast of flames, tilted upwards, and the pilot mashed the throttles.

As Ranger Two, circling the mount with Three through Six, came to land, Marisa and Christina backed away from the landing zone. In the glaring heat and light of hydrogen drives, three Scarlet Saviors emerged from the Paleowright Chapel.

"Fork," called Margret.

The matriarch jerked.

Irons threw his spear.

Christina spied them in the glaring, flickering shadows and arched her back just enough, but Marisa— the spear veered strangely skyward.

The second and third Saviors threw their spears, their aim true.

Christina's shield was on her shoulder. She was moving but too slow. The spear hit an invisible wall scant inches in front of her.

The third spear's aim unerring, Marisa saw the point coming, her head facing it, and in that instant, the fork closed. The spear deflected at a ninety-degree angle.

Rachael, at the Upper Gate, slumped to the cobbles like a rag doll.

Irons drew his rachier, and the three Saviors charged.

Lettern, running all the way from the Upper Gate, yelled, "Alon, get down!" Christina heaved herself at Marisa, and the pair landed on the flagstones.

"Stop!" Lettern commanded.

Irons kept charging.

Lettern raised her rifle, lowered her aim, and *Bang!*

The bullet zipped over Christina's back.

Irons stumbled, dropping his rachier, shot in the leg.

Ratcheting another round in the chamber, "Stop!" Lettern commanded.

The second Savior, driven by long-preached dogma, kept coming.

*Bang!*

Uloch saw it all.

*Cla-junk,* another round rammed into the chamber, and the third Savior swiveled into Lettern's sights. He came to a stop.

"Get back!" she ordered and fired a shot that whizzed past his ear.

He back pedaled in a hurry.

Irons, kneeling, regained his rachier and struggled to rise.

Christina approached him and sheathed her sword. "Stay down, captain. This fight is over."

Standing, he limped towards her.

Lettern moved to get a better shot.

Christina didn't budge. "The Ancients have come tonight, Captain." They eyed each other. "Sheath your weapon. Reflect on what you have seen. The Church is *not* what they would have you believe."

"We're the last," Ivan said to Marisa.

The landing zone was surrounded by hundreds of Drakans. They stood just beyond the flaring heat of the lift thrusters.

The crew chief of the lander waited. Two Assault Marines crouched between them and the Drakans.

"It's a sad night, Ivan."

"How so, Lady?"

"Too many died for Church glory. Wait for me." She walked into the dark.

Uloch watched her come, surrounded by his elite.

"We have your wounded," she said. "Tomorrow, noon. Clear the parade grounds. We will return them to you."

He didn't speak. He didn't have to. She could see the hatred in his eyes.

She left him and the Citadel that night, and the Drakan Empire, forever changed.

# Chapter 42
## Sick Bay

*Tempest Dare, Dianis Orbit*

The rumble was deafening; every fiber of her body shook, crushed into the crash-seat webbing. The lander's blast from the planet relentless.

Marisa tried to reach a hand across the padded armrest to Ivan, strapped in beside her. With a grotesque curl of her lips, she groaned, "Is this normal?"

"Yes-s," he stuttered back.

Slowly at first, then more swiftly, the noise, the shaking, and the oppressive force on her chest abated.

In the new, relative calm, Ivan said, "These assault pilots only know one speed, full. Since we don't have any wounded on board, they're burning gas. Usually, the inertial dampeners work better, but we're not in adaptive armor. If the dampeners hadn't been working at all, our guts would liquefy and spew out all our holes."

She gave a nasty grimace and looked away. Dispelling the imagery, she asked,

"What are inertial dampers?"

He smirked. "Yeah, sorry. Those are the things that cancel the gravity we felt from the thrust of the engines."

"Ah."

Christina sat, strapped in, on a crash couch on the opposite bulkhead.

Marisa took solace from the Alon's apparent discomfort, though she wasn't complaining about it.

Ivan pointedly studied Marisa's armor, specifically the sword-shoulder pauldron.

"What?" Marisa asked.

"You've battle-tested your armor." There were three hard divots in the titanium and gouges where the dark grey annealing had been scraped clean.

"Ah. Hoplites. They were good. Damn good. They were after me. Thought because I was a woman I'd be easy prey."

He nodded solemnly.

"Who do I have to thank for it? The armor. those spear thrusts were sharp."

"Anna Lexa, our in-country armorer. When she heard the provincial representative to the Avarian Federation was going to battle, she offered to make a set for you."

"How did she get it to fit so well?"

"She retrieved your measurements from the shift system. Every body is precisely scanned and measured before a shift."

Marisa raised her chin in understanding while Christina watched them from across the aisle.

"Do you know what they call you, those Hoplites?" asked Ivan.

She shook her head.

"Jeremy overheard them by recon bot as you were negotiating with Uloch outside of Glory Hall. They call you the Iron Witch."

Marisa grimaced, then shook her head.

"That was a brave thing you did, leading seven Marines down those steps."

She kept her grimace.

"What's that?" Ivan pointed to his ear and held his hand up. "Oh?" Pause. "What's it about?" Pause. The interlude lengthened. "I see. Roger. I'll let them know."

The assault lander was in the vacuum of space, making its return approach, at boost, to the *Tempest Dare*.

"Clienen and Captain Trich want to speak with you as soon as we dock." Then he said, across the aisle to Christina, "Meridia and Lettern will escort you to sick bay so you can see Alex."

Christina assented, but didn't ask any questions.

*Odd,* thought Marisa. Christina had not been part of the rescue force shifted onto the carrier.

Ivan studied Christina openly, frankly.

She returned the study unfettered.

"When will I get to see Atch?" Marisa asked.

"Ah," answered Ivan, as if the whole point of their mission was mundane and relegated to history. "Let me ask."

She listened to him converse, one-sided, with someone who seemed in charge.

"He's been shifted down to the Central Station medical bay. We'll send you down there as well."

"Central Station? What is his condition? You have doctors there? Why not treat him here?"

Ivan held up his hand before she could ask more. "Hold on. One question at a time. First, Atch is still officially an IDB chief inspector. Central Station is his home."

Marisa took issue with that, but bit her tongue. Tivor, Marinda Hall was Atch's home.

"An IDB chief surgeon has been assigned to the Margel, and he's onboard the *Tempest*. He cleared Atch for transfer dirtside. It spares a bed on the *Tempest* for more provincials. You'll be speaking with the chief surgeon as well."

There were no windows in the assault lander, so Marisa had to rely on Ivan's narrative as to the bumps, jerks, and groans the boat made during the docking process in the *Tempest's* hangar bay. Eventually, air hissed around the rear boarding ramp as it cracked open and lowered. The occupants unbuckled their restraints, and there, at the end of the ramp, were Meridia and Lettern, along with Major Vuulanin and two Marines in full armor. Marisa's walk down the ramp stopped. Her hand went to Christina's. Meridia and Lettern were both carrying Marine assault plasma rifles. Lettern's face was grim, but Meridia gave a thumbs up. "We got this. Alon, let's go see Alex."

Christina arched an eyebrow at Marisa, but gently pulled her hand free. "I'll be fine."

"Lettern? What's up?" asked Marisa.

Lettern pulled her plasma close and checked the charge indicator. "As IDB CivMon, Alon is in my care. *Nothing* is gonna happen to her."

Meridia shrugged. "The director gave the order. Lettern's in charge of Alon's escort. That would be us."

Christina walked down the ramp. "Then take me to Alex."

When Vuulanin and his charges had departed, Ivan walked Marisa to where Director Hor and Captain Trich observed the disembarkation.

"That was dramatic," Marisa said to the pair of officers. "Lettern packing a plasma on board your ship, captain?"

Trich grimaced and said, "Follow me."

They trailed behind the captain in silence, all the way to his cabin. On the way, Marisa noticed how the crew members they encountered gave Trich a wide berth. It was not a happy ship.

Inside his cabin, with two Marine guards posted outside, Trich inclined his head to Clienen.

"Lady--," he hesitated, "so much has happened." He chose an oblique course, "We have Christina's welfare close to our hearts. I have, therefore, classified a drone feed from the *Trilonair* as IDB Ultra Secret."

Ivan blinked, searching Clienen for import.

Clienen said to him, "The classification was approved by the executive director."

Ivan's countenance didn't change.

"And I've ordered," said Trich, "all copies of the drone feed wiped on the *Trilonair,* here on the *Tempest,* and the executive director did the same for the *Shields*. One copy was sent to fleet HQ for high-security archiving."

Marisa and Ivan both shared a confused look.

Clienen explained. "The *Trilonair* had a surveillance drone following Christina's party as they made their way from Pred to Stith Drakas. En route, they stopped at a heretofore unknown Loch Norim site, where the Alon entered the site, actuated unknown controls, and then led her entire party down into the facility, where they disappeared off all scans. They remained there for an entire day, from which they then emerged and continued with their mission."

Marisa swallowed. "Okay. So, you know there is a new Loch Norim site, and it is functional."

Ivan glanced at her. She caught the drift of what he was implying: Being disingenuous and ignoring Christina's role in the event.

"Okay," she braced herself. "The Alon is a Loch Norim."

"She is either a Loch Norim, or she knows the ways of the Loch Norim," stated Trich. "The result is the same."

Clienen came to the point. "Sedge is dead. He was murdered."

Marisa went pale, mouth open.

Ivan took an arm and settled her in a chair.

Trich said, "He was assassinated. On my ship. By a ULUP commissioner who killed two other commissioners and sabotaged this ship by seeding an AI virus into our core terminal system. We are still eighty percent disabled. Disabled! An Avarian Assault Carrier disabled! We are a massive piece of space debris."

Marisa didn't give one twit for Trich's ship, but she did for Sedge.

"He was killed for what he knew," said Clienen.

She moved her mouth, but no words came. So many dead, and now Sedge. Her hands moved to her face, and tears rolled between her fingers.

They gave her space.

Ivan cocked his head, a realization coming to him. "Who?"

"Everyone is working on it," Clienen elaborated. "The Matrincy, Fleet, Internal Security. It has something to do with an obscure threat called Nemesis, or Tochman Lower Five Outer, or something between the two. Whoever killed Sedge didn't want their secret known."

"Does Lettern know? And Ogden?" Marisa asked.

"Yes. And they will have told Christina by now." Clienen watched her, ready to call for medical aid. She'd not been treated for any injuries she may have.

"Lady, I don't mean to be insensitive to your grievance, to the loss of a man so clearly honored and respected," Trich apologized. "But consider this: The knowledge of our systems and the planning and audacity our enemy has perpetrated in the execution of this plot. The timing--" Trich shook his head grimly. "Not only did they want Sedge dead, but they killed your mission commander just before he was to shift planet-side. *And* they completely disabled the primary support platform for the mission: Our newest assault carrier. This was no simple, one-man operation."

"The Tochman Lower Five commissioner," added Clienen, "knew he was on a suicide mission. That he would never get off the ship. He was a zealot. Whoever he worked for are ...."

Trich nodded. "Willing to die to keep their secret. In the middle of all the unknowns, that's what worries me the most. What secret are they protecting?"

He had Marisa's attention. "What is Tochman Lower, whatever," she tossed her hand angrily, "and what is Nemesis?"

Clienen and Trich shared a glance, uncertain who should explain.

Finally, Clienen said, "Tochman is a star system thirty light years from here, which is a long way beyond Federation space. And Nemesis-- that's a myth, or so we thought until a Marine armor cam recorded an audio feed through a compartment door. In his final moments, the Lower Five commissioner clearly says *Nemesis.*"

She shook her head. "What is the myth?"

"The demise of the Loch Norim," finished Trich.

"And that's about all we know," said Clienen.

Marisa couldn't tell if they were being truthful or evasive. "So, you are afraid for Christina?"

Trich gave her a tight-lipped grimace. "We can't protect her dirtside, and I don't know if a woman like her would consign herself to our custody, not after what happened to Sedge."

"As of now, anonymity is her best protection," offered Clienen. "We did have plans to sample her DNA to test it against the cryopods in Mount Mars. No longer. We don't want her DNA. Our internal security is suspect. It's grave for me to say that. It took secret knowledge to seed an AI virus into the *Tempest*. If Christina's DNA is matched to Sedge and leaked, she would be a hunted woman."

Ivan said to Clienen, "If the enemy was able to infiltrate ULUP and gain access to the *Tempest's* data systems...."

"No telling what they know or where they are," said Trich.

Marisa arched an eyebrow, "They're not planet-side? On Dianis?"

Ivan asked, "Are you sure? The Paleowrights do their best to keep Dianis ignorant of all things Ancient. Who knows what secrets they've found and hoarded over these hundreds of years?"

She took a ragged breath and exhaled a hacking cough. "I need to see Atch. He will know what to do."

"And you will, Lady," hurried Trich, "but first, you need to tell us what to do with the prisoners. I need to clear the *Tempest* and make plans for an emergency boost out of system."

She blinked. "You mean the wounded Drakans?"

"Yes," said Ivan, "and Rachael. She suffered a cerebral hemorrhage and is in sick bay."

"Which she is being treated for," said Clienen, "but they found a tumor in her brain."

It was all coming too fast, overwhelming; each new revelation bore its own terror. Struggling, Marisa turned from Clienen to Ivan. "The Curse? The Timber's Curse?"

Ivan gave a subtle head waggle. "What the Timber's Curse is needs to be better defined. But for certain, she has a brain tumor that needs to be removed. The chief surgeon onboard will explain more."

"But I did bring Outish onboard," said Clienen. "He's down there now."

"*And?*" Trich pressed him.

"The Matrincy wants to shift in their own experts to evaluate Rachael."

Marisa's eyes narrowed. "Who?"

"They didn't say."

"Then let's hold them off," Marisa reasoned, "until I can hear what the surgeon and Outish have to say."

Ivan held up his hand and tapped his ear. "Roger," he replied to the unheard voice. "What are they doing?" He nodded to himself and then said, "We're coming down." He looked to Trich, "The ULUP investigators have arrived. One is an Avarian, a former Internal Security agent, and the other is an auditor from Torren Twi Two. Lettern says he's weird."

"Why did they come?" Marisa asked Trich.

"Fleet agreed to it. They've shifted in a team of cyber forensics experts to triage the intrusion and discover how the anti-AI agents were installed. ULUP wants to know, too."

Marisa shook her head. "ULUP killed Sedge. That's what they need to focus on."


Alex woke. The ceiling was strange, the lighting bright and came seemingly from everywhere. He tried to move, but an object, an apparatus of some sort with blinking lights, pinned his shoulder in place. Another similar contraption was strapped to his right-side ribs. In his peripheral vision, to the left, a person sat in a chair. They were perched on a stool, and then he recognized the Lamaran braid of golden wheat. He was overcome with relief.

She looked up from her knitting and smiled. It was the radiance of love. He closed his eyes; a wave of exhaustion overcame him, but her presence was a comforting blanket. "Where did you get the yarn?" he managed, his throat dry as the desert.

He felt the bed shift and her warm breath on his cheek. She kissed him on his forehead. "Mother provides," her whisper drifted, mixing with his dreams.

Above the low whir of a pump or a fan, Alex heard voices and opened his eyes.

Christina sat there perched on her stool of glistening metal, her hands busily knitting he knew not what, but her focus was across the room. He knew that look and tried peering past the machine attached to his shoulder.

Setting her work aside, Christina rose and reached across him. In her closeness, he could smell she was freshly bathed. She expertly rotated the device on his shoulder so he could see past it.

In the bed beside him was Rachael. On the other side of her stood the prince, arms across his chest, eyes closed, seemingly asleep, except for the occasional flicker of his tongue. Marisa, Outish, and a man he didn't know were discussing Rachael's condition. Lettern stood at the closed door to the compartment of what he now assumed was an apothecary or infirmary of some sort. There were the two beds in the chamber, and Lettern had a Marine assault plasma rifle in a sling across her chest. She had exchanged her Drakan Auxiliary armor for something akin to the armor he'd seen the Marines in when fighting Quorat.

Alex glanced at Christina, and the two Defenders appraised her.

Christina leaned close, not to interrupt Marisa's interrogation of the IDB chief medical officer, and said of Lettern's presence, "Mother's Guardian."

"Formidable." He wanted to say something to make light of the moment, but his side hurt too much, so he said instead, "I can rest in peace."

"The prince is a conduit to Rachael's spirit ward. He calls to the Hallowed Reed." Christina leaned back to sit on her stool.

"ULUP will have a problem with this." Alex overheard the IDB officer say to Marisa.

"I don't care," Marisa replied.

"I know you don't, Lady. But we should still have a plausible explanation."

Outish spoke next. "The Federation will want to know if this treatment course can work. The Matriarch charged me with the research!"

"I know she did," answered the chief medical officer, "But it will take my testimony in front of the Senate to convince them to ignore ULUP's charge of Deliberate Indigenous Interference."

Christina, Alex, and Lettern watched Marisa for her reaction. Clearly, as the provincial representative for Dianis, her opinion mattered. Outish, fervent in his belief they could cure Rachael of the hypothalamus cancer tumor *and* keep her sixthsense skills, did not have the credibility as a junior IDB astrobiologist compared to the senior medical officer of Federation IDB.

"Outy," said Marisa, "I don't see a problem with his proposal. We move Rachael to Central Station ...," and she looked to Fire Eye, whose yellow orbs were open and staring at her, "and we bring in the IDB oncologists, and using your research, test a serum on her. We'll need her da's permission."

Lettern nodded.

"When she wakes," said the medical officer, "her memory may have gaps, but the cerebral hemorrhage treatment is progressing along the desired pathways. She will have some motor skill regressions, but those will come back."

"Okay," said Outish. "I have all the marsediminium samples I need. Mbecca should help us. She can find us similar patients with whom we can do tumor comparisons, symptoms analysis, and select the serum formula."

"What?" asked the medical officer, picking up on Marisa's reservation of engaging Mbecca.

It was one thing to treat Rachael in isolation, but it was another to expose Mbecca and her patients to the IDB and the Matrincy. The ramifications of broadening the involvement between Clan Mearsbirch and the Matrincy bothered Marisa. This was what Atch, and particularly Baryy, had been afraid of. She wanted to interrogate Outish on the idea further, but not in front of the polished and clever chief medical officer. "Atch needs to be asked about this," she hedged. "Once he learns of Rachael's condition, I'm sure he'll agree to bring her to Central Station." The implication being she could convince him of it.

Having reached an interim agreement on Rachael's treatment, Marisa and the officer followed a Marine guard from the intensive care ward to a larger medical bay where patients were taken for routine post-operative recovery.

Marisa halted in the sliding hatch for the bay. She was shocked by the size. There were four rows of beds, semi-enclosed autodocs, separated by two aisles, positioned the length of the room for some eighty beds in all. "So many," she said.

"Forty-seven Drakans and twenty-three assault force," answered Ivan, who was waiting inside with a group of officers. "There would be more Drakans, but we couldn't retrieve them. It wasn't safe."

Marisa walked to the first bed. A Drakan pikeman, judging by the tunic and helmet in the open gear locker, looked at her with a mixture of fear and awe. Her gauntlets were shoved in her sword belt, so she reached out and grasped his hand. "How are you feeling?"

"Are you an Ancient?" he asked.

She smiled and laughed. "No," she said it loudly so that others could hear. "I am a Tivorian. An Isueltan, just like you."

"What are they going to do to us?"

The fear in the question stunned her, but did not surprise her.

"Well, first they will—"

"Beware of what you tell them, Lady."

Marisa turned to look at the person speaking.

The man standing behind her was completely bald, had blue skin, and a perfectly round mouth with lips around the mouth. He wore some sort of uniform she didn't recognize. "They are indigenous prisoners of war on a Class A warship," the man continued, "and subject to ULUP conventions of indigenous isolation and quarantine."

She looked to Ivan to explain, but the chief medical officer intervened instead. "Quarantine protocols have been established and followed, Em Auditor. The Federation fleet is proficient in their application. There is little risk—"

"Perhaps, IDB officer, you do not understand the gravity of the situation. These, these," and he pointed at the Drakan pikeman, "should never have been brought here. This is a grievous and terminus breach of ULUP conventions. There is no recovery of this offense. All of these," and he pointed a finger at Marisa, "Class F specimens must be fully mind wiped and returned to the planet forthwith, and whoever authorized—"

Marisa's cutlass scraped clear of its scabbard and hovered at her hip.

"What! You dare!" the ULUP auditor spewed at her, "Who allowed her the possession of a weapon?"

No one moved as the cutlass tip whipped up, pointing inches from the commissioner's throat. Marisa's eyes, orbs of hatred, were shorn of all empathy. "*We*," she growled in a low voice that curled Ivan's toes, "are *not* specimens. And you'll be mindwiping no one, ever, of anything while I carry this sword, and he," she pointed with her off-hand at a Scarlet Savior sergeant who lay, in an opposite bed, listening intently, "is not an indigenous *prisoner* of *war,* but a fellow human who fought bravely for his cause and is entitled to remember—"

"Orengen," the man cursed, "you demonstrate your ignorance, *Lady,*" the auditor spat at her, "I am not human; do not project your human sentiments onto me."

Ivan sensed it; the blow was coming, but niether Trich, Clienen, nor he prepared to stop her.

Marisa's gaze narrowed. She was being baited. The ULUP auditor had a trick up his sleeve, but a shadow of doubt crossed his circular mouth and his blue skin faded when the cutlass did not move or waver.

Muscles flexed in Marisa's jaw. "You want us mind wiped. Us humans. Us Dianis provincials so we cannot help in the Turboii War, so our sensitives can not thwart Nemesis yet again, so that the Loch Norim cannot chain the Ovid." It was a string of guesses, a gamble on her part, but as a trader princess, she'd learned when to provoke a *tell,* an uncontrolled response, with an unexpected accusation.

The auditor's browless eyes widened, "What do you—" His focus slanted from Marisa to someone behind her.

Without turning, she saw Trich, standing behind the auditor, give her a smug, conspiratorial wink. Trusting him, she turned to view their visitor.

"Lady Marisa Pontifract of House Marinda, Dianis Provincial Representative to the Avarian Federation." The matriarch held out her bare signet hand.

Marisa's anger burned unabated. She wanted to kill.

Turning back to the ULUP auditor, she said, "*We,* have unfinished business." Her cutlass slammed home in its sheath, and she spun on the matriarch. "Madam Matriarch, Senator."

Marisa grasped the proffered hand, Matrincy fashion, and stroked the Matrincy signet ring of the Grand Councilor. Gathering her wits and trying to calm her boiling blood, Marisa said, "I had not expected you. We are unresolved on the Matrincy's request to attend Rachael."

The matriarch covered Marisa's hand with her other and stepped in close to the irritation of the auditor. "Lady, honestly, do you think I *ever* ask for permission?" A ghost of warmth crossed her face, and then she looked aside. "And you, sir, Em Auditor, did I hear you threaten the Dianis Representative to the Avarian Federation with mindwipe?"

"She drew a weapon and directed it at my presence, and you know the penalty for armed threat of bodily injury." The auditor's blue skin turned a shade darker, and his circular lip went flat.

"How disingenuous of you, Em Auditor, and you will address me by my rank." The matriarch replied with an icy smile. "As you know, the Law of Identity Defense allows the use of force to protect one's memories in the event of unfounded memory erasure."

"It is not unfounded, Madame Matriarch. As *you know*, ULUP is quite clear—"

"Captain Trich," the matriarch interrupted, "you have two hundred and twenty-seven Dianis provincials, what Em Auditor here refers to as indigen specimens, on board your ship. What are your orders as to the disposition of those provincials?"

The captain feigned a look of surprise. "That's up to the Lady Pontifract. She is their representative."

The auditor wheeled and snapped at the captain, "That is ludicrous, she has no power or authority—"

"That may be true, sir Auditor, but my orders from Fleet are clear. And after what ULUP did to my ship, you are damned fortunate I let you come aboard."

Rebuffing him, the auditor said, "There will be repercussions for your behavior towards me and conduct toward ULUP, captain."

"Ah yes, let's talk about that, Em Auditor," said the matriarch. "Lady, are you aware that Clan Mearsbirch, through you, has a claim of *Grievous Conduct* against ULUP for the wanton murder of Sedge?"

The auditor started spewing a vehement protest, but unfazed, the matriarch persisted. To Marisa, she said, "Yes, in the act of an official ULUP intervention, they did terminate the life of Sedge, a Dianis provincial who freely followed and placed himself in the care of no less than three ULUP commissioners. Shocking. The case will be prosecuted to its fullest extent by IDB Avaria, so the executive director has assured me."

To the auditor, whom the matriarch waved a hand and his mouth, in mid-sentence, went limp, "Em Auditor, it was so fitting the Lady should remind us all of my role in the Senate. Ianata," and this she said to Marisa, though it was clear the message was meant for the auditor, "is a conservative faction in the Senate. It is our goal to bolster human defenses for the protection of all sentient species against the depredations of the Turboii and to do so, we seek to remove the Federation from ULUP. It's no secret—"

"Which you can *not* do!" the auditor railed, "The treaties are binding beyond any withdrawal convention!"

"That's what he thinks," the matriarch said softly to Marisa, but clear enough for those around to hear, "just like he thinks his force repulsor would protect him from your sword."

A look of alarm crossed the auditor's face.

Ivan shook his head at the auditor. "I was wondering why you dare tempt her. At three inches, with her arm strength and a straight jab of that point, the repulsor would not have stopped the blade."

"You knew this and made no move to stop her?" The auditor wheeled on Captain Trich.

Trich shrugged. "You're still alive," though he bore a disappointed frown.

# Chapter 43
## Consequence

*The Citadel*

Larech led Commandant Fritach up from the pit cells in Ages Castle. General Lord Orn Blannach and Decurion Uloch were waiting for them in the Upper Bailey.

"The prisoner is gone," Fritach reported.

"Did he survive the bats?" asked Uloch.

The commandant shook his head, "Don't know. But they killed hundreds of bats getting to him. Both jailers are dead. They sealed the bat entrance, and we found this," he held up a mangled Mk2 Dragonfly defense bot whose nano-dissembler pack was clawed away before it could actuate.

Blannach peered closely at the mechanism, then waited for an explanation.

"One of their flies, Lord General, look at this," and Fritach pointed to the venom injector in the thorax. He didn't have to explain what the apparatus was.

"They fought the bats with those?" asked the decurion.

Larch shrugged. "We found other bats cut in half cleanly. Others were crushed against the walls. It was a battle, decurion. I found one of these." He showed them a Tivor Marine cutlass.

"They took casualties," surmised Blannach.

"Good," declared the decurion, "even our bats are fierce."

Blannach surveyed the ground and route between the prison and the Ages Castle. His critical eye imagining the battle. "If the Church had not taken the prisoner to the dungeons?"

"You mean stolen, Lord General?" asked Fritach.

They'd seen the dead guards in the prison and heard firsthand the wounded recount the tale of the Scarlet Saviors' attack.

Larech held his tongue, but he'd told Fritach his own story.

"The emperor will be informed of *all* that has transpired," answered Blannach. "If the Iron Witch had found the Ancient in the prison, what would have happened?"

They collectively considered the implications. Larech was the first to respond, "The Al Suri was the first at the prison. She had the men to take the prison, seize the prisoner, and then--"

"They would have left," Fritach completed the statement.

"How can you be so sure?" growled the decurion.

"Because the trader would have been alive. He bore us no ill will. We saved his life, and the Al Suri," he tossed a shoulder, "she fought Helprig and Irons before and showed them mercy in Wedgewood. They would have left."

Uloch glared at him, but there were over eighty dead and wounded Drakans and an untold number taken by the Ancients.

"Then, are you prepared to present your findings to the emperor?" Blannach asked Fritach. "He will be most displeased."

"Ach, Lord General, on this day, who is pleased?"

"The Iron Witch is," said Uloch.

The commandant gave a quick shake of his bald ebon head. "Nach. The Church tortured her trader, her lover."

Emperor Elexir Tyr Violorich, resplendent in his purple robes, ermine cape, and audience crown, made a stark contrast to the blackened stones of the Areaum.

Larech explained the scene of the previous night, of the Ancient ships blasting down in flames, landing, and then roaring off with the Tivorians and Timberkeeps. He recounted, in precise Washen agent detail, while the emperor listened closely, of the heavily armored Ancients they called *assault Marines*, the weapons they carried, and the fact the Ancients felt safe with just four to guard all the Areaum.

"Is it true, Decurion," the emperor asked, "as the agent tells it?"

Uloch gave a grim regard to Larech, then answered. "It is true. We had massed hundreds by the time the Iron Witch left, and she was not afraid."

"But those weapons only wounded the Savior captain and his sergeant. They are both alive."

"The Ancients did not shoot. Irons and the other were the work of the spy, the woman dressed as an Auxiliary Scout. She carried a different weapon," said Uloch.

Fritach expounded on what they had learned of the weapons the enemy carried, and Larech tied it to the rumors they had heard that night in the foundry in Wedgewood.

The emperor listened to it all. At key points, he and the Lord General exchanged glances.

Scuffing the soot-stained stones with his boot, the emperor went to a spot where the drive thrusters of the assault landers had burned the stones white, vaporizing the surface layers. "I want all of this fixed, Lord Blannach. There is to be no sign that they were ever here."

"Yes, sire."

"And bring me Helprig."

Fritach motioned for the agents at the Paleowright chapel to bring out Viscount Helprig.

The clergyman was literally dragged out of the chapel, trailing his wounded leg, and calling out, "This is Diunesis holy ground. I cannot be removed by force. You are violating Church—" but then he saw the emperor and cut his protest short.

The agents held him up by the arms, but the emperor made a motion, and they forced Helprig down to his knees. "But, sire, lord, what is this? I am—"

"Shut up, you fool," ordered Blannach, "You will speak when addressed."

Helprig's jaw worked, but the emperor's dispassionate inspection of him stayed his tongue.

With a dismissive wave of his signet hand, the emperor said, "Fritach, you have something to say to him?"

"Thank you, sire. Helprig, your predicant has confessed."

"Ca--, confessed?"

"Under your orders, you did forcibly remove a person, under the protection of the Drakan Empire, invoking mayhem and murder, and pronounced said person to torture and death."

"But he was—" Helprig squawked.

At a gesture of Fritach's goatee, an agent pulled a dirk and thrust it under Helprig's chin, holding it there. Blood began to dribble.

"You stole through the night, like a common thief, through the Sally Port, knowing fully you were to be escorted to the emperor for a personal meeting. You performed such subterfuge to thwart the emperor's wishes and torture the prisoner, an Ancient whom we were to present to the emperor."

Helprig wanted to speak, but the blade dug deeper.

"Yes, Helprig, present. Achelous the Ancient. The emperor, the empire, would have benefited by meeting him."

"An Ancient, Helprig," the emperor said, quietly. "You chained and tortured an Ancient and brought the wrath of the heavens upon us here on the hallowed ground of my forebears. We who worship the Ancient have now suffered their fury."

The emperor watched as the stream of blood from Helprig's jaw trickled down his neck. He looked away, his gaze and thoughts inscrutable. "How long until the twelve hour?"

"A half glass, your highness," answered Larech.

"Then we will go there now." Without looking back, the emperor said, "Send Helprig's head to the archbishop. Inform him the Ancients have returned to Isuelt."

# Chapter 44
## A Finger's Touch

*Tempest Dare, Dianis Orbit*

"Atch?"

"Yes, Lace."

"What are you doing?"

"Going for a walk."

"Momma, come with!" Boyd came running and jumped into her arms, oblivious to his mother's distraction. Marisa caught him. He was giggling, and she started to swing him.

"Lady?"

She swung the boy high, Boyd's little face a beacon of joy.

"Lady?"

A voice called. She stopped.

"Lady." Something was pushing at her shoulder.

Marisa opened her eyes, and a young female officer stood there. Through the fog of exhaustion, she focused on the unfamiliar uniform. The collar pips could be that of an ensign, maybe. Then she saw the shoulder board: *Tempest Dare*.

It all came crashing down around her: The joy of the dream, the warmth of Boyd's laugh, the sound of Atch's voice.

"It is time, Lady," the ensign said. "We are moving the wounded to the shift zone."

Marisa nodded and climbed out of the med bay bunk. She was wearing a set of *Tempest Dare* duty fatigues with her name and a strange insignia on the collars.

"I'll carry your armor down for you," offered the ensign.

"Oh."

The Drakans were all about military decorum, and she was a provincial like them. If she was to build peace, eventually, with them, she would need to start with familiarity, then trust. Parading around in an Ancient uniform was not the way to start.

"I'll wear the armor."

The ensign helped her buckle the pieces on. "We cleaned it for you, but Chief Darinarishcan said you wouldn't want it repaired."

"Darinarishcan?" Marisa asked, then caught herself, "Oh, Ivan." She smiled. "Sorry, I'm so out of it. How long did I sleep?"

"Six hours, Ma'am. Do you want a stim shot?"

She watched the junior officer open a med locker and withdraw two small pneumatic injectors, one green and one yellow. "Slow acting or fast?" the officer asked.

Marisa eyed the injectors warily.

The officer smiled. "Slow." She pulled up Marisa's sleeve and, without asking, jabbed the green into her wrist.

First, a burn, gentle, then a tingle spread up her arm and dissipated. The fogginess of the past night cleared, and so, too, the anxiety and fears.

"Ready?" asked the ensign.

Marisa's reluctant expression said yes.

At the shift platform, Marisa watched eight Special Forces troopers shift planet-side. "Special Forces?" she asked Ivan, who was coordinating with the navy corpsmen.

"Yes, the matriarch is coming. Emperor Violorich is at the Citadel, at the Parade Grounds with his command staff. They have a thousand Drakans formed up in ranks."

"Where is she?"

"Behind you."

Despite the surge of the stim shot, Marisa felt the prospect, the weight of a new and long day dragging her down. Turning, she saw both the matriarch and Alon regarding her. Taking a breath, her dark eyes met those of the matriarch. Alon, looking refreshed, her armor gleaming, came forward. She held out her hand.

Marisa tried to smile.

Alon reached down and took her hand, her grip soft, then stronger, the firmness reassuring. "Mother is with you."

Holding Alon's hand, Marisa moved closer to the matriarch. "Why today? Why go down there?" she was shaking her head. "Surely it isn't safe."

While the Special Forces captain beside the matriarch wore a sour expression, he came to the matriarch's defense. "We'll be fully shielded. Two assault birds are overhead, and we'll have the battle drones in position. *Trilonair's* Field gen will be locked to the Matriarch's signet and set to instant retrieve."

The matriarch, as always, at least with Marisa, showed her enigmatic grin. "My dear, my Lady. There is an emperor to meet. A real one. Not some trumped-up buffoon. How could I resist? Besides, I need to deliver a message, personally."

Marisa, on the cusp of citing obvious provincial interference and the ULUP repercussions, just frowned. She was keenly aware that she and Christina were both alive because of the matriarch's meddling, though Rachael had paid a price.

Intrigue ultimately overcame Marisa's hesitation. She wanted to hear the matriarch's message delivered to the emperor.

"Unless you don't want me to go?" asked the matriarch.

Marisa eased her expression to neutral. "I know you are not asking permission."

The matriarch laughed.

"Captain," Marisa addressed him, "you are a patient man."

Another laugh.

On the Parade Grounds, in the glorious noon sun, the Angraris wind streamed the arrayed flags and pendants of the massed centuries and regiments. In front of a thousand stoic and awed Drakan faces, Ivan organized the downshift of the wounded pikemen, Saviors, and Halberdiers. Assault Marines formed a square, and inside the square, flashing beacons marked the shift zone. The Drakan battalions and centuries were arranged in precisely ordered ranks around the zone. It was meant to be the ultimate show of empire power.

In front of the Main Gate, Emperor Violorich, with Decurion Uloch and a host of other officers, waited.

Opposing the Drakans, a similar row of Tivorians, Timberkeeps, and Avarians were arrayed.

Ogden, his rifle slung over his shoulder, stood to the fore. Marisa was two paces behind, with Christina one step behind her and to the right. They had positioned themselves ten paces in front of the emperor's party, as Jeremy, relayed by Ivan, reported was the proper protocol for introductions to the sovereign. Shifted in a discrete distance behind the Alon was the matriarch with the Special Forces captain and sergeant on either side of her, their projection bubble shields active. Floating menacingly above both troopers was a Phantom aerial battle drone, their weapons obvious to even an uneducated provincial. A thousand meters above, an assault shuttle, plasmas cannons charged and loaded with Marines, hovered on a low thrust burn.

Ivan, wearing his IDB uniform and clearly not a provincial, singled out Agent Larech standing to the left of Commandant Fritach, who stood immediately to the left of the emperor. "To whom may we pass the care of your wounded and provide further instruction for their treatment? You will find wound dressings that may be unfamiliar."

Larech spoke to Commandant Fritach, and then Larech gave a bow to Ivan, "We have doctors and stretcher bearers ready." He signaled Ivan should follow him.

With all the Federation uniforms, drones, and assault ships on display, Marisa was relieved that she, Ogden, and Alon were in their provincial armor, cleaned for the occasion, but battle-worn, not parade dress.

With the exception of Ogden, they were women, and the Drakans were men, and in the Citadel, for this moment, humility was best. She was not there to antagonize or gloat, but to plead the case of the wounded.

Fidgeting, Ogden wanted to be done with introductions and assume a position he preferred, as Marisa's adjutant, at her left and one step behind. To all, his Doroman-Timberkeep heritage was clear, and the rifle on his shoulder meant as a reminder. There was no point in hiding the weapon or perpetuating its secret. For Ogden, the rifle was now his preferred weapon of choice. Many of the Drakan wounded had fallen because of it.

Signaling him, Marisa called out. "Master Smith, Warden of the Second, you may make our introductions."

"Oi, Lady." Ogden, burly, wearing his smith's leathers, conical helm with ox horns, and long beard, strode forward to his equal, a man who he recognized. "Sir. To whom shall I represent the opposition leadership?" The word *opposition* was carefully chosen. By rights, Marisa could have chosen *victorious* leadership, but she was here to build familiarity and, eventually, in the future, trust. Claiming victory, however obvious, was not a goal. However, by having Ogden make the opening introduction -- a Timberkeep -- served as an esteemed recognition for all Doromen.

Decurion Uloch stepped forward and gave a brief, stiff bow. "General Commandant Fritach," he said, without taking his eyes from Ogden, "Do you accept their representations?"

"Ach, yes." Fritach took one formal step forward, then presented to Ogden, offering a Drakan handshake.

Never having done it Drakan style before, Ogden cocked his head, eyed the hand, then reached out a beefy, calloused mitt and shook it. "Oi, good to meet you, sir." He didn't really know if it was good to meet the commandant, but said it all the same.

"And to you as well, Master Smith, I have heard much of you."

Ogden was taken aback. "Me?"

"Ha, ach. The famous weaponsmith of Wedgewood. You know of the Washentrufel?"

Ogden pursed his lips, his beard moving. "I've heard Atch and others speak of it."

To which the commandant brightened. "Atch? By which you mean Achelous the Trader?" and Fritach glanced at Marisa.

"Oi, that be him."

"Then, you must make introductions to his Lady," at which Marisa involuntarily shifted. "And the rifle you carry on your shoulder, we should talk about it."

Caught off guard, Ogden said, "Oola, I don't think so."

Fritach laughed, "No, I suppose not. Our emperor is a powerful man, and his time is precious, please," and he waved his hand towards Marisa.

Relieved to get on with it, Ogden walked the commandant to Marisa and made their formal introductions, relying on Fritach to cite his own title.

"Lady," Fritach held her hand, "your trader, he is well?"

Marisa realized, partly in surprise, that Fritach was genuinely concerned. "I am told he is, though I have not seen him yet."

Clearly relieved, Fritach turned to share a glance with his emperor. "I, on behalf of the empire, apologize for any foul treatment that may have befallen him while under our protection. I assure you, Major Startoren did his utmost to extricate your, shall we say, *Ancient* from Viscount Helprig's vassals at the earliest possible."

If Fritach was looking for a reaction to the label *Ancient*, Marisa didn't show it.

"But, alas, the viscount violated our trust in him by usurping Drakan territorial sovereignty and took your trader from Drakan protection, to which he has paid for it with his head." Fritach motioned to a Halberdier holding a sack.

The soldier opened the sack and lifted Helprig's head by the hair.

Marisa's olive skin drained pale.

"I would send it to your Ancient trader with our apologies, but it is bound to the archbishop instead."

She swallowed. "No, that's fine. Atch wouldn't want it."

"Oi, Lady. Margern would take it," said Ogden.

Marisa gave a short nod. "I'm sure she would." Then, to Fritach, she asked, "May I make a presentation to the emperor?"

Fritach turned and asked the unvoiced question of his liege.

Violorich responded, "You may bring the Lady forward."

The seconds, Ogden and Commandant Fritach, made the introductions.

Marisa said, "Your Highness, we have forty-seven of your wounded. Thirty-two of them," Marisa pivoted and pointed to where Ivan coordinated with the navy corpsmen and Citadel doctors on the transfer and future care of the injured, "you see being returned to you today. There are fifteen that are what the Avarians term as critical condition and should not be moved."

"Avarians?" he asked, his voice gritty.

The question served as a stark reminder of where she had been just a few short months ago. "Yes, Your Highness. That is what the Ancients call themselves."

She saw the emperor's attention drawn to something behind her. Hearing the low whir of the battle-drone fans, she surmised the matriarch was moving in. "Emperor, I am here to advocate for the fair treatment of your wounded.

"Fair treatment?" demanded the emperor, "Of what concern is that of yours?"

She met his glare with one of her own, not as a subservient woman but as an equal leader. "Cultures." She pointedly omitted the use of his honorific. "Some regressive and controlling societies such as," and she put a fine point on it, "the Church may punish or shame those who were given succor by their enemies. Your men fought bravely for their cause. They were brought aboard the Avarian ship because they are fellow humans and needed aid. Whether they were Drakan, Tivor, or Timberkeep, it does not matter. Their pain was real. Such is the human way. Be it galactic," she pointed to the stars, "or provincial," and she pointed at the ground. "My galactic, my trader, the Avarian," pride resonated in her voice, "taught me that we humans are alone in the galaxy. We are Fed upon, preyed upon by alien species who would farm us like cattle. Only through our care for each other, our mutual defense have we survived. And so, I am here to ask you to honor your wounded. Many did not have a chance to resist our aid. Some tried but were rendered unconscious. But understand, they are all returned to you with their memories intact. They are unchanged except for their wounds."

The emperor's glare eased. "Memories? What of their memories?"

She said to Fritach, "Commandant, consider your disadvantage if your men were returned to you with their memories wiped, devoid of all that happened. Both here and on the ship? What would that mean to them? Their honor? Their identities?" She spoke to his own self-interest. "And what of your knowledge? The Washentrufel? If wounded had their memories wiped, what of your information of events. The knowledge you are always wrestling from the Church in their game of concealing and hoarding it. All for power, theirs, not yours."

The emperor asked, "You would not do that?" A sneer began to form. "Destroy their minds? It would be to your advantage."

"No, Your H*ighness, I* would not," she responded.

The whir of drone fans drew closer. Marisa could feel the static discharge of a shield projector tease her hair.

"Lady Pontifract, Princess of House Marinda, would you indulge me in joining your conversation? I assure you, my interruption is most relevant."

Marisa turned to face the matriarch. She gave a deep Tivorian bow that impressed even the matriarch with its graceful elegance. By invoking her official title, and asking *permission* of the Dianis Provincial Representative to the Avarian Federation, the matriarch was strictly adhering to Federation and IDB protocol. Fate lines were fluxing.

"Your Highness," Marisa addressed the emperor, "I have the honor to present to you the Grand Counselor of the

Matrincy, Senator li Ianata of the Avarian Federation Senate, and amongst her other titles, Rights and Honors Representative for Federation non-aligned worlds, of which Dianis is. Our planet is not part of the Avarian Federation, but we *are* in Federation space." Marisa looked to Fritach, "And, simply put, commandant, the matriarch is the most powerful human in the galaxy by any measure you should choose."

The matriarch laughed, a generous and pleasurable expression reserved for a friend. "Lady Pontifract, you so glorify me." But to emphasize Marisa's point, she said, "Captain, can you withdraw these Phantom drones and drop these cloying shields? Honestly, we are under a flag of truce." She looked up at the white flag with a green slash across it. "I assume, Lord General Blannach, that you intend to honor the truce?"

The supreme commander of the Drakan military flourished a bow. "Indeed—" and he looked to Marisa for the correct honorific, to which she supplied, "Madam Matriarch."

"For the duration of this conclave," he completed.

"Very well then." The matriarch pointedly looked at the captain, resplendent in his black and silver polished powered armor and gleaming plasma rifle. The projection shields were dropped, and the drones withdrew a few paces behind.

Christina, who up to that point had not spoken, picked up on Blannach's interpretation of the captain's hesitancy as insubordination said to the Drakans, "The captain takes his responsibility to keep the matriarch safe quite seriously. He is not happy the matriarch is here. Billions, not millions, of lives rest on the matriarch. That she has come in person is a sign of honor and trust." Christina left out her own thoughts of how important Dianis was to the matriarch and the war. Critical enough for the matriarch to travel planet-side and meet with a leader, albeit an emperor, whose forces would not survive an hour against a Turboii-Sizar invasion. *Today,* that is. To Christina, it was patently obvious what the matriarch's plans were.

"Did you hear that, captain?" the matriarch asked. "You have the Al Suri Ascalon's condolences." She said it to the Drakan high command.

Marisa watched their expressions. The matriarch, as always, was a wild card. How the Drakan men would view the matriarch's dress particularly interested Marisa. The matron had opted to wear her Matrincy ceremonial robes, not those of an Auro Na priestess, Federation Senator, or one of her holo-vid gowns, for which she was famous. The ceremonial robes were all black and shimmering midnight blue. The cowl of her close-fitting robe –buttoned tight down the front of the bodice -- framed her long coal-black dreadlocks. Her bodice was, of course, open at the top, exposing a view of her svelte bosom. While her dress was beguiling, complete with a mythical beast imprinted in iridescence, it was the Matrincy aquamarine-5 jewels that attracted the most attention. Contrasting with her pale skin, black eyeliner, black brows, and ruby lips, the inverted U of the Matrincy symbol hung from its diadem, fitting perfectly between her brows. At the top of the upside-down U was the aquamarine-5 gem. The diadem was of either silver or, perhaps, albaminia; Marisa couldn't tell. Last, and most provocatively, was the Matrincy séance chain, ever so delicate in its infinitely fine craftsmanship, that dangled across her left cheek from a nostril piercing to her left earlobe. Six tiny silver daggers, evenly spaced, hung from the chain resting on her jaw. Each dagger, Marisa had learned from Ivan, counted a phase in spirit meditation and was there to revive a person with a prick of pain should they slip too far into the ether.

The reactions of the Drakan males varied. To his credit, the emperor was appreciative, but skeptical. Marisa glanced to Fritach and found him watching *her* watch the emperor. They exchanged recognition of negotiators in parlay, not adversaries in war.

"Emperor Elexir Tyr Violorich," the matriarch addressed him in a neutral manner where tone of voice mattered, then she added, "sir," as a generous note of respect to his subordinates, "the Lady Pontifract did undertake, at peril to herself, to protect your men. She is a Diesian. In the galaxy, that means she comes from your planet, Dianis. When your men were threatened with the loss of their memories—" and incredibly, the matriarch was able to point to a Scarlet Savior sergeant who had just been down-shifted.

Marisa suspected Andromeda had a role in that bit of seeming magic.

"Sergeant," the matriarch called to him. "Will you present yourself to your emperor? I have a question for you."

The sergeant, who'd been stabbed and slashed in the fracas with Alex and a Lamaran, looked at the Alon with a mixture of respect, fear, and anger. Then he saw Blannach's ascent, and he approached, coming to attention the best his wounds and bandages would allow.

"Sergeant, are you of your whole mind? Do you remember what transpired from the time you were wounded to now?" the matriarch asked.

Blannach again gave a clue for permission to speak.

"I do."

The matriarch gave her mischievous, *I have a secret* smile, "Are you familiar with the Iron Witch's cutlass, sergeant? Have you seen it drawn?"

His eyes darted to the wire-wrapped hilt of Marisa's sword. "I have."

"What was her intent? Why did she draw it?"

"Ach, she was going to kill the blue man. Was it a man? I don't know. He had a round mouth. He wanted to take our memories. *Wipe* them, he said. She was going to kill him. No one was stopping her."

The emperor noted the obvious pain on Marisa's face. Angst at the memory of the event.

"And you did not kill him, Lady?" Fritach asked.

When Marisa didn't answer, the matriarch did. "I, fortunately or unfortunately, intervened at that moment and warned the blue man of his folly. So yes, the ULUP auditor does still live." She peered at Marisa fondly. "The lady is not beholden to me. Dianis is not a Federation world," she gave a head-waggle, "it may be in the future, but ... Lady Pontifract stands for Dianis. It does not matter the race or culture."

"To which I come to my interest," the matriarch said directly to the emperor. Carefully, with slow ceremony, she removed the glove of her signet-ring hand, exposing immaculate manicuring and glittering burgundy nail polish. She raised the hand and pointed the index finger upwards. "I come bearing a gift. You, Lord Emperor, will fight whom you may for whatever goals you deem, but understand no human is your real enemy. No Diesian, your true foe. What I offer you is a vision, a brief glimpse, of who humanity's ultimate enemy is." Holding the finger aloft, she said, "A touch and I will give you the vision I have seen of this world and all our true enemy."

"Fritach, what trickery is this?" asked the emperor.

The commandant, thoughtful, his dark, clean-shaven pate glistening in the noon sunlight there on the Citadel, hesitated, then, "Perhaps, Madam Matriarch, it best you show your dream to Agent Larech."

The agent's face was impassive, but Marisa caught the tension in his shoulders.

Larech made an assertion, "You masqueraded as the Auro Na High Priestess of the Seahorse Isles."

Marisa suspected the agent was guessing, but an accurate guess, nonetheless.

"I did," the matriarch answered brightly and rocked her head, "and it was most fun. The Oligarch of Oridia is such a gentleman, but Ghost-I, from Neuland, he was a boor."

"She's a decimar," said Fritach flatly. The Drakan high command was schooled in Auro Na sixthsense rankings.

The emperor's eyes bored into Marisa, "And you, Iron Witch, you too are an Auro Na temptress."

Marisa shook her head slowly, "No. Lord. I am *not*." Her eyes strayed to Decurion Uloch. "Call me what you wish," and she put an index finger on the pommel of her cutlass, "on the stairs of Glory Hall, there was room for nothing but steel."

"The Church hides the truth from you," Christina said. "They hoard knowledge and make you guess at every word, the smallest secret that is no secret. And now you have the guiding light of humanity, Mother's Ward, offering you knowledge beyond the archbishop's greatest fear, and you balk?"

"Ach!" The mention of the Church tore it for the commandant. "Then show me this dream, I would know this wonder. This new evil."

"Is it safe?"

To Marisa's surprise, the emperor asked it of her.

She peered at him, then turned to take the measure of the matriarch. "Lord, this dream the matriarch has not shared with me, but I fear I know of the enemy, the Turboii, the Sizars, to which she refers." Pausing, she pursed her lips, staring at the emperor. "I am alive today, as is the Alon, because of a dream shared by the matriarch. Her foretelling reflects the world as it will be. To ignore them is to tempt fate, to stand before an Angraris gale and will it calm."

The matriarch waggled her finger. "Knowledge is power." Her tone was not light and teasing, but hard. Unyielding.

Removing a glove, the emperor strode forward, perhaps to show all Drakans he had no fear of the witch in black. He held up his finger.

A quick tap, before he could move, the matriarch touched their fingers. "Done."

He blinked, his eyes wide. For a moment, he swayed and then steadied. Peering suspiciously at her, he said, "What—" Then more images came. "Who—" more of the dream floated into his consciousness. He stood back, scowling.

Fritach and Blannach moved, but the emperor shooed them away. A scene unfolded in his mind's eye. "Where is that?" he asked the matriarch.

She lifted a brow. "You tell me. It's your planet. Are those Drakan banners?"

He took a deep breath and spun on a heel. "Blannach, give our-- visitors a minute to leave. This conclave is over."

The Parade Ground empty, Fritach, Blannach, and the emperor rode in the royal coach to the palace. The emperor stared out the window, pensive, brooding.

The coach arrived at the Citadel's palace, but the emperor made no move to rise.

"Sire," asked Fritach, "are you--"

"Ill?" responded the emperor. He let the coach sit idle, the coachmen and honor guard waiting to open the door.

Eventually, he said, "Blannach."

"Sire?"

The emperor pulled his brooding gaze from the window. "We must attack. And soon. They grow too strong."

"The rifles," mused Fritach.

"They dared to attack us at our very heart," said Blannach. "They spilled our blood in Glory Hall. Such an affront, the hubris, it must be avenged, and on a scale that is insurmountable."

"They threaten our very existence," growled the emperor. "Helprig, in his madness, has done us a service."

"How so, Sire?" asked Fritach.

"He spite them, drawing them out. Better now, General, than a year from now when they are stronger."

"And the dream, sire? What did the matriarch show you?"

A quick shake of his head, the emperor answered, "Tricks of a sorceress, beguiling and befuddling their intent. Bah, the real enemy! The real enemy stood in front of us, plain. He carried the rifle on his shoulder. That is our foe; don't be fooled by whisperings of witches."

"And the Ancients?" asked Fritach. "Do we fight them as well?"

The emperor's snake eyes regarded him. "They will not fight. They are cowards."

# Chapter 45
## The Dig

*Dianis*

Huddled over her cramped engineer console, Krch moved the target landing cursor to the center of the river, above the largest pool on the river.

"Copy," came the pilot's voice. He tilted the Intruder's yoke, and the craft angled in a turn.

Butch, the commander, who she still called Haz, short for hazmat man, occupied the copilot-commander's chair beside the pilot. If he didn't like her target selection, he'd say so.

Skimming low along the river using hydrogen, not ion or anti-grav drives, the Intruder passed over the three-person ground-security crew. At its widest point, the pool in the river was two hundred yards across.

Bringing the craft to a halt, just feet above the water, the pilot announced on the local short-range net, "Settling."

When the hull touched the surface, Krch activated sonar, mapping the bottom. Adjusting the landing cursor to the deepest part of the river, she heard the pilot say, "Copy."

Hissing and popping echoed along the hull, and steam, in frothing gouts, rose from the hydro drives until they were fully submerged. They'd waited for the stormy weather for a week now. The cold front concealed their intrusion profile and the heat signature of the steam boiling from the hull. A stealth drone in geo-sync orbit pinged the Intruder with a laser tight beam, feeding data from its passive sensors. Haz grunted in satisfaction. "Clean entry."

Slowly, as the ship settled to the bottom of the pond, the hissing and popping stopped. "Down," announced the pilot.

"Top third still above water," said the security lead.

Haz looked over his shoulder at Krch. "Clear?"

She nodded, her mouth tubes limp. "Clears."

"Extending expeller pipes." The pilot waited for the pipes to reach maximum length. "Here we go. Dredgers engaged."

A low thrumming sounded, and then the Intruder began to tremble as the dredge blades bit into the river bottom. Larger than most Intruders but smaller than a typical planetary mining machine, the ship sank deeper into the pond bottom as the pilot wiggled the ship gently, digging out a bed much the same way a spawning fish would, scraping the bottom with its tail to deposit eggs.

Mud and rock were spewed from the expeller pipes, and the ground crew immediately went to work directing the dredge material into a rough arc behind the ship.

When a dredge blade hit rock, the ship began to bounce and shudder in earnest until the pilot managed to feather the down angle.

Haz watched Krch for a reassurance.

"It's goodss, ground radar shows rubbles, sandstones, no granite -- yets," she answered.

"Top is covered," signaled the ground crew.

Monitoring the depth gauge, the orange glow of the controls bathing her face, Krch watched the engineering readouts. While she was not a starship engineer, she knew enough to spot trouble. She'd been trained by Haz on the new, non-geologist functions for her post. They were running a crew of six, the smallest she'd been on. It wasn't because the outfit was cheap, far from it; the Intruder was brand new and customized just for this op. Crew size was predicated on one thing: Shift size of their shielded Field generator. Due to its low output signature and disturbance profile, their shift zone could only handle five hundred pounds or two fully equipped crew members. They'd practiced the emergency shift routines back at dry dock. In case their op was compromised by the IDB, they could out shift all six crewmembers in ninety seconds in three shifts of two, assuming all crew were mustered and ready to go. A detonation charge, nuclear, would take care of the equipment. The nuclear device was another example of no expense spared, and Haz had been clear to all crew members that in the event of a busted op, you either got shifted out in a hundred and eighty seconds or were vaporized by the auto self-destruct charge that was tamper proof. Even he didn't have the control codes for it. If a predetermined series of events were detected by the nuke's AI, one hundred and eighty seconds later, it would go *boom*.

At the fifty-foot depth marker, the top of the hull and nacelles would be ten feet under water, the minimum depth they needed for the compressed sediment of the sarcophagus, the structure that would conceal the ship from aerial overflights using radar. The compressed sediment also served the purpose of consuming dredge material. Eventually, depending on how much aquamarine-5 they mined, they would accumulate a considerable amount of mine tailings. "Forty-five feet," Krch reported. The surface team was now directing the dredge material to form an earthen dam that would gradually increase the size of the pond and provide a greater area to distribute the mine tailings underwater and out of view from prying satellites.

Krch pondered the nuke as the surface crew reported their progress in camouflaging the earthen dam to look natural, dragging uprooted trees in place and seeding the mud with fast-growing vegetation, along with the liberal use of camo nets.

She could understand the desire to destroy physical and aura evidence if they were discovered, but to obliterate, vaporize it, seemed extreme. "Forty-eight feet," she called out. Her gaze strayed aft to the cargo bay where the shielded Field gen and shift zone were. She'd never seen the likes of it before, and Haz was not interested in talking about it other than to say the "outfit" had built it themselves. Which, in her opinion, was greasy eenu turds. No contract mining firm could have built it. Unless, of course, Haz meant *outfit* to be something else entirely.

"Fifty-feet," she announced.

"Secure ship for mining ops. Let's get the airlock installed, people." Haz unbuckled from his seat as the pilot shut down the engines and flight systems.

Krch made her way aft and donned her dive suit, and grabbed one of the portable mining rigs. Cycling through the airlock into the pressurized dive chamber, she climbed a ladder, took a breath, and did one of her least favorite things: Went swimming. Jumping into the dive pool, she swam to the murky, sediment-caked bottom. She hooked up the portable drill to the expeller pipe pump and began digging, mining a tunnel straight down. Using her suit's sonar in the gloom, she dug a pit wide enough to stand in. The surface team reported they were bringing the pieces of the mine airlock down to the pit.

Krch settled her flippers on the bottom, mud and silt swirling before her face plate. It wasn't how she expected to return, but there she was, both feet on Dianis. If miss-perfect-Margret and the IDB only knew. She should laugh in victory, but swimming in swirling muck gave her the willies.

# Chapter 46
## Aorolmin's Grand Ball

*Tivor*

Marisa first fussed over Boyd, then peppered his nanny with a string of questions and asked Eliot again when the *Far Shore* was due in.

Achelous gave Eliot a subtle grin, and the huntsmaster answered with the same response as before, "At noon, Lady, its top gallants have been sighted off the point."

"Oh," she caught herself, then looked between the two men, Achelous sitting at the great table in the Hall and Eliot hovering at the Hall doors. She blushed, her olive skin turning a tinge of rose. "Sorry, I...."

"Lace, come sit with me for a moment. Will you?" Achelous moved the chair beside him. Marisa was dressed in formal lunch attire, her hair elegantly coiled high and pinned by a ruby stiletto that winked red with the sun from the Hall skylights. Long ruby earrings dangled against her perfect neck. A curl of hair was carefully pulled from the coil and spun beside each earring. She wore a white chiffon blouse and a slit black skirt. The elaborate shawl that went with the outfit was casually draped on a chair back. Today, on this rare occasion, she wore the House Marinda royal signet ring: A ruby set with diamonds, and the Marinda ruby necklace, inter-spaced with sapphires, that rested on her chest. When he'd seen how she dressed and was told to dress similarly, he'd remarked about the omission of the House tiara. To which she had huffed, "This is enough jewelry."

She came to sit beside him, her back straight. She searched his eyes, then looked away.

He leaned forward and scooted his chair a little closer. Her nerves wound so tight he wanted to comfort her but not patronize. Much had transpired during his captivity. He was catching up, but many details, important ones, eluded him.

Stories were half told, then told again, but different. A steady stream of well-wishers, visitors, and medics had come through the Hall as he regained his strength and use of his foot and hand. He and Outish, as old friends, perhaps as father and son, had joked of the troubles with regeneration; neither of their hands were yet completely healed. Ivan, Clienen, and Ogden visited often. He was introduced to Lettern and Meridia and heard of their exploits. He'd known of Lettern before his capture, but now, as an IDB CivMon agent, he'd come to appreciate her fierce, unconscious determination. He'd laughed at and with Ivan at Meridia's exploits, what Ivan termed misadventures. But when it came to Meridia's solo mission to Hebert, where he'd met Fire Eye—Achelous looked to the corner of the foyer and swallowed. The pain, the hurt, at least it had dulled from days of personal torment. When Meridia had asked him, in front of Ivan, if he'd done the right thing by avenging Baryy, Achelous had said, "It wasn't vengeance. You were performing your lawful duty of arresting the assailants of an IDB agent." That, of course, was true *and* the official party line. What Achelous personally felt was far more complex. Meridia should never had needed to go to Hebert.

A gentle but firm hand pulled his gaze from the foyer and directed his face at her. Marisa put her forehead against his. "It's over," she whispered. "Helprig did that. Not you." She'd told him that a hundred times. "*You,*" and she said it fiercely, "fight for Dianis. I know that now more than ever. You are, and forever will be, my hero."

He felt his spirit, his soul crumble, then soar under her gaze, her ebon eyes nearly touching his grey.

Eliot approached, "Excuse me, but the incoming shift signal is lit. Our visitor is on their way."

They both took a deep breath, and Marisa rose. "I'll go meet her."

She spared him the trial. He walked with a severe limp; the regeneration pain only bearable because of neural dampeners.

Clienen had insisted on having a shift zone erected near Marinda Hall, and Marisa had gone further by building a new addition solely dedicated to *Federation business*. Much had changed, both during his captivity and during his recovery at Central Station. He'd been at Marinda Hall for less than a week. That Clienen, Ivan, and Marisa were keeping things from him was certain. He expected a myriad of ULUP issues, laws broken and waived, had to be resolved. He knew the Matrincy, in conjunction with the Federation, had given Marisa and Boyd a guarantee, in perpetuity, against extradition or mindwipe. Which, as native provincials, was highly unlikely to begin with. That he himself had been granted an award for Ultimate Cause was phenomenal. It had taken him some time to come to terms with that outcome. So many people had to advocate on his behalf for such an award. He'd expressed his gratitude to Clienen and the IDB executive director. However, when he'd broached the subject of reinstatement, he'd been awarded with stony silence. His security clearance had been downgraded to Confidential. Even Jeremy, in the form of Buzz Too, who sat on a perch playing catch with Boyd, was mum as to his future. Achelous shook his head. The recon bot was an expensive toy, and yet there it was, in Marinda Hall, as Marisa's familiar.

"Brawk, if I eat one more energy pellet, I will poop an eenu."

Boyd squealed in laughter. "One more! One more!"

Buzz launched from his perch, fleeing from the Hall, "Awk, awk, food torture. He's stuffing me for dinner!"

Boyd squealed again and chased after the parrot, his nanny in pursuit.

After a time, Achelous heard Marisa's voice and that of another coming from the hallway to the Federation Atrium.

"Are you coming to the ball tonight?" He heard Marisa ask.

To which a voice he recognized from the Fednet Interconn answered, "Thank you, Lady, the invitation was most gracious. We shall see." There was a moment of silence, and then, "It depends."

Marisa appeared at the Hall passage, and beside her was the matriarch. Never did he, a back-world IDB chief, expect to meet her, and yet, just like Buzz, here she was, in Marinda Hall. In the flesh, no holo-projection surrogate.

Achelous stood and took a few obligatory and halting steps in their direction.

"Chief Inspector Achelous Forushen, we finally meet."

"Madam Matriarch," he bowed and took her proffered bare signet hand. At this point in his life, he had no secrets to keep from her.

She covered his hand with her other and peered at him frankly. "Achelous Forushen, in the flesh. You exist, after all," she smirked. "You are a popular man."

"Please," begged Marisa, "Let's sit. I have a fine Tuggern dark set for lunch. It is perfectly aged."

"How delicious," said the matriarch, "I do so love provincial food."

The Special Forces captain and sergeant took up opposing positions in the Hall. Four other troopers were stationed out of sight. The light security was due to the new, layered security systems installed at Marinda Manor.

"Achelous Forushen," the matriarch said again once seated, shaking her head, "how the Federation revolves around you. You may be even more famous than me," she teased, "at least by current reference count on the Interconnect."

Achelous didn't know what to say. They had planned for the matriarch's visit for some days, whose purpose, he was told, was to "complete terms and contracts."

"So many people, so many events were spawned by your actions, Chief Inspector. It defies calculation, certainly casual observation."

"Am I to apologize, Madam Matriarch?" his question was sincere, and he was prepared to deliver it.

Taken aback, "What?" she snorted most un-ladylike, "Apologize? For being you?" she glanced across the table to Marisa. "No."

He sensed some form of subtle signal pass between the two women. Though he'd not been there, he'd seen the drone feed of the matriarch's visit to the Citadel three weeks ago. She was dressed now as then, in full Matrincy regalia.

"Chief Forushen, for you to apologize for your actions would be to deny the rightful course of Dianis."

He scowled, "So many--" his voice caught.

"Deaths, yes," she said it brutally. "And you think they could have been avoided? That Agent Maxmun's death would have been otherwise?" Her lips pressed tight. "That Sedge, the Loch Norim warlord, would still be walking the planet?" A quick shake of her head, "Nay. Their fates were sealed when forces forked Fate, and the IDB was withdrawn from this planet. What the conspirators did not calculate, in their condescension, was the rise of Chief Achelous Forushen. One can not intercede with Fate and expect an optimum outcome," she sniffed at the understatement.

"Even though you have, Madam," observed Marisa.

"Yes. My efforts are but a muddle, trifling's, tweaks at the edges. Not something so bold and audacious as having the IDB pulled from Dianis. I am loath to do a tweak, and I am prepared to accept the consequences. Only when the original course is too ... unacceptable, dare I meddle."

Marisa thought of Rachael and her sacrifice. Though she was recovering, the matriarch had willingly sent the girl to her peril.

"Sir," the matriarch said to Achelous, "Would you have done what you did had the IDB not been withdrawn?"

"No."

"But you would have loved Marisa nonetheless."

"Yes."

The matriarch nodded her head. "I do not know, can not read all the threads; they are infinite, but Mother is irresistible. She will find her champions."

It was the first time Marisa heard the matriarch invoke Mother.

A silence settled in the hall.

"And so we come to our contracts," said the matriarch. "Lady, do you have the attestment and accompanying insignia?"

Marisa rose, left the room, and then returned with a polycritic sheet and a jewelry box. She sat with the attestment and box in front of her. She met his eyes.

He saw uncertainty and worry. He immediately became concerned: Was the Matrincy, the matriarch, demanding something of her ... a sacrifice?

"Chief, are you aware that your career in the IDB is over?"

He was holding his breath. Glancing between the two, whatever the matriarch was about to say, Marisa was in on it. Slowly, he settled back in his chair. Whatever their plan, he'd have to go along, but he didn't like being out of the know, out of control. The tables were turned on him. Surveying the Hall, Boyd's highchair, this was his home. His trust in Marisa complete. "Not in so few words. You're the first to come out and say it."

"That's because you have a decision to make, and others are waiting for you to make it. But I," the matriarch shifted in her chair, relaxing a bit herself, "know you. Not because we have touched or because I have seen the future, which in this case I have not, but because of your honor."

Marisa looked down, focusing on the polycritic.

He wanted to reach out and touch her hand.

"Your love for all that is here dictates one response, and in that response, you will sacrifice one love for another."

He tried to focus on the matriarch, to glean her meaning, but Marisa's distress was—

"The lady was offered a trade. She now needs you to fulfill it. Your award for Ultimate Cause protects you to the day the Lady and I made our bargain. That day has passed. You cannot stay on Dianis, not as Chief Achelous Forushen of the IDB. On that, ULUP and the IDB are clear and unbending."

He measured his breathing, letting his embed moderate the flow of adrenalin and temper his growing anxiety. He swallowed. "And how do I stay here?" his voice almost a whisper.

"Lady, present him with your proposal."

Marisa looked up. With challenge in her gaze, she slid the attestment across the table, but held onto the jewelry box.

He read the document, wherein it stated,

> *As a councilor of the Matrincy, I, Achelous Forushen, shall contract in matrimony, for the term of my remaining lifetime, one Princess Marisa Pontifract, House Marinda, of the Dianis Royal Tivorian Court. In so doing, become the trusted and faithful representative of the Matrincy to the planet Dianis, entitled to all writs, warrants, and licenses, thereby granted such a stature and position.*

A smug expression forming, the matriarch said, "When the Federation signed on to ULUP, the Matrincy demanded and received an exception to the treaty. Matrincy counselors, one per planet, are excluded from ULUP laws under a narrow set of conditions, one of those being they wed a provincial, who of sound mind and free will voluntarily engage in a matrimony contract with the councilor, and they, with IDB inspection, peacefully cohabitate for their duration on the protected planet."

Marisa was waiting.

"ULUP thought the terms of the exclusion impossible to achieve because how was a Matrincy councilor to meet the conditions if they were not allowed on the planet in the first place? And yet, here we are. Matriarchs, not included." She laughed.

Achelous was ignoring the matriarch, his focus on Marisa. It pained him when the awareness came that her fear and her trepidations were predicated on his response to her *marriage* proposal. "Lace," he thought of all the things he could say, should say. How they had lived, loved, and hidden their bonding in secret and that now it was no longer necessary. He could say all that and more. Instead, he said, "Will you marry me?"

The tears welled up. She stood, and walking in a dream, came to him. Lifting his chin, she kissed him. Sliding onto his lap, she hugged him tight.

"Well then," the matriarch quipped, "I will take that as a yes."

They hugged and kissed, intent on each other.

"Captain," she called, "I think we will withdraw. Marisa? Marisa, dear?"

"Yes?" Marisa muffled a response.

"You may tell the aorolmin I will attend the ball, and be sure to get your future husband's thumbprint on the attestment. It needs his aura signature to be official."

"Yes, Ma'am."

"The coach is ready, Lady," Eliot called from beyond the master suite door.

"Thank you, Eliot." Marisa opened the door and stopped still. She was wearing what she hoped was a stunning formal ball gown, but Eliot's Avant Garde hunter's attire caught her off guard. He averted his eyes, trying to ignore her scrutiny. She walked around him, eyeing him up and down.

"Is there a problem, Lady?"

"No. No, Eliot. I am just savoring this moment. Perhaps I see some new fashion trends."

"I was assured by Jeremy it would be most appropriate for this evening."

"Indeed." She gave him a mischievous wrinkle, "You're taking fashion advice from a parrot?"

He did his best rendition of her, rolling his eyes and stumped away, "I will see you in the coach."

Achelous was adjusting his new formal suit, hand-delivered by a young Matrincy adept. He fumbled with the collar pips.

"Let me," she said, "it should be *my* honor to be the first to pin them on you."

Inserting the pip stud through the suit's collar holes, a suit tailored to be worn with pips, she asked, "So what exactly does a planetary counselor do?"

"Well, there's not many of them. It depends on the planet they are assigned to. But there was an encrypted note attached to the suit when it arrived. Penned by the Misses."

"Misses?"

"Yeah, inside the Matrincy, that's what they call the matriarch, out of her earshot, of course. The note said,

> *Bend the rules, work the case of the IDB's departure, help Marisa uplift, and beware all foes. There are more than you know.*"

His collar pips attached, the white, sky-blue, and grass-green of the Mother Dianis Lilly swirling in the opalescence of the orbs. Marisa had both hands on his chest.

He felt her mood change.

"Sedge is dead," she said.

The woman in his arms was soft and yielding, but her voice edged with steel.

"They murdered him on a Federation assault carrier and disabled it. Who can do that?"

His brows creased. "Someone with great capacity to do harm. They deceived ULUP. Ivan told me there is intel potentially connecting the IDB's withdrawal to the attack on the *Tempest Dare*."

Marisa's back was stiff. "He told me there's speculation, the Church, Helprig was manipulated into kidnapping you. Ivan said the attack on the *Tempest Dare* was nearly perfect, only an hour off target."

"What target?"

"An hour sooner, the assault would have been delayed. Helprig would have made it to the castle."

They stood there, his hands around her waist.

He let her go, thinking. Taking her hand, they slowly walked down the staircase into the great room. Halfway down, he paused. "They wanted to disrupt the assault. If Sedge was the sole target there were easier ways to do it. "

"But the risk they took," she said. "It's clear they, whoever they are, thought Sedge was a threat. They didn't want him loose, sharing his knowledge, his secrets, especially with the Federation." She shifted her grasp to his elbow, helping him down the staircase. A Marinda Marine sergeant, posted at the foot of the stairs, offered to help.

"Ovids," he said. "The commissioner from Tochman Lower Five had genetic manipulation. Clienen said they were genes from a human branch thought to have died out. It predates the Federation. They lived in the Ovid sector. They were believed to be a slave race that died out when their owners left them."

As the sergeant waited, Achelous added, "There's so much we don't know."

Tivor Castle had been restored to its pre-assault architecture. Gone were the structures mocking the Citadel. Never had the aorolmin thrown such an extravagant affair. Compared to his forebears, who were renowned for their spontaneous celebrations, he was a hermit. Today, however, he had a reason for celebrating, not the least being the return of his rescue mission from the Citadel.

The banquet itself a luxurious affair, with food and wine imported from far reaches of Isuelt. Wine, the barrels stamped with the *House Marinda Trade* label, was decanted in rivers on all the tables. Berga, venison, mountain gnu, and other delicacies were plentiful. The who's who of Tivor aristocracy, prominent trade houses, ship captains, and the Tivor officer's corps, with their personal invites, had turned out. The belle of the ball, feted by the aorolmin and adored by well-wishers, was the Lady Pontifract, a glimmering beauty in her sea-green satin gown, with a plunging neckline, which she adorned with the House Marinda tiara. Next was Christina Tara, Al Suri Ascalon, who regaled all in the rare display of a Lamaran Empire gown with sequins of real gold dotted with silver flashing. The dress matched her diadem and her flaxen braid. whence she obtained the gown, everyone speculated.

At Woodwern and Margern's urging, who had made the trip via coach to visit New Ungern, Lettern, representing all Doromen, came dressed in a sleek black silk jumper whose hem fell mid thigh. Not surprisingly, the muscles in her thighs matched those of her arms. She wore two glittering diamond bracelets and matching earrings that dangled along her neck. Gifts from a former assault Marine corporal who said he never spent his pay, and now was the time.

Lastly, much to the fit and consternation of Avarian Special Forces, was the galactic exotic that awed and transformed all visitors into gawkers: The matriarch in her Matrincy High Form hooded gown, with all the Matrincy meditation jewelry, accessories, and ornamentation. Where Christina was fair, light, and inviting, the matriarch was mysterious, dark, and contemplative. The contrast made stark as they were seated next to each other at the matriarch's request.

Achelous surreptitiously watched his new boss, though how far below her in Matrincy hierarchy he was not sure, speak animated and engagingly with the Alon.

"I've never known the Alon to talk so much," Marisa whispered in his ear, three seats away from the Alon on the other side of the aorolmin, Woodwern, and Margern.

"Hmm, I can't hear what they are saying, but if the matriarch thought she was going to control the conversation, I think she is wrong. And yes, this is a different side of the Alon."

The aorolmin's steward rang the attention bell. After repeated attempts, the ballroom hubbub eventually quieted. "There will be a fifteen-minute interlude while the West Stage is reconfigured for our ceremony, and then the floor will be cleared for dancing. Please make your preparations."

"Ceremony?" Achelous asked Marisa.

She shook her head in surprise. "No idea. I didn't see any ceremony on the list of festivities."

During the interlude, Ogden found Meridia and Lettern, and apologized to the agent: Lettern was needed for a conclave called by Margern.

In the aorolmin's smoking room, Ordern Smoothgrain, chieftain of the Red Elm Timberkeep clan, sat near the windows overlooking the gardens. A Red Elm warrior in his Red Elm tabard closed the door behind Ogden and Lettern as they entered.

"Please, have a seat, everyone," said Woodwern. "Margern and I thought it best to have a quick hoot and moot," he chuckled, "if you will, before the ceremony. We've been having a debate and think it is settled."

Lettern took a seat beside Ordern on the cushioned bench that fronted the windows to the gardens. Ogden stood beside them. Beyond the castle wall, the tall masts of the aorolmin's fleet could be seen docked at the quays.

"The aorolmin knows we are here," Margern offered, "but this is business of the Doroman Nation."

Lettern quickly scanned the attendees; like her, they were all Doromen, though two or three she did not recognize. Chief Torgren Razorleaf, of Cedar Floral, she had met just that morning. She suspected one or two of the others might also be chiefs, but Woodwern, in a hurry to conclude the moot during the interlude, skipped introductions. Nevertheless, it struck Lettern that this might be the first time that so many Doromen chieftains had gathered in a nation meeting.

"I've offered to host a nation hoot and moot in New Ungern for all Doromen clans, but we need to saw some wood first," which was his way of saying *work out the details.*

The news of bringing Timber, Plains, and Rock clans under one roof for a hoot was big news, and Lettern sat on the edge of the cushion, waiting for more.

"We have all sung our praises and composed ballads in honor of Sedge, the Warlord," said Margern. "We, according to our custom, did not have a funeral pyre, but instead acceded to the Alon's request and surrendered his body to her."

"To which we come to our first point of settlement," said Woodwern, "I have Ogden's agreement with the Alon's opinion." Woodwern was looking at Lettern. "That Captain Perrin be hired as the Clan Mearsbirch militia commander. In charge of all wards."

Lettern's eyes lifted to Ogden.

Ogden knew what she was thinking. Of all the Mearsbirch wards, he was the senior warden. "Oi, it won't be me," he whispered to her. "My time is best spent at the anvil." Then louder, "We've a thousand rifles to make, and the Second Ward is the most I can manage."

Her expression flipped from doubt to surprise at the number of rifles.

Margern said, "It's not enough. To arm Tivor and all the Timber clans, we'll need six thousand rifles."

Lettern inhaled. The entire room turned peer at her. Arming, training, and deploying six thousand Riflemen would transform Isuelt, but to what? She'd seen firsthand the strengths *and* weaknesses of the rifles. In the Citadel, they'd taken casualties when the few axemen they had struggled to hold off the Drakan pikemen while the rifles were reloaded.

Ordern Smoothgrain asked, "Lettern, your prowess on the battlefield is renown; we must know, when the Drakans come, to whom will you serve? Your clan or the Ancients?"

Stunned they should ask and alarmed that it had been a conversation beyond her ears, she answered, "My clan."

"And your Ancient?" Ordern asked.

Ogden said, "Ivan has made it plain that Achelous will be directed to aid the IDB in enforcing ULUP, which means Meridia—"

"We don't know what it means for Illy," she rebutted, but in truth, she knew what Ivan would force. "But I will fight with my clan. Illy--"

"Fair enough," acquiesced Margern. "Your knowledge of the Ancients, the Avarians, will be important to our defense."

"You're so sure the Drakans are coming?" Lettern asked, hoping.

Woodwern nodded. "Our pathics with Darnkilden are reporting new Drakan units arriving *all* along the 'Kilden border."

"We must prepare," declared Margern. "March now and help Darnkilden hold the frontier, or?" she looked to Ordern.

Ordern replied, "Arrange, as Sedge would say, a defense in depth."

"Too much is in the wind," Chief Razorleaf asserted. "The leaves blow in a swirl. Oridia, Neuland, Mestrich, the Plains and Rock, they must all decide."

"The Sea Haven League is moving to bolster Darnkilden, but the League has much coastline to defend," noted Ordern.

Finally, Woodwern came to the point he wanted to make before they adjourned the conclave. "We, all Timber clans, need a new warlord. Perrin could do it, but he is not a Doroman, and a Doroman is needed if we are to marshal the Plains and Rock with us."

Lettern rose and smoothed her skirt. "Who?"

"Ordern Smoothgrain is my and Margern's nominee. Ogden agrees."

"I as well," said Chief Razorleaf.

"I too," said the other two Doroman chiefs Lettern did not know.

Ogden was waiting for Lettern to speak.

She looked to Ordern. "Sedge would approve."

"Then it is agreed," Woodwern said to the chieftain of Red Elm. "We look to you to marshal our defenses. I will send word to Oridia, Darnkilden, and the League that the Timber wards are uniting."

In the main ballroom, a steward's page arranged the red carpet up the steps of the West Stage. Satisfied with the preparations, the steward keyed the orchestra seated behind the stage. They began playing a jaunty melody that Marisa did not recognize, but surmised to be a Timberkeep favorite as all the Doromen began clapping in unison. Soon, they were joined by the Tivorians. The orchestra increased in volume and tempo. The throng were seated in chairs arranged in an arc before the stage, the dignitaries in the front row.

At a prearranged signal, Lettern jumped up and whirled a strip of ribbons above her head. She held on to her skirt as she twirled and did a woodland jig in precise footwork to the first step of the stage. Outish, to Achelous's amazement, in unison, jumped up as well, whooped, twirled a New Ungern bough above his head, and tried to mimic the same jig on his way to the stage.

The Doromen roared and rose from their chairs, clapping and stomping. Compelled to follow suit, slowly at first, Tivorians began to rise and stomp, though they knew not what for. The secret was on them, a Doroman secret, but they wanted in on it.

Lettern's shapely legs were clearly part of the act, as was Outish's clumsy but energetic attempt to match her. The crowd, convinced by the Doromen that this was acceptable, joined in the ruckus.

Lettern and Outish took their places on the first set of steps, facing each other. They bent forward, wiggled their bottoms, and slapped their butts. Then they kissed each other on both cheeks.

"Ho, ho, ho!" the Doromen chanted. The steward signaled to the orchestra, and they changed tunes to one higher in chord and no less rollicking and frivolous.

While Lettern and Outish kept up a muted rendition of their jig on the first step, Alon and Ogden jumped up. The Alon whirled a white scarf above her head, and Ogden unveiled a length of chain to which the Doromen roared in laughter. The pair did their own unique jig. The Alon elegant and fluid in her execution, whereas to Marisa's surprise, Ogden's performance was also superb, clearly well practiced.

She leaned into Achelous while they clapped and stomped, "He's done that before."

Alon and Ogden performed their dance to the second step of the stage. Lettern and Outish moved aside for the audience to watch.

Bending forward, swaying their bottoms to the orchestra's rollicking, they slapped their butts and when Ogden did it, Marisa burst out laughing. The crowd was in an ecstatic frenzy. The pair kissed each other on both cheeks, twirled, and hooted. Even Achelous, unable to remain serious, laughed at Ogden's twirl as compared to the Alon's magical spin, her Lamaran gown billowing.

"Ho, ho, ho!" the Doromen chanted.

The steward cued the orchestra, and they changed their tune again, this one more serious but still carrying bawdy overtones.

Marisa felt a tap on her shoulder.

The matriarch held out her hand.

Marisa took the hand. When she did and turned to look to Achelous for assurance, she was rocked. Ivan was doing the same to him.

Achelous begged a moment from Ivan and used the multi-func to boost the neural dampener to maximum.

The crowd was stomping and clapping, showing no sign their appetite had been sated. Bending to it with renewed vigor, the orchestra reached a new crescendo.

The new pair were led to the front, up to the third step, one below the stage.

Ivan and the matriarch steered their charges into the correct positions, and then, the matriarch, her expression firm, flourished her hand in a resounding directive that the pair were to follow suit of their thirds and seconds.

Laughter washed across the ballroom at the matriarch's stern command they perform.

Marisa was ready.

Though his foot felt like a lead club, Achelous followed suit, trying his best not to embarrass her.

They step danced to the music, Marisa, the agile one. Carried away in the moment, she did a twirl reminiscent of the Alon's, though in the low-cut, tight-fitting gown much more daring. Whistles and hollering congratulated her.

They bent forward, slapped their bottoms, left, right, then kissed each other, but not on the sides of their face; on the lips.

Apparently satisfied, the Doromen chanted, "Ho, ho, ho," one last time and quieted, ceasing their clapping and stomping.

From the left side of the stage, the aorolmin entered, and from the right, Woodwern. Ascending to the stage, the matriarch took a position between and back from the Leaders.

The aorolmin waited for the steward to gain control of the audience. Silencing the enlivened orchestra helped.

"Lords and ladies, fellow dignitaries, Tivorians, Doromen, and visitors from afar," the steward's resonant voice rang out, "we shall now conduct the ceremony. Listen, for these presents are binding."

Marisa stared at Achelous; her red lips curled in a sanguine smile. He had only eyes for her. The stage was in tunnel vision. He could sense the matriarch to his right and Ogden to his left, but they were worlds away.

Woodwern was saying something, but Achelous wasn't listening. He wanted to fall into Marisa's ebon eyes, to lose himself in her embrace. Ogden nudged him. There were giggles in the audience. The aorolmin looked at him with his best stern expression, "Not yet, you don't."

The crowd roared.

"E-hem," Woodwern straighten, facing the aorolmin. "Do you, the honorable Aorolmin of the Duchy of Tivor, thus give your liege woman, the Princess Marisa Pontifract of your House Marinda, into this union of body and soul, before Mother herself, to foster and bring life to Mother's Womb for as ever their souls persist?"

"I do," answered the aorolmin.

Woodwern faced the matriarch. "Do you, the honorable Madam Matriarch of the Avarian Federation and Matrincy, thus give your officer, the Dianis Planetary Councilor Achelous Forushen, into this union of body and soul before Mother herself, to foster and bring life to Mother's Womb for as ever their souls persist?"

"I do," she answered with a preeminently satisfied smile.

The Alon took Marisa's hand, and Ogden took Achelous's. They clasped them together, the Alon draping her scarf over the hands and Ogden placed the links of chain, snapping a clasp to enclose the circle of iron.

Lettern and Outish came up the steps. Lettern wrapped her colored ribbons around their hands, and Outish completed with laying the Ungerngerist bough over it all.

"With Mother's never-failing blessing," Woodwern called out strongly, "I claim a Union of Souls!"

Cheering and clapping filled the ballroom.

At Achelous's confused expression, the aorolmin asked, "What?"

"Don't, don't you ask us first?"

"No," came the immediate response.

More laughing and cheering. "You're standing here. You should have thought about before now."

They roared.

Before her husband could make a bigger fool of himself, Marisa reached out, grabbed him by both lapels, yanked him close, and kissed him.


The End.

# A Word From Frank

I write to entertain *you*. That is my passion. This story has *shifted* you, in the time of your choosing, from Earth to Dianis, where you could find relief from your Earthly trials. Through the story, from the comfort of your abode, you could follow your favorite characters as they faced peril and intrigue. I sincerely hope you enjoyed your time. Please use this link Goodreads: The Citadel or the QR Code below and post your thoughts by clicking on the *Write Customer Review* button. I'd love to hear who your favorite character is.

*The Citadel* on Goodreads

A preview of the next chronicle, *The Loch Norim,* follows.

# *Preview*
# *The Loch Norim*

### *The Angraris Ocean*

The *Black Gull* hoisted its Sea Haven League battle pendant, removing any doubt as to its origins or intent. They'd been following their quarry, a Drakan blockade runner, ever since the Drakan came abreast of Toll Haven.

At the sight of the Sea Haven colors, the schooner obligingly hoisted all sails and beat to Bareen, three leagues distant.

"It would have been simpler to take them at sea," said the *Black Gull's* captain.

"With casualties," intoned Christina. "We've no idea what they would do with the prisoner."

"Throw him over the side," said the first mate.

"Aye, with weights," acknowledged the captain. "Wouldn't want to be caught with the likes of him on board."

Sailing past Bareen and having watched the schooner scuttle into safe harbor, the *Black Gull* made for a deep lagoon south of the city.

At the lagoon, the sight of the Sea Haven warship threw the pirate haven into a frenzy: Buccaneers and their sloops hastily pulled anchor and fled. A steady stream of sails vacated the bay.

Entering the lagoon and docking at the rickety quay, the first mate reported all the search party's eenus were successfully put ashore.

"I bid you Mother's Farewell, captain. I'd wish you peace."

"Aye, and Mother's Farewell to you, Alon." With his glass, he spied the beach and the sands beyond. The Sea Haven League was at war, and peace was not in the offing.

Riding through the night, the party came to the main road leaving Bareen, winding its way through the desert scrub, past reeds of the Great Latitude Swamp, and ultimately to Hebert in the northwest. Finding a suitable lookout where they could conceal their mounts, the party made camp without fire and waited.

During the next day, several caravans came and went. Alex sighted them from a dune, their eenus and oxen wavering in the swamp heat.

At peace, appreciating the sciroccos rifling the marsh grass and cattails, Alex felt his breathing languish at low ebb as he watched the cattails sway. His wounds from the Citadel were healed, but he still felt pain when he swung his arm in a certain motion.

Dune sand shifted behind him.

Christina settled in, crouching close behind. She put her arm around his waist. He grasped her hand.

"Anything?" she asked, a breath close to his ear.

"There," he pointed, "the reeds move against the wind. It comes from that caravan."

Noting how the reeds ruffled, Alex and Alon rose and descended the back side of the dune.

Alex announced, "He's coming."

Their two fellow Defenders, Feolin and his new apprentice, were waiting expectantly.

Stoicism in their movements, the Defenders broke the sparse camp and prepared to mount up.

Prince Fire Eye slipped around a reed bank, his body glistening with swamp muck.

Rachael grinned at him. Though the Lizardman gave no overt clues, she could tell he was content, at home in the alien landscape where desert met marsh.

Alon, in the impassive manner of the reptile, conferred the prince a questioning look.

He flicked his tongue twice.

"How many guards?" asked Alex.

He held up both hands: *Ten.*

They moved out. Fire Eye trailed the caravan while the Defenders kept a distance behind. The party followed the troop north until the caravanserai pitched camp.

Biding time till the dead of night, they reconnoitered the bivouac. "They're Bareen mercs," Alex said to Alon. "Their trade goods are light."

She waited for him to make his point, mainly so Feolin and Rachael could hear. Christina understood what he was driving at.

"When they deliver the prisoner, they'll sign up with the archbishop to fight against Wedgewood."

Rachael tensed. In a crouch behind a barrel cactus, she reached into her pouch and retrieved several forty-caliber bullets. Wedgewood was her home; she was a Timberkeep.

"Remember, young apprentice, it is Mother's Will you serve," said Alon.

The light of the dying campfires tinged Rachael's young blue eyes like the orbs of a cat, feral, hungry. "Mother's Will," she breathed, "we protect the harmed, the harmless, and all Mother's Believers. Are these Mother's Believers?" she asked.

Balance the good with the bad. No student was perfect. What Christina wanted most for Feolin's young apprentice was to be guided by Mother and not driven by hate.

"Go," said Alex.

Fire Eye and Rachael moved out. The pair, ever since the Citadel, had formed a unique bond.

Crouching paces behind Fire Eye, Rachael hovered a bullet above her hand as he crab-crawled on all fours to the periphery of the campfire illumination. Christina, Alex, and Feolin were in a stack to Rachael's rear.

Rising, the prince swept into the camp, his twin scimitars flashing.

Lead slugs whizzed from Rachael's throwing hand. She'd been practicing. Now, she could launch snap-throws on the run.

Two Bareen mercs on watch went down in a flurry of scimitar swipes, and two more were felled by bullet strikes.

There was a commotion in a tent. A muffled voice asked, "Barook? You there?"

With Feolin close on her heels holding a torch he pulled from a tent pole, Rachael whipped open the tent flap of

Barook's inquisitor. A man rose from a bedroll. When he saw the girl, a teenager perhaps, framed in the opening, he called, "Thief!" and reached for a scimitar. A second form lay on the sand in the center of the tent.

Rachael stepped in, a bullet orbiting lazily above her hand. In the torchlight, she noticed the prone form was bound, staked, and gagged. The scimitar wielder unsheathed his weapon and advanced on her, expecting her to flee like a mouse in a cupboard.

She gave him a wicked smile. "Drop your weapon."

Astonished anger lit the mercenary. "You insolent urchin!"

He charged and died.

Pulling a dirk, she went to the captive while saying, "I gave him a chance, Feo."

"Aye, lass, you did."

Untying the gag, Rachael slit the prisoner's stake-bonds and blanched at the sight of his bloody trousers. "Ugh, I'm going to gag. That smell."

"Let me," said Feolin.

Rachael scooched aside while the prisoner watched her, transfixed by the white lily necklace that hung about her neck. His gaze went to the hilt of a shiny new dirk, a gift from Ogden for her apprentice appointment. On it was an engraved lily.

"Timmy?" the prisoner hissed. "Defenders?" he asked, seeing Feolin's shield painted with the Life Defender's heraldic.

"Yup," said Rachael, "and you're one of us now."

"Arg, uh," the prisoner grunted as Feolin slit the trouser leg open and began cleaning the putrefying wound on his thigh. "No, I'll not—"

"Oh yes, you will. You are one of us. Even if I *am* a Timberkeep." Rachael's voice, a young woman or teenager, carried a resonance and latent anger that stayed further complaints.

Christina entered the tent.

"It's the best I can do," said Feolin.

When Christina came into the torchlight and removed her helm, her flaxen Lamaran braid hanging loose, the prisoner stiffened. He began to struggle.

Ill and feverish from the infected bullet wound, the prisoner was still quite strong. It took Rachael and Feolin to hold him while Christina pulled out a pouch and several syringes.

Alon reached to his face and lifted an eyelid, checking a pupil. Opening the pouch, she readied the bandage.

This part fascinated Rachael. The medical instruments Alon brought for the mission were neither Dianis provincial nor Avarian galactic.

"Hold him tight," said Alon, and they did while she injected the contents of all three syringes into the wound. The prisoner spasmed, arching his back. After a few tense moments, he lay still.

Dressing the wound with a special fabric, Christina removed a small device with an aquamarine-5 crystal the size of her thumb and attached it to the fabric. Gently, she pressed on the crystal. It began to glow a low-intensity blue. "That will use your own life force, your own aura to heal you, Captain, so leave it on."

"I'm not a captain," he hesitated, "not anymore."

"Oh yes, you are, Captain Irons," Rachael chided. "I told Og we were coming to get you, and I *am* bringing *the* Captain Irons back to Wedgewood."

"To hang. To burn," he said.

In the flickering lamplight, their shadows wavering on the tent ceiling, Christina peered at him. "No, captain. Mother's Mercy is here. You were cast off, forsaken by the Church, sentenced to death for your archbishop's retribution, payment for Helprig's disgrace. Mother cares not of your past deeds. You are one of us now."

# Acknowledgements

It's an honor to have friends who look forward to reading, and yes, reviewing your next novel. A diverse set of opinions and perspectives twists and turns the tale from unforeseen angles, testing it for continuity. That is real gratification when the finished product emerges refined and tempered by their inputs. The cast of characters who play an integral role in that process are Tom, Terry, Jeff, Danya, and Micheal. My many heartfelt thanks to them. Reading a story that is not yet polished takes special patience. The evolution of the chronicles has been as much a journey for them as it is for me. Again, thank you so much.

# *About the Author*

Living along the Mississippi River, Frank Dravis has leveraged his many life experiences to write the the *Dianis, A World In Turmoil* chronicles. He was born and raised in Detroit, Michigan, where he and his father cruised the Great Lakes. His father often went out on the roughest days when they were the only craft cresting white caps. Frank spent six years in the US Navy chasing Soviet submarines. His love of the sea is reflected in the chronicles, a love he has shared with his wife and two girls.

A hunter, Frank has taken game with a variety of weapons, including the bow, rifle, shotgun, and muzzleloader, the weapon modeled in *The Foundry* and used as the tool of choice in the fight against the Drakan Empire in *The Citadel.*

He assists his wife in her passion for horses as stable hand and hay schlepper. Equines appear in the Dianis series, not as horses, but as eenus.

Frank's care for Earth and the stewardship of their land in Wisconsin are reflected in the culture and ethos of the Timberkeeps.

He has two degrees, a Bachelor of Computer Science and a Master of Business Administration. Both of those degrees are integral to his careers as a writer, software engineer, marketing executive, and chief information officer. The scientific acumen he gained through those endeavors is leveraged in the chronicles to make the Dianis brand of science fiction practically possible somewhere in the galaxy.

.

# Social Media

For current information on the Dianis a World in Turmoil series, please visit us on the Web at https://www.dianisworld.com and on Facebook at Dianis Facebook where additional maps, images, character info, details behind key concepts, and the status of *The Loch Norim* (book four) can be found.

*Quorat's Intruder at Contractor Haven*

Most importantly, if you like the book, please post a review on Goodreads at Books by Frank Dravis

# Titles In The Dianis Chronicles

*The Foundry, Book 1*
*The Matriarch, Book 2*
*The Citadel, Book 3*
*The Loch Norim, Book 4 (draft)*
*And more to come*